Praise for #1 ~~New~~ ~~York Times~~
bestselling author Debbie Macomber

"It's impossible not to cheer for [Debbie] Macomber's characters.... When it comes to creating a special place and memorable, honorable characters, nobody does it better than Macomber."
—*BookPage* on *Twenty Wishes*

"Popular romance author Debbie Macomber has a gift for evoking the emotions that are at the heart of the genre's popularity."
—*Publishers Weekly*

"Macomber is a master storyteller."
—*RT Book Reviews*

Praise for *USA TODAY* bestselling author
Marie Ferrarella

"A touching, heartwarming story about three genuinely lonely souls who find each other. This book will delight and engage."
—*RT Book Reviews* on
Finding Happily-Ever-After

"[Marie] Ferrarella's engaging romance takes a sad occasion and turns it into joy. The characters are fascinating and will leave readers eager to hear their stories."
—*RT Book Reviews* on *Innkeeper's Daughter*

Debbie Macomber is a number one *New York Times* and *USA TODAY* bestselling author. Her books include *1225 Christmas Tree Lane, 1105 Yakima Street, A Turn in the Road, Hannah's List* and *Debbie Macomber's Christmas Cookbook*, as well as *Twenty Wishes, Summer on Blossom Street* and *Call Me Mrs. Miracle.* She has become a leading voice in women's fiction worldwide and her work has appeared on every major bestseller list, including those of the *New York Times, USA TODAY, Publishers Weekly* and *Entertainment Weekly.* She is a multiple award winner, and won the 2005 Quill Award for Best Romance. There are more than one hundred million copies of her books in print. Two of her MIRA Books Christmas titles have been made into Hallmark Channel Original Movies, and the Hallmark Channel has launched a series based on her bestselling Cedar Cove stories. For more information on Debbie and her books, visit her website, DebbieMacomber.com.

USA TODAY bestselling and RITA® Award-winning author **Marie Ferrarella** has written more than two hundred books for Harlequin, some under the name Marie Nicole. Her romances are beloved by fans worldwide. Visit her website, MarieFerrarella.com.

#1 *New York Times* Bestselling Author

DEBBIE MACOMBER

Ready for MARRIAGE

 HARLEQUIN® BESTSELLING AUTHOR COLLECTION

ISBN-13: 978-0-373-01019-6

Ready for Marriage
Copyright © 2015 by Harlequin Books S.A.

The publisher acknowledges the copyright holder
of the individual works as follows:

Ready for Marriage
Copyright © 1994 by Debbie Macomber

Finding Happily-Ever-After
Copyright © 2010 by Marie Rydzynski-Ferrarella

Recycling programs
for this product may
not exist in your area.

Printed in U.S.A.

™ www.Harlequin.com

CONTENTS

READY FOR MARRIAGE

Debbie Macomber

Dedicated to
Carole Grande and her family
for their loving support
through the years

Chapter 1

She could always grovel at Evan's feet. Knowing him as well as she did, Mary Jo Summerhill figured he'd probably like that. The very fact that she'd made this appointment—and then had the courage to show up—proved how desperate she was. But she'd had no choice; her parents' future rested in her hands and she knew of no better attorney to help with this mess than Evan Dryden.

If only he'd *agree* to help her...

Generally, getting in touch with an old boyfriend wouldn't create such anxiety, but Evan was more than just someone she'd dated a few times.

They'd been in love, deeply in love, and had planned to marry. In ways she hadn't yet fully grasped, Mary Jo still loved him. Terminating their relationship had nearly devastated her.

And him.

Mary Jo wasn't proud of the way she'd ended it. Mailing him back the beautiful pearl engagement ring had been cowardly, but she'd known she couldn't tell him face-to-face. She should've realized Evan would never leave it at that. She'd been a fool to think he'd take back the ring without confronting her.

He'd come to her angry and hurt, demanding an explanation. It quickly became apparent that he wouldn't accept the truth, and given no option, Mary Jo concocted a wild story about meeting another teacher and falling in love with him.

Telling such a bold-faced lie had magnified her guilt a hundredfold. But it was the only way she could make Evan believe her. The only way she could extricate herself from his life.

Her lie had worked beautifully, she noted with a twinge of pain. He'd recovered—just like his mother had said he would. He hadn't wasted any time getting on with his life, either.

Within a matter of months he was dating again. Pictures of Evan, with Jessica Kellerman at his side, had appeared regularly in the newspaper society pages. Unable to resist finding out more, Mary Jo had researched the Kellerman family. Her investigation had told her everything she needed to know. Jessica would make the perfect Dryden wife. The Kellermans were wealthy and established, unlike the Summerhills, who didn't rate so much as a mention in Boston's social register.

Later the same year, Mary Jo had heard about the extravagant Dryden family wedding. She been out of town that week at a teaching seminar, so she'd missed the newspaper coverage, and she'd avoided the society pages ever since. She didn't need any reminders of the wedding that had been the social event of the year.

That was nearly three years ago. Evan and Jessica were an old married couple by now. For all she knew, they might already have started a family. The twinge of regret became a knot in her stomach. Evan would make a wonderful father. They'd talked of a family, and she remembered how eager he was for children.

This wasn't exactly the best time for her to reenter his life, but she had no alternative. Her parents' future depended on Evan.

"Mr. Dryden will see you now," the receptionist said, breaking into Mary Jo's thoughts.

She nearly lost her nerve right then and there. Her heart pounded furiously. In a dead panic she tightened her hold on her purse strap, fighting the urge to dash straight out of her chair and out of the office.

"If you'll come this way."

"Of course," Mary Jo managed, although the words came out in gurglelike sounds, as if she were submerged in ten feet of water.

She followed the receptionist down a wide, plush-carpeted hallway to Evan's office. His name was on the door, engraved on a gold plate. The receptionist ushered her in, and left.

Mary Jo recognized Evan's personal assistant immediately, although they'd never met. Mrs. Sterling was exactly the way he'd described her. Late middle-age. Short and slim, with the energy of a Tasmanian devil. Formidably efficient. He'd claimed the woman could easily reorganize the world if she had to, and that she'd willingly take on any project he asked of her. She was loyal to a fault.

"Evan asked me to send you right in," Mrs. Sterling said, leading her to the closed inner door. She opened it, then asked, "Can I get you a cup of coffee?" Her tone was friendly but unmistakably curious.

"No, thank you." Mary Jo stepped over the threshold, her heart in her throat. She wondered how she'd feel seeing Evan again after all this time. She'd already decided that a facade was necessary. She planned to approach him as if they were long-lost friends. Casual friends. With a smile, she'd shake his hand, inquire about Jessica and catch up on events in his life.

Now that there were only a few feet between her and the man she loved, Mary Jo found she couldn't move, could barely even breathe.

Nothing could have prepared her for the force of these emotions. Within seconds she was drowning in feelings she didn't know how to handle. She felt swamped and panicky, as if she were going down for the third time.

She conjured up Gary's face, the man she'd dated off and on for the past few months, but that didn't help. Next she struggled to come up with some clever comment, some joke, anything. Instead, all she could remember was that the man she'd loved three years ago, loved now, was married to someone else.

Evan sat at his desk, writing; only now did he look up. Their eyes met and for the briefest moment, he seemed to experience the same sense of loss and regret she was feeling. He blinked and the emotion disappeared, wiped out with a mere movement of his eyes.

"Hello, Evan," she said, amazed at how offhand she sounded. "I imagine it's a surprise to see me after all this time."

He stood and extended his hand for a perfunctory shake, and when he spoke his voice was crisp and professional. "Mary Jo. It's great to see you."

Mary Jo nearly laughed out loud. Evan never did know how to tell a good lie. He was anything but pleased to see her again.

He motioned toward the chair on the other side of his desk. "Sit down."

She did, gratefully, uncertain how much longer her knees would support her. She set her purse on the carpet and waited for her heart rate to return to normal before she told him the purpose of her visit.

"Did Mary offer you a cup of coffee?"

"Yes. I'm fine, thank you," she said hurriedly. Her hands were trembling.

Evan sat down again and waited.

"I—guess you're wondering why I'm here...."

He leaned back in his chair, looking cool and composed. It'd been three long years since she'd seen him. He hadn't changed, at least not outwardly. He remained one of the handsomest men she'd ever seen. His hair was as dark as his eyes, the color of rich Swiss chocolate. His features were well defined, almost chiseled, but that was too harsh a word for the finely cut, yet pronounced lines of his face. Walter

Dryden, Evan's father, was a Massachusetts senator, and it was commonly accepted that Evan would one day enter politics himself. He certainly had the smooth, clean-cut good looks for such a calling.

What had made him fall in love with Mary Jo? She'd always wondered, always been fascinated by that question. She suspected it had to do with being different from the other women he'd dated. She'd amused him, hadn't taken him too seriously, made him laugh.

"You have something you wanted to discuss with me?" he prompted, his tone revealing the slightest hint of irritation.

"Yes...sorry," she said, quickly returning her attention to the matter at hand. "My parents...actually, my father...he retired not long ago," she said, rushing the words together, "and he invested his savings with a financial company, Adison Investments. Have you ever heard of the firm?"

"No, I can't say I have."

This didn't surprise Mary Jo. Wealthy men like Evan had huge financial portfolios with varied and multiple investments. Her father had taken his life's savings and entrusted it to a man he'd met and trusted completely.

"Dad invested everything he had with the company," she continued. "According to the terms of the agreement, he was to receive monthly interest checks. He hasn't. At first there were a number of plausible excuses, which Dad readily accepted. He wanted to believe this Bill Adison so much that it was easier to accept the excuses than face the truth."

"Which is?" Evan asked.

"I...I don't know. That's why I'm here. My father worked for thirty-five years as a construction electrician. He's raised six children, scrimped and saved all that time to put something extra away for his retirement. He wanted to be able to travel with Mom. They've dreamed of touring the South Pacific, and now I'm afraid they're going to be cheated out of everything."

Evan scribbled down a few notes.

"I'm coming to you because I'm afraid my brothers are about to take things into their own hands. Jack and Rich went to Adison's office last week and made such a fuss they were almost arrested. It'd destroy my parents if my brothers ended up in jail over this. As far as I can see, the only way to handle it is through an attorney."

Evan made another note. "Did you bring the papers your father signed?"

"No. I didn't tell anyone I was coming to see you. I thought if I could convince you to take this case for my family, I'd bring my parents in and you could discuss the details with them. You need to understand that it's more than the money. My dad's embarrassed that he could have trusted such a man. He feels like an old fool." Her father had become very depressed. Adison Investments had robbed him of far more than his retirement savings. They'd taken his self-confidence and left him feeling vulnerable and inept.

"There are strict laws governing investments in this state."

Anxious to hear what he had to say, Mary Jo

leaned forward in her chair. This was the very reason she'd swallowed her pride and come to Evan. He had the knowledge and political clout to be effective in ways her family never could.

"Then you can help us?" she asked eagerly. Evan's hesitation sent her heart plummeting. "I'll be happy to pay you whatever your fee is," she added, as if that was his sole concern. "I wouldn't expect you to charge less than you'd receive from anyone else."

Evan stood and walked over to the window, his back to her. "Our firm specializes in corporate law."

"That doesn't mean you can't take this case, does it?"

Evan clenched his hands at his sides, then flexed his fingers. "No, but these sorts of cases have a tendency to become involved. You may end up having to sue."

"My family's willing to do whatever to takes to settle this matter," she said with a stubborn tilt to her jaw.

"Lawsuits don't come cheap," he warned, turning around to face her.

"I don't care and neither do my brothers. True, they don't know I made an appointment to see you, but once I tell them, I'm sure they'll be willing to chip in whatever they can to cover your fee." They wouldn't be able to afford much. Mary Jo was the youngest of six and the only girl. Her brothers were all married and raising young families. There never seemed to be enough money to go around. The burden of the expense would fall on her shoulders, but Mary Jo accepted that.

"You're sure you want me to handle this?" Evan asked, frowning.

"Positive. There isn't anyone I trust more," she said simply. Her eyes met his and she refused to look away.

"I could recommend another attorney, someone far more qualified in the area of investment fraud—"

"No," she broke in. "I don't trust anyone but you." She hadn't meant to tell him that and, embarrassed, quickly lowered her gaze.

He didn't say anything for what seemed like a very long time. Mary Jo held her breath, waiting. If he expected her to plead, she'd do it willingly. It was fair compensation for the appalling way she'd treated him. "Please," she said, her voice low and trembling.

Evan's shoulders lifted in a drawn-out sigh. "Before I decide, fill me in on what you've been doing for the past three years."

Mary Jo hadn't anticipated this, wasn't prepared to discuss her life. "I'm still teaching."

"Kindergarten?"

"Yes," she said enthusiastically. She loved her job. "Five-year-olds are still my favorites."

"I notice you're not wearing a wedding band."

Her gaze automatically fell to her ring finger, and she pinched her lips tightly together.

"So you didn't marry lover boy, after all."

"No."

"What happened?" he asked. He almost seemed to enjoy questioning her. Mary Jo felt as though she were on the witness stand being cross-examined.

She shrugged, not wanting to become trapped in

a growing web of untruths. She'd regretted that stupid lie every day for the past three years.

"It didn't work out?" he suggested.

This was agony for her. "You're right. It didn't work out."

He grinned then, for the first time, as if that delighted him.

"Are you seeing someone now?"

"I don't believe that information's necessary to the case. You're my attorney, not my confessor."

"I'm nothing to you," he said and his words were sharp. "At least not yet."

"Will you take the case or won't you?" she demanded.

"I haven't decided."

He did want her to grovel. And they said hell hath no fury like a *woman* scorned. Apparently women didn't hold the patent on that.

"Gary Copeland," she said stiffly, without emotion. "Gary and I've been seeing each other for several months."

"Another teacher?"

"He's a fireman."

Evan nodded thoughtfully.

"Will you or won't you help my parents?" she asked again, growing tired of this silly game.

He was silent for a moment, then said abruptly, "All right. I'll make some inquiries and learn what I can about Adison Investments."

Mary Jo was so relieved and grateful she sagged in her chair.

"Make an appointment with Mrs. Sterling for next

week, and bring your father with you. Friday would be best. I'll be in court most of the week."

"Thank you, Evan," she whispered, blinking rapidly in an effort to fight back tears.

She stood, eager now to escape. Resisting the urge to hug him, she hurried out of his office, past Mrs. Sterling and into the hallway. She was in such a blind rush she nearly collided with a woman holding a toddler in her arms.

"Oh, I'm so sorry," Mary Jo said, catching herself. "I'm afraid I wasn't watching where I was going."

"No problem," the other woman said with a friendly smile. She held the child protectively against her hip. The little boy, dressed in a blue-and-white sailor suit, looked up at her with eyes that were dark and solemn. Dark as rich Swiss chocolate.

Evan's eyes.

Mary Jo stared at the tall lovely woman. This was Jessica, Evan's wife, and the baby in her arms was Evan's son. The flash of pain nearly paralyzed her.

"I shouldn't have been standing so close to the door," Jessica went on to say. "My husband said he was taking us to lunch, and asked me to meet him here."

"You must be Jessica Dryden," Mary Jo said, finding the strength to offer her a genuine smile. She couldn't take her eyes off Evan's son. He now wore a cheerful grin and waved small chubby arms. If circumstances had been different, this child might have been her own. The void inside her widened; she'd never felt so bleak, so empty.

"This is Andy." Jessica did a small curtsy with her son in her arms.

"Hello, Andy." Mary Jo gave him her hand, and like a proper gentleman, he took it and promptly tried to place it in his mouth.

Jessica laughed. "I'm afraid he's teething. Everything goes to his mouth first." She walked with Mary Jo toward the elevator, bouncing the impatient toddler against her hip. "You look familiar," she said casually. "Do I know you?"

"I don't think so. My name's Mary Jo Summerhill."

Jessica's face went blank, then recognition swept into her eyes as her smile slowly evaporated. Any censure, however, was quickly disguised.

"It was nice meeting you," Mary Jo said, speeding up as they neared the door.

"Evan's mentioned you," Jessica told her.

Mary Jo stopped suddenly. "He has?" She couldn't help it. Curiosity got the better of her.

"Yes. He…thought very highly of you."

That Jessica used the past tense didn't escape Mary Jo. "He's a top-notch attorney."

"He's wonderful," Jessica agreed. "By the way, I understand we have a mutual friend. Earl Kress."

Earl had been a volunteer at Mary Jo's school. He'd tutored slow readers, and she'd admired his patience and persistence, and especially his sense of humor. The children loved him.

Earl mentioned Evan's name at every opportunity. He seemed to idolize Evan for taking on his civil suit against the school district—and winning.

Earl had graduated from high school functionally illiterate. Because he was a talented athlete, he'd been passed from one grade to the next. Sports were important to the schools, and the teachers were coerced into giving him passing grades. Earl had been awarded a full-ride college scholarship but suffered a serious knee injury in football training camp two weeks after he arrived. Within a couple of months, he'd flunked out of college. In a landmark case, Earl had sued the school district for his education. Evan had been his attorney.

The case had been in the headlines for weeks. During the trial, Mary Jo had been glued to the television every night, eager for news. As a teacher, she was, of course, concerned with this crucial education issue. But in all honesty, her interest had less to do with Earl Kress than with Evan. Following the case gave her the opportunity to see him again, even if it was only on a television screen and for a minute or two at a time.

She'd cheered when she heard Earl had won his case.

In the kind of irony that life sometimes presents, Mary Jo met Earl about a year later. He was attending college classes and volunteering part-time as a tutor at the grade school. They'd become friends. She admired the young man and missed him now that he'd returned to the same university where he'd once failed. Again he'd gone on a scholarship, but this time it was an academic one.

"Yes, I know Earl," Mary Jo said.

"He told Evan he'd been working with you. We were surprised to learn you weren't married."

Evan knew! He'd made her squirm and forced her to tell him the truth when all along he'd been perfectly aware that she was still single. Mary Jo's hands knotted at her sides. He'd taken a little too much delight in squeezing the information out of her.

"Darling," a husky male voice said from behind Mary Jo. "I hope I didn't keep you waiting." He walked over to Jessica, lifted Andy out of her arms and kissed her on the cheek.

Mary Jo's jaw fell open as she stared at the couple.

"Have you met my husband?" Jessica asked. "Damian, this is Mary Jo Summerhill."

"How…hello." Mary Jo was so flustered she could barely think.

Evan wasn't married to Jessica. His *brother* was.

Chapter 2

"Can you help us?" Norman Summerhill asked Evan anxiously.

Mary Jo had brought both her parents. Evan was reading over the agreement her father had signed with Adison Investments. With a sick feeling in the pit of her stomach, she noticed he was frowning. The frown deepened the longer he read.

"What's wrong?" Mary Jo asked.

Her mother's hands were clenched so tightly that her fingers were white. Financial affairs confused and upset Marianna Summerhill. From the time Marianna had married Norman, she'd been a housewife and mother, leaving the financial details of their lives to her husband.

Mary Jo was fiercely proud of her family. Her

father might not be a United States senator, but he was an honest and honorable man. He'd dedicated his life to his family, and worked hard through the years to provide for them. Mary Jo had been raised firmly rooted in her parents' love for each other and for their children.

Although close to sixty, her mother was still a beautiful woman, inside and out. Mary Jo had inherited her dark hair and brown eyes and her petite five-foot-four-inch frame. But the prominent high cheekbones and square jaw were undeniably from her father's side of the family. Her brothers towered above her and, like her parents, were delighted their youngest sibling was a girl.

That affection was returned. Mary Jo adored her older brothers, but she knew them and their quirks and foibles well. Living with five boys—all very different personalities—had given her plenty of practice in deciphering the male psyche. Evan might have come from a rich, upper-crust family, but he was a man, and she'd been able to read him like a book from the first. She believed that her ability to see through his playboy facade was what had originally attracted him. That attraction had grown and blossomed until...

"Come by for Sunday dinner. We eat about three, and we'd enjoy getting to know you better," her mother was saying. "It'd be an honor to have you at our table again."

The words cut into Mary Jo's thoughts like a scythe through wheat. "I'm sure Evan's too busy for that, Mother," she blurted out.

"I appreciate the invitation," Evan said, ignoring Mary Jo.

"You're welcome to stop by the house any time you like, young man," her father added, sending his daughter a frown of disapproval.

"Thank you. I'll keep it in mind," Evan said absently as he returned his attention to the investment papers. "If you don't object, I'd like an attorney friend of mine to read this over. I should have an answer for you in the next week or so."

Her father nodded. "You do whatever you think is necessary. And don't you worry about your fee."

"Dad, I already told you! I've talked to Evan about that. This is my gift to you."

"Nonsense," her father argued, scowling. "I was the one who was fool enough to trust this shyster. If anyone pays Evan's fee, it'll be me."

"We don't need to worry about that right now," Evan interjected smoothly. "We'll work out the details of my bill later."

"That sounds fair to me." Norman Summerhill was quick to agree, obviously eager to put the subject behind him. Her father had carried his own weight all his life and wouldn't take kindly to Mary Jo's accepting responsibility for this debt. She hoped she could find a way to do so without damaging his formidable pride.

"Thank you for your time," she said to Evan, desperate to leave.

"It was good to see you again, young man," Norman said expansively, shaking hands with Evan. "No need to make yourself scarce. You're welcome for dinner any Sunday of the year."

"Daddy, please," Mary Jo groaned under her breath. The last thing she wanted was to have Evan show up for Sunday dinner with her five brothers and their assorted families. Her one dinner with his family had sufficiently pointed out the glaring differences between their backgrounds.

"Before you go," Evan said to Mary Jo, "my brother asked me to give you this. I believe it's from Jessica." He handed her a sealed envelope.

"Thank you," Mary Jo mumbled. For the better part of their meeting, he'd avoiding speaking to her. He hadn't been rude or tactless, just businesslike and distant. At least toward her. With her parents, he'd been warm and gracious. She doubted they'd even recognized the subtle difference between how he'd treated them and how he'd treated her.

Mary Jo didn't open the envelope until she'd arrived back at her cozy duplex apartment. She stared at it for several minutes, wondering what Jessica Dryden could possibly have to say to her.

No need to guess, she decided, and tore open the envelope.

Dear Mary Jo,
I just wanted you to know how much I enjoyed meeting you. When I asked Evan why you were in to see him, he clammed right up. I should've known better—prying information out of Evan is even more difficult than it is with Damian.

From your reaction the other day, I could tell
you assumed I was married to Evan. Damian
and I got quite a chuckle out of that. You see,
just about everyone tried to match me up with
Evan, but I only had eyes for Damian. If you're
free some afternoon, give me a call. Perhaps
we could have lunch.
Warmest regards,
Jessica

Jessica had written her telephone number beneath
her signature.

Mary Jo couldn't understand why Damian's wife
would seek her out. They were virtual strangers. Perhaps Jessica knew something Mary Jo didn't—something about Evan. The only way to find out was to
call.

Although Mary Jo wasn't entirely sure about
doing this, she reached for the phone.

Jessica Dryden answered almost immediately.

"Mary Jo! I'm so glad to hear from you," she said.
"I wondered what you'd think about my note. I don't
usually do that sort of thing, but I was just so pleased
you'd been to see Evan."

"You said he's mentioned me?"

"A number of times. Look, why don't you come
over one afternoon soon and we can talk? You're not
teaching right now, are you?"

"School let out a week ago."

"That's what I thought. Could you stop by next
week? I'd really enjoy talking to you."

Mary Jo hesitated. Her first introduction to Evan's

family had been a catastrophe, and she'd come away knowing their love didn't stand a chance. A second sortie might prove equally disastrous.

"I'd like that very much," Mary Jo found herself saying. If Evan had been talking about her, she wanted to know what he'd said.

"Great. How about next Tuesday afternoon? Come for lunch and we can sit on the patio and have a nice long chat."

"That sounds great," Mary Jo said.

It wasn't until later that evening, when she was filling a croissant with a curried shrimp mixture for dinner, that Mary Jo stopped to wonder exactly *why* Jessica was so eager to "chat" with her.

She liked Gary. She really did. Though why she felt it was necessary to remind herself of this, she didn't know. She didn't even want to know.

It had been like this from the moment she'd broken off her relationship with Evan. She'd found fault with every man she'd dated. Regardless of how attractive he was. Or how successful. How witty, how considerate...it didn't matter.

Gary was very *nice,* she repeated to herself.

Unfortunately he bored her to tears. He talked about his golf game, his bowling score and his prowess on the handball court. Never anything that was important to her. But his biggest fault, she'd realized early on in their relationship, was that he wasn't Evan.

They'd dated infrequently since the beginning of the year. To be honest, Mary Jo was beginning to think that, to Gary, her biggest attraction was her mother's cooking. Invariably, Gary stopped by early on Sunday afternoon, just as she was about to leave for her parents' home. It'd happened three out of the past five weeks. She suspected he'd been on duty at the fire hall the two weeks he'd missed.

"You look lovely this afternoon," he said when she opened her front door to him now. He held out a bouquet of pink carnations, which she took with a smile, pleased by his thoughtfulness.

"Hello, Gary."

He kissed her cheek, but it seemed perfunctory, as if he felt some display of affection was expected of him. "How've you been?" he muttered, easing himself into the old rocking chair next to the fireplace.

Although Mary Jo's rooms were small, she'd carefully decorated each one. The living room had an Early American look. Her brother Lonny, who did beautiful woodwork, had carved her an eagle for Christmas, which she'd hung above the fireplace. In addition to her antique rocking chair, she had a small sofa and an old oak chest that she'd restored herself. Her mother had crocheted an afghan for the back of the sofa in a patriotic blend of red, white and blue.

Her kitchen was little more than a wide hallway that led to a compact dining space in a window alcove. Mary Jo loved to sit there in the morning sunshine with a cup of coffee and a book.

"You're lucky, you know," Gary said, gesturing around the room.

"How do you mean?"

"Well, first off, you don't have to work in the summer."

This was an old argument and Mary Jo was tired of hearing it. True, school wasn't in session for those two and a half months, but she didn't spend them lolling on a beach. This was the first summer in years that she wasn't attending courses to upgrade her skills.

"You've got the time you need to fix up this place the way you want it," he went on. "You have real decorating talent, you know. My place is a mess, but then I'm only there three or four days out of the week, if that."

If he was hinting that he'd like her to help him decorate his apartment, she refused to take the bait.

"Are you going over to your parents' this afternoon?" Gary asked cheerfully. "I don't mean to horn in, but your family doesn't seem to mind, and the two of us have an understanding, don't we?"

"An...understanding?" This was news to Mary Jo.

"Yeah. We're...I don't know, going together, I guess."

"I thought we were just friends." That was all Mary Jo intended the relationship to be.

"Just friends." Gary's face fell. His gaze wandered to the carnations he'd brought.

"When was the last time we went out on a date?" she asked, crossing her arms. "A real date."

"You mean to the movies or something?"

"Sure." Surveying her own memory, she could count on one hand the number of times he'd actually spent money taking her out. The carnations were an exception.

"We went to the Red Sox game, remember?"

"That was in April," she reminded him.

Gary frowned. "That long ago? Time certainly flies, doesn't it?"

"It sure does."

Gary rubbed his face. "You're right, Mary Jo. I've taken you for granted, haven't I?"

She was about to say they really didn't have much of an understanding, after all, did they. Yet a serious relationship with Gary didn't interest her and, difficult as it was to admit now, never had. She'd used him to block out the loneliness. She'd used him so her parents wouldn't worry about her. They firmly believed that a woman, especially a young woman, needed a man in her life, so she'd trotted out Gary in order to keep the peace. She wasn't exactly proud of her motives.

Gary reached for her hand. "How about a movie this afternoon?" he suggested contritely. "We'll leave right after dinner at your parents'. We can invite anyone who wants to come along. You wouldn't mind, would you?"

Gary was honestly trying. He couldn't help it that he wasn't Evan Dryden. The thought slipped uncensored into her mind.

"A movie sounds like a great idea," she said firmly. She was going, and furthermore, she was determined to have a wonderful time. Just because Evan Dryden had briefly reentered her life was no reason to wallow in the impossible. He was way out of her league.

"Great." A smile lighted his boyish face. "Let's drive over to your mom and dad's place now."

"All right," Mary Jo said. She felt better already. Her relationship with Gary wasn't ideal—it wasn't even close to ideal—but he was her friend. Love and marriage had been built on a whole lot less.

Before they left the house, Gary grabbed the bouquet of carnations. Mary Jo blinked in surprise, and he hesitated, looking mildly chagrined. "I thought we'd give these to your mother. You don't mind, do you?"

"Of course not," she mumbled, but she did, just a little.

Gary must have realized it because he added, "Next time I'll bring some just for you."

"You owe me one, Mr. Copeland."

He laughed good-naturedly and with an elaborate display of courtesy, opened the car door for her.

Mary Jo slid into the seat and snapped her seat belt in place. During the brief drive to her parents' house, less than two miles away, she and Gary didn't speak; instead, they listened companionably to part of a Red Sox game.

Her nephews and nieces were out in the huge side yard, playing a rousing game of volleyball when they arrived. Gary parked his car behind her oldest brother's station wagon.

"I get a kick out of how much fun your family has together," he said a bit wistfully.

"We have our share of squabbles, too." But disagreements were unusual and quickly resolved. Three of her brothers, Jack, Rich and Lonny, were construction electricians like their father. Rob and Mark had both become mechanics and opened a shop together.

They were still struggling to get on their feet financially, but both worked hard. With time, they'd make a go of it; Mary Jo was convinced of that.

"I wonder what your mother decided to cook today," Gary mused, and Mary Jo swore he all but licked his chops.

Briefly she wondered if Gary bothered to eat during the week, or if he stored up his appetite for Sunday dinners with her family.

"I've been introduced to all your brothers, haven't I?" he asked, frowning slightly as he helped her out of the car.

Mary Jo had to think about that. He must have been. Not every brother came every Sunday, but over the course of the past few months surely Gary had met each of her five brothers.

"I don't recognize the guy in the red sweatshirt," he said as they moved up the walk toward the house.

Mary Jo was distracted from answering by her mother, who came rushing down the porch steps, holding out her arms as if it'd been weeks since they'd last seen each other. She wore an apron and a smile that sparkled with delight. "Mary Jo! I'm so glad you're here." She hugged her daughter close for a long moment, then turned toward Gary.

"How sweet," she said, taking the bouquet of carnations and kissing his cheek.

Still smiling, Marianna turned back to her daughter. "You'll never guess who came by!"

It was then that Mary Jo noticed Evan walking toward them. Dressed in jeans and a red sweatshirt, he carried Lenny, her six-year-old nephew, tucked under one arm, and Robby, his older brother by a year, under the other. Both boys were kicking and laughing.

Evan stopped abruptly when he saw Mary Jo and Gary. The laughter drained out of his eyes.

"Hello," Gary said, stepping forward. "You must be one of Mary Jo's brothers. I don't believe we've met. I'm Gary Copeland."

Chapter 3

"**W**hat are you *doing* here?" Mary Jo demanded the minute she could get Evan alone. With a house full of people, it had taken her the better part of two hours to corner him. As it was, they were standing in the hallway and could be interrupted at any moment.

"If you'll recall, your mother invited me."

"The only reason you're here is to embarrass me." The entire meal had been an exercise in frustration for Mary Jo. Evan had been the center of attention and had answered a multitude of questions from her parents and brothers. As for the way he'd treated Gary—every time she thought about it, she seethed. Anyone watching them would think Evan and Gary were old pals. Evan had joked with Gary, even going so far as to mention that Mary Jo's ears grew red whenever she was uncomfortable with a subject.

The second he'd said it, she felt the blood rush to her ears. Soon they were so hot she was afraid Gary might mistake them for a fire engine.

What upset her most was the fact that Evan had her family eating out of his hand. Everyone acted as though he was some sort of celebrity! Her mother had offered him the first slice of chocolate cake, something Mary Jo could never remember happening. No matter who was seated at the dinner table, her father had always been served first.

"I didn't mean to make you uncomfortable," Evan said now, his eyes as innocent as a preschooler's.

Mary Jo wasn't fooled. She knew exactly why he'd come—to humiliate her in front of her family. Rarely had she been angrier. Rarely had she felt more frustrated. Tears filled her eyes and blurred her vision.

"You can think what you want of me, but don't *ever* laugh at my family," she said from between gritted teeth. She whirled away and had taken all of two steps when he caught hold of her shoulder and yanked her around.

Now he was just as angry. His dark eyes burned with it. They scowled at each other, faces tight, hands clenched.

"I would never laugh at your family," he said evenly.

Mary Jo straightened her shoulders defiantly. "But you look forward to make a laughingstock out of *me*. Let me give you an example. You knew I wasn't married, yet you manipulated me into admitting it. You *enjoy* making me uncomfortable!"

He grinned then, a sly off-center grin. "I figured you owed me that much."

"I don't owe you anything!" she snapped.

"Perhaps not," he agreed. He was laughing at her, had been from the moment she'd stepped into his high-priced office. Like an unsuspecting fly, she'd carelessly gotten caught in a spider's web.

"Stay out of my life," she warned, eyes narrowed.

Evan glared back at her. "Gladly."

Just then Sarah, one of Mary Jo's favorite nieces, came skipping down the hallway as only a five-year-old can, completely unaware of the tension between her and Evan. Sarah stopped when she saw Mary Jo with Evan.

"Hi," she said, looking up at them.

"Hello, sweetheart," Mary Jo said, forcing herself to smile. Her mouth felt as if it would crack.

Sarah stared at Evan, her eyes wide with curiosity. "Are you going to be my uncle someday?"

"No," Mary Jo answered immediately, mortified. It seemed that even her own family had turned against her.

"Why not?" Sarah wanted to know. "I like him better than Gary, and he likes you, too. I can tell. When we were eating dinner, he kept looking at you. Like Daddy looks at Mommy."

"I'm dating Gary," Mary Jo insisted, "and he's taking me to a movie. You can come if you want."

Sarah shook her head. "Gary likes *you,* but he doesn't like kids very much."

Mary Jo's heart sank. She'd noticed that about Gary herself. He wasn't accustomed to small children; he tolerated them, but kid noise irritated him. Evan, on the other hand, was an instant hit with both the adults and the kids. Nothing her nieces or nephews said or did seemed to bother him. If anything, he appeared to enjoy himself. He'd played volleyball and baseball with her brothers, chess with her father, and wrestled with the kids—ten against one.

"I hope you marry Evan," Sarah said, her expression serious. Having stated her opinion, she skipped on down to the end of the hallway.

"Mary Jo."

Before she could say anything else to Evan—although she didn't know what—Gary came looking for her. He stopped abruptly when he saw who she was with.

"I didn't mean to interrupt anything," he said, shoving his hands in his pockets, obviously uncomfortable.

"You didn't," Mary Jo answered decisively. "Now, what movie do you think we should see?" She turned her back on Evan and walked toward Gary, knowing in her heart that Sarah was right. Evan was the man for her. Not Gary.

"I'm absolutely thrilled that you came," Jessica Dryden said, opening the front door. Mary Jo stepped into the Dryden home, mildly surprised that a maid or other household help hadn't greeted her. From what she remembered of the older Drydens' home, Whispering Willows, the domestic staff had been with them for nearly thirty years.

"Thank you for inviting me," Mary Jo said, looking around. The house was a sprawling rambler decorated with comfortable modern furniture. An ocean scene graced the wall above the fireplace, but it wasn't by an artist Mary Jo recognized. Judging by the decor and relaxed atmosphere, Damian and Jessica seemed to be a fairly typical young couple.

"I fixed us a seafood salad," Jessica said, leading Mary Jo into the large, spotless kitchen. She followed, her eyes taking in everything around her. Jessica and Damian's home was spacious and attractive, but it was nothing like Whispering Willows.

"You made the salad yourself?" Mary Jo asked. She didn't mean to sound rude, but she'd assumed Jessica had kitchen help.

"Yes," Jessica answered pleasantly. "I'm a fairly good cook. At least Damian hasn't complained. Much," she added with a dainty laugh. "I thought we'd eat on the patio. That is, if you don't mind. It's such a beautiful afternoon. I was working in the garden earlier and I cut us some roses. They're so lovely this time of year."

Sliding glass doors led to a brick-lined patio. A round glass table, shaded by a brightly striped umbrella, was set with two pink placemats and linen napkins. A bouquet of yellow roses rested in the middle.

"Would you like iced tea with lunch?" Jessica asked next.

"Please."

"Sit down and I'll bring everything out."

"Let me help." Mary Jo wasn't accustomed to being waited on and would've been uncomfortable letting Jessica do all the work. She followed her into the kitchen and carried out the pitcher of tea while Jessica brought the seafood salad.

"Where's Andy?" Mary Jo asked.

"Napping." She set the salad bowl and matching plates on the table and glanced at her watch. "We'll have a solid hour of peace. I hope."

They sat down together. Jessica gazed at her earnestly and began to speak. "You must think I'm terribly presumptuous to have written you that note, but I'm dying to talk to you."

"I'll admit curiosity is what brought me here," Mary Jo confessed. She'd expected to feel awkward and out of place, but Jessica was so easygoing and unpretentious Mary Jo felt perfectly at ease.

"I've known Evan from the time I was a kid. We grew up next door to each other," Jessica explained. "When I was a teenager I had the biggest crush on him. I made an absolute fool of myself." She shook her head wryly.

Mary Jo thought it was no wonder she found herself liking Jessica so much. They obviously had a great deal in common—especially when it came to Evan!

"As you may be aware, I worked with Evan when he represented Earl Kress. Naturally Evan and I spent a lot of time together. We became good friends and he told me about you."

Mary Jo nervously smoothed the linen napkin across her lap. She wasn't sure she wanted to hear what Jessica had to say.

"I hurt him badly, didn't I?" she asked, keeping her head lowered.

"Yes." Apparently Jessica didn't believe in mincing words. "I don't know what happened between you and the man you left Evan for, but clearly it didn't work out the way you expected."

"Few things in life work out the way we expect them to, do they?" Mary Jo answered cryptically.

"No." Jessica set down her fork. "For a while I was convinced there wasn't any hope for Damian and me. You see, I loved Damian, but everyone kept insisting Evan and I should be a couple. It gets confusing, so I won't go into the details, but Damian seemed to think he was doing the noble thing by stepping aside so I could marry Evan. It didn't seem to matter that I was in love with *him*. Everything was complicated even more by family expectations. Oh, my heavens," she said with a heartfelt sigh, "those were very bleak days."

"But you figured everything out."

"Yes," Jessica said with a relaxed smile. "It wasn't easy, but it was sure worth the effort." She paused, resting her hands in her lap. "This is the reason I asked you to have lunch with me. What happens between you and Evan is none of my business. And knowing Evan, he'd be furious with me if he knew I was even speaking to you, but…" She stopped and took in a deep breath. "You once had something very special with Evan. I'm hoping that with a little effort on both your parts you can reclaim it."

A cloak of sadness seemed to settle over Mary Jo's shoulders, and when she spoke her words were little more than a whisper. "It isn't possible anymore."

"Why isn't it? I don't know why you've come to Evan. That's not my affair. But I do realize how much courage it must have taken. You're already halfway there, Mary Jo. Don't give up now."

Mary Jo wished she could believe that, but it was too late for her and Evan now. Whatever chance they'd had as a couple had been destroyed long ago.

By her own hand.

Her reasons for breaking off the relationship hadn't changed. She'd done it because she had to, and she'd done it in such a way that Evan would never forgive her. That was part of her plan—for his sake.

"I almost think Evan hates me," she murmured. Speaking was painful; there was a catch in her voice.

"Nonsense," Jessica said briskly. "I don't believe that for a moment."

Mary Jo wished she could accept her friend's words, but Jessica hadn't been there when Evan suggested she hire another attorney. Jessica hadn't seen the look in Evan's eyes when she'd confronted him in the hallway of her family home. Nor had she been there when Mary Jo had introduced him to Gary.

He despised her, and the ironic thing was that she couldn't blame him.

"Just remember what I said," Jessica urged. "Be patient with Evan, and with yourself. But most of all, don't give up, not until you're absolutely convinced it'll never work. I speak from experience, Mary Jo—the rewards are well worth whatever it costs your pride. I can't imagine my life without Damian and Andy."

After a brief silence, Mary Jo resolutely changed the subject, and the two women settled down to their meal. Conversation was lighthearted—books and movies they'd both enjoyed, anecdotes about friends and family, opinions about various public figures.

They were continuing a good-natured disagreement over one of the Red Sox pitchers as they carried their plates inside. Just as they reached the kitchen, the doorbell chimed.

"I'll get that," Jessica said.

Smiling, Mary Jo rinsed off the plates and placed them in the dishwasher. She liked Jessica very much. Damian's wife was open and natural and had a wonderful sense of humor. She was also deeply in love with her husband.

"It's Evan," Jessica said, returning to the kitchen. Her voice was strained and tense. Evan stood stiffly behind his sister-in-law. "He dropped off some papers for Damian."

"Uh, hello, Evan," Mary Jo said awkwardly.

Jessica's gaze pleaded with her to believe she hadn't arranged this accidental meeting.

Andy let out a piercing cry, and Mary Jo thought the toddler had the worst sense of timing of any baby she'd ever known.

Jessica excused herself, and Mary Jo was left standing next to the dishwasher, wishing she was anywhere else in the world.

"What are you doing here?" he demanded the minute Jessica was out of earshot.

"You showed up at *my* family's home. Why is it so shocking that I'm at your brother's house?"

"I was invited," he reminded her fiercely.

"So was I."

He looked for a moment as if he doubted her.

"Fine. I suppose you and Jessica have decided to become bosom buddies. That sounds like something you'd do."

Mary Jo didn't have a response to such a patently unfair remark.

"As it happens," Evan said in an obvious attempt to put his anger behind him, "I was meaning to call you this afternoon, anyway."

"About my parents' case?" she asked anxiously.

"I've talked with my colleague about Adison Investments, and it looks as if it'll involve some lengthy litigation."

Mary Jo leaned against the kitchen counter. "Lengthy is another word for expensive, right?"

"I was prepared to discuss my fee with you at the same time," he went on in a businesslike tone.

"All right," she said, tensing.

"I can't see this costing anything less than twenty or thirty thousand."

She couldn't help a sharp intake of breath. That amount of money was a fortune to her parents. To her, too.

"It could go even higher."

Which was another way of saying he wasn't willing to handle the case. Mary Jo felt the sudden need to sit down. She walked over to the table, pulled out a chair and sank into it.

"I'd be willing to do what I can, but—"

"Don't lie to me, Evan," she said, fighting back her hurt and frustration. She'd come to him because he had the clout and the influence to help her family. Because he was a damn good attorney. Because she'd trusted him to be honest and ethical.

"I'm not lying."

"That kind of money is far beyond what my parents or I can afford. It may not be a lot to you or your family, but there's no way we could hope to raise that much in a short amount of time."

"I'm willing to take payments."

How very generous of him, she mused sarcastically.

"There might be another way," he said.

"What?"

"If you agree, of course."

Mary Jo wasn't sure she liked the sound of this.

"A summer job. You're out of school, aren't you?" She nodded.

"My personal assistant, Mrs. Sterling, is taking an extended European vacation this summer. I'd intended to hire a replacement, but as I recall your computer and dictation skills are excellent."

"My computer skills are very basic and I never took shorthand."

He grinned as if that didn't matter. Obviously, what did matter was making her miserable for the next two months.

"But you're a fast learner. Am I right or wrong?" he pressed.

"Well…I do pick up things fairly easily."

"That's what I thought." He spread out his hands. "Now, do you want the job or not?"

Chapter 4

"Mr. Dryden's a real pleasure to work for. I'm sure you won't have any problems," Mrs. Sterling said, looking relieved and happy that Mary Jo would be substituting for her. "Evan's not the least bit demanding, and I can't think of even one time he's been unreasonable."

Mary Jo suspected that might not be the case with her.

"I could have retired with my husband, but I enjoy my job so much I decided to stay on," Mrs. Sterling continued. "I couldn't bear leaving that young man. In some ways, I think of Evan as my own son."

"I'm sure he reciprocates your feelings," Mary Jo said politely. She didn't know how much longer she could endure listening to this list of Evan's finer qualities. Not that she doubted they were true. For Mrs. Sterling.

Thus far, Evan had embarrassed her in front of her family and blackmailed her into working for him. She had a problem picturing him as Prince Charming to her Cinderella. As for his being a "real pleasure" to work for, Mary Jo entertained some serious reservations.

"I'm glad you've got the opportunity to travel with your husband," Mary Jo said.

"That's another thing," Evan's personal assistant gushed. "What boss would be willing to let his personal assistant go for two whole months like this? It's a terrible inconvenience to him. Nevertheless, Mr. Dryden encouraged me to take this trip with Dennis. Why, he *insisted* I go. I promise you, they don't come any better than Mr. Dryden. You're going to thoroughly enjoy your summer."

Mary Jo's smile was weak at best.

Evan wanted her under his thumb, and much as she disliked giving in to the pressure, she had no choice. Twenty or thirty thousand dollars would financially cripple her parents. Evan knew that. He was also well aware that her brothers weren't in any position to contribute.

With the slump in the economy, new construction starts had been way down. Jack, Rich and Lonny had collected unemployment benefits most of the winter and were just scraping by now. Rob and Mark's automotive business was barely on its feet.

She was the one who'd gone to Evan for help, and she was the one who'd accepted the financial respon-

sibility. When she'd told her parents she'd be working for Evan, they were both delighted. Her mother
seemed to think it was the perfect solution. Whether
Evan had planned it this way or not, his employ-
ing her had smoothed her father's ruffled feathers
about Evan's fee. Apparently, letting her pick up any
out-of-pocket expenses was unacceptable to Norman Summerhill, but an exchange of services, so to
speak, was fine.

Evan, who could do no wrong as far as her parents were concerned, came out of this smelling like
a rose—to use one of her dad's favorite expressions.

Mary Jo wondered if she was being unfair to assume that Evan was looking for vengeance, for a
means of making her life miserable. Perhaps she'd
misjudged him.

Perhaps. But she doubted it.

"I'm taking my lunch now," Mrs. Sterling said,
pulling open the bottom drawer of her desk and taking out her handbag. She hesitated. "You will be all
right here by yourself, won't you?"

"Of course." Mary Jo made an effort to sound infinitely confident, even if she wasn't. Evan's legal
assistant, Peter McNichols, was on vacation for the
next couple of weeks, so she'd be dealing with Evan
entirely on her own.

Mary Jo wasn't emotionally prepared for that just
yet. The shaky, unsure feeling in the pit of her stomach reminded her of the first time she'd stood in front
of a classroom filled with five-year-olds.

No sooner had Mrs. Sterling left than Evan summoned Mary Jo. Grabbing a pen and pad, she hurried

into his office, determined to be the best substitute personal assistant he could have hired.

"Sit down," he instructed in a curt, businesslike tone.

Mary Jo complied, sitting on the very edge of the chair, her back ramrod-straight, her shoulders stiff.

He reached for a small, well-worn black book and flipped through the flimsy pages, scrutinizing the names. Mary Jo figured it had to be the typical bachelor's infamous "little black book." She knew he had a reputation, after all, as one of Boston's most eligible bachelors. Every six months or so, gossip columns speculated on Evan Dryden's current love interest. A little black book was exactly what she expected of him.

"Order a dozen red roses to be sent to Catherine Moore," he said, and rattled off the address. Mary Jo immediately recognized it as being in a prestigious neighborhood. "Suggest we meet for lunch on the twenty-fifth. Around twelve-thirty." He mentioned one of Boston's most elegant restaurants. "Have you got that?" he asked.

"I'll see to it right away," Mary Jo said crisply, revealing none of her feelings. Evan had done this on purpose. He was having her arrange a lunch date with one of his many conquests in order to humiliate her, to teach her a lesson. It was his way of telling her he'd completely recovered from their short-lived romance. There were any number of women who'd welcome his attentions.

Well, Mary Jo got the message, loud and clear. She got up, ready to return to her desk.

"There's more," Evan said.

Mary Jo sat back down and was barely able to keep up with him as he listed name after name, followed by phone number and address. Each woman was to receive a dozen red roses and an invitation to lunch, with time and place suggested.

When he'd finished, Mary Jo counted six names, each conjuring up a statuesque beauty. No doubt every one of them could run circles around her in looks, talent and, most important, social position.

Mary Jo didn't realize one man would know that many places to eat with so many different women, but she wisely kept her opinion to herself. If he was hoping she'd give him the satisfaction of a response, he was dead wrong.

She'd just finished ordering the flowers when Damian Dryden stepped into the office.

"Hello," he said. His eyes widened with surprise at finding her sitting at Mrs. Sterling's desk.

Mary Jo stood and extended her hand. "I'm Mary Jo Summerhill. We met briefly last week." She didn't mention the one other time she'd been introduced to Damian, certain he wouldn't remember.

It was well over three years ago. Evan and Mary Jo had been sailing, and they'd run into Damian at the marina. Her first impression of Evan's older brother was that of a shrewd businessman. Damian had seemed rather distant. He'd shown little interest in their cheerful commentary on sailing and the weather. From conversations she'd previously had with Evan regarding his brother, she'd learned he was a serious and hardworking lawyer, and that was certainly how he'd struck her—as someone with no time for fun or frivolity. Now he was a Superior Court judge, but he often dropped by the family law firm. Apparently the two brothers were close friends.

The man she'd met on the dock that day and the one who stood before her now might have been two entirely different men. Damian was still serious and hardworking, but he seemed more relaxed now, more apt to smile. Mary Jo was convinced that marriage and fatherhood had made the difference, and she was genuinely happy for him and for Jessica.

"You're working for the firm now?" Damian asked.

"Mrs. Sterling will be traveling in Europe this summer," Mary Jo said, "and Evan, uh, offered me the job." Which was a polite way of saying he'd coerced her into accepting the position.

"But I thought—" Damian stopped abruptly, then grinned. "Is Evan in?"

"Yes. I'll tell him you're here." She reached for the intercom switch and announced Damian, who walked directly into Evan's office.

Mary Jo was acquainting herself with the filing system when she heard Evan burst out laughing. It really wasn't fair to assume it had anything to do with her, but she couldn't help believing that was the case.

Damian left a couple of minutes later, smiling. He paused in front of Mary Jo's desk. "Don't let him give you a hard time," he said pleasantly. "My wife mentioned having you over for lunch last week, but she didn't say you'd accepted a position with the firm."

"I...I didn't know it myself at the time," Mary Jo mumbled. She hadn't actually agreed to the job until much later, after she'd spent a few days examining her limited options.

"I see. Well, it's good to have you on board, Mary Jo. If you have any questions or concerns, don't hesitate to talk to Evan. And if he does give you a hard time, just let me know and I'll straighten him out."

"Thank you," she said, and meant it. Although she couldn't very well see herself complaining to one brother about the other...

She decided to change her attitude about the whole situation. She'd forget about Evan's probable motives and, instead, start looking at the positive side of this opportunity. She'd be able to help her parents now, without dipping into her own savings. Things could definitely be worse.

Mary Jo didn't learn just how *much* worse until Wednesday—the first day she was working on her own. Mrs. Sterling had spent the first two days of the week acquainting Mary Jo with office procedures and the filing system. She'd updated her on Evan's current cases, and Mary Jo felt reasonably confident she could handle whatever came up.

He called her into his office around eleven. "I need the William Jenkins file."

"I'll have it for you right away," she assured him. Mary Jo returned to the outer office and the filing cabinet, and sorted through the colored tabs. She located three clients named Jenkins, none of whom was William. Her heart pounded with dread as she hurried to another drawer, thinking it might have been misfiled.

Five minutes passed. Evan came out of his office, his movements as brusque and irritated as his voice. "Is there a problem?"

"I...can't seem to find the William Jenkins file," she said, hurriedly going through the files one more time. "Are you sure it isn't on your desk?"

"Would I have asked you to find it if I had it on my desk?" She could feel his cold stare directly between her shoulder blades.

"No, I guess not. But it isn't out here."

"It has to be. I distinctly remember giving it to Mrs. Sterling on Monday."

"She had me replace all the files on Monday," Mary Jo admitted reluctantly.

"Then you must have misfiled it."

"I don't recall any file with the name Jenkins," she said stubbornly. She didn't want to make an issue of this, but she'd been extremely careful with every file, even double-checking her work.

"Are you telling me I *didn't* return the file? Are you calling me a liar?"

This wasn't going well. "No," she said in a slow, deliberate voice. "All I'm saying is that I don't recall replacing any file with the name Jenkins on it." Their gazes met and locked in silent battle.

Evan's dark eyes narrowed briefly. "Are you doing this on purpose, Mary Jo?" he asked, crossing his arms over his chest.

"Absolutely not." Outraged, she brought her chin up and returned his glare. "You can think whatever you like, but I'd never do anything so underhanded as hide an important file."

She wasn't sure if he believed her or not, and his lack of trust hurt her more than any words he might have spoken. "If you honestly suspect I'd sabotage your office, then I suggest you fire me immediately."

Evan walked over to the cabinet and pulled open the top drawer. He was searching through the files, the same way she had earlier.

Silently Mary Jo prayed she hadn't inadvertently missed seeing the requested file. The humiliation of having him find it would be unbearable.

"It isn't here," he murmured, sounding almost surprised.

Mary Jo gave an inward sigh of relief.

"Where could it possibly be?" he asked impatiently. "I need it for an appointment this afteroon."

Mary Jo edged a couple of steps toward him. "Would you mind if I looked in your office?"

He gestured toward the open door. "Be my guest."

She sorted through the stack of files on the corner of his desk and leafed through his briefcase, all to no avail. Glancing at the clock, she groaned inwardly. "You have a lunch appointment," she reminded him.

"I need that file!" he snapped.

Mary Jo bristled. "I'm doing my best."

"Your best clearly isn't good enough. *Find that file.*"

"I'll do a much better job of it if you aren't here breathing down my neck. Go have lunch, and I'll find the Jenkins file." She'd dismantle the filing cabinets one by one until she'd located it, if that was what it took.

Evan hesitated, then checked his watch. "I won't be long," he muttered, reaching for his jacket and thrusting his arms into the sleeves. "I'll give you a call from the restaurant."

"All right."

"If worse comes to worst, we can reschedule the client," he said as he buttoned the jacket. Evan had always been a smart dresser, she reflected irrelevantly. No matter what the circumstances, he looked as if he'd just stepped off a page in *Esquire* or *GQ*.

"Listen," Evan said, pausing at the door. "Don't worry about it. The file has to surface sometime." He seemed to be apologizing, however indirectly, for his earlier bout of bad temper.

She nodded, feeling guilty although she had no reason. But the file was missing and she felt responsible, despite the fact that she'd never so much as seen it.

Since she'd brought her lunch to work, Mary Jo nibbled at it as she sorted through every single file drawer in every single cabinet. Mrs. Sterling was meticulously neat, and not a single file had been misplaced.

Mary Jo was sitting on the carpet, files spread around her, when Evan phoned.

"Did you find it?"

"No, I'm sorry, Evan…Mr. Dryden," she corrected quickly.

His lengthy pause added to her feelings of guilt and confusion. She'd been so determined to be a good replacement. She'd vowed she was going to give him his money's worth. Yet here it was—her first day of working alone—and already she'd failed him.

By the time Evan was back at the office, she'd reassembled everything. He made the call to reschedule the appointment with William Jenkins, saving her the task of inventing an excuse.

At three o'clock her phone rang. It was Gary, and the instant she recognized his voice, Mary Jo groaned.

"How'd you know where to reach me?" she asked, keeping her voice low. Evan was sure to frown on personal phone calls, especially from a male friend. After their confrontation that morning, she felt bad enough.

"Your mom told me you were working for Daddy Warbucks now."

"Don't call him that," she said heatedly, surprised at the flash of anger she experienced.

Gary didn't immediately respond—as if he, too, was taken aback by her outburst. "I apologize," he said, his voice contrite. "I didn't phone to start an argument. I wanted to tell you I've taken our talk last Sunday to heart. How about dinner and dancing this Saturday? We could go to one of those all-you-can-eat places that serve barbecued ribs, and shuffle our feet a little afterward."

"Uh, maybe we could talk about this later."

"Yes or no?" Gary cajoled. "Just how difficult can it be? I thought you'd be pleased."

"It isn't a good idea to call me at the office, Gary."

"But I'll be at the fire station by the time you're off work," he explained. "I thought you wanted us to spend more time together. That's what you said, isn't it?"

Was that what she'd said? She didn't think so. Not exactly. "Uh, well…" Why, oh why, was life so complicated?

"I'm glad you spoke up," Gary continued when she didn't, "because I tend to get lazy in a relationship. I want you to know how much I appreciate your company."

"All right, I'll go," she said ungraciously, knowing it was the only way she'd get him off the phone quickly. "Saturday evening. What time?"

"Six okay? I'll pick you up."

"Six is fine."

"We're going to have a great time, Mary Jo. Just you wait and see."

She wasn't at all convinced of that, but she supposed she didn't have any right to complain. Eager to please, Gary was doing exactly what she'd asked of him. And frankly, dinner with Gary was a damn sight better than sitting home alone.

No sooner had she hung up the phone than Evan opened his door and stared at her, his look hard and disapproving. He didn't say a word about personal phone calls. He didn't have to. The heat radiated from her cheeks.

"Th-that was Gary," she said, then wanted to kick herself for volunteering the information. "I told him I can't take personal calls at the office. He won't be phoning again."

"Good," he said, and closed the door. It clicked sharply into place, as if to underline his disapproval. She returned to the letter she was typing into the computer.

Just before five, Mary Jo collected the letters that required Evan's signature and carried them to his office. He was reading over a brief, and momentarily looked up when she knocked softly and entered the room.

"Is there anything else you'd like me to do before I leave?" she asked, depositing the unsigned letters on the corner of his desk.

He shook his head. "Nothing, thank you. Good night, Ms. Summerhill."

He sounded so stiff and formal. As if he'd never held her, never kissed her. As if she'd never meant anything to him and never would.

"Good night, Mr. Dryden." She turned quickly and walked out of the office.

After their brief exchange regarding the missing file, they'd been coolly polite to each other during the rest of the day.

If his intention was to punish her, he couldn't have devised a more effective means.

Because she loved Evan. She'd never stopped loving him, no matter how she tried to convince herself otherwise. Being with him every day and maintaining this crisp, professional facade was the cruelest form of punishment.

Once she was home, Mary Jo kicked off her low heels, slumped into the rocking chair and closed her eyes in a desperate attempt to relax. She hadn't worked for Evan a full week yet, and already she wondered if she could last another day.

The rest of the summer didn't bear thinking about.

"What I don't understand," Marianna Summerhill said as she chopped up chicken for the salad, "is why you and Evan ever broke up."

"Mom, please, it was a long time ago."

"Not so long. Two, three years."

"Do you want me to set the table?" Mary Jo asked, hoping to distract her mother. That she hadn't seen through this unexpected dinner invitation only showed how weary she was, how low her defenses. Her mother had phoned the evening before, when Mary Jo was still recovering from working on her own with Evan; she'd insisted Mary Jo join them for dinner and "a nice visit."

"So, how's the job going?" her father asked, sitting down at the kitchen table. The huge dining room table was reserved for Sunday dinners.

"Oh, just great," Mary Jo said, working up enough energy to offer him a reassuring smile. She didn't want her parents to know what the job was costing her emotionally.

"I was just saying to Mary Jo what a fine young man Evan Dryden is." Her mother set the salad in the center of the table and pulled out a chair.

"He certainly is a decent sort. You were dating him a while back, weren't you?"

"Yes, Dad."

"Seems to me the two of you were real serious." When she didn't answer, he added, "As I recall, he gave you an engagement ring, didn't he? You had him come to dinner that one time. Whatever happened, Mary Jo? Did our family scare him off?"

Mary Jo was forever bound to hide the truth. Evan had been an instant hit with her family. They'd thrown open their arms and welcomed him, delighted that Mary Jo had found a man to love. Not for the world would she let her parents be hurt. Not for the world would she tell them the truth.

How could she possibly explain that their only daughter, whom they adored, wasn't good enough for the high-and-mighty Drydens? The minute Mary Jo met Evan's mother, she'd sensed the older woman's disappointment in her. Lois Dryden was looking for more in a daughter-in-law than Mary Jo could ever be.

Their private chat after dinner had set the record straight. Evan was destined for politics and would need a certain kind of wife, Mrs. Dryden had gently explained. Mary Jo didn't hear much beyond that.

Mrs. Dryden had strongly implied that Mary Jo would hinder Evan's political aspirations. She might very well ruin his life. There'd been some talk about destiny and family expectations and the demands on a political wife—Mary Jo's memories of the conversation were vague. But her understanding of Mrs. Dryden's message had been anything but.

Evan needed a woman who would be an asset—socially and politically. As an electrician's daughter, Mary Jo couldn't possibly be that woman. End of discussion.

"Mary Jo?"

Her mother's worried voice cut into her thoughts. She shook her head and smiled. "I'm sorry, Mom, what were you saying?"

"Your father asked you a question."

"About you and Evan," Norman elaborated. "I thought you two were pretty serious."

"We were at one time," she admitted, seeing no

other way around it. "We were even engaged. But we…drifted apart. Those things happen, you know. Luckily we realized that before it was too late."

"But he's such a dear boy."

"He's a charmer, Mom," Mary Jo said, making light of his appeal. "But he's not the man for me. Besides, I'm dating Gary now."

Her parents exchanged meaningful glances.

"You don't like Gary?" Mary Jo prodded.

"Of course we like him," Marianna said cautiously. "It's just that…well, he's very sweet, but I just don't think Gary's right for you."

Frankly, Mary Jo didn't, either.

"It seems to me," her father said slowly as he buttered a slice of bread, "that your young man's more interested in your mother's cooking than he is in you."

So the family had noticed. Not that Gary'd made any secret of it. "Gary's just a friend, Dad. You don't need to worry—we aren't really serious."

"What about Evan?" Marianna studied Mary Jo carefully, wearing the concerned expression she always wore whenever she suspected one of her children was ill. An intense, narrowed expression—as if staring at Mary Jo long enough would reveal the problem.

"Oh, Evan's a friend, too," Mary Jo said airily, but she didn't really believe it. She doubted they could ever be friends again.

Late Friday afternoon, just before she began getting ready to leave for the weekend, Evan called

Mary Jo into his office. He was busy writing, and she waited until he'd finished before she asked, "You wanted to see me?"

"Yes," he said absently, picking up a file folder. "I'm afraid I'm going to need you tomorrow."

"On Saturday?" She'd assumed the weekends were her own.

"I'm sure Mrs. Sterling mentioned I might occasionally need you to travel with me."

"No, she didn't," Mary Jo said, holding her shoulders rigid. She could guess what was coming. Somehow he was going to keep her from seeing Gary Saturday night. A man who lunched with a different woman every day of the week wanted to cheat her out of one dinner date with a friend.

"As it happens, I'll need you tomorrow afternoon and evening. I'm driving up to—"

"As it happens I already have plans for tomorrow evening," she interrupted defiantly.

"Then I suggest you cancel," he said impassively. "According to the terms of our agreement, you're to be at my disposal for the next two months. I need you this Saturday afternoon and evening."

"Yes, but—"

"May I remind you, that you're being well compensated for your time?"

It would take more than counting to ten to cool Mary Jo's rising temper. She wasn't fooled. Not for a second. Evan was doing this on purpose. He'd overheard her conversation with Gary.

"And if I refuse?" she asked, her outrage and defiance evident in every syllable.

Evan shrugged, as if it wasn't his concern one way or the other. "Then I'll have no choice but to fire you."

The temptation to throw the job back in his face was so strong she had to close her eyes to control it. "You're doing this intentionally, aren't you?" she said angrily. "I have a date with Gary Saturday night— you know I do—and you want to ruin it."

Evan leaned forward in his black leather chair; he seemed to weigh his words carefully. "Despite what you might think, I'm not a vindictive man. But, Ms. Summerhill, it doesn't really matter *what* you think."

She bit down so hard, her teeth hurt. "You're right, of course," she said quietly. "It doesn't matter what I think." She whirled around and stalked out of his office.

The force of her anger was too great to let her sit still. For ten minutes, she paced the floor, then sank into her chair. Resting her elbows on the desk, she buried her face in her hands, feeling very close to tears. It wasn't that this date with Gary was so important. It was that Evan would purposely ruin it for her.

"Mary Jo."

She dropped her hands to find Evan standing in front of her desk. They stared at each other for a long, still moment, then Mary Jo looked away. She wanted to wipe out the past and find the man she'd once loved. But she knew that what *he* wanted was to hurt her, to pay her back for the pain she'd caused him.

"What time do you need me?" she asked in an expressionless voice. She refused to meet his eyes.

"Three-thirty. I'll pick you up at your place."

"I'll be ready."

In the ensuing silence, Damian walked casually into the room. He stopped when he noticed them, glancing from Evan to Mary Jo and back again.

"I'm not interrupting anything, am I?"

"No." Evan recovered first and was quick to reassure his older brother. "What can I do for you, Damian?"

Damian gestured with the file he carried. "I read over the Jenkins case like you asked and jotted down some notes. I thought you might want to go over them with me."

The name leapt out at Mary Jo. "Did you say *Jenkins?*" she asked excitedly.

"Why, yes. Evan gave me the file the other day and asked me for my opinion."

"I did?" Evan sounded genuinely shocked.

Damian frowned. "Don't you remember?"

"No," Evan said. "Mary Jo and I've been searching for that file since yesterday."

"All you had to do, little brother," Damian chided, "was ask me."

The two men disappeared into Evan's office while Mary Jo finished tidying up for the day. Damian left as she was gathering her personal things.

"Evan would like to see you for a moment," he said on his way out the door.

Setting her purse aside, she walked into Evan's office. "You wanted to see me?" she asked coldly, standing just inside the doorway.

He stood at the window, staring down at the street far below, his hands clasped behind his back. His shoulders were slumped as if he'd grown weary. He turned to face her, his expression composed, even cool. "I apologize for the screw-up over the Jenkins file. I was entirely at fault. I did give it to Damian to read. I'm afraid it completely slipped my mind."

His apology came as a surprise. "It's no problem," she murmured.

"About tomorrow," he said next, lowering his voice slightly, "I won't be needing you, after all. Enjoy your evening with lover boy."

Chapter 5

"Is Evan coming?" Mary Jo's oldest brother, Jack, asked as he passed the bowl of mashed potatoes to his wife, Carrie.

"Yeah," Lonny piped in. "Where's Evan?"

"I heard you were working for him now," Carrie said, adding under her breath, "Lucky you."

Mary Jo's family was sitting around the big dining room table. Her parents, Jack, Carrie and their three children, Lonny and his wife, Sandra, and their two kids—they'd all focused their attention on Mary Jo.

"Mr. Dryden doesn't tell me his plans," she said, uncomfortable with their questions.

"You call him 'Mr. Dryden?'" her father asked, frowning.

"I'm his employee," Mary Jo replied.

"His father's a senator," Marianna reminded her husband, as if this was crucial information he didn't already know.

"I thought you said Evan's your friend." Her father wasn't going to give up, Mary Jo realized, until he had the answers he wanted.

"He *is* my friend," she returned evenly, "but while I'm an employee of the law firm it's important to maintain a certain decorum." That was a good response, she thought a bit smugly. One her father couldn't dispute.

"Did you invite him to Sunday dinner, dear?" her mother wanted to know.

"No."

"Then that explains it," Marianna said with a disappointed sigh. "Next week I'll see to it myself. We owe him a big debt of thanks."

Mary Jo resisted telling her mother that a man like Evan Dryden had more important things to do than plan his Sunday afternoons around her family's dinner. He'd come once as a gesture of friendliness, but they shouldn't expect him again. Her mother would learn that soon enough.

"How's the case with Adison Investments going, M.J.?" Jack asked, stabbing his fork into a marinated vegetable. "Have you heard anything?"

"Not yet," Mary Jo answered. "Evan had Mrs. Sterling type up a letter last week. I believe she mailed Mom and Dad a copy."

"She did," her father inserted.

"From my understanding, Evan, er, Mr. Dryden, gave Adison Investments two weeks to respond. If he hasn't heard from them by then, he'll prepare a lawsuit."

"Does he expect them to answer?" Rich burst out, his dark eyes flashing with anger.

"Now, son, don't get all riled up over this. Evan and Mary Jo are handling it now, and I have complete faith that justice will be served."

The family returned their attention to their food, and when the conversation moved on to other subjects, Mary Jo was grateful. Then, out of the blue, when she least expected it, her mother asked, "How was your dinner date with Gary?"

Taken aback, she stopped chewing, the fork poised in front of her mouth. Why was her life of such interest all of a sudden?

"Fine," she murmured when she'd swallowed. Once again the family's attention was on her. "Why is everyone looking at me?" she demanded.

Lonny chuckled. "It might be that we're wondering why you'd date someone like Gary Copeland when you could be going out with Evan Dryden."

"I doubt very much that Evan dates his employees," she said righteously. "It's bad business practice."

"I like Evan a whole lot," five-year-old Sarah piped up. "You do, too, don't you, Aunt Mary Jo?"

"Hmm…yes," she admitted, knowing she'd never get away with a lie, at least not with her own family. They knew her too well.

"Where's Gary now?" her oldest brother asked as though he'd only just noticed that he hadn't joined them for dinner. "It seems to me he's generally here. You'd think the guy had never tasted home cooking."

Now was as good a time as any to explain, Mary Jo decided. "Gary and I decided not to see each other anymore, Jack," she said, hoping to gloss over the details. "We're both doing different things now, and we've…drifted apart."

"Isn't that what you were telling me about you and Evan Dryden?" her father asked thoughtfully.

Mary Jo had forgotten that. Indeed, it was exactly what she'd said.

"Seems to me," her father added with a knowing parental look, "that you've been doing a lot of drifting apart from people lately."

Her mother, bless her heart, cast Mary Jo's father a frown. "If you ask me, it's the other way around." She nodded once as if to say the subject was now closed.

In some ways, Mary Jo was going to miss Gary. He was a friend and they'd parted on friendly terms. She hadn't intended to end their relationship, but over dinner Gary had suggested they think seriously about their future together.

To put it mildly, she'd been shocked. She'd felt comfortable in their rather loose relationship. Now Gary was looking for something more. She wasn't.

She knew he'd been disappointed, but he'd accepted her decision.

"I like Evan better, anyway," Sarah said solemnly. It seemed to be a recurring theme with her. She nodded once, the way her grandmother had just done, and the pink ribbons on her pigtails bobbed. "You'll bring him to dinner now, won't you?"

"I don't know, sweetheart."

"I do," her mother said, smiling confidently. "A

mother knows these things, and it seems to me that
~~Evan Dryden is the perfect man for our Mary Jo."~~

Evan was in the office when Mary Jo arrived early
Monday morning. She quickly prepared a pot of coffee and brought him a mug as soon as it was ready.

He was on the phone but glanced up when she entered his office and smiled as he accepted the coffee. She returned to the outer office, amazed—and
a little frightened—by how much one of his smiles
could affect her.

Mary Jo's greatest fear was that the longer they
worked together the more difficult it would be to
maintain her guard. Without being aware of it, she
might reveal her true feelings for Evan.

The phone rang and she automatically reached
for it, enjoying her role as Evan's personal-assistant.
She and Evan had had their share of differences, but
seemed to have resolved them. In the office, anyway.

"Mary Jo." It was Jessica Dryden.

Mary Jo stiffened, fearing Evan might hear her
taking a personal call. She didn't want anything to
jeopardize their newly amicable relationship. The
door to his office was open and he had a clear view
of her from his desk.

"May I help you?" she asked in her best personal
assistant voice.

Jessica hesitated at her cool, professional tone.
"Hey, it's me. Jessica."

"I realize that."

Jessica laughed lightly. "I get it. Evan must be
listening."

"That's correct." Mary Jo had trouble hiding a smile. One chance look in her direction, and he'd know this was no client she had on the line.

"Damian told me you're working for Evan now. What happened?" Jessica's voice lowered to a whisper as if she feared Evan would hear her, too.

Mary Jo carefully weighed her words. "I believe that case involved blackmail."

"Blackmail?" Jessica repeated, and laughed outright. "This I've got to hear. Is he being a real slave driver?"

"No. Not exactly."

"Can you escape one afternoon and meet me for lunch?"

"I might be able to arrange a lunch appointment. What day would you suggest?"

"How about tomorrow at noon? There's an Italian restaurant around the corner in the basement of the Wellman building. The food's great and the people who own it are like family."

"That sounds acceptable."

Evan appeared in the doorway between his office and hers. He studied her closely. Mary Jo swallowed uncomfortably at the obvious censure in his expression.

"Uh, perhaps I could confirm the details with you later."

Jessica laughed again. "Judging by your voice, Evan's standing right there—and he's figured out this isn't a business call."

"I believe you're right," she said stiffly.

Jessica seemed absolutely delighted. "I can't wait

to hear all about this. I'll see you tomorrow, and Mary Jo…"

"Yes?" she urged, eager to get off the line.

"Have you thought any more about what I said? About working things out with Evan?"

"I…I'm thinking."

"Good. That's just great. I'll see you tomorrow, then."

Mary Jo replaced the receiver and darted a look in Evan's direction. He averted his eyes and slammed the door. As if he was furious with her. Worse, as if she disgusted him.

Stunned, Mary Jo sat at her desk, fighting back a rush of outrage. He was being unfair. At the very least, he could've given her the opportunity to explain!

The morning, which had started out so well, with a smile and a sense of promise, had quickly disintegrated into outright hostility. Evan ignored her for the rest of the morning, not speaking except about office matters. And even then, his voice was cold and impatient. The brusque, hurried instructions, the lack of eye contact—everything seemed to suggest that he could barely tolerate the sight of her.

Without a word of farewell, he left at noon for his lunch engagement and came back promptly at one-thirty, a scant few minutes before his first afternoon appointment. Mary Jo had begun to wonder if he planned to return at all, worrying about how she'd explain his absence.

The temperature seemed to drop perceptibly the moment Evan walked in the door. She tensed, debating whether or not to confront him about his attitude.

Evan had changed, Mary Jo mused defeatedly. She couldn't remember him ever being this temperamental. She felt she was walking on the proverbial eggshells, afraid of saying or doing something that would irritate him even more.

Her afternoon was miserable. By five o'clock she knew she couldn't take much more of this silent treatment. She waited until the switchboard had been turned over to the answering service; that way there was no risk of being interrupted by a phone call.

The place was quiet—presumably staff in the nearby offices had gone home—when she approached his door. She knocked, then immediately walked inside. He was working and seemed unaware of her presence. She stood there until he glanced up.

"Could I speak to you for a moment?" she asked, standing in front of his desk. She heard the small quaver in her voice and groaned inwardly. She'd wanted to sound strong and confident.

"Is there a problem?" Evan asked, raising his eyebrows as if surprised—and not pleasantly—by her request.

"I'm afraid my position here isn't working out."

"Oh?" Up went the eyebrows again. "And why isn't it?"

It was much too difficult to explain how deeply his moods affected her. A mere smile and she was jubilant, a frown and she was cast into despair.

"It…it just isn't," was the best she could do.

"Am I too demanding?"

"No," she admitted reluctantly.

"Unreasonable?"

She lowered her gaze and shook her head.

"Then what is it?"

She gritted her teeth. "I want you to know that I've never made a personal phone call from this office during working hours."

"True, but you've received them."

"I assured you Gary wouldn't be phoning again."

"But he did," Evan inserted smoothly.

"He most certainly did not."

"Mary Jo," he said with exaggerated patience, as though he were speaking to a child, "I heard you arranging a lunch date with him myself."

"That was Jessica. Damian mentioned running into me at the office and she called and suggested we meet for lunch."

"Jessica," Evan muttered. He grew strangely quiet.

"I think it might be best if I sought employment elsewhere," Mary Jo concluded. "Naturally I'll be happy to train my replacement." She turned abruptly and started to leave.

"Mary Jo." He sighed heavily. "Listen, you're right. I've behaved like a jerk all day. I apologize. Your personal life, your phone calls—it's none of my business. I promise you this won't happen again."

Mary Jo paused, unsure what to think. She certainly hadn't expected an apology.

"I want you to stay on," he added. "You're doing an excellent job, and I've been unfair. Will you?"

She should refuse, walk out while she had the excuse to do so. Leave without regrets. But she couldn't. She simply couldn't.

She offered him a shaky smile and nodded. "You

know, you're not such a curmudgeon to work for, after all."

"I'm not?" He sounded downright cheerful. "This calls for a celebration, don't you think? Do you still enjoy sailing as much as you used to?"

She hadn't been on the water since the last time they'd taken out his sailboat. "I think so," she murmured, head spinning at his sudden reversal.

"Great. Run home and change clothes and meet me at the marina in an hour. We'll take out my boat and discover if you've still got your sea legs."

The prospect of spending time with Evan was too wonderful to turn down. For her sanity's sake, she should think twice before accepting the invitation, but she didn't. Whatever the price, she'd pay it—later.

"Remember when I taught you to sail?" Evan asked, his eyes smiling.

Mary Jo couldn't keep herself from smiling back. He'd been infinitely patient with her. She came from a long line of landlubbers and was convinced she'd never be a sailor.

"I still remember the first time we pulled out of the marina with me at the helm. I rammed another sailboat," she reminded him, and they both laughed.

"You'll meet me?" Evan asked, oddly intense after their moment of lightness.

Mary Jo doubted she could have refused him anything. "Just don't ask me to motor the boat out of the slip."

"You've got yourself a deal."

A little while earlier, she'd believed she couldn't

last another hour with Evan. Now here she was,
agreeing to meet him after work for a sailing lesson.

Rushing home, she threw off her clothes, not bothering to hang them up the way she usually did. She
didn't stay longer than the few minutes it took to pull
on a pair of jeans, a sweatshirt and her deck shoes.
If she allowed any time for reflection, Mary Jo was
afraid she'd talk herself out of going. She wanted
these few hours with Evan so much it hurt.

Right now she refused to think about anything
except the evening ahead of them. For this one night
she wanted to put the painful past behind them—
wipe out the memory of the last three lonely years.

She could see Evan waiting for her when she arrived at the marina. The wind had turned brisk, perfect for sailing, and the scent of salt and sea was
carried on the breeze. Grabbing her purse, she trotted
across the parking lot. Evan reached for her hand as
if doing so was an everyday occurrence. Unthink-
ingly, Mary Jo gave it to him.

Both seemed to recognize in the same instant
what they'd done. Evan turned to her, his eyes questioning; he seemed to expect Mary Jo to remove her
hand from his. She met his gaze evenly and offered
him a bright smile.

"I brought us something to eat," he said. "I don't
know about you, but I'm starved."

Mary Jo was about to make some comment about
his not eating an adequate lunch, when she recalled
that he'd been out with Catherine Moore. Mary Jo
wondered if the other woman was as elegant as her
name suggested.

Evan leapt aboard, then helped her onto the small deck. He went below to retrieve the jib and the mainsail, and when he emerged Mary Jo asked, "Do you want me to rig the jib sail?"

He seemed surprised and pleased by the offer.

"That was the first thing you taught me, remember? I distinctly recall this long lecture about the importance of the captain and the responsibilities of the crew. Naturally, *you* were the distinguished captain and I was the lowly crew."

Evan laughed and the sound floated out to sea on the tail end of a breeze. "You remember all that, do you?"

"Like it was yesterday."

"Then have a go," he said, motioning toward the mast. But he didn't actually leave all the work to her. They both moved forward and attached the stay for the jib to the mast, working together as if they'd been partners for years. When they were finished, Evan motored the sleek sailboat out of its slip and toward the open waters of Boston Harbor.

For all her earlier claims about not being a natural sailor, Mary Jo was still astonished by how much she'd enjoyed her times on the water. Her fondest memories of Evan had revolved around the hours spent aboard his boat. There was something wildly romantic about sailing together, gliding across the open water with the wind in their faces. She would always treasure those times with Evan.

Once they were safely out of the marina, they raised the mainsail and sliced through the emerald-green waters toward Massachusetts Bay.

"So you've been talking to Jessica?" he asked with a casualness that didn't deceive her.

"Mostly I've been working for you," she countered. "That doesn't leave me much time for socializing."

The wind whipped Evan's hair about his face, and he squinted into the sun. From the way he pinched his lips together, she guessed he was thinking about her date with Gary that weekend. She considered telling him it was over between her and Gary, but before she'd figured out how to bring up the subject, Evan spoke again.

"There's a bucket of fried chicken below," he said with a knowing smile, "if you're hungry, that is."

"Fried chicken," she repeated. She had no idea why sailing made her ravenous. And Evan was well aware of her weakness for southern-fried chicken. "Made with a secret recipe of nine special herbs and spices? Plus coleslaw and potato salad?"

Evan wiggled his eyebrows and smiled wickedly. "I seem to remember you had a fondness for a certain brand of chicken. There's a bottle of Chardonnay to go with it."

Mary Jo didn't need a second invitation to hurry below. She loaded up their plates, collected the bottle and two wineglasses and carried everything carefully up from the galley.

Sitting beside Evan, her plate balanced on her knees, she ate her dinner, savoring every bite. She must have been more enthusiastic than she realized, because she noticed him studying her. With a chicken leg poised near her mouth, she looked back at him.

"What's wrong?"

He grinned. "Nothing. I appreciate a woman who enjoys her food, that's all."

"I'll have you know I skipped lunch." But she wasn't going to tell him it was because every time she thought about him with Catherine Moore, she lost her appetite.

"I hope your employer values your dedication."

"I hope he does, too."

When they'd eaten, Mary Jo carried their plates below and packed everything away.

She returned and sat next to Evan. They finished their wine, then he let her take a turn at the helm. Almost before she was aware of it, his arms were around her. She stood there, hardly breathing, then allowed herself to lean back against his chest. It was as if those three painful years had been obliterated and they were both so much in love they couldn't see anything beyond the stars in their eyes.

Those had been innocent days for Mary Jo, that summer when she'd actually believed that an electrician's daughter could fit into the world of a man as rich and influential as Evan Dryden.

If she closed her eyes, she could almost forget everything that had happened since....

The wind blew more strongly and dusk began to darken the water. Mary Jo realized with intense regret that it was time for them to head back to the marina. Evan seemed to feel the same unwillingness to return to land—and reality.

They were both quiet as they docked. Together, they removed and stowed the sails.

Once everything was locked up, Evan walked her

to the dimly lighted parking area. Mary Jo stood by the driver's side of her small car, reluctant to leave.

"I had a wonderful time," she whispered. "Thank you."

"I had a good time, too. Perhaps *too* good."

Mary Jo knew what he was saying; she felt it herself. It would be so easy to forget the past and pick up where they'd left off. Without much encouragement, she could easily find herself in his arms.

When he'd held her those few minutes on the boat, she'd experienced a feeling of warmth and completeness. Of happiness.

Sadness settled over her now, the weight of it almost unbearable. "Thank you again." She turned away and with a trembling hand inserted the car key into the lock. She wished Evan would leave before she did something ridiculous, like break into tears.

"Would you come sailing with me again some time?" he asked, and Mary Jo could have sworn his voice was tentative, uncertain. Which was ridiculous. Evan was one of the most supremely confident men she'd ever known.

Mary Jo waited for an objection to present itself. Several did. But not a single one of them seemed worth worrying about. Not tonight...

"I'd enjoy that very much." It was odd to be carrying on a conversation with her back to him, but she didn't dare turn around for fear she'd throw herself in his arms.

"Soon," he suggested, his voice low.

"How soon?"

"Next Saturday afternoon."

She swallowed and nodded. "What time?"

"Noon. Meet me here, and we'll have lunch first."

"All right."

From the light sound of his footsteps, she knew he'd moved away. "Evan," she called, whirling around, her heart racing.

He turned toward her and waited for her to speak.

"Are you sure?" Mary Jo felt as if her heart hung in the balance.

His face was half-hidden by shadows, but she could see the smile that slowly grew. "I'm very sure."

Mary Jo's hands shook as she climbed into her car. It was happening all over again and she was *letting* it happen. She was trembling so badly she could hardly fasten her seat belt.

What did she hope to prove? She already *knew* that nothing she could do would make her the right woman for Evan. Eventually she'd have to face the painful truth—again—and walk away from him. Eventually she'd have to look him in the eye and tell him she couldn't be part of his life.

Mary Jo didn't sleep more than fifteen minutes at a stretch that night. When the alarm went off, her eyes burned, her head throbbed and she felt as lifeless as the dish of last week's pasta still sitting in her fridge.

She got out of bed, showered and put on the first outfit she pulled out of her closet. Then she downed a cup of coffee and two aspirin.

Evan was already at the office when she arrived. "Good morning," he said cheerfully as she walked in the door.

"Morning."

"Beautiful day, isn't it?"

Mary Jo hadn't noticed. She sat down at her desk and stared at the blank computer screen.

Evan brought her a cup of coffee and she blinked up at him. "I thought I was the one who was supposed to make coffee."

"I got here a few minutes early," he explained. "Drink up. You look like you could use it."

Despite her misery, she found the strength to grin. "I could."

"What's the matter? Bad night?"

She cupped the steaming mug with both hands. "Something like that." She couldn't very well confess *he* was the reason she hadn't slept. "Give me a few minutes and I'll be fine." A few minutes to dredge up the courage to tell him she had other plans for Saturday and couldn't meet him, after all. A few minutes to control the searing disappointment. A few minutes to remind herself she could survive without him. The past three years had proved that.

"Let me know if there's anything I can get you," he said.

She was about to suggest an appointment with a psychiatrist, then changed her mind. Evan would think she was joking; Mary Jo wasn't so sure it *was* a joke. What sensible woman would put herself through this kind of torture?

"I've already sorted through the mail," Evan announced. "There's something here from Adison Investments."

That bit of information perked Mary Jo up. "What did they say?"

"I haven't read it yet, but as soon as I do, I'll tell you. I'm hoping my letter persuaded Adison to agree to a refund."

"That's what you hope, not what you expect."

Evan's dark eyes were serious. "Yes."

He walked into his office but was back out almost immediately. Shaking his head, he handed Mary Jo the brief letter. She read the two curt paragraphs and felt a sense of discouragement. She had to hand it to Bill Adison. He came across as confident. Believable. He had to be, otherwise her father would never have trusted him. Adison reiterated that he had a signed contract and that the initial investment wouldn't be returned until the terms of their agreement had been fully met. Never mind that he hadn't upheld *his* side of the contract.

"Do you want to make an appointment with my parents?" she asked, knowing Evan would want to discuss the contents of the letter with her mother and father.

Evan took a moment to consider the question. "No. I think it'd be better for me to stop by their house myself and explain it to them. Less formal that way."

"Fine," she said, praying he wouldn't suggest Sunday. If he arrived on Sunday afternoon, one or more of her family members would be sure to tell him she'd broken up with Gary. No doubt her niece Sarah would blurt out that Evan could marry her now.

"I should probably talk to them today or tomorrow."

Mary Jo nodded, trying to conceal her profound relief.

"Why don't we plan on going there this evening after work?"

The "we" part didn't escape her.

"I'll call my folks and tell them," she said, figuring she'd set a time with them and then—later—make some plausible excuse for not joining Evan. Like a previous date. Or an emergency appointment with a manicurist. She'd break one of her nails and...

She was being ridiculous. She *should* be there. She *would* be there. She owed it to her parents. And it was business, after all, not a social excursion with Evan. Or a date. There was nothing to fear.

Mary Jo had just arrived at this conclusion when Evan called her into his office.

"Feeling better?" he asked, closing the door behind her.

"A little." She managed a tremulous smile.

He stared at her for an uncomfortable moment. She would've walked around him and seated herself, but he blocked the way.

"I know what might help," he said after a moment.

Thinking he was going to suggest aspirin, Mary Jo opened her mouth to tell him she'd already taken some. Before she could speak, he removed the pen and pad from her unresisting fingers and set them aside.

"What are you doing?" she asked, frowning in confusion.

He grinned almost boyishly. "I am, as they say in the movies, about to kiss you senseless."

Chapter 6

"You're going to kiss me?" Mary Jo's heart lurched as Evan drew her into his arms. His breath was warm against her face, and a wonderful, wicked feeling spread through her. She sighed and closed her eyes.

Evan eased his mouth over hers and it felt so natural, so familiar. So right.

He kissed her again, and tears gathered in Mary Jo's eyes. He wrapped her tightly in his arms and took several long breaths.

"I wanted to do this last night," he whispered.

She'd wanted him to kiss her then, too, yet—paradoxically—she'd been grateful he hadn't. It occurred to her now that delaying this moment could have been a mistake. They'd both thought about it, wondered how it would be, anticipated being in each

other's arms again. And after all that intense speculation, their kiss might have disappointed them both.

It hadn't.

Nevertheless, Mary Jo was relieved when the
phone rang. Evan cursed under his breath. "We need
to talk about this," he muttered, still holding her.

The phone pealed a second time.

"We'll talk later," she promised quickly.

Evan released her, and she leapt for the telephone
on his desk. Thankfully, the call was for him. Thankfully, it wasn't Jessica. Or her mother. Or Gary.

Mary Jo left his office and sank slowly into her
chair, trying to make sense of what had happened.

All too soon Evan was back. He sat on the edge
of her desk. "All right," he said, his eyes as bright
and happy as a schoolboy's on the first day of summer vacation. "We're going to have this out once
and for all."

"Have this out?"

"I don't know what happened between you and the
man you fell in love with three years ago. But apparently it didn't last, which is fine with me."

"Evan, please!" She glanced desperately around.
"Not here. Not now." She was shaking inside. Her
stomach knotted and her chest hurt with the effort
of holding back her emotions. Eventually she'd have
to tell Evan there'd never been another man, but she
wasn't looking forward to admitting that lie. Or her
reasons for telling it.

"You're right." He sounded reluctant, as if he
wanted to settle everything between them then and
there. "This isn't the place. We need to be able to talk

freely." He looked at his watch and his mouth tightened. "I've got to be in court this morning."

"Yes, I know." She was pathetically grateful that he'd be out of the office for a few hours. She needed time to think. She'd already made one decision, though: she refused to lie to him again. She was older now, more mature, and she recognized that, painful though it was, Evan's mother had been right. Mary Jo could do nothing to enhance Evan's career.

But she wasn't going to run away and hide, which was what she'd done three years ago. Nor could she bear the thought of pitting Evan against his parents. The Drydens were a close family, like her own. No, she'd have to find some other approach, some other way of convincing him this relationship couldn't possibly work. Just *how* she was going to do this, she had no idea.

Forcing her attention back to her morning tasks, she reached for the mail and quickly became absorbed in her work. In fact, she was five minutes late meeting Jessica.

Her friend was waiting in the Italian restaurant, sitting at a table in the back. A grandmotherly woman was holding Andy, using a bread stick to entertain the toddler.

"Lucia, this is my friend Mary Jo," Jessica said when she approached the table.

"Hello," Mary Jo murmured, pulling out a chair.

"Leave lunch to me," Lucia insisted, giving Andy back to his mother, who placed him in the high chair beside her. Jessica then handed her son another bread stick, which delighted him. Apparently Andy didn't understand he was supposed to *eat* the bread. He seemed to think it was a toy to wave gleefully over-head, and Mary Jo found herself cheered by his an-tics.

The older woman returned with large bowls of minestrone, plus a basket of bread so fresh it was still warm. "You eat now," she instructed, waiting for them to sample the delectable-smelling soup. "Enjoy your food first. You can talk later."

"It would be impossible *not* to enjoy our food," Jessica told Lucia, who beamed with pride.

"Lucia's right, of course," Jessica said, "but we've got less than an hour and I'm dying to hear what's happening with you and Evan."

"Not much." Which was the truth. For now, any-way. Mary Jo described how Evan had coerced her into working for him. She'd expected expressions of sympathy from her friend. Instead, Jessica seemed downright pleased.

"Damian said there'd been some misunderstand-ing about a file. He said Evan had suspected you of being careless—or worse—and when Damian showed up with it, Evan felt wretched."

"That's all behind us now." The uncertainty of their future loomed before them, and that was what concerned her most. Mary Jo weighed the decision to confide in Jessica about their kiss that morning. If Jessica had been someone other than Evan's sister-in-law, she might've done so. But it would be unfair to involve his family in this.

Jessica dipped her spoon into the thick soup. "I explained earlier that Evan and I became fairly close while I was working for the firm. What I didn't mention was how often he talked about you. He really loved you, Mary Jo."

Uncomfortable, Mary Jo lowered her gaze.

"I'm not saying this to make you feel guilty, but so you'll know that Evan's feelings for you were genuine. You weren't just a passing fancy to him. In some ways, I don't believe he's ever gotten over you."

Mary Jo nearly choked on her soup. "I wish that was true. I've arranged no less than six lunch appointments for him. All the names came directly out of his little black book. The invitations were accompanied by a dozen red roses." Until that moment, Mary Jo hadn't realized how jealous she was, and how much she'd been suffering while he'd wined and dined his girlfriends.

"Don't get me wrong," Jessica said. "Evan's dated other women. But there's never been anyone serious."

Mary Jo energetically ripped off a piece of bread. "He's gone out of his way to prove the opposite."

"What were these women's names?"

Lucia returned to the table with a large platter heaped with marinated vegetables, sliced meats and a variety of cheeses. Andy stretched out his hand, wanting a piece of cheese, which Jessica gave him.

"One was Catherine Moore."

A smile hovered at the edges of Jessica's mouth. "Catherine Moore is around seventy and she's his great-aunt."

Shocked, Mary Jo jerked up her head. "His great-aunt? What about…" and she rolled off the other names she remembered.

"All relatives," Jessica said, shaking her head. "The poor boy was desperate to make you jealous."

Mary Jo had no intention of admitting how well his scheme had worked. "Either that, or he was being thoughtful," she suggested offhandedly—just to be fair to Evan. She wanted to be angry with him, but found she was more amused.

"Trust me," Jessica said, smiling broadly. "Evan was desperate. He's dated, true, but he seldom goes out with the same woman more than three or four times. His mother's beginning to wonder if he'll ever settle down."

At the mention of Lois Dryden, Mary Jo paid close attention to her soup. "It was my understanding that Evan was planning to go into politics."

"I believe he will someday," Jessica answered enthusiastically. "In my opinion, he should. Evan has a generous, caring heart. He genuinely wants to help people. More importantly, he's the kind of man who's capable of finding solutions and making a difference.

"He's a wonderful diplomat, and people like him. It doesn't matter what walk of life they're from, either. The best way I can describe it is that Evan's got charisma."

Mary Jo nodded. It was the truth.

"Although he went into corporate law," Jessica continued, "I don't think his heart's ever really been in it. You should've seen him when he represented Earl Kress. He was practically a different person. No, I don't think he's at all happy as a corporate attorney."

"Then why hasn't he decided to run for office?"

"I'm not sure," Jessica said. "I assumed, for a while, that he was waiting until he was a bit older, but I doubt that's the reason. I know his family encourages him, especially his mother. Lois has always believed Evan's destined for great things."

"I...got that impression from her, as well."

"Evan and Damian have had long talks about his running for office. Damian's encouraged him, too, but Evan says the time's not right."

Mary Jo's heart felt heavy. Everything Jessica said seconded Lois Dryden's concerns about the role Evan's wife would play in his future.

"You're looking thoughtful."

Mary Jo managed a small smile. "I never understood what it was about me that attracted Evan."

"I know exactly what it was," Jessica said without a pause. "He told me himself, and more than once. He said it was as though you knew him inside and out. Apparently you could see right through him. I suspect it has something to do with the fact that you have five older brothers."

"Probably."

"Evan's been able to charm his way around just about everyone. Not you. You laughed at him and told him to save his breath on more than one occasion. Am I right?"

Mary Jo nodded, remembering the first day they'd met on the beach. He'd tried to sweet-talk her into a dinner date, and she'd refused. She'd realized immediately that Evan Dryden didn't know how to take no for an answer. In the end they'd compromised. They'd built a small fire, roasted hot dogs and marshmallows and sat on the beach talking until well past midnight.

They saw each other regularly after that. Mary Jo knew he was wealthy by the expensive sports car he drove, the kind of money he flashed around. In the beginning she'd assumed it was simply because he was a high-priced attorney. Fool that she'd been, Mary Jo hadn't even recognized the name.

It wasn't until much later, after she was already head over heels in love with him, that she learned the truth. Evan was more than wealthy. He came from a family whose history stretched back to the *Mayflower*.

"You were different from the other women he'd known," Jessica was saying. "He could be himself with you. One time he told me he felt an almost spiritual connection with you. It's something he's never expected to find with anyone else."

"Evan told you all that?" Mary Jo asked breathlessly.

"Yes, and much more," Jessica said, leaning forward. "You see, Mary Jo, I know how much Evan loved you—and still loves you."

Mary Jo felt as if she was about to break into deep, racking sobs. She loved Evan, too. Perhaps there *was* hope for them. Jessica made her feel they might have a future. She seemed to have such faith that, whatever their problems, love and understanding could work them out.

Mary Jo returned to the office, her heart full of hope. She'd been wrong not to believe in their love, wrong not to give them a chance. Her insecurities had wasted precious years.

When Evan walked in, it was almost five o'clock. Mary Jo resisted the urge to fly into his arms, but immediately sensed something was wrong. He was frowning and every line of his body was tense.

"What happened?" she asked, following him into his office.

"I lost," he said pacing. "You know something? I'm a damn poor loser."

She *had* noticed, but he hadn't experienced loss often enough to grow accustomed to accepting it. "Listen, it happens to the best of us," she assured him.

"But it shouldn't have in this case. We were in the right."

"You win some and you lose some. That's the nature of the legal game."

He glared at her and she laughed outright. He reminded her of one of her brothers after a highly contested high-school basketball game. Mark, the youngest, had always loved sports and was fiercely competitive. He'd had to be in order to compete against his four brothers. In his desire to win, Evan was similar to Mark.

"I can always count on you to soothe my battered ego, can't I?" he asked, his tone more than a little sarcastic.

"No. You can always count on me to tell you the truth." *Almost always,* she amended sadly, recalling her one lie.

"A kiss would make me feel better."

"Certainly not," she said briskly, but it was difficult to refuse him. "Not here, anyway."

"You're right," he admitted grudgingly, "but at least let me hold you." She wasn't given the opportunity to say no, not that she would've found the strength to do so.

He brought her into his arms and held her firmly against him, breathing deeply as if to absorb everything about her. "I can't believe I'm holding you like this," he whispered.

"Neither will anyone else who walks into this room." But she didn't care who saw them. She burrowed deeper into his embrace and rested her head against the solid strength of his chest.

He eased himself away from her and framed her face with his hands. His eyes were intense as he gazed down on her. "I don't care about the past, Mary Jo. It's water under the bridge. None of it matters. The only thing that matters is *right now.* Can we put everything else behind us and move forward?"

She bit her lower lip, her heart full of a new confidence. Nothing in this world would ever stand between them again. She would've said the words, but couldn't speak, so she nodded her head in abrupt little movements.

She found herself pulled back into his arms, the embrace so hard it threatened to cut off her breath, but she didn't care. Breathing hardly seemed necessary when Evan was holding her like this. She wanted to laugh and to weep at once, to throw back her head and shout with a free-flowing joy that sprang from her soul.

"We'll go to your parents' place," Evan said, "talk to them about Adison's response, and then I'll take you to dinner and from there—"

"Stop," Mary Jo said, breaking free of his hold and raising her right hand. "You'll take me to dinner? Do you honestly think we're going to escape my mother without being fed?"

Evan laughed and pulled her into his arms again. "I suppose not."

Evan was, of course, welcomed enthusiastically by both her parents. He and Norman Summerhill discussed the Adison situation, while Mary Jo helped her mother prepare a simple meal of fried chicken and a pasta-and-vegetable salad. Over dinner, the mood was comfortable and lighthearted.

As it turned out, though, the evening included a lot more than just conversation and dinner. Her brothers all played on a softball team. They had a game scheduled that evening, and one of the other players had injured his ankle in a fall at work. The instant Evan heard the news, he volunteered to substitute.

"Evan," Mary Jo pleaded. "This isn't like handball, you know. These guys take their game seriously."

"You think handball isn't serious?" Evan kissed her on the nose and left her at her parents' while he hurried home to change clothes.

Her mother watched from the kitchen, looking exceptionally pleased. She wiped her hands on her apron skirt. "I think you did a wise thing breaking up with Gary when you did."

"I'm so happy, Mom," Mary Jo whispered, grabbing a dish towel and some plates to dry.

"You love him."

Mary Jo noticed it wasn't a question.

"I never stopped loving him."

Her mother placed one arm around Mary Jo's shoulders. "I knew that the minute I saw the two of you together again." She paused, apparently considering her next words. "I've always known you loved Evan. Can you tell me what happened before—why you broke it off?"

"I didn't believe I was the right woman for him."

"Nonsense! Anyone looking at the two of you would realize you're perfect for each other. Who would say such a thing to you?"

Mary Jo was intelligent enough not to mention Lois Dryden. "He's very wealthy, Mom."

"You can look past that."

Mary Jo's laugh was spontaneous. Her sweetheart of a mother saw Evan's money as a detriment—and in some ways, it was.

"His father's a senator."

"You think his money bought him that position?" Marianna scoffed. "If you do, you're wrong. He was elected to that office because he's a decent man with an honest desire to help his constituents."

Her mother could make the impossible sound plausible. Mary Jo wished she could be more like her.

"Now, freshen up," Marianna said, untying her apron, "or we'll be late for your brothers' game."

Evan was already in the outfield catching fly balls

when Mary Jo and her parents arrived. He looked as if he'd been a member of the team for years.

The game was an exciting one, with the outcome unpredictable until the very end of the ninth inning. Mary Jo, sitting in the bleachers with her family—her parents, a couple of sisters-in-law, some nieces and nephews—screamed herself hoarse. Their team lost by one run, but they all took the defeat in stride—including Evan, who'd played as hard as any of them.

Afterward, the team went out for pizza and cold beer. Mary Jo joined Evan and the others, while her parents returned to the house, tired from the excitement.

Evan threw his arm over her shoulders and she wrapped her own arm around his waist.

"You two an item now or something?" her brother Rob asked as they gathered around a long table at the pizza parlor.

"Yeah," Rich chimed in. "You look awful chummy all of a sudden. What's going on?"

"Yeah, what about good ol' Gary?" Mark wanted to know.

Evan studied her, eyebrows raised. "What *about* Gary?" he echoed.

"You don't need to worry about him anymore," Jack explained, carrying a pitcher of ice-cold beer to the table. "M.J. broke up with him over the weekend."

"You did?" It was Evan who asked the question.

"Yup." Once more her brother was doing the talking for her. "Said they were drifting in opposite directions or some such garbage. No one believed her. We know the *real* reason she showed Gary the door."

"Will you guys *please stop?*" Mary Jo insisted, her ears growing redder by the minute. "I can speak for myself, thank you very much."

Jack poured them each a beer and slid the glasses down the table. "You know M.J. means business when she says *please stop.* Uh-oh—look at her ears. Let's not embarrass her anymore, guys, or there'll be hell to pay."

Evan barked with laughter, and her brothers smiled approvingly. He fit in with her family as if he'd been born into it. This was his gift, Mary Jo realized. He was completely at ease with her brothers—as he would be with a group of government officials or lawyers or "society" people. With *anyone.* He could drink beer and enjoy it as much as expensive champagne. It didn't matter to him if he ate pizza or lobster.

But Mary Jo was definitely more comfortable with the pizza-and-beer way of life. Hours earlier she'd been utterly confident. Now, for the first time that night, her newfound resolve was shaken.

Evan seemed aware of her mood, although he didn't say anything until later, when they were alone, driving to her place. Reluctant to see the evening end, Mary Jo gazed at the oncoming lights of the cars zooming past. She couldn't suppress a sigh.

Evan glanced over at her. "Your family's wonderful," he said conversationally. "I envy you coming from such a large, close-knit group."

"You're close to your brother, too."

"True. More so now that we're older." He reached for her hand and squeezed it gently. "Something's troubling you."

She stared out the side window. "You're comfortable in my world, Evan, but I'm not comfortable in yours."

"World? What are you talking about? In case you haven't noticed, we're both right here in the same world—the planet earth."

She smiled, knowing he was making light of her concerns. "If we'd been with your family, do you think we'd be having pizza and beer? More likely it'd be expensive French wine, baguettes and Brie."

"So? You don't like baguettes and Brie?"

"Yes, but…" She paused, since it wouldn't do any good to argue. He didn't understand her concerns, because he didn't share them. "We're different, Evan."

"Thank goodness. I'd hate to think I was attracted to a clone of myself."

"I'm an electrician's daughter."

"A lovely one, too, I might add."

"Evan," she groaned. "Be serious."

"I *am* serious. It'd scare the socks off you if you knew *how* serious."

He exited the freeway and headed down the street toward her duplex. As he parked, he said, "Invite me in for coffee."

"Are you really interested in coffee?"

"No."

"That's what I thought," she said, smiling to herself.

"I'm going to kiss you, Mary Jo, and frankly, I'm

a little too old to be doing it in a car. Now invite me inside—or suffer the consequences."

Mary Jo didn't need a second invitation. Evan helped her out of the car and took her arm as they walked to her door. She unlocked it but didn't turn on the lights as they moved into her living room. The instant the door was closed, Evan maneuvered her in his arms so that her back was pressed against it.

Her lips trembled as his mouth sought hers. It was a gentle caress more than it was a kiss, and she moaned, wanting, *needing* more of him.

Evan's hand curved around the side of her neck, his fingers stroking her hair. His mouth hovered a fraction of an inch from hers, as if he half expected her to protest. Instead, she raised her head to meet his lips again.

Groaning, Evan kissed her with a passion that left her breathless and weak-kneed.

Mary Jo wound her arms around his neck and stood on the tips of her toes. They exchanged a series of long kisses, then Evan laid his head on her shoulder and shuddered.

Mary Jo was convinced that if he hadn't been holding her upright, she would've slithered to the floor.

"We'd better stop while I have the strength," Evan whispered, almost as if he was speaking to himself. His breathing was ragged and uneven. He moved away from her, and in the dark stillness of her living room, illumined only by the glow of a streetlight, she watched him rake his hands through his thick, dark hair.

"I'll make us that coffee," she said in a purposeful voice. They both squinted when she flipped on the light.

"I really don't need any coffee," he told her.

"I know. I don't, either. It's an excuse for you to stay."

Evan followed her into the kitchen and pulled out a chair. He sat down and reached for her, wrapping his arms around her waist, drawing her down onto his lap. "We have a lot of time to make up for."

Unsure how to respond, Mary Jo rested her hands on his shoulders. It was so easy to get caught up in the intensity of their attraction and renewed love. But despite her earlier optimism, she couldn't allow herself to ignore the truth. Except that she didn't know how to resolve this, or even if she could.

Evan left soon afterward, with a good-night kiss and the reminder that they'd be together again in the morning.

Mary Jo sat in her rocking chair in the dark for a long time, trying to sort out her tangled thoughts. Loving him the way she did, she was so tempted to let her heart go where it wanted to. So tempted to throw caution to the winds, to ignore all the difficult questions.

Evan seemed confident that their love was possible. Jessica did, too. Mary Jo desperately wanted to believe them. She wanted to overlook every objection. She wanted what she would probably never receive—his family's approval. Not Damian and Jessica's; she had that. His parents'.

Sometimes loving someone wasn't enough. Mary Jo had heard that often enough and she recognized the truth of it.

Too tired to think clearly, she stood, setting the rocker in motion, and stumbled into her bedroom.

Saturday, Mary Jo met Evan at the yacht club at noon. They planned to sail after a leisurely lunch. She'd been looking forward to this from the moment Evan had invited her on Wednesday.

The receptionist ushered her to a table outside on the patio, where Evan was waiting for her. There was a festive, summery atmosphere—tables with their striped red-yellow-and-blue umbrellas, the cheerful voices of other diners, the breathtaking view of the marina. Sailboats with multicolored spinnakers could be seen against a backdrop of bright blue sky and sparkling green sea.

Evan stood as she approached and pulled out her chair. "I don't think you've ever looked more beautiful."

It was a line he'd used a thousand times before, Mary Jo was sure of that, although he sounded sincere. "You say that to all your dates," she chided lightly, picking up the menu.

"But it's true," he returned with an injured air.

Mary Jo laughed and spread the linen napkin across her lap. "Your problem is that you're such a good liar. You'd be perfect in politics since you lie so convincingly." She'd been teasing, then suddenly realized how rude she'd been. His father was a politician!

"Oh, Evan, I'm sorry. That was a terrible thing to say." Mary Jo felt dreadful, reminded anew that she was the type of person who could offend someone without even being aware of it. She simply wasn't circumspect enough.

He chuckled and brushed off her apology. "Dad would get a laugh out of what you said."

"Promise me you won't ever tell him."

"That depends," he said, paying exaggerated attention to his menu.

"On what?" she demanded.

He wiggled his eyebrows. "On what you intend to offer me for my silence."

She smiled and repeated a line her brothers had often used on her. "I'll let you live."

Evan threw back his head and laughed boisterously.

"Evan?" The woman's voice came from behind Mary Jo. "What a pleasant surprise to find you here."

"Mother," Evan said, standing to greet Lois Dryden. He kissed her on the cheek. "You remember Mary Jo Summerhill, don't you?"

Chapter 7

"Of course I remember Mary Jo," Lois Dryden said cheerfully. "How nice to see you again."

Mary Jo blinked, wondering if this was the same woman she'd had that painful heart-to-heart chat with all those years ago. The woman who'd suggested that if Mary Jo really loved Evan she would call off their engagement. Not in those words exactly; Mrs. Dryden had been far too subtle for that. Nevertheless, the message had been there, loud and clear.

"I didn't know you two were seeing each other again," Lois continued. "This is a...surprise."

Mary Jo noticed she didn't say it was *pleasant* surprise. Naturally, Evan's mother was much too polite to cause even a hint of a scene. Not at the yacht club, at any rate. Now, if she'd been at Whispering Willows, the Dryden estate, she might swoon or have a fit of vapors, or whatever it was wealthy women did to convey their shock and displeasure. Mary Jo knew she was being cynical, but couldn't help herself.

Evan reached for her hand and clasped it in his own. His eyes smiled into hers. "Mary Jo's working for me this summer."

"I...I hadn't heard that."

"Would you care to join us?" Evan asked, but his eyes didn't waver from Mary Jo's. Although he'd issued the invitation, it was obvious that he expected his mother to refuse. That he *wanted* her to refuse.

"Another time, perhaps. I'm lunching with Jessica's mother. We're planning a first-birthday party for Andrew, and, well, you know how the two of us feel about our only grandchild."

Evan chuckled. "I sure do. It seems to me that either Damian or I should see about adding another branch to the family tree."

Mary Jo felt the heat of embarrassment redden her ears. Evan couldn't have been more blatant. He'd all but announced he intended to marry her. She waited for his mother to comment.

"That would be lovely, Evan," Lois said, but if Evan didn't catch the tinge of disapproval in his mother's voice, Mary Jo did. Nothing had changed.

The lines were drawn.

Lois made her excuses and hurried back into the yacht club. Mary Jo's good mood plummeted. She made a pretense of enjoying her lunch and decided to put the small confrontation behind her. Her heart was set on enjoying this day with Evan. She loved sailing as much as he did, and as soon as they were out in the bay, she could forget how strongly his mother disapproved of her. *Almost* forget.

They worked together to get the sailboat ready. Once the sails were raised, she sat next to Evan. The wind tossed her hair about her face, and she smiled into the warm sunshine. They tacked left and then right, zigzagging their way through the water.

"Are you thirsty?" Evan asked after they'd been out for an hour or so.

"A cold soda sounds good."

"Great. While you're in the galley, would you get one for me?"

Laughing, she jabbed him in the ribs, but she went below and brought back two sodas. She handed him his, then reclaimed her spot beside him.

Evan slipped his arm around her shoulders and soon she was nestled against him, guiding the sailboat, with Evan guiding her. When she veered off course and the sails slackened, he placed his hand over hers and gently steered them back on course.

Mary Jo had found it easy to talk to Evan from the moment they'd met. He was easygoing and congenial, open-minded and witty. But this afternoon he seemed unusually quiet. She wondered if he was brooding about the unexpected encounter with his mother.

"It's peaceful, isn't it?" Mary Jo said after several long minutes of silence.

"I think some of the most profound moments of my life have taken place on this boat. I've always come here to find peace, and I have, though it's sometimes been hard won."

"I'm grateful you introduced me to sailing."

"I took the boat out several times after...three years ago." His hold on her tightened. "I've missed you, Mary Jo," he whispered, and rubbed the side of his jaw against her temple. "My world felt so empty without you."

"Mine did, too," she admitted softly, remembering the bleak, empty months after their breakup.

"Earl Kress stopped by the office a while back, and I learned that you weren't married. Afterward, I couldn't get you out of my mind. I wondered what had happened between you and this teacher you loved. I wanted to contact you and find out. I must've come up with a hundred schemes to worm my way back into your life."

"W-why didn't you?" She felt comfortable and secure in his arms, unafraid of the problems that had driven them apart. She could deal with the past; it was the future that terrified her.

"Pride mostly," Evan said quietly. "A part of me was hoping you'd come back to me."

In a way she had, on her knees, needing him. Funny, she couldn't have approached him for herself, even though she was madly in love with him, but she'd done it for her parents.

"No wonder you had that gleeful look in your eye when I walked into your office," she said, hiding a smile. "You'd been waiting for that very thing."

"I wanted to punish you," he told her, and she heard the regret in his voice. "I wanted to make you suffer like I had. That was the reason I insisted you work for me this summer. I'd already hired Mrs. Sterling's replacement, but when I had the opportunity to force you into accepting the position, I couldn't resist."

This wasn't news to Mary Jo. She'd known the moment he'd offered her the job what his intention was. He'd wanted to make her as miserable as she'd made him. And his plan had worked those first few days. She'd gone home frustrated, mentally beaten and physically exhausted.

"A woman of lesser fortitude would have quit the first day, when you had me ordering roses and booking lunch dates."

"Those weren't any love interests," he confessed. "I'm related to each one."

"I know." She tilted back her head and kissed the underside of his jaw.

"How?" he asked, his surprise evident.

"Jessica told me."

"Well, I certainly hope you were jealous. I went through a great deal of unnecessary trouble if you weren't."

"I was green with it." She could have downplayed her reaction, but didn't. "Every time you left the office for another one of your dates, I worked myself into a frenzy. Please, Evan, don't ever do that to me again."

"I won't," he promised, and she could feel his smile against her hair. "But you had your revenge several times over, throwing Gary in my face. I disliked the man as soon as I met him. There I was, hoping to catch you off guard by showing up at your parents' for dinner, and my plan immediately backfires when you arrive with your boyfriend in tow."

"You really didn't like Gary?"

"He's probably a nice guy, but not when he's dating *my* woman."

"But you acted like Gary was an old pal! I was mortified. My entire family thought it was hilarious. You had more to say to Gary than to me."

"I couldn't let you know how jealous I was, could I?"

Mary Jo snuggled more securely in his arms. A seagull's cry came from overhead, and she looked up into the brilliant blue sky, reveling in the sunshine and the breeze and in the rediscovery of their love.

"Can we ever go back?" Evan asked. "Is it possible to pretend those years didn't happen and take up where we left off?"

"I…I don't know," Mary Jo said. Yet she couldn't keep her heart from hoping. She closed her eyes and felt the wind on her face. Those years had changed her. She was more confident now, more sure of herself, emotionally stronger. This time she'd fight harder to hold on to her happiness.

One thing was certain. If she walked out of Evan's life again, it wouldn't be in silence or in secrecy.

She remembered the pain of adjusting to her life without Evan. Pride had carried her for several months. She might not come from old Boston wealth, but she had nothing to be ashamed of. She was proud of her family and refused to apologize for the fact that they were working class.

But pride had only taken her so far, and when it had worn down, all she had left was the emptiness of her dreams and a life that felt hollow.

Like Evan, she'd forced herself to go on, dragging from one day to the next, but she hadn't been fully alive—until a few days ago, when he'd taken her in his arms and kissed her. Her love for him, her regret at what she'd lost, had never gone away.

"I want to give us another chance," Evan murmured. The teasing had gone out of his voice. "Do you?"

"Yes. Oh, yes," Mary Jo said ardently.

He kissed her then, with a passion and a fervor she'd never experienced before. She returned his kiss in full measure. They clung tightly to each other until the sails flapped in the breeze and Evan had to steer them back on course.

"I love you, Mary Jo," Evan said. "Heaven knows, I tried not to. I became…rather irresponsible after we split up, you know. If it hadn't been for Damian, I don't know what I would've done. He was endlessly patient with me, even when I wouldn't tell him what was wrong. My brother isn't stupid. He knew it had something to do with you. I just couldn't talk about it. The only relief I found was here, on the water."

Turning, Mary Jo threw her arms around his middle and pressed her face against his chest, wanting to absorb his pain.

"When you told me you'd fallen in love with another man, I had no recourse but to accept that it was over. I realized that the moment you told me how difficult it was for you. Loving him while you were still engaged to me must have been hell."

A sob was trapped in her throat. This was the time to admit there'd never been another man, that it was all a lie....

"Can you tell me about him?"

"No." She jerked her head from side to side. She couldn't do it, just couldn't do it. She was continuing the lie—because telling him would mean revealing his mother's part in all of this. She wouldn't do that.

His free arm cradled her shoulders, his grip tight.

"I'd more or less decided that if I couldn't marry you," Evan said after a lengthy pause, "I wasn't getting married at all. Can't you just see me twenty or thirty years down the road, sitting by a roaring fire with my ever-faithful dog sleeping at my side?"

The mental picture was so foreign to the devil-may-care image she'd had of him these past few years that she laughed out loud. "Nope, I can't quite picture that."

"What about fatherhood? Can you picture me as a father?"

"Easily." After watching him with Andrew and her own nieces and nephews, she realized Evan was a natural with children.

"Then it's settled," he said, sounding greatly relieved.

"What's settled?" she asked, cocking her head to one side to look up at him. His attention was focused straight ahead as he steered the sailboat.

"We're getting married. Prepare yourself, Mary Jo, because we're making up for lost time."

"Evan—"

"If you recall, when I gave you the engagement

ring, we planned our family. Remember? Right down
to the timing of your first pregnancy."

Mary Jo could hardly manage a nod. Those were
memories she'd rarely allowed herself to examine.

"We both thought it was important to wait a couple of years before we started our family. You were
supposed to have our first baby this year. Hey, we're
already behind schedule! It seems to me we'd better
take an extended honeymoon."

Mary Jo laughed, the wind swallowing the sound
the moment it escaped her lips.

"Two, three months at the very least," Evan went
on, undaunted. "I suggest a South Pacific island, off
the tourist track. We'll rent a bungalow on the beach
and spend our days walking along the shore and our
nights making love."

He was going much too fast for her. "Do you mind
retracing a few steps?" she asked. "I got lost somewhere between you sitting by a roaring fire with your
faithful dog and us running into Gauguin's descen-
dants on some South Pacific beach."

"First things first," Evan countered. "We agreed
on four children, didn't we?"

"Evan!" She couldn't keep from laughing, her
happiness spilling over.

"These details are important, and I'd like them
decided before we get involved in another subject. I
wanted six kids, remember? I love big families. But
you only wanted two. If you'll think back, it took
some fast talking to get you to agree to a compromise of four. You did agree, remember?"

"What I remember was being railroaded into a

crazy conversation while you went on about building us this huge mansion."

"Ah, yes, the house. I'd nearly forgotten. I wanted one large enough for all the kids. With a couple of guest rooms. That, my beautiful Mary Jo, isn't a mansion."

"It is when you're talking seven bedrooms and six thousand square feet."

"But," Evan said, his eyes twinkling, "you were going to have live-in help with the children, especially while they're younger, and I wanted to be sure we had a place to escape and relax at the end of the day."

"I found an indoor swimming pool, hot tub and exercise room a bit extravagant." Mary Jo had thought he was teasing when he'd showed her the house plans he'd had drawn up, but it had soon become apparent that he was completely serious. He was serious now, too.

"I still want to build that home for us," he said, his dark eyes searching hers. "I love you. I've loved you for three agonizing years. I want us to be married, and soon. If it were up to me, we'd already have the license."

"You're crazy." But it was a wonderful kind of crazy.

"You love me."

Tears filled her eyes as she nodded. "I do. I love you so much, Evan." She slid her arms around his neck. "What am I going to do with you?"

"Marry me and put me out of my misery."

He made it seem so easy and she was caught up

in the tide of his enthusiasm, but she couldn't agree. Not yet. Not until she was convinced she was doing the right thing for both of them.

"Listen," Evan said, as though struck by a whole new thought. "I have a judge in the family who can marry us as soon as I make the necessary arrangements. We can have a private ceremony in, say, three days' time."

"My parents would be devastated, Evan. I know for a fact that my father would never forgive us if we cheated him out of the pleasure of escorting me down the aisle."

Evan grimaced. "You're right. My mother's the same. She actually enjoys planning social events. It's much worse now that my dad's a senator. She's organized to a fault." He grinned suddenly, as if he found something amusing in this. "My father made a wise choice when he married Mom. She's the perfect politician's wife."

The words cut through Mary Jo like an icy wind. They reminded her that she'd be a liability to Evan should he ever decide to run for political office.

Often the candidates' spouses were put under as much scrutiny as the candidates themselves. The demands placed on political wives were often no less strenuous than those placed on the politicians.

"Evan," she said, watching him closely. "I'm not anything like your mother."

"So? What's that got to do with our building a big house and filling all those bedrooms with children?"

"I won't make a good politician's wife."

He looked at her as if he didn't understand what she was saying.

Mary Jo had no option but to elaborate. "I've heard, from various people, that you intend to enter politics yourself."

"Someday. I'm in no rush. My family, my mother especially, seems to think I have a future in that area, but it isn't anything that's going to happen soon. When and if the time comes, the two of us will decide together. But for now it's a moot point."

Mary Jo wasn't willing to accept that. "Evan, I'm telling you here and now I'd hate that kind of life. I'm not suited for it. Your mother enjoys arranging spectacular society events and giving interviews and living her life a certain way, but I don't. I'm uncomfortable in a roomful of strangers—unless they're five-year-olds."

"All right," Evan said with an amused air. "Then I won't enter politics. My mother has enough to keep her busy running my father's career. You're far more important to me than some elected position. Besides, I have the feeling Mother would've driven me crazy."

His words should have reassured her, but didn't. It seemed ludicrous to pin their future together on something as fleeting as this promise, so lightly made. Her greatest fear was that Evan would change his mind and regret ever marrying her.

"Let's go talk to your parents," Evan said, apparently unaware of the turmoil inside her.

"About what?"

His head went back and he frowned. "Making the arrangements for the wedding, what else? My mother will put up a fight, but I believe a small, private ceremony with just our immediate families would be best."

"Oh, Evan, please, don't rush me," Mary Jo pleaded. "This is the most important decision of our lives. We both need to think this through very carefully."

He gaze narrowed. "What's there to think about? I love you, and you love me. That's all that matters."

How Mary Jo wished that was true.

It took even more courage to drive over to Whispering Willows than Mary Jo had expected. She'd spent most of the night alternating between absolute delight and abject despair. She awoke Sunday morning sure that she'd never find the answers she needed until she'd talked to Evan's mother.

That was how Mary Jo came to be standing outside the Drydens' front door shortly before noon. With a shaking hand, she rang the bell.

She'd assumed one of the household staff would answer. Instead, Lois Dryden herself appeared at the door. The two women stared at each other.

Mary Jo recovered enough to speak first. "I'm sorry to disturb you, Mrs. Dryden, but I was wondering if I could have a few minutes of your time."

"Of course." The older woman stepped aside to let Mary Jo enter the lavish house. The foyer floor was of polished marble, and a glittering crystal chandelier hung from the ceiling, which was two-and-a-half stories high.

"Perhaps it would be best if we talked in my husband's office," Lois Dryden said, ushering Mary Jo to the darkly paneled room down the hall. This must be the room Evan had described in his absurd scenario of lonely old bachelor sitting by the fire with his dog.

"Would you like some something cold to drink? Or perhaps coffee?"

"No, thank you," Mary Jo answered. She chose the dark green leather wing chair angled in front of the fireplace. Mrs. Dryden sat in its twin.

"I realize you were surprised to see me with Evan yesterday."

"Yes," Lois agreed, her hands primly folded in her lap, "but who my son chooses to date is really none of my concern."

"That's very diplomatic of you. But I suspect you'd rather Evan dated someone other than me."

"Mary Jo, please. We got started on the wrong foot all those years ago. It was entirely my fault, and I've wished many times since that I'd been more thoughtful. I have the feeling I offended you and, my dear girl, that wasn't my intention."

"I'm willing to put the past behind us," Mary Jo suggested, managing a small smile. "That was three years ago, and I was more than a little overwhelmed by your family's wealth and position. If anyone's at fault, it was me."

"That's very gracious of you, my dear." Mrs. Dryden relaxed in her chair and crossed her ankles demurely.

"I love Evan," Mary Jo said, thinking it would be best to be as forthright as possible. "And I believe he loves me."

"I'm pleased for you both." No telltale emotion sounded in her voice. They could've been discussing the weather for all the feeling her words revealed.

"Evan has asked me to marry him," she announced, carefully watching the woman who sat across from her for any signs of disapproval.

"I'm very pleased." A small and all-too-brief smile accompanied her statement. "Have you set the date? I hope you two understand that we'll need at least a year to plan the wedding. This type of event takes time and careful preparation."

"Evan and I have decided on a small, private ceremony."

"No," Lois returned adamantly. "That won't be possible."

"Why not?" Mary Jo asked, taken aback by the vehemence in the older woman's voice.

"My husband is a senator. The son of a man in my husband's position does not sneak away and get married in…in secret."

Mary Jo hadn't said anything about sneaking away or secrecy, but she wasn't there to argue. "I come from a large family, Mrs. Dryden. We—"

"There were ten of you or some such, as I recall." Her hands made a dismissive motion.

Mary Jo bristled. The woman made her parents sound as if they'd produced a warren of rabbits, instead of a large, happy family.

"My point," Mary Jo said, controlling her irritation with some difficulty, "is that neither my parents nor I could afford a big, expensive wedding."

"Of course," Lois said in obvious relief. "We

wouldn't expect your relatives to assume the cost of such an elaborate affair. Walter and I would be more than happy to foot the bill."

"I appreciate the offer, and I'm sure my parents would, too, but I'm afraid we could never accept your generosity. Tradition says the bride's family assumes the cost of the wedding, and my father is a very traditional man."

"I see." Mrs. Dryden gnawed her lower lip. "There must be some way around his pride. Men can be such sticklers over things like this." For the first time she seemed almost friendly. "I'll come up with a solution. Just leave it to me."

"There's something you don't understand. An ostentatious wedding isn't what I want, either."

"But you must! I've already explained why it's necessary. We wouldn't want to create even a breath of scandal with some hushed-up affair. Why, that could do untold damage to my husband and to Evan's political future."

"Breath of *scandal?*"

"My dear girl, I don't mean to be rude, and please forgive me if I sound like an old busybody, but there are people who'd delight in finding the least little thing to use against Walter."

"But I'm marrying Evan, not Walter."

"I realize that. But you don't seem to grasp that these matters have to be handled…delicately. We need to start planning immediately. The moment the announcement is made, you and your family will be the focus of media attention."

Mary Jo's head began to spin. "I'm sure you're

mistaken. Why should anyone care about me or my family?"

Lois was wringing her hands. "I don't suppose it does any harm to mention it, although I must ask you not to spread this information around. Walter has been contacted by a longtime friend who intends to enter the presidential campaign next year. This friend has tentatively requested Walter to be his running mate, should he garner the party's nomination."

Mary Jo developed an instant throbbing headache.

"My husband and I must avoid any situation that might put him in an unflattering light."

"We could delay the wedding." She'd been joking, but Evan's mother looked relieved.

"Would you?" she asked hopefully.

"I'll talk to Evan."

At the mention of her youngest son, Lois Dryden frowned. "Shouldn't he be here with you? It seems a bit odd that you'd tell me about your engagement without him."

"I wanted the two of us to chat first," Mary Jo explained.

"An excellent idea," Lois said with a distinct nod of her head. "Men can be so difficult. If you and I can agree on certain…concerns before we talk to Evan and my husband, I feel sure we can work everything out to our mutual satisfaction."

"Mrs. Dryden, I'm a kindergarten teacher. I think you should know I feel uncomfortable with the idea of becoming a media figure."

"I'll do whatever I can to help you, Mary Jo. It's a lot to have thrust on you all at once, but if you're going to marry my son, you have to learn how to handle the press. I'll teach you how to use them to your advantage and how to turn something negative into a positive."

Mary Jo's headache increased a hundredfold. "I don't think I've been clear enough, Mrs. Dryden. I'm more than uncomfortable with this—I refuse to become involved in it."

"Refuse?" She repeated the word as if unsure of the meaning.

"I've already told you about my feelings for Evan," Mary Jo continued. "I love your son so much…" Her voice shook and she stopped speaking for a moment. "I'm not like you or your husband, or Evan, for that matter. Nor do I intend to be. When Evan asked me to marry him, I told him all this."

A frown creased Lois Dryden's brow. "I don't understand."

"Perhaps I'm not explaining it well. Basically, I refuse to live my life seeking the approval of others. I want a small, private wedding and Evan has agreed."

"But what about the future, when Evan decides to enter politics? Trust me, Mary Jo, the wife's position is as public as that of her husband."

"I'm sure that's true. But I'd hate the kind of life you're describing. Evan knows that and understands. He's also agreed that as long as I feel this way, he won't enter politics."

His mother vaulted from her chair. "But you can't do this! Politics is Evan's destiny. Why, from the time he was in grade school his teachers have told me what a natural leader he is. He was student-body

president in high school *and* in college. From his
early twenties on, he's been groomed for this very
thing. I can visualize my son in the White House
someday."

His mother had lofty plans indeed. "Is this what
Evan wants?"

"Of course it is," she said vehemently. "Ask him
yourself. His father and brother have had countless
conversations with him about it. If my son were to
marry a woman who didn't appreciate his abilities
or understand his ambitions, it might destroy him."

If the words had come from anyone other than
Lois Dryden, Mary Jo would've thought them absurd and melodramatic. But this woman believed
implicitly in what she said.

"Evan's marrying the right kind of woman is crucial to your plans for his future, isn't it?" Mary Jo
asked with infinite sadness.

Mrs. Dryden looked decidedly uncomfortable.
"Yes."

"I'm not that woman."

The older woman sighed. "I realize that. The
question is, what do you intend to do about it?"

Chapter 8

"I love Evan," Mary Jo insisted again, but even as she spoke, she realized again that loving him wasn't enough. Although she'd matured and wasn't the skittish, frightened woman she'd been three years earlier, nothing had really changed. If she married Evan, she might ruin his promising career. It was a heavy burden to carry.

Mary Jo couldn't change who and what she was, nor should she expect Evan to make all the concessions, giving up his future.

"I'm sure you do love my son," Lois said sincerely.

"And he loves me," Mary Jo added, keeping her back straight and her head high. She angled her chin at a proud, if somewhat defiant, tilt, unwilling to accept defeat. "We'll work this out somehow," she said confidently. "There isn't anything two people who love each other can't resolve. We'll find a way."

"I'm sure you will, my dear." Lois Dryden's mouth formed a sad smile that contradicted her reassurances. "In any case, you're perfectly right. You should discuss this with Evan and reach a decision together."

The older woman smoothed an invisible wrinkle from her dove-gray skirt. "Despite what you may think, Mary Jo, I have no personal objections to your marrying my son. When the two of you separated some time ago, I wondered if it had something to do with our little talk. I don't mind telling you I suffered more than a few regrets. I never intended to hurt you, and if I did, I beg your forgiveness."

"You certainly opened my eyes," Mary Jo admitted. Evan's mother had refined that talent over the past few years, she noted silently.

"I might sound like a interfering old woman, but I do hope you'll take our little talk to heart. I trust you'll seriously consider what we've discussed." She sighed. "I love Evan, too. God has blessed me with a very special family, and all I want is what's best for my children. I'm sure your parents feel the same way about you."

"They do." The conversation was becoming more and more unbearable. Mary Jo desperately wanted to leave. And she needed to talk to Evan, to share her concerns and address their future. But deep down she'd caught a fearful glimpse of the truth.

Mary Jo stood up abruptly and offered Mrs. Dryden her hand. "Thank you for your honesty and your insights. It wasn't what I wanted to hear, but I suppose it's what I needed to know. I'm sure this was just as difficult for you. We have something in common, Mrs. Dryden. We both love your son. Evan wouldn't be the man he is without your love and care. You have a right to be proud."

Evan's mother took Mary Jo's hand in both of her own and held it firmly for a moment. "I appreciate that. Do keep in touch, won't you?"

Mary Jo nodded. "If you wish."

The older woman led her to the front door and walked out to the circular driveway with her. Mary Jo climbed into her car and started the engine. As she pulled away, she glanced in her rearview mirror to find Lois Dryden's look both thoughtful and troubled.

Normally Mary Jo joined her family for their Sunday get-togethers. But not this week. Needing time and privacy to sort out her thoughts, she drove to the marina. She parked, then made her way slowly to the waterfront. The wind coming off the ocean was fresh and tangy with salt. She had to think, and what better place than here, where she'd spent countless happy hours in Evan's company?

How long she sat on the bench overlooking the water she didn't know. Time seemed to be of little consequence. She gazed at the boats moving in and out of their narrow passageways. The day had turned cloudy, which suited her somber mood.

Standing, she walked along the pier, once again reviewing her conversation with Evan's mother. Her steps slowed as she realized no amount of brooding would solve the problems. She had to talk to Evan, and soon, before she lost her nerve.

She found a pay phone, plunked in a quarter and dialed his home number.

"Mary Jo. Thank goodness! Where were you?" Evan asked. "I've been calling your place every fifteen minutes. I have some wonderful news."

"I…had an errand to run," she said, not ready to elaborate just then. He was obviously excited. "What's your good news?"

"I'll tell you the minute I see you."

"Do you want to meet somewhere?" she asked.

"How about Rowe's Wharf? We can take a stroll along the pier. If you want, we can visit the aquarium. I haven't been there in years. When we're hungry we can find a seafood restaurant and catch a bite to eat." He paused and laughed at his weak joke. "No pun intended."

"That'll be great," she said, finding it difficult to rouse the proper enthusiasm.

"Mary Jo?" His voice rose slightly. "What's wrong? You sound upset."

"We need to talk."

"All right," he agreed guardedly. "Do you want me to pick you up?" When she declined, he said, "I'll meet you there in half an hour, okay?"

"Okay." It was ironic, Mary Jo mused, that Evan could be so happy while she felt as if her entire world was about to shatter.

When she finished speaking to Evan, Mary Jo phoned her mother and told her she wouldn't be joining them for dinner. Marianna knew instantly that something wasn't right, but Mary Jo promised to explain later.

From the marina she drove down Atlantic Avenue and found a suitable place to park. It had been less than twenty-four hours, and already she was starved for the sight of Evan. It seemed unthinkable to live the rest of her life without him.

He was standing on the wharf waiting for her when she arrived. His face lighted up as she approached, and he held out both hands to her.

Mary Jo experienced an immediate sense of comfort the moment their fingers touched. In another second, she was securely wrapped in his arms. He held her against him as though he didn't intend to ever let her go. And she wished she didn't have to leave the protective shelter of his arms.

"I've missed you," he breathed against her temple. "I've missed you so much." He threaded his fingers lovingly through her windblown hair.

"We spent nearly all of yesterday together," she reminded him lightly, although she shared his feelings. Even a few hours apart left her wondering how she'd managed to survive all those years without him. How she'd ever do it again...

"I love you, Mary Jo. Don't forget that."

"I won't." His words were an immense comfort. She buried her face in his neck and clung to him, wanting to believe with everything she possessed that there was a way for them to find happiness together.

"Now tell me your good news," she murmured. Evan eased her out of his arms, but tucked her hand inside his elbow. His eyes were shining with excitement.

"Damian and I had a long talk last evening," Evan said. "I phoned to tell him about the two of us, and he's absolutely delighted. Jessica, too. They both send their congratulations, by the way."

"Thank them for me," she said softly. "So, come on, tell me your news." She leaned against him as they walked leisurely down the wharf.

"All right, all right. Damian's been in contact with a number of key people over the past few weeks. The general consensus is that the time for me to make my move into the political arena is now."

Mary Jo felt as though a fist had plowed into her midsection. For a moment she remained frozen. She couldn't breathe. Couldn't think. She was dimly aware of Evan beside her, still talking.

"Now?" she broke in. "But I thought…you said…"

"I know it probably seems too early to be discussing next year's elections," Evan went on to say, his face alive with energy. "But we've got some catching up to do. I won't file for office until after the first of the year, but there're a million things that need to be done before then."

"What office do you intend to run for?" Her mind was whirling with doubts and questions. The sick feeling in the pit of her stomach refused to go away. She felt both cold and feverishly hot at the same time.

"I'm running for city council. There's nothing I'd enjoy more. And, Mary Jo," he said with a broad grin, "I know I can make a difference in our city. I have so many ideas and I've got lots of time, and I don't mind working hard." He raised her hand to his lips and kissed the knuckles. "That's one of the reasons I want us to get married as soon as it can be arranged.

We'll work together, side by side, the way my father and mother did when he ran for the Senate."

"I—"

"You'll need to quit your teaching job."

So many objections rose up in her she didn't know which one to address first. "Why can't I teach?"

He looked at her as if the question surprised him. "You don't have to work anymore, and besides, I'm going to need you. Don't you see? This is just the beginning. There's a whole new life waiting for the two of us."

"Have you talked this over with your parents?" Mrs. Dryden must've already known, Mary Jo thought.

"Dad and I discussed it this morning, and he agrees with Damian. The timing is right. Naturally, he'd like to see me run for mayor a few years down the road, and I might, but there's no need to get ahead of ourselves. I haven't been elected to city council yet."

"What did your mother have to say?"

"I don't know if Dad's had the chance to talk to her yet. What makes you ask?"

"I...visited her this morning," Mary Jo said, studying the water. It was safer to look out over Boston Harbor than at the man she loved.

"You spent the morning with my mother?" Evan stopped. "At Whispering Willows?"

"Yes."

His eyebrows shot straight toward his hairline. "Why would you go and visit my mother?"

Mary Jo heaved in a deep breath and held it until her chest ached. "There's something you should know, Evan. Something I should've told you a long time ago."

She hesitated, hardly able to continue. Eventually she did, but her voice was low and strained. "When I broke our engagement three years ago, it wasn't because I'd fallen in love with another man. There was never anyone else. It was all a big lie."

She felt him stiffen. He frowned and his eyes narrowed, first with denial and then with disbelief. He shook off her hand and she walked over to the pier, waiting for him to join her.

It took him several minutes.

"I'm not proud of that lie," she told him, "and I apologize for stooping to such cowardly methods. You deserved far better, but I wasn't strong enough or mature enough to confront you with the truth."

"Which was?" She could tell he was making a strenuous effort to keep his voice level and dispassionate. But his fists were clenched. She could feel his anger, had anticipated it, understood it.

"Various reasons," she confessed. "I invented another love interest because I knew you'd believe me, and...and it avoided the inevitable arguments. I couldn't have dealt with a long-drawn-out debate."

"That makes no sense whatsoever." He sounded angry now, and Mary Jo couldn't blame him. "You'd better start at the beginning," he suggested after a long silence. "What was it we would have argued about?"

"Our getting married."

"Okay," he said, obviously still not understanding.

"It all began the evening you took me to meet your family," Mary Jo said. "I'd known you were wealthy, of course, but I had no idea how prominent your family was. I was naive and inexperienced, and when your mother asked me some…pertinent questions, I realized a marriage between us wouldn't work."

"What kind of 'pertinent' questions?" The words were charged with contained fury.

"Evan, please, it doesn't matter."

"The hell it doesn't!"

Mary Jo closed her eyes. "About my family and my background, and how suitable I'd be as a political wife. She stressed the importance of your marrying the right woman."

"It appears my mother and I need to have a chat."

"Don't be angry, Evan. She wasn't rude or cruel, but she brought up a few truths I hadn't faced. Afterward, I was convinced a marriage between us would never survive. We have so little in common. Our backgrounds are nothing alike, and I was afraid that in time you'd…you'd regret having married me."

He made a disgusted sound. "And so you invented this ridiculous lie and walked out of my life, leaving me lost and confused and so shaken it…" He paused as if he'd said more than he'd intended.

"I behaved stupidly—I know that. But I hurt, too, Evan. Don't think it was easy on me. I suffered. Because I loved you then and I love you still."

He sighed heavily. "I appreciate your honesty, Mary Jo, but let's put the whole mess behind us. It doesn't concern us anymore. We're together now and will be for the next fifty years. That's all that matters."

Tears blurred Mary Jo's eyes as she watched the airport shuttle boat cross Boston Harbor. The waters churned and foamed—like her emotions, she thought.

"It's quite apparent, however," Evan went on, "that I need to have a heart-to-heart with my dear, sweet, interfering mother."

"Evan, she isn't the one to blame. Breaking up, lying to you—that was *my* bad idea. But it isn't going to happen again."

"I won't let you out of my life that easily a second time."

"I don't plan on leaving," she whispered. He placed his arm around her shoulder, and Mary Jo slid her own arm around his waist. For a moment they were content in the simple pleasure of being together.

"Because of that first meeting with your mother, I felt it was important to talk to her again," Mary Jo said, trying to explain why she'd gone to see Mrs. Dryden that morning. "She's a wonderful woman, Evan, and she loves you very much."

"Fine. But I will not allow her to interfere in our lives. If she doesn't understand that now, she will when I finish talking to her."

"Evan, please! She did nothing more than open my eyes to a few home truths."

"What did she have to say this morning?"

"Well…she had some of the same questions as before."

"Such as?" he demanded.

"You want us to be married soon, right?"

He nodded. "The sooner the better." Bending his head, he kissed a corner of her mouth. "As I said earlier, we have three years of lost time to make up for. Keep that house with all those empty bedrooms in mind."

Despite the ache in her heart, Mary Jo smiled. "Your mother told me that a small, private wedding might cause problems for your father."

"Whose wedding is this?" Evan cried. "We'll do this our way, sweetheart. Don't worry about it."

"It could be important, Evan," she countered swiftly. "Your father can't be associated with anything that…that could be misinterpreted."

Evan laughed outright. "In other words, she prefers to throw a large, gala wedding with a cast of thousands? That's ridiculous."

"I…think she might be right."

"That's the kind of wedding you want?" Evan asked, his eyes revealing his disbelief.

"No. It isn't what I want at all. But on the other hand, I wouldn't want to do anything to hurt your father."

"Trust me, Mary Jo, you won't." He gave her an affectionate squeeze. "Now you listen. We're going to be married and we'll have the kind of wedding *we* want, and Mother won't have any choice but to accept it."

"But, Evan, what if our rushed wedding did cause speculation?"

"What if it did? Do you think I care? Or my father, either, for that matter? My mother is often guilty of making mountains out of molehills. She loves to worry. In this day and age, it's ridiculous to get upset about such things."

"But—"

He silenced her with a kiss thorough enough to leave her feeling that anything was possible. "I love you, Mary Jo. If it was up to me, we'd take the next plane to Las Vegas and get married this evening."

"People might gossip." She managed to dredge up one last argument.

"Good. The more my name's in circulation, the better."

Mary Jo's spirits had lightened considerably. She so desperately wanted to believe him, she didn't stop to question what he was saying.

"It's settled, then. We'll be married as soon as we can make the arrangements. Mom can fuss all she wants, but it isn't going to do her any good."

"I... There are some other things we need to talk over first."

"There are?" He sounded exasperated.

She leaned against the pier, knotting and unknotting her hands. "You're excited about running for city council, aren't you?"

"Yes," he admitted readily. "This is something I want, and I'm willing to work for it. I wouldn't run for office if I wasn't convinced I could make some positive changes. This is exactly the right way for me to enter politics, especially while Dad's in the Senate."

She turned to study him. "What if I asked you not to run?"

Evan took a moment to mull over her words. "Why would you do that?"

"What if I did?" she asked again. "What would you do then?"

"First, I'd need to know exactly what you objected to."

"What if I reminded you I wasn't comfortable in the spotlight? Which, I might add, was something we discussed just yesterday. I'm not the kind of person who's comfortable living my life in a fishbowl."

"It wouldn't be like that," he protested.

Her smile was sad. Evan didn't understand. He'd grown up accustomed to having people interested in his personal life. Even now, his dating habits often provided speculation for the society pages.

"It *would* be like that, Evan. Don't kid yourself."

"Then you'll adjust," he said with supreme confidence.

"I'll adjust," she repeated slowly. "What if I don't? Then what happens? I could be an embarrassment to you. My family might be, as well. Let me give you an example. Just a few days ago, Jack and Rich were so upset over this investment problem my father's having that they were ready to go to Adison's office again and punch him out. If we hadn't stopped them, they'd have been thrown in jail. The press would have a field day with that."

"You're overreacting."

"Maybe," she agreed grudgingly, then added with emphasis, "but I don't think so. I told you before how I feel about this. You didn't believe me, did you? You seem to think a pat on the head and a few reassurances are all I need. You've discounted everything I've said to you."

"Mary Jo, please—"

"In case you haven't noticed, I—I have this terrible habit of blushing whenever I'm the center of attention. I'm not the kind of woman your mother is. She enjoys the spotlight, loves arranging social events. She has a gift for making everyone feel comfortable and welcome. I can't do that, Evan. I'd be miserable."

Evan said nothing, but his mouth tightened.

"You may think I'm being selfish and uncaring, but that isn't true. I'm not the right woman for you."

"Because my mother said so."

"No, because of who and what I am."

Evan sighed. "I can see that you've already got this all worked out."

"Another thing. I'm a good teacher and I enjoy my job. I'd want to continue with my kindergarten class after we were married."

Evan took several steps away from her and rubbed his hand along the back of his neck. "Then there's nothing left for me to say, is there? I'll talk to Damian and explain that everything's off. I won't run for city council, not if it makes you that uncomfortable."

"Oh, Evan." She was on the verge of tears. This was exactly what she'd feared. Exactly what she didn't want. "Don't you see?" she pleaded, swallowing a sob. "I can't marry you knowing I'm holding you back from your dreams. You may love me now, but in time you'd grow to resent me, and it would ruin our marriage."

"You're more important to me than any political office," Evan said sharply. "You're right, Mary Jo, you did tell me how you felt about getting involved in politics, and I did discount what you said. I grew up in a family that was often in the limelight. This whole thing is old hat to me. I was wrong not to have considered your feelings."

She closed her eyes in an effort to blot out his

willingness to sacrifice himself. "It just isn't going to work, Evan. In the beginning you wouldn't mind, but later it would destroy us. It would hurt your family, too. This isn't only your dream, it's theirs."

"Leave my family to me."

"No. You're a part of them and they're a part of you. Politics has been your dream from the time you were a boy. You told me yourself that you believe you can make a difference to the city's future."

By now, the tears were running down her face. Impatiently she brushed them aside and forced herself to continue. "How many times are you going to make me say it? *I'm not the right woman for you.*"

"You *are* the right woman," he returned fiercely. His hands gripped her shoulders and he pulled her toward him, his eyes fierce and demanding. "I'm not listening to any more of this. We've loved each other for too long. We're meant to be together."

Mary Jo stared out at the harbor again. "There's someone else out there—from the right family, with the right background. A woman who'll share your ambition and your dreams, who'll work with you and not against you. A woman who'll…love you, too."

"I can't believe you're saying this." His grip tightened on her shoulder until it was almost painful, but she knew he didn't even realize it. "It's *you* I love. It's *you* I want to marry."

Mary Jo shook her head sadly.

"If you honestly think there's another woman for me, why didn't I fall in love with someone else? I had three whole years to find this phantom woman you mention. Why didn't I?"

"Because your eyes were closed. Because you were too wrapped up in your own pain to look. For whatever reasons… I don't know…"

"Is this what you want? To walk out of my life a second time as if we meant nothing to each other?" He was beginning to attract attention from passersby, and he lowered his voice.

"No," she admitted. "This is killing me. I'd give anything to be the kind of woman you need, but I can only be me. If I ask you to accept who I am, then…I can't ask you to be something you're not."

"Don't do this," he said from between clenched teeth. "We'll find a way."

How she wanted to believe that. How she wished it was possible.

Evan drew a deep breath and released her shoulders. "Let's not make any drastic decisions now. We're both emotionally spent. Nothing has to be determined right this minute." He paused and gulped in another deep breath. "Let's sleep on it and we can talk in the morning. All right?"

Mary Jo nodded. She couldn't have endured much more of this.

The following morning Evan phoned the office shortly after she'd arrived and told her he'd be in late. His voice was cool, without a hint of emotion, as he asked her to reschedule his first two appointments.

Mary Jo thought she might as well have been speaking to a stranger. She longed to ask him how he was or if he'd had any further ideas, but it was clear he wanted to avoid speaking to her about anything personal.

With a heavy heart, she began her morning duties. Around nine-thirty, the office door opened and Damian walked in. He paused as if he wasn't sure he'd come to the right room.

"Evan won't be in until eleven this morning," she explained.

"Yes, I know." For a man she'd assumed was utterly confident, Damian appeared doubtful and rather hesitant. "It wasn't Evan I came to see. It was you."

"Me?" She looked up at Damian, finding his gaze warm and sympathetic. "Why?"

"Evan stopped by the house yesterday afternoon to talk to both Jessica and me. He was confused and…"

"Hurt," Mary Jo supplied for him. She knew exactly what Evan was feeling because she felt the same way.

"My talking to you may not solve anything, but I thought I should give it a try. I'm not sure my brother would appreciate my butting into his personal business, but he did it once for me. I figure I owe him one." Damian's smile was fleeting. "I don't know if this is what you want to hear, but Evan really loves you."

A lump developed in her throat and she nodded. "I realize that." She loved him just as much.

"From what Evan said to us, I gather he's decided against running for city council. He also told us why he felt he had to back out. Naturally, I support any decision he chooses to make."

"But…" There had to be a "but" in all this.

"But it would be a shame if he declined."

"I'm not going to let that happen," Mary Jo said calmly. "You see, I love Evan and I want what's best for him, and to put it simply, that isn't me."

"He doesn't believe that, Mary Jo, and neither do I."

She could see no reason to discuss the issue. "Where is he now?" she asked softly.

"He went to talk to our parents."

Their parents. If anyone could get him to face the truth, it was Lois Dryden. Mary Jo had approached the woman, strong and certain of her love, and walked away convinced she'd been living in a dreamworld. Lois Dryden was capable of opening Evan's eyes as no one else could.

"We both need time to think this through," Mary Jo murmured. "I appreciate your coming to me, Damian, more than I can say. I know you did it out of love, but what happens between Evan and me, well, that's our concern."

"You didn't ask for my advice, but I'm going to give it to you, anyway," Damian said. "Don't be so quick to give up."

"I won't," she promised.

Mary Jo was sitting at her desk sorting mail when Evan arrived shortly after eleven. She stood up to greet him, but he glanced past her and said tonelessly, "I can't fight both of you." Then he walked into his office and shut the door.

His action said more than his words. In her heart, Mary Jo had dared to hope that if Evan confronted his parents and came away with his convictions intact, there might be a chance for them.

But obviously that hadn't happened. One look plainly revealed his resignation and regret. He'd accepted from his parents what he wouldn't from her. The truth.

Sitting back down, Mary Jo wrote her letter of resignation, printed it and then signed it. Next she phoned a temporary employment agency and made arrangements for her replacement to arrive that afternoon.

When she'd finished, she tapped on his closed door and let herself into his office.

"Yes?" Evan said.

She found him standing in front of the window, hands clasped behind his back. After a moment, he turned to face her.

With tears blocking her throat, she laid the single sheet on his desk and crossed the room to stand beside him.

His gaze went from the letter to her and back. "What's that?"

"My letter of resignation. My replacement will be here within the hour. I'll finish out the day—show her around and explain her duties."

She half expected him to offer a token argument, but he said nothing. She pressed her hand against the side of his face and smiled up at him. His features blurred as tears filled her eyes.

"Goodbye, Evan," she whispered.

Chapter 9

A week passed and the days bled into one another until Mary Jo couldn't distinguish morning from afternoon. A thousand regrets hounded her at all hours of the day and night.

Blessed with a loving family, Mary Jo was grateful for their comfort, needed it. There was, for all of them, some consolation in the news that came from Evan. Through his new personal assistant, he'd been in touch with her father regarding Adison Investments.

Mary Jo heard from him, too. Once. In a brief letter explaining that Adison would be forthcoming with the return of the original investment money, plus interest. Since he'd calculated his fee for an extended lawsuit, she owed him nothing.

Mary Jo read the letter several times, searching

for a message. Anything. But there were only three short sentences, their tone crisp and businesslike, with no hidden meaning that she could decipher. Tears blurred her eyes as she lovingly ran her finger over his signature. She missed him terribly, felt empty and lost, and this was as close as she'd ever be to him again—her finger caressing his signature at the end of a letter.

Another week passed. Mary Jo was no less miserable than she'd been the first day after she'd stopped working for Evan. She knew it would take time and effort to accept the infeasibility of her love for him, but she wasn't ready. Not yet. So she stayed holed up in her apartment, listless and heartbroken.

The fact that the summer days were glorious— all sunshine and blue skies—didn't help. The least Mother Nature could've done was cooperate and match her mood with dark gray clouds and gloomy weather.

She dragged herself out of bed late one morning and didn't bother to eat until early afternoon. Now she sat in front of the television dressed in her nightie and munching dry cornflakes. She hadn't been to the grocery store in weeks and had long since run out of milk. And just about everything else.

The doorbell chimed, and Mary Jo shot an accusing glance in the direction of her front door. It was probably her mother or one of her sisters-in-law, who seemed to think it was up to them to boost her spirits. So they invented a number of ridiculous excuses to pop in unexpectedly.

The love and support of her family was important,

but all Mary Jo wanted at the moment was to be left alone. To eat her cornflakes in peace.

She set the bowl aside, walked over to the door and squinted through the peephole. She caught a glimpse of a designer purse, but unfortunately whoever was holding it stood just outside her view.

"Who is it?" she called out.

"Jessica."

Mary Jo pressed her forehead against the door and groaned. She was an emotional and physical wreck. The last person she wanted to see was anyone related to Evan.

"Mary Jo, please open the door," Jessica called. "We need to talk. It's about Evan."

Nothing could have been more effective. She didn't want company. She didn't want to talk. But the minute Jessica said Evan's name, Mary Jo turned the lock and opened the door. Standing in the doorway, she closed her eyes against the painfully bright sun.

"How are you?" Jessica asked, walking right in.

"About as bad as I look," Mary Jo mumbled, shutting the door behind her. "What about Evan?"

"Same as you." She strode into the room, removed a stack of papers from the rocking chair and planted herself in it as if she intended to stay for a while.

"Where's Andy?" Mary Jo asked, still holding the doorknob.

Jessica crossed her legs, rocking gently. "My mother has him—for the *day*."

Mary Jo noted the emphasis. Jessica was going to stay here until she got what she wanted.

"I told Mom I had a doctor's appointment, and I

do—later," Jessica said. "I think I'm pregnant again." A radiant happiness shone from her eyes.

"Congratulations." Although Mary Jo was miserable, she was pleased for her friend, who was clearly delighted.

"I know it's none of my business," Jessica said sympathetically, "but tell me what happened between you and Evan."

"I'm sure he's already explained." Mary Jo wasn't up to discussing all the painful details. Besides, it would solve nothing.

Jessica laughed shortly. "Evan talk? You've got to be joking. He wouldn't say so much as a word. Both Damian and I've tried to get him to tell us what happened, but it hasn't done a bit of good."

"So you've come to me."

"Exactly."

"Please don't do this, Jessica," Mary Jo said, fighting back the tears. "It's just too painful."

"But you both love each other so much."

"That's why our breakup's necessary. It isn't easy on either of us, but this is the way it has to be."

Jessica threw her hands in the air. "You're a pair of fools! There's no talking to Evan, and you're not much better. What's it going to take to get you two back together?"

"A miracle," Mary Jo answered.

Jessica took some time to digest this. "Is there anything I can do?"

"No," Mary Jo said sadly. There wasn't anything anyone could do. But one thing was certain: she couldn't continue like this. Sliding from one day to the next without a thought to the future. Immersed in the pain of the past, barely able to live in the present.

"You're sure?"

"I'm thinking of leaving Boston," she said suddenly. The impulse had come unexpectedly, and in a heartbeat Mary Jo knew it was the right decision. She couldn't live in this town, this state, without constantly being bombarded with information about the Dryden family. Not a week passed that his father wasn't in the news for one reason or another. It would only get worse once Evan was elected to city council.

Escape seemed her only answer.

"Where would you go?" Jessica pressed.

Anywhere that wasn't here. "The Northwest," she said, blurting out the first destination that came to mind. "Washington, maybe Oregon. I've heard that part of the country's beautiful." Teachers were needed everywhere and she shouldn't have much trouble obtaining a position.

"So far away?" Jessica seemed to breathe the question.

The farther the better. Her family would argue with her, but for the first time in two weeks, Mary Jo had found a reason to look ahead.

Her parents would tell her she was running away, and Mary Jo would agree, but sometimes running was necessary. She remembered her father's talks with her older brothers; he'd explained that there might come a day when they'd find themselves in a no-win situation. The best thing to do, he'd told them, was to walk away. Surely this was one of those times.

"Thank you for coming," Mary Jo said, looking

solemnly at her friend. "I appreciate it. Please let me know when the baby's born."

"I will," Jessica said, her eyes sad.

"I'll have my mother send me the results of the election next year. My heart will be with Evan."

It would always be with him.

Jessica left soon afterward, flustered and discouraged. They hugged and, amid promises to keep in touch, reluctantly parted. Mary Jo counted Evan's sister-in-law as a good friend.

Mary Jo was filled with purpose. She dressed, made a number of phone calls, opened the door and let the sunshine pour in. By late afternoon, she'd accomplished more than she had in the previous two weeks. Telling her parents her decision wouldn't be easy, but her mind was made up. It was now Tuesday. Tomorrow she'd give the school her notice and let her landlord know, too. First thing next Monday morning, she was packing what she could in her car and heading west. As soon as she'd settled somewhere she'd send for her furniture.

Before Mary Jo could announce her decision, her father phoned her with the wonderful news that he'd received a cashier's check returning his investment. Not only that, Evan had put him in contact with a reputable financial adviser.

"That's great," Mary Jo said, blinking back tears. Hearing the relief in her father's voice was all the reward she'd ever need. Although it had ultimately broken her heart, asking Evan to help her parents had been the right thing to do. Her father had gotten far more than his investment back. In the process he'd restored his pride and his faith in justice.

"I need to talk to you and Mom," Mary Jo said, steeling herself for the inevitable confrontation. "I'll be over in a few minutes."

The meeting didn't go well. Mary Jo hadn't expected that it would. Her parents listed their objections for nearly an hour. Mary Jo's resolve didn't waver. She was leaving Boston; she would find a new life for herself.

To her surprise, her brothers sided with her. Jack insisted she was old enough to make her own decisions. His words did more to convince her parents than hours of her own arguments.

The Friday before she planned to leave, Mary Jo spent the day with her mother. Marianna was pickling cucumbers in the kitchen, dabbing her eyes now and then when she thought Mary Jo wasn't looking.

"I'm going to miss you," Marianna said, shaking her head.

Mary Jo's heart lurched. "I'll miss you, too. But, Mom, you make it sound like you'll never hear from me again. I promise to phone at least once a week."

"Call when the rates are cheaper, understand?"

Mary Jo suppressed a smile. "Of course."

"I talked to Evan," her mother said casually as she was inserting cloves of garlic into the sterilized canning jars.

Mary Jo froze, and her breath jammed in her chest.

"I told him you'd decided to leave Boston, and you know what he said?"

"No." The word rose from her throat on a bubble of hysteria.

"Evan said you'd know what was best." She paused as if carefully judging her words. "He didn't sound like himself. I'm worried about that boy, but I'm more concerned about you."

"Mom, I'm going to be fine."

"I know that. You're a Summerhill and we're strong people."

Mary Jo followed her mother, dropping a sprig of dill weed into each of the sparkling clean jars.

"You never told me what went wrong between you and Evan, not that you had to. I've got eyes and ears, and it didn't take much to figure out that his family had something to do with all this."

Her mother's insight didn't come as any surprise, but Mary Jo neither confirmed nor denied it.

"The mail's here," Norman Summerhill said, strolling into the kitchen. "I had one of those fancy travel agencies send us a couple of brochures on the South Pacific. When you're finished packing those jars, let's sit down and read them over."

Marianna's nod was eager. "We won't be long."

Her father set the rest of the mail on the table. The top envelope caught Mary Jo's attention. The return address was a bankruptcy court. She didn't think anything of it until later when her father opened the envelope.

"I wonder what this is?" he mumbled, frowning in confusion. He stretched his arm out in front of him to read it.

"Norman, for the love of heaven, get your glasses," Marianna chastised.

"I can see fine without them." He winked at Mary Jo. "Here, you read it for me." Mary Jo took the cover letter and scanned the contents. As she did, her stomach turned. The bankruptcy court had written her parents on behalf of Adison Investments. They were to complete the attached forms and list, with proof, the amount of their investment. Once all the documents were submitted, the case would be heard.

The legal jargon was difficult for Mary Jo to understand, but one thing was clear. Adison Investments hadn't returned her father's money.

Evan had.

"It's nothing, Dad," Mary Jo said, not knowing what else to say.

"Then throw it out. I don't understand why we get so much junk mail these days. You'd think the environmentalists would do something about wasting all those trees."

Mary Jo stuck the envelope in her purse, made her excuses and left soon afterward. She wasn't sure what she was going to do, but if she didn't escape soon, there'd be no hiding her tears.

Evan had done this for her family because he loved her. This was his way of saying goodbye. Hot tears burned in her eyes, and sniffling, she rubbed the back of her hand across her face.

The blast of a car horn sounded from behind her and Mary Jo glanced in the direction of the noise. Adrenaline shot through her as she saw a full-size sedan barreling toward her.

The next thing she heard was metal slamming against metal. The hideous grating noise blasted her ears and she instinctively brought her hands up to her face. The impact was so strong she felt as though she were caught in the middle of an explosion.

Her world went into chaos. There was only pain. Her head started to spin, and her vision blurred. She screamed.

Her last thought before she lost consciousness was that she was going to die.

"Why didn't you call me right away?" a gruff male voice demanded.

It seemed to come from a great distance away and drifted slowly toward Mary Jo as she floated, unconcerned, on a thick black cloud. It sounded like Evan's voice, but then again it didn't. The words came to her sluggish and slurred.

"We tried to contact you, but your personal assistant said you couldn't be reached."

The second voice belonged to her father, Mary Jo determined. But he, too, sounded odd, as if he were standing at the bottom of a deep well and yelling up at her. The words were distorted and they vibrated, making them difficult to understand. They seemed to take a very long time to reach her. Perhaps it was because her head hurt so badly. The throbbing was intensely painful.

"I came as soon as I heard." It was Evan again and he sounded sorry. He sounded as if he thought he was to blame. "How seriously is she hurt?"

"Doc says she sustained a head injury. She's unconscious, but they claim she isn't in a coma."

"She'll wake up soon," her mother said in a soothing tone. "Now sit down and relax. Everything's going to be all right. I'm sure the doctor will be happy to answer any of your questions. Mary Jo's going to be fine, just wait and see."

Her mother was comforting Evan as if he were one of her own children, Mary Jo realized. She didn't understand why Evan should be so worried. Perhaps he was afraid she was going to die. Perhaps she already had, but then she decided she couldn't be dead because she hurt too much.

"What have they done to her head?"

Mary Jo was eager to hear that answer herself.

"They had to shave off her hair."

"Relax." It was her father speaking. "It'll grow back."

"It's just that she looks so…" Evan didn't finish the sentence.

"She'll be fine, Evan. Now sit down here by her side. I know it's a shock seeing her like this."

Mary Jo wanted to reassure Evan herself, but her mouth refused to open and she couldn't speak. Something must be wrong with her if she could hear but not see or speak. When she attempted to move, she found her arms and legs wouldn't cooperate. A sense of panic overwhelmed her and the pounding pain intensified.

Almost immediately she drifted away on the same dark cloud and the voices slowly faded. She longed to call out, to pull herself back, but she lacked the strength. And this way, the pain wasn't as bad.

The next sound Mary Jo heard was a soft thumping. It took her several minutes to recognize what it meant. Someone was in her room, pacing. Whoever it was seemed impatient, or maybe anxious. She didn't know which.

"How is she?" A feminine voice that was vaguely familiar drifted toward Mary Jo. The pain in her head was back, and she desperately wanted it to go away.

"There's been no change." It was Evan who spoke. Evan was the one pacing her room. Knowing he was there filled her with a gentle sense of peace. She'd recover if Evan was with her. How she knew this, Mary Jo didn't question.

"How long have you been here?" The feminine voice belonged to Jessica, she decided.

"A few hours."

"It's more like twenty-four. I met Mary Jo's parents in the elevator. They're going home to get some sleep. You should, too. The hospital will call if there's any change."

"No."

Mary Jo laughed to herself. She'd recognize that stubborn streak of his anywhere.

"Evan," Jessica protested. "You're not thinking clearly."

"Yeah, I know. But I'm not leaving her, Jessica. You can argue all you want, but it won't make a damn bit of difference."

There was a short silence. Mary Jo heard a chair being dragged across the floor. It was coming toward her. "Mary Jo was leaving Boston, did you know?"

"I know," Evan returned. "Her mother called to tell me."

"Were you going to stop her?"

It took him a long time to answer. "No."

"But you love her."

"Jess, please, leave it alone."

Evan loved her and she loved him, and it was hopeless. A sob swelled within her chest and Mary Jo experienced a sudden urge to weep.

"She moved," Evan said sharply, excitedly. "Did you see it? Her hand flinched just now."

Mary Jo felt herself being pulled away once more into a void where there was no sound. It seemed to close in around her like the folds of a dark blanket.

When Mary Jo opened her eyes, the first thing she saw was a patch of blue. A moment later, she realized it was the sky outside the hospital window. A scattering of clouds shimmied across the horizon. She blinked, trying to figure out what she was doing in this bed, this room.

She'd been in a car accident, that was it. She couldn't remember any details—except that she'd thought she was dying. Her head had hurt so badly. The throbbing wasn't nearly as bad now, but it was still there and the bright sunshine made her eyes water.

Rolling her head to the other side demanded a great deal of effort. Her mother was sitting at her bedside reading from a Bible and her father was standing on the other side of the room. He pressed his hands against the small of his back as if to relieve tired muscles.

"Mom." Mary Jo's voice was husky and low.

Marianna Summerhill vaulted to her feet. "Norman! Norman, Mary Jo's awake." Having said that, she covered her face with her hands and burst into tears.

It was very unusual to see her mother cry. Mary Jo looked at her father and saw that his eyes, too, were brimming with tears.

"So you decided to rejoin the living," her father said, raising her hand to his lips. "Welcome back."

Smiling required more strength than she had.

"How do you feel?" Her mother was dabbing at her eyes with a tissue. She was so pale that Mary Jo wondered if she'd been ill herself.

"Weird," she said hoarsely.

"The doctor said he expected you to wake up soon."

There was so much she wanted to ask, so much she had to say. "Evan?" she managed to croak.

"He was here," her mother answered. "From the moment he learned about the accident until just a few minutes ago. No one could convince him to leave."

"He's talking with some fancy specialist right now," her father explained. "I don't mind telling you, he's been beside himself with worry. We've all been scared."

Her eyes drifted shut. She felt so incredibly weak, and what energy she had evaporated quickly.

"Sleep," her mother cooed. "Everything's going to be fine."

No, no, Mary Jo protested, fighting sleep. Not yet. Not so soon. She had too many questions that needed answering. But the silence enveloped her once more.

It was night when she stirred again. The sky was dark and the heavens were flecked with stars. Moonlight softly illuminated the room.

She assumed she was alone, then noticed a shadowy figure against the wall. The still shape sat in the chair next to her bed. It was Evan, and he was asleep. His arms were braced against the edge of the mattress, supporting his head.

The comfort she felt in knowing he was with her was beyond measure. Reaching for his hand, she covered it with her own, then yawned and closed her eyes.

"Are you hungry?" Marianna asked, carrying in the hospital tray and setting it on the bedside table.

Mary Jo was sitting up for the first time. "I don't know," she said, surprised by how feeble her voice sounded.

"I talked to the doctor about the hospital menu," her mother said, giving her head a disparaging shake. "He assured me you'll survive on their cooking until I can get you home and feed you properly."

It probably wasn't all that amusing, but Mary Jo couldn't stop smiling. This was the first day she'd really taken note of her surroundings. The room was filled with fresh flowers. They covered every available surface; there were even half a dozen vases lined up on the floor.

"Who sent all the flowers?" she asked.

Her mother pointed toward the various floral arrangements. "Your brothers. Dad and I. Those two are from Jessica and Damian. Let me see—the teachers at your old school. Oh, the elaborate one is from the Drydens. That bouquet of pink carnations is from Gary."

"How sweet of everyone." But Mary Jo saw that there were a number of bouquets her mother had skipped. Those, she strongly suspected, were from Evan.

Evan.

Just thinking about him made her feel so terribly sad. From the time she'd regained consciousness, he'd stopped coming to the hospital. He'd been there earlier, she was sure of it. The memories were too vivid not to be real. But as soon as she was out of danger, he'd left her life once more.

"Eat something," Marianna insisted. "I know it's not your mama's cooking, but it doesn't look too bad."

Mary Jo shook her head and leaned back against the pillow. "I'm not hungry."

"Sweetheart, please. The doctors won't let you come home until you've regained your strength."

Evan wasn't the only one with a stubborn streak. She folded her arms and refused to even glance at the food. Eventually, she was persuaded to take a few bites, because it was clear her lack of appetite was distressing her mother.

When the tray was removed, Mary Jo slept. Her father was with her when she awoke. Her eyes met his, which were warm and tender.

"Was the accident my fault?" She had to know. She remembered so little of what had happened.

"No. The other car ran a red light."

"Was anyone else hurt?"

"No," he said, taking her hand in both of his.

"I'm sorry I worried you."

A slight smile crossed his face. "Your brothers were just as worried. And Evan."

"He was here, wasn't he?"

"Every minute. No one could get him to leave, not even his own family."

But he wasn't there now. When she really needed him.

Her father gently patted her hand, and when he spoke it was as if he'd been reading her thoughts. "Life has a way of making things right. Everything will turn out just like it's supposed to. So don't you fret about Evan or his family or anything else. Concentrate on getting well."

"I will." But her heart wasn't in it. Her heart was with Evan.

A week passed, and Mary Jo regained more of her strength each day. With her head shaved, she looked as if she'd stepped out of a science-fiction movie. All she needed were the right clothes and a laser gun and she'd be real Hollywood material.

If she continued to improve at this pace, she should be discharged from the hospital within the next few days. That was good news—not that she didn't appreciate the excellent care she'd received.

Mary Jo spent part of the morning slowly walking the corridors in an effort to rebuild her strength. She still tired easily and took frequent breaks to chat with nurses and other patients. After a pleasant but exhausting couple of hours, she decided to go back to bed for a while.

As she entered her room, she stopped abruptly. Lois Dryden stood by the window, looking out of place in her tailored suit.

Lois must have sensed her return. There was no disguising her dismay when she saw Mary Jo's shaved, bandaged head. She seemed incapable of speech for a moment.

Mary Jo took the initiative. "Hello, Mrs. Dryden," she said evenly.

"Hello, my dear. I hope you don't mind my dropping in like this."

"No, of course I don't mind." Mary Jo made her way to the bed and got in, conscious of her still-awkward movements.

"I was very sorry to hear about your accident."

Mary Jo adjusted the covers around her legs and leaned back against the raised mattress. "I'm well on the road to recovery now."

"That's what I understand. I heard there's a possibility you'll be going home soon."

"I hope so."

"Is there anything I can do for you?"

The offer surprised Mary Jo. "No, but thank you."

Lois walked away from the window and stood at

the foot of the bed, the picture of conventional propriety with her small hat and spotless white gloves. She looked directly at Mary Jo.

"I understand Jessica has come by a number of times," she said.

"Yes," Mary Jo responded. "She's been very kind. She brought me some books and magazines." Except that Mary Jo hadn't been able to concentrate on any of them. No sooner would she begin reading than she'd drift off to sleep.

"I suppose Jessica told you she and Damian are expecting again."

Without warning, Mary Jo's heart contracted painfully. "Yes. I'm delighted for them."

"Naturally, Walter and I are thrilled with the prospect of a second grandchild."

It became important not to look at Evan's mother, and Mary Jo focused her gaze out the window. The tightness in her chest wouldn't go away, and she knew the source of the pain was emotional. She longed for a child herself. Evan's child. They'd talked about their home, planned their family. The picture of the house he'd described, with a yard full of laughing, playing children flashed into her mind.

That house would never be built now. There would be no children. No marriage. No Evan.

"Of course, Damian's beside himself with happiness."

Somewhere deep inside, Mary Jo found the strength to say, "I imagine he is."

"There'll be a little less than two years between

the children. Andrew will be twenty months old by the time the baby's born."

Mary Jo wondered why Mrs. Dryden was telling her all this and could think of nothing more to say. She found the conversation exhausting. She briefly closed her eyes.

"I...I suppose I shouldn't tire you anymore."

"Thank you for stopping by," Mary Jo murmured politely.

Lois stepped toward the door, then hesitated and turned back to the bed. Mary Jo noticed that the older woman's hand trembled as she reached out and gripped the foot of the bed.

"Is something the matter?" Mary Jo asked, thinking perhaps she should ring for the nurse.

"Yes," Evan's mother said. "Something is very much the matter—and I'm the one at fault. You came to me not long ago because you wanted to marry my son. I discouraged you, and Evan, too, when he came to speak to his father and me."

"Mrs. Dryden, please—"

"No, let me finish." She took a deep breath and leveled her gaze on Mary Jo. "Knowing what I do now, I would give everything I have if you'd agree to marry my son."

Chapter 10

Mary Jo wasn't sure she'd heard Evan's mother correctly. "I don't understand."

Instinctively, she knew that Mrs. Dryden was someone who rarely revealed her emotions. She knew the older woman rarely lost control of a situation—or of herself. She seemed dangerously close to losing it now.

"Would…would you mind if I sat down?"

"Please do." Mary Jo wished she'd suggested it herself.

Lois pulled the chair closer to the bed, and Mary Jo was surprised by how delicate, how fragile, she suddenly appeared. "Before I say anything more, I must ask your forgiveness."

"Mine?"

"Yes, my dear. When you came to me, happy and excited, to discuss marrying my son, I was impressed by your…your courage. Your sense of responsibility. You'd guessed my feelings correctly when Evan brought you to dinner three or so years ago. Although you were a delightful young woman, I couldn't picture you as his wife. My son, however, was enthralled with you."

Mary Jo started to speak, but Mrs. Dryden shook her head, obviously determined to finish her confession. "I decided that very night that it was important for us to talk. I'd never intended to hurt you or Evan, and when I learned you were no longer seeing each other, I realized it might have had something to do with what I'd said to you."

"Mrs. Dryden, please, this isn't necessary."

"On the contrary. It's very necessary. If you're to be my daughter-in-law, and I sincerely hope you will be, then I feel it's vital for us to…to begin afresh."

Mary Jo's pulse began to hammer with excitement. "You meant what you said earlier, then? About wanting me to marry Evan?"

"Every word. Once we know each other a little better, you'll learn I almost never say what I don't mean. Now, please, allow me to continue."

"Of course. I'm sorry."

Mrs. Dryden gave her an ironic smile. "Once we're on more familiar terms, you won't need to be so apprehensive of me. I'm hoping we can be friends, Mary Jo. After all, I pray you'll be the mother of my grandchildren." She smiled again. "Half of them, anyway."

Mary Jo blinked back tears, deeply moved by the other woman's unmistakable contrition and generosity.

"Now...where was I? Oh, yes, we were talking about three years ago. You and Evan had decided not to see each other again, and frankly—forgive me for this, Mary Jo—I was relieved. But Evan seemed to take the breakup very badly. I recognized then that I might have acted too hastily. For months, I contemplated calling you myself. I'm ashamed to tell you I kept putting it off. No," she said and her voice shook, "I was a coward. I dreaded facing you."

"Mrs. Dryden, it was a long time ago."

"You're right, it was, but that doesn't lessen my guilt." She paused. "Evan changed that autumn. He'd always been such a lighthearted young man. He still joked and teased, but it wasn't the same. The happiness had gone out of his eyes. Nothing held his interest for long. He drifted from one brief relationship to another. He was miserable, and it showed."

In those bleak, lonely months, Mary Jo hadn't fared much better, but she said nothing about that now.

"It was during this time that Walter decided to run for the Senate, and our lives were turned upside down. Our one concern was Evan. The election was important to Walter, and in some ways, Evan was a problem. Walter discussed the situation with him— Oh, dear. None of this applies to the present situation. I'm getting sidetracked."

"No. Go on," Mary Jo pleaded.

"I have to admit I'm not proud of what we did. Walter and I felt strongly that Jessica Kellerman was the right woman for Evan, and we did what we could to encourage a relationship. As you know, Damian and Jessica fell in love. You'd think I'd have learned my lesson about interfering in my sons' lives, but apparently not."

Mary Jo wished she could say something to reassure Lois.

"Early this summer, Walter and I noticed a…new happiness in Evan. He seemed more like he used to be. Later we learned that you were working for him. I decided then and there that if you two decided to rekindle your romance, I'd do nothing to stand in your way."

"You didn't," Mary Jo said quickly.

"Then you came to me and insisted on a small, private wedding. It was obvious you didn't understand the social demands made of a husband in politics. I could see you were getting discouraged, and I did nothing to reassure you. At the time it seemed for the best."

"Mrs. Dryden, you're taking on far more blame than you should."

"That's not all, Mary Jo." She clutched her purse with both gloved hands and hung her head. "Evan came to speak to Walter and me about the two of you. I don't believe I've ever seen him so angry. No other woman has ever held such power over my son. You see, Evan and I've always been close and it… pains me to admit this, but I was jealous. I told him that if you were willing to break off another engagement over the first disagreement, then you weren't the woman for him.

"I must've been more persuasive than I realized. Later Evan told me he couldn't fight both of us and that he'd decided to abide by your wishes."

"He said that to me, too," Mary Jo murmured.

"It's been several weeks now, but nothing's changed. My son still loves you very much. After your accident, he refused to leave the hospital. I came here myself early one morning and found Evan sitting alone in the hospital chapel." She paused and her lower lip trembled. "I knew then that you weren't some passing fancy in his life. He loves you as he's never loved another woman and probably won't again."

Mary Jo leaned forward. "I'll never be comfortable in the limelight, Mrs. Dryden," she said urgently. "But I'm willing to do whatever it takes to be the kind of wife Evan needs."

Mrs. Dryden snapped open her purse, took out a delicate white handkerchief and dabbed her eyes. "It's time for another confession, I'm afraid. I've always believed Evan would do well in politics. I've made no secret of my ambitions for my son, but that's what they were—*my* ambitions. Not his. If Evan does decide to pursue a political career, it should be his decision, not mine.

"In light of everything that's taken place, I'm determined to stay out of it entirely. Whatever happens now depends on Evan. On you, too, of course," she added hurriedly, "but I promise you, I won't interfere. I've finally learned my lesson."

Unable to speak, Mary Jo reached for the other woman's hand and held it tightly.

"I'd like it if we could be friends, Mary Jo," Lois

added softly. "I'll do my damnedest to stop being an interfering old woman."

"My mother learned her lessons with my oldest brother, Jack, and his wife. You might like to speak to her sometime and swap stories," Mary Jo suggested.

"I'd like that." She stood and bent to kiss Mary Jo's cheek. "You'll go to Evan, then, when you're able?"

Mary Jo grinned. "As soon as I look a bit more presentable."

"You'll look wonderful to Evan now, believe me." The older woman touched her hand softly. "Make him happy, Mary Jo."

"I'll do my best."

"And please let me know when your mother and I can talk. We have a million things to discuss about the wedding."

Mary Jo ventured, a bit hesitantly, "The wedding will be small and private."

"Whatever you decide."

"But perhaps we could have a big reception afterward and invite the people you wouldn't want to offend by excluding them."

"An excellent idea." Lois smiled broadly.

"Thank you for coming to see me."

A tear formed in the corner of Lois's eye. "No. Thank *you,* my dear."

From the day of Lois Dryden's visit, Mary Jo's recovery was little short of miraculous. She was discharged two days later and spent a week recuperating at her parents' home before she felt ready to confront Evan.

According to Jessica, he was frequently out on his sailboat. With her friend's help, it was a simple matter to discover when he'd scheduled an outing.

Saturday morning, the sun was bright and the wind brisk—a perfect sailing day. Mary Jo went down to the marina. Using Damian's key, she let herself in and climbed aboard Evan's boat to wait for him.

She hadn't been there long when he arrived. He must've seen her right away, although he gave no outward indication that he had.

She still felt somewhat uncomfortable about her hair, now half an inch long. She'd tried to disguise it with a turban, but that only made her look as if she should be reading palms or tea leaves. So she left it unadorned.

"Mary Jo?"

"It hard to tell without the hair, right?" she joked.

"What are you doing here?" Evan wasn't unfriendly, but he didn't seem particularly pleased to see her.

"I wanted to talk, and this is the place we do our best talking. Are you taking the boat out this morning?"

He ignored the question. "How are you?" The craft rocked gently as he climbed on deck and sat down beside her.

"Much better. Still kind of weak, but I'm gaining strength every day."

"When were you released from the hospital?"

Evan knew the answer as well as she did, Mary Jo was sure. Why was he making small talk at a time like this?

"You already know. Your mother told you, or Jessica." She paused. "You were at the hospital, Evan."

His mouth tightened, but he said nothing.

"There were periods when I could hear what was going on around me. I was awake, sort of, when you first got there. Another time, I heard you pacing my room, and I heard you again when Jessica came by once." She took Evan's hand and threaded her fingers through his. "One of the first times I actually woke was in the middle of the night, and you were there, asleep."

"I've never been more frightened in my life," he said hoarsely, as if the words had been wrenched from his throat. He slid his arms around her then, but gently, with deliberate care. Mary Jo rested her head against his shoulder, and his grip on her tightened just a little. He buried his face in the curve of her shoulder; she felt his warm strength. After a moment, he let her go.

"I understand my parents' investment was returned to them—with interest," she said, her tone deceptively casual.

"Yes," he admitted. "They were among the fortunate few to have their money refunded."

"*Their* money?" She raised his hand to her mouth, kissing his knuckles. "Evan, I know what you did."

He frowned. He had that confused, what-are-you-talking-about expression down to an art.

"You might've been able to get away with it but, you see, the papers came."

"What papers?"

"The day of my accident my parents received a notice from the bankruptcy court—as I'm sure you know. If their investment had been returned, how do you explain that?"

He shrugged. "Don't have a clue."

"Evan, please, it's not necessary to play games with me."

He seemed to feel a sudden need to move around. He stood, stretched and walked to the far end of the sailboat. Pointedly, he glanced at his watch. "I wish I had time to chat, but unfortunately I'm meeting a friend."

"Evan, we need to talk."

"I'm sorry, but you should've let me know sooner. Perhaps we could get together some other time." He made an elaborate display of staring at the pier, then smiling and waving eagerly.

A tall, blond woman, incredibly slender and beautifully tanned, waved back. She had the figure of a fashion model and all but purred when Evan hopped out of the boat and met her dockside. She threw her arms around his neck and kissed him, bending one shapely leg at the knee.

Mary Jo was stunned. To hear his mother speak, Evan was a lost, lonely man, so in love with her that his world had fallen apart. Clearly, there was something Mrs. Dryden didn't know.

In her rush to climb out of the sailboat, Mary Jo practically fell overboard. With her nearly bald head and the clothes that hung on her because of all the weight she'd lost, she felt like the little match girl standing barefoot in the snow. Especially beside this paragon of feminine perfection.

She suffered through an introduction that she

didn't hear, made her excuses and promptly left. When she was back in her car, she slumped against the steering wheel, covering her face with both hands.

Shaken and angry, she returned to her parents' place and called Jessica to tell her what had happened. She was grateful her parents were out.

Mary Jo paced the living room in an excess of nervous energy until Jessica came to the house an hour later, looking flustered. "Sorry it took me so long, but I took a cab and it turned out to be the driver's first day on the job. We got lost twice. So what's going on?" She sighed. "I don't know what I'm going to do with the two of you."

Mary Jo described the situation in great detail, painting vivid word pictures of the other woman.

Jessica rolled her eyes. "And you *fell* for it?"

"Fell for what?" Mary Jo cried. "Bambi was all over him. I didn't need anyone to spell it out. I was mortified. Good grief," she said, battling down a sob, "look at me. Last week's vegetable casserole has more hair than I do."

Jessica laughed outright. "Mary Jo, be sensible. The man loves you."

"Yeah, I could tell," she muttered.

"Her name's Barbara, not that it matters. Trust me, she doesn't mean a thing to him."

The doorbell chimed and the two women stared at each other. "Are you expecting company?"

"No."

Jessica lowered her voice. "Do you think it could be Evan?"

On her way to the door, Mary Jo shook her head dismally. "I doubt it."

"Just in case, I'd better hide." Jessica backed out of the room and into the kitchen.

To her complete surprise, Mary Jo found Lois Dryden at the door.

"What happened?" the older woman demanded.

Mary Jo opened the door and let her inside. "Happened?"

"With Evan."

"Jessica," Mary Jo called over her shoulder. "You can come out now. It's a Dryden, but it isn't Evan."

"Jessica's here?" Lois said.

"Yes," Jessica said. "But what are *you* doing here?"

"Checking up on Mary Jo. I got a call from Damian. All he said was that he suspected things hadn't gone well with Evan and Mary Jo this morning. He said Mary Jo had phoned and Jessica had hurried out shortly afterward. I want to know what went wrong."

"It's a long story," Mary Jo said reluctantly.

"I tried calling you," Lois explained, "then realized you must still be staying with your family. I was going out, anyway, and I thought this might be an excellent opportunity to meet your mother."

"She's out just now." Mary Jo exhaled shakily and gestured at the sofa. "Sit down, please."

Her parents' house lacked the obvious wealth and luxury of Whispering Willows, but anyone who stepped inside immediately felt welcome. A row of high-school graduation pictures sat proudly on the fireplace mantel. Photos of the grandchildren were scattered about the room. The far wall was lined with bookcases, but some shelves held more trophies than books.

"So you went to see Evan this morning," his mother said, regarding her anxiously. "I take it the meeting was…not a success?"

"Evan had a *date,*" Mary Jo said, glancing sharply at Jessica.

"Hey," Jessica muttered, "all you asked me to do was find out the next time he was going sailing. How was I supposed to know he was meeting another woman?"

"Who?" Lois asked, frowning.

"Barbara," Mary Jo said.

Lois made a dismissive gesture with her hand. "Oh, yes, I know who she is. She's a fashion model who flies in from New York every now and then. You have nothing to worry about."

"A fashion model." Mary Jo's spirits hit the floor.

"She's really not important to him."

"That may be so," Mary Jo pointed out, "but he certainly seemed pleased to see her." Depressed, she slouched down on the sofa and braced her feet against the edge of the coffee table.

Lois's back stiffened. "It seems to me I'd better have a chat with that boy."

"Mother!" Jessica cried at the same moment Mary Jo yelped in protest.

"You promised you weren't going to interfere, remember?" Jessica reminded her mother-in-law. "It only leads to trouble. If Evan wants to make a fool of himself, we're going to have to let him."

"I disagree," Lois said. "You're right, of course, about my talking to him—that would only make matters worse—but we can't allow Mary Jo to let him think he's getting away with this."

"What do you suggest we do?" Jessica asked.

Lois bit her bottom lip. "I don't know, but I'll think of something."

"Time-out," Mary Jo said, forming a *T* with her hands—a technique she often used with her kindergarten class. "I appreciate your willingness to help, but I'd really like to do my own plotting, okay? Don't be offended, but…" Her words trailed off, and her expression turned to one of pleading.

Jessica smiled and took for her hand. "Of course," she said.

Mary Jo looked at Lois, and the woman nodded. "You're absolutely right, my dear. I'll keep my nose out." She reached over and gave Mary Jo a hug.

"Thank you," Mary Jo whispered.

Mary Jo didn't hear from Evan at all the following week. She tried to tell herself she wasn't disappointed—but of course she was. When it became clear that he was content to leave things between them as they were, she composed a short letter and mailed it to him at his office. After all, it was a business matter.

Without elaborating, she suggested she work for him the next four summers as compensation for the money he'd given her parents.

Knowing exactly when he received his morning mail, she waited anxiously by her phone. It didn't take long. His temporary personal assistant phoned and set up an appointment for the next morning. By the time she hung up the receiver, Mary Jo was downright gleeful.

The day of her appointment, she dressed in her best suit and high heels, and arrived promptly at eleven. His personal assistant escorted her into his office.

Evan was at his desk, writing on a legal pad, and didn't look up until the other woman had left the room.

"So, is there a problem?" she asked flatly.

"*Should* there be a problem?"

She lifted one shoulder. "I can't imagine why you'd ask to see me otherwise. I can only assume it has something to do with my letter."

He leaned back in his chair and rolled a gold pen between his palms. "Where did you come up with this harebrained idea that I forked over fifty thousand dollars to your mother and father."

"Evan, I'm not stupid. I know exactly what you did. And I know why."

"I doubt that."

"I think it was very sweet, but I can't allow you to do it."

"Mary Jo—"

"I believe my suggestion will suit us both nicely. Mrs. Sterling would love having the summers free to travel. If I remember correctly, her husband recently retired, and unless she has the freedom to do as she'd like now and then, you're going to lose her."

Evan said nothing, so she went on, "I worked out

all right while I was here, didn't I? Well, other than losing that one file, which wasn't my fault. Naturally, I hope you won't continue trying to make me jealous. It almost worked, you know."

"I'm afraid I don't know what you're talking about."

"Oh, Evan," she said with an exaggerated sigh. "You must think I'm a complete fool."

He arched his thick brows. "As it happens, I do."

She ignored that. "Do you honestly believe you could convince me you're attracted to…to Miss August? I know you better than you think, Evan Dryden."

His lips quivered slightly with the beginnings of a smile, but he managed to squelch it immediately.

"Are you agreeable to my solution?" she asked hopefully.

"No," he said.

The bluntness of his reply took her by surprise and her head snapped back. "No?"

"You don't owe me a penny."

At least he wasn't trying to get her to believe the money came from Adison Investments.

"But I can't let you do this!"

"Why not?" He gave the appearance of growing bored. Slumped in his chair, he held the pen at each end and twirled it between his thumb and index finger.

"It isn't right. You don't owe them anything, and if they knew, they'd return it instantly."

"You won't tell them." Although he didn't raise his voice, the tone was determined.

"No, I won't," she admitted, knowing it would devastate her parents, "but only if you allow me to reimburse you myself."

He shook his head. "No deal."

Mary Jo knew he could be stubborn, but this was ridiculous. "Evan, please, I *want* to do it."

"The money was a gift from me to them, sent anonymously with no strings attached. And your plan to substitute for Mrs. Sterling—it *didn't* work out this summer. What makes you think it will in the future? As far as I'm concerned, this issue about the money is pure nonsense. I suggest we drop it entirely." He set the pen down on his desk, as if signaling the end of the conversation.

Nonsense. Mary Jo reached for her purse. "Apparently we don't have anything more to say to each other."

"Apparently not," he agreed without emotion.

Mary Jo stood and, with her head high, walked out of the office. It wasn't until she got to the elevator that the trembling started.

"Are you going to tell me what's bothering you?" Marianna asked Mary Jo. They were sitting at the small kitchen table shelling fresh peas Marianna had purchased from the local farmers' market. Both women quickly and methodically removed the peas from their pods and tossed them into a blue ceramic bowl.

"I'm fine," Mary Jo insisted, even though it was next to impossible to fool her mother. After years of raising children and then dealing with grandchildren, Marianna Summerhill had an uncanny knack of recognizing when something was wrong with any of her family.

"Physically, yes," her mother agreed. "But you're troubled. I can see it in your eyes."

Mary Jo shrugged.

"If I was guessing, I'd say it had something to do with Evan. You haven't seen hide nor hair of him in two weeks."

Evan. The name alone was enough to evoke a flood of unhappiness. "I just don't understand it!" Mary Jo cried. "To hear his mother talk, you'd think he was fading away for want of me."

"He isn't?"

"Hardly. He's dated a different woman every night this week."

"He was mentioned in some gossip column in the paper this morning. Do you know anything about a Barbara Jackson?"

"Yes." Mary Jo clamped her lips together. If he was flaunting his romantic escapades in an effort to make her jealous, he'd succeeded.

"I imagine you're annoyed."

"'Annoyed' isn't it." She snapped a pea pod so hard, the peas scattered across the table like marbles shooting over a polished hardwood floor. Her mother's smile did nothing to soothe her wounded pride. "What I don't get," she muttered, "is *why* he's doing this."

"You haven't figured that out yet?" Marianna asked, her raised voice indicating her surprise. The peas slid effortlessly from the pod to the bowl.

"No, I haven't got a clue. Have *you* figured it out?"

"Ages ago," the older woman said casually.

Mary Jo jerked her head toward her mother. "What do you mean?"

"You're a bright girl, Mary Jo, but when it comes to Evan, I have to wonder."

The words shook her. "What do you mean? I *love* Evan!"

"Not so I can tell." This, too, was said casually.

Mary Jo pushed her mound of pea pods aside and stared at her mother. "Mom, how can you say that?"

"Easy. Evan isn't sure you love him. Why should he be? He—"

Mary Jo was outraged. "Not sure I love him? I can't believe I'm hearing this from my own mother!"

"It's true," Marianna continued, her fingers working rhythmically and without pause. "Looking at it from Evan's point of view, I can't say I blame him."

As the youngest in a big family, Mary Jo had had some shocking things said to her over the years, but never by her own mother. And never this calmly— as if they were merely discussing the price of fresh fruit.

Her first reaction had been defensive, but she was beginning to realize that maybe Marianna knew something she didn't. "I don't understand how Evan could possibly believe I don't love him."

"It's not so hard to understand," Marianna answered smoothly. "Twice you've claimed to love him enough to marry him, and both times you've changed your mind."

"But—"

"You've turned your back on him when you were confronted with any resistance from his family. You've never really given him the opportunity to answer your doubts. My feeling is, Evan would've stood by you come hell or high water, but I wonder if the reverse is true."

"You make it sound so...so simple, but our situation is a lot more difficult than you understand."

"Possibly."

"His family is *formidable*."

"I don't doubt that for an instant," came Marianna's sincere reply. "Let me ask you one thing, though, and I want you to think carefully before you answer. Do you love Evan enough to stand up to opposition, no matter what form it takes?"

"Yes," Mary Jo answered heatedly.

Marianna's eyes brightened with her wide smile. "Then what are you going to do about it?"

"Do?" Mary Jo had tried twice and been thwarted by his pride with each attempt. One thing was certain—Evan had no intention of making this easy for her.

"It seems to me that if you love this man, you're not going to take no for an answer. Unless, of course..." Her mother hesitated.

"Unless what?"

"Unless Evan isn't as important to you as you claim."

Chapter 11

Mary Jo pushed up the sleeves of her light sweater and paced the floor of her living room. Her mother's comments about the way she'd treated Evan still grated. But what bothered her most was that her mother was right.

No wonder Evan had all but ignored her. He couldn't trust her not to turn her back and run at the first sign of trouble. After all her talk of being older, wiser and more mature, Mary Jo had to admit she was as sadly lacking in those qualities as she'd been three years before. And she was furious.

With herself.

What she needed now was a way to prove her love to Evan so he'd never have cause to doubt her again. One problem was that she had no idea how long it would take for that opportunity to present itself. It might be months—maybe even another three long years. Mary Jo was unwilling to wait. Evan would just have to take her at her word.

But why should he, in light of their past? If he refused, Mary Jo couldn't very well blame him. She sighed, wondering distractedly what to do next.

She could call Jessica, who'd been more than generous with advice. But Mary Jo realized that all Jessica could tell her was what she already knew. Mary Jo needed to talk to Evan herself, face-to-face, no holds barred.

Deciding there was no reason to postpone what had to be done, she carefully chose her outfit—a peach-colored pantsuit with gold buttons, along with a soft turquoise scarf and dangly gold earrings.

When she arrived at his office, Mary Jo was pleasantly surprised to find Mrs. Sterling.

"Oh, my, don't you look lovely this afternoon," the older woman said with a delighted smile. She seemed relaxed and happy; the trip had obviously done her good.

"So do you, Mrs. Sterling. When did you get back?"

"Just this week. I heard about your accident. I'm so pleased everything turned out all right."

"So am I. Is Evan in?"

"I'm sorry, no, but I expect him any time. Why don't you make yourself at home there in his office? I'll bring you some coffee. I don't think he'll be more than a few minutes."

"Thanks, I will." Mary Jo walked into the office and sank onto the sofa. In her determination to see this through, she naively hadn't considered the possibility of Evan's being out of the office. And she was afraid that the longer she waited, the more her courage would falter.

She was sipping the coffee Mrs. Sterling had brought her and lecturing herself, trying to bolster her courage, when she heard Evan come in. Her hands trembled as she set the cup aside.

By the time Evan strolled into the room, still rattling off a list of instructions for Mrs. Sterling, Mary Jo's shoulders were tensed.

His personal assistant finished making her notes. "You have a visitor," she announced, smiling approvingly in Mary Jo's direction.

Evan sent a look over his shoulder, but revealed no emotion when he saw who it was. "Hello, Mary Jo."

"Evan." She pressed her palms over her knees, certain she must resemble a schoolgirl feeling the principal after some misdemeanor. "I'd like to talk to you, if I may."

He frowned and glanced at his watch.

"Your schedule is free," Mrs. Sterling said emphatically, and when she walked away, she closed the door.

"Well, it seems I can spare a few minutes," Evan said without enthusiasm as he moved behind his desk and sat down.

Mary Jo left the sofa and took the chair across from him. "First I'd like to apologize."

"No," he said roughly. "There's nothing to apologize for."

"But there is," she told him. "Oh, Evan, I've nearly ruined everything."

His eyebrows rose, and his expression was skeptical. "Come now, Mary Jo."

She slid forward in her seat. "It all started the summer we met when—"

"That was years ago, and if you don't mind, I'd prefer to leave it there." He reached for his gold pen, as if he needed to hold on to something. "Rehashing it all isn't going to help either of us."

"I disagree." Mary Jo would not be so easily discouraged this time. "We need to clear up the past. Otherwise once we're married—"

"It seems to me you're taking a lot for granted," he said sharply.

"Perhaps, but I doubt it."

"Mary Jo, I can't see how this will get us anywhere."

"I do," she said hurriedly. "Please listen to what I have to say, and if you still feel the same afterward, then…well, I'll just say it another way until you're willing to accept that I love you."

His eyebrows rose again. "I have a date this evening."

"Then I'll talk fast, but I think you should know you aren't fooling me."

"Do you think I'm lying?"

"Of course not. You may very well have arranged an evening with some woman, but it's me you love."

His handsome features darkened in a frown, but she took heart from the fact that he didn't contradict her.

Mary Jo studied her own watch. "How much time do I have before you need to leave?"

Evan shrugged. "Enough."

He wasn't doing anything to encourage her, but that was fine; she knew what she wanted, and she wasn't going to let a little thing like a bad attitude stand in her way.

It took her a few mintes to organize her thoughts and remember what she'd so carefully planned to say. Perhaps that was for the best. She didn't want to sound as if she'd practiced in front of a mirror, although she'd done exactly that.

"You were saying?" Evan murmured.

She bit her lip. "Yes. I wanted to talk to you about the house."

"What house?" he asked impatiently.

"The one with the seven bedrooms. The one we've discussed in such detail that I can see it clear as anything. The house I want to live in with you and our children."

She noticed that his eyes drifted away from hers.

"I've been doing a lot of thinking lately," Mary Jo continued. "It all started when I was feeling sorry for myself, certain that I'd lost you. I…found the thought almost unbearable."

"You get accustomed to it after a while," he muttered dryly.

"I never will," she said adamantly, "not ever again."

He leaned forward in his chair as if to see her better. "What brought about this sudden change of heart?"

"It isn't sudden. Well, maybe it is. You see, it's my mother. She—"

"Are you sure it wasn't *my* mother? She seems to

have her hand in just about everything that goes on between you and me."

"Not anymore." This was something else Mary Jo wanted to correct. "According to Jessica, your mother's been beside herself wondering what's going on with us. We have to give her credit, Evan—she hasn't called or pressured me once. She promised she wouldn't, and your mother's a woman of her word."

"Exactly what did she promise?"

"Not to meddle in our lives. She came to me when I was still in the hospital, and we had a wonderful talk. Some of the problems between us were of my own making. Your mother intimidated me, and I was afraid to go against her. But after our talk, I understand her a little better and she understands me."

She waited for him to make some comment, but was disappointed. From all outward appearances, Evan was merely enduring this discussion, waiting for her to finish so he could get on with his life.

"I'm not Lois's first choice for a daughter-in-law. There are any number of other women who'd be a far greater asset to you and your political future than I'll ever be."

"I'm dating one now."

The information was like a slap in the face, but Mary Jo revealed none of her feelings.

"Above and beyond anything else, your mother wants your happiness, and she believes, as I do, that our being together will provide that."

"Nice of her to confer with me. It seems the two of you—and let's not forget dear Jessica—have joined forces. You're all plotting against me."

"Absolutely not. I've talked to Jessica, but not recently. It was my mother who helped me understand what was wrong."

"And now *she's* involved." He rolled his eyes as if to say there were far too many mothers interfering in his life.

"All my mother did was point out a few truths. If anything, we should thank her. She told me you've got good reason to question the strength of my love for you. I was floored that my own mother could suggest something like that. Especially since she knew how unhappy and miserable I've been."

The hint of a smile lifted his mouth.

"Mom said if I loved you as much as I claim to, I would've stood by your side despite any opposition. She...she said if our situations had been reversed, you would've stood by me. I gave up on you too easily, and, Evan, I can't tell you how much I regret it." She lowered her gaze to her hands. "If I could undo the past, step back three years—or even three weeks—I'd do anything to prove how much I love you. I believe in you, Evan, and I believe in our love. Never again will I give you cause to doubt it. Furthermore—"

"You mean there's more?" He sounded bored, as if this was taking much longer than he'd expected.

"Just a little," she said, and her voice wavered with the strength of her conviction. "You're going to make a wonderful member of city council, and I'll do whatever's necessary to see that it happens. It won't be easy for me to be the focus of public attention, but in time, I'll learn not to be so nervous.

Your mother's already volunteered to help me. I can do this, Evan, I know I can. Another three or four years down the road, I'll be a pro in front of the cameras. Just wait and see."

He didn't speak, and Mary Jo could feel every beat of her heart in the silence that followed.

"That's all well and good," Evan finally said, "but I don't see how it changes anything."

"You don't?" She vaulted to her feet. "Do you love me or not?" she demanded.

He regarded her with a look of utter nonchalance. "Frankly, I don't know what I feel for you anymore."

In slow motion, Mary Jo sank back into her seat. She'd lost him. She could see it in his eyes, in the way he looked at her as if she was nothing to him anymore. Someone he'd loved once, a long time ago, but that was all.

"I see," she mumbled.

"Now, if you'll excuse me, I have some business I need to attend to."

"Ah…" The shock of his rejection had numbed her, and it took her a moment to get to her feet. She clutched her purse protectively to her stomach. "I…I'm sorry to have bothered you." She drew on the little that remained of her pride and dignity to carry her across the room.

"No bother," Evan said tonelessly.

It was at that precise moment that Mary Jo knew. She couldn't have explained exactly how, but she *knew*. Relief washed over her like the warm blast of a shower after a miserable day in the cold. *He loved her*. He'd always loved her.

Confident now, she turned around to face him.

He was busily writing on a legal pad and didn't look up.

"Evan." She whispered his name.

He ignored her.

"You love me."

His hand trembled slightly, but that was all the emotion he betrayed.

"It isn't going to work," she said, walking toward him.

"I beg your pardon?" He sighed heavily.

"This charade. I don't know what you're trying to prove, but it isn't working. It never will. You couldn't have sat by my hospital bed all those hours and felt nothing for me. You couldn't have given my parents that money and not cared for me."

"I didn't say I didn't care. But as you said yourself, sometimes love isn't enough."

"Then I was wrong," she muttered. "Now listen. My mother and yours are champing at the bit to start planning our wedding. What do you want me to tell them? That the whole thing's off and you don't love me anymore? You don't honestly expect anyone to believe that, do you? *I* don't."

"Believe what you want."

She closed her eyes for a moment. "You're trying my patience, Evan, but don't think you can get me to change my mind." She moved closer. There was more than one way of proving her point. More than one way to kick the argument out from under him. And she wasn't going to let this opportunity pass her by.

She stepped over to his desk and planted both

hands on it, leaning over the top so that only a few inches separated their faces. "All right, Dryden, you asked for this."

His eyes narrowed as she edged around the desk. His head followed her movements. He turned in his chair, watching her speculatively.

Just then she threw herself on his lap, wound her arms around his neck and kissed him. She felt his surprise and his resistance, but the latter vanished almost the instant her mouth settled over his.

It'd been so long since they'd kissed. So long since she'd experienced the warm comfort of his embrace.

Groaning, Evan kissed her back. His mouth was tentative at first, then hard and intense. His hold tightened and a frightening kind of excitement began to grow inside her. As she clung to him, she could feel his heart beating as fast as hers, his breathing as labored.

Cradling his face with her hands, she spread eager, loving kisses over his mouth, his jaw, his forehead. "I love you, Evan Dryden."

"This isn't just gratitude?"

She paused and lifted her head. "For what?"

"The money I gave your family."

"No," she said, teasing a corner of his mouth with the tip of her tongue. "But that *is* something we need to discuss."

"No, we don't." He tilted her so that she was practically lying across his lap. "I have a proposition to make."

"Decent or indecent?" she asked with a pretended leer.

"That's for you to decide."

She looped her arms around his neck again, hoisted herself upright and pressed her head against his shoulder.

"You'll marry me?" he asked.

"Oh, yes—" she sighed with happiness "—and soon. Evan, let's make this the shortest engagement on record."

"On one condition. You never mention that money again."

"But—"

"Those are my terms." He punctuated his statement with a kiss so heated it seared her senses.

When it ended, Mary Jo had difficulty breathing normally. "Your terms?" she repeated in a husky whisper.

"Do you agree, or don't you?"

Before she could answer, he swept away her defenses and any chance of argument with another kiss. By the time he'd finished, Mary Jo discovered she would have concurred with just about anything. She nodded numbly.

Evan held her against him and exhaled deeply. "We'll make our own wedding plans, understood?"

Mary Jo stared at him blankly.

"This is our wedding and not my mother's—or your mother's."

She smiled and lowered her head to his shoulder. "Understood."

They were silent for several minutes, each savoring the closeness.

"Mom was right, wasn't she?" Mary Jo asked

softly. "About how I needed to prove that my love's more than words."

"If you'd walked out that door, I might always have wondered," Evan confessed, then added, "You wouldn't have gotten far. I would've come running after you, but I'm glad I didn't have to."

"I've been such a fool." Mary Jo lovingly traced the side of his neck with her tongue.

"I'll give you fifty or sixty years to make it up to me, with time off for good behavior." He paused, then said, "You've made a concession to my career, and I'm going to do the same. I know you love teaching and if you want to continue, it's fine with me."

The happiness on her face blossomed into a full smile. She raised her head and waited until their eyes met before she lowered her mouth to his. The kiss was long, slow and thorough. Evan drew in a deep breath when it was over.

"What was that for?"

"To seal our bargain. From this day forward, Evan Dryden, we belong to each other. Nothing will ever come between us again."

"Nothing," he agreed readily.

The door opened and Mrs. Sterling poked her head in. "I just wanted to make sure everything worked out," she said, smiling broadly. "I can see that it has. I couldn't be more pleased."

"Neither could I," Mary Jo said.

Evan drew her mouth back to his and Mary Jo heard the office door click shut in the background.

Epilogue

Three years later

"Andrew, don't wake Bethanne!" Jessica called out to her four-year-old son.

Mary Jo laughed as she watched the child bend to kiss her newborn daughter's forehead. "Look, they're already kissing cousins."

"How are you feeling?" Jessica asked, carrying a tall glass of iced tea over to Mary Jo, who was sitting under the shade of the patio umbrella.

"Wonderful."

"Evan is thrilled with Bethanne, isn't he?"

"Oh, yes. He reminded me of Damian when you had Lori Jo. You'd think we were the only two women in the world to ever have given birth."

Jessica laughed and shook her head. "And then the grandparents…"

"I don't know about you," Mary Jo teased, "but I could become accustomed to all this attention."

Jessica eyed her disbelievingly.

"All right, all right. I'll admit I was a bit flustered when the mayor paid me a visit in the hospital. And it was kind of nice to receive flowers from all those special-interest groups—the ones who think Evan is easily influenced. Clearly, they don't know my husband."

Jessica sighed and relaxed in her lounge chair. "You've done so well with all this. Evan's told Damian and me at least a hundred times that you as much as won that council position for him."

Mary Jo laughed off the credit. "Don't be silly."

"You were the one who walked up to the microphone at that rally and said anyone who believed Evan wasn't there for the worker, should talk to you or your family."

Mary Jo remembered the day well. She'd been furious to hear Evan's opponent state that Evan didn't understand the problems of the everyday working person. Evan had answered the accusation, but it was Mary Jo's fervent response that had won the hearts of the audience. As it happened, television cameras had recorded the rally and her impassioned reply had been played on three different newscasts. From that point on, Evan's popularity had soared.

Bethanne stirred, and Mary Jo reached for her daughter, cradling the infant in her arms.

A sound in the distance told her that Evan and his brother were back from their golf game.

"They're back soon," Jessica said when the men strolled onto the patio. Damian poured them each a glass of iced tea.

Evan took the seat next to his wife. "How long has it been since I told you I love you?" he asked in a low voice.

Smiling, Mary Jo glanced at her watch. "About four hours."

"Much too long," he said, kissing her. "I love you."

"Look at that pair," Damian said to his wife. "You'd think they were still on their honeymoon."

"So? What's wrong with that?" Jessica reached over and squeezed his hands.

He smiled at her lovingly. "Not a thing, sweetheart. Not a damn thing."

* * * * *

FINDING
HAPPILY-EVER-AFTER

Marie Ferrarella

To
Jacinta
who won Nik's heart.
Welcome to the family.

Chapter 1

He was accustomed to some disorder. It was there, on his desk, in his office at the university. But that was a controlled disorder. If pressed, Christopher Culhane knew exactly how to lay his hands on almost any textbook in his extensive library, be it math or one of the physics disciplines, as well as on any notes that he'd jotted down in the past six to nine months.

This, however, he thought as he looked around what he assumed was the living room, had to be what the inside of Dorothy's house had looked like immediately after the twister had landed it on top of the Wicked Witch of the East.

Maybe even worse, he silently amended. He'd always known that Rita, his younger sister, wasn't much for housekeeping. Growing up, she'd never been able to keep her room in any semblance of order despite their mother's numerous pleas and threats to come in with a bulldozer. Looking back, Rita's room had been downright neat in comparison to what he was seeing now.

How could a sane person live like this? The answer to that troubled him on several levels.

With a suppressed sigh, Chris scrubbed his hands over his face, trying very hard to pull himself together. The past thirty-six hours had been one hell of an emotionally draining ride. A ride that he fervently hoped to God he'd never come close to having to go through again.

"Are you okay, Uncle Chris?" a small, inordinately adult-sounding voice asked, fear vibrating in every syllable.

His nephew, Joel, peered at his face with blatant concern. Joel was small and slight for his age, which made him look even younger than five years old. But the moment he opened his mouth, he negated that impression and sounded like an old man trapped in a child's body.

"You're not having a headache or anything, are you?" he wanted to know. His brown eyes were wide with worry.

Chris shook his head sadly. "No."

Given what the boy had been through, Chris thought, it was a legitimate question, as was the obvious anxiety that surrounded it. According to the story Joel had related, both to the police and then to him, his mother had complained about an excruciating headache just before she collapsed on the floor.

Unlike all the other times she'd fallen down because alcohol or drugs—or both—had temporarily gotten the better of her, this time Rita Johnson did not open her eyes no matter how hard Joel shook her, pleading with her to wake up.

But the brain aneurysm that had ruptured with no apparent warning, other than an overwhelming headache minutes before snuffing out Rita's life, had other ideas.

It was Joel who called 911 and Joel who had told the policeman summoned to the hospital about his mother having a brother in the area. The boy had solemnly added that his mother "didn't want Uncle Chris coming around 'cause he didn't like what she was doing."

Chris had gotten the news just as he finished teaching his last physics class of the day. The dean's administrative assistant had handed him a note asking him to call Blair Memorial Hospital and speak to a Dr. MacKenzie. The sparse message only said that it was about his sister.

An icy feeling had passed over him as he'd dialed the number on the paper.

It had gone downhill from there.

Almost three years had gone by since he'd last seen Rita. That had been her choice. Despite slurring her words, Rita had made that perfectly clear. She'd angrily shouted for him to get out of her house and out of her life, that she'd had "enough to deal with without having you always staring down your disapproving nose at me!"

Trying to reason with her had been useless. He'd had to satisfy himself with covertly driving by the house every so often to catch a glimpse of his nephew and assure himself that the boy was doing all right.

The checks he sent regularly for the boy's care partially saw to that. He knew that his sister did love her child. She wouldn't have allowed him to starve or do completely without. He also knew that if he tried to police her, she'd do something to spite him, so the best method in this case was to give her money earmarked for Joel and stand back. He could only hope that, in her own strange way, Rita gave the boy the emotional support he needed.

Arriving at the hospital to identify his sister, Chris struggled with his own emotions. He had just turned away from Rita's lifeless body when he saw the huge, sad brown eyes looking at him from beneath the thick fringe of dark brown hair. The last time he'd been in the same room with Joel, the boy had been a little more than two years old and already on his way to being a prodigy.

Mourning the fact that this was all such a huge waste of a life, Chris approached the boy slowly. Even though he had conducted himself with exceptional maturity up to this point, Joel was still a five-year-old who had just lost his mother and needed comforting.

Chris had no idea how to talk to someone that young.

He dealt exclusively with adults, and had for some

time now. Children were just short human beings he occasionally noted as being part of the background or scenery, like flowers or benches or buildings. He had no direct contact with any of them. He was completely unprepared to break the news to the boy that his mother had died ten minutes after she'd been brought to Blair Memorial.

As it turned out, he didn't have to say very much at all. Joel had looked up at him with stoic, old eyes and said rather than asked, "My mother's dead, isn't she?"

When he'd answered his nephew haltingly in the affirmative, Joel slowly nodded his head. He was amazingly self-contained. In the day and a half that they'd been together since then, he still hadn't heard the boy cry. He was beginning to think that he never would.

It was eerily unnatural.

At a loss as to his next move, Chris had brought Joel back to the home that the boy had shared with his mother. He was utterly astonished at the chaotic scene that met him the moment he unlocked the door. Though it might have once been confined to a small area, the unbridled mess now spread out until it invaded every room in the house. There were newspapers stacked high in the corners, decaying food left on paper plates that turned up in the most unlikely places. And layers of dirty laundry seemed to be scattered everywhere.

The moment they walked in, Joel instantly began to pick things up. The systematic way he moved about told Chris that Joel was the one who tried, albeit unsuccessfully, to put things in order, not Rita. The boy obviously needed the semblance of some kind of order, especially now, when it was his very life that was in chaos. So, the first thing Chris did, right after calling the closest funeral parlor to make arrangements, was to place a call to a local cleaning service.

To his surprise, the woman who answered said they could be there the next morning. Sooner, she assured him kindly, if need be. There was no extra charge for speed. Because he was emotionally wiped out, Chris opted for the morning.

"I'm sorry about the mess," he apologized to the woman who appeared on the doorstep bright and early, armed with a warm smile and a willing crew. The woman, a Ms. Cecilia Parnell, came in first and quietly surveyed what she must have viewed as the aftermath of a blitz attack.

Cecilia smiled in response to the tall, good-looking young man's words, doing her best to melt away any outer discomfort on her client's part.

"Don't be. If there wasn't a mess, you wouldn't be needing my company's services and we'd all be selling tools in a hardware store," she told him cheerfully. She made her way around the stacks of papers, touching things at random as if to get a feel for what needed to be done and how long it would take. "If you don't mind my asking, how long has it been since you—?" She allowed her voice to trail off, not actually saying the word *cleaned* in case he would find it offensive and think that she was in any way criticizing him.

"Oh, it's not my house," Chris informed her quickly. The glut of clutter embarrassed him. "The house is my sister's."

His sister, Cecilia thought, would never give Martha Stewart a run for her money. "And you want to surprise her?" she guessed.

Chris felt his heart twist inside his chest. He shouldn't have stood on ceremony. He should have come over, should have insisted that he be part of Rita's life. Who knows? She might still be alive if he had, he thought as guilt tore off huge, jagged pieces of him.

"It's too late for that," he said. The moment the words were out, Chris realized how enigmatic that had to have sounded to the woman. She was looking at him curiously. He took a breath and explained, "My sister just died."

Sympathy instantly swept over Cecilia, her mother's heart going out to the young man. "Oh, I'm so sorry." She looked around again. Behind her, she heard Kathy and Ally, two of her carefully selected crew, setting up their equipment. Horst was bringing in the industrial-strength vacuum cleaner and muttering something to himself in German. "So you're trying to clean the house up in order to sell it?" She needed to know what his intentions were in order to ascertain just how deeply they were to clean. It was a hard real-estate market these days. A house up for sale had to sparkle right down to the support beams. Even her best friend, Maizie, who could sell hamburgers to a vegetarian, complained about it.

"No!" Quiet up until now, Joel jumped up the moment he heard the word *sell*. He looked stricken as he tugged on Chris's arm. "Don't sell it! You *can't* sell it. This is my home."

There was no way he intended to cause the boy any further pain. Awkwardly, Chris put his arm around the extremely thin shoulders. "I'm not selling the house, Joel. I just want you to be able to walk around here without bumping into things. Or coming down with anything," he added under his breath. He was fairly certain there were three kinds of mold growing in the kitchen alone. Possibly four.

Cecilia quickly connected the dots. "Your nephew?" she asked her client kindly.

He nodded. His arm still around Joel's shoulders, he moved him slightly forward. "This is Joel," he told the woman charged with what amounted to turning straw into gold.

Surprised when the boy offered his hand, Cecilia solemnly shook it. "Pleased to meet you, Joel." She raised her eyes to Chris's face. "And the boy's father?"

Ah, the million-dollar question. "Haven't a clue," he answered, swallowing a sigh. The moment he'd assessed the situation, he'd put in for a two-week leave of absence, citing a family emergency. He hoped it was enough. "Finding him is going to be my first order of business—right after getting this place habitable again."

Oh, yes, dear God, yes! Cecilia had stopped listening after her client had uttered the words *finding him.* Finally, Cecilia thought as relief wove its way through her.

Just when she thought it would never happen for her, or rather, for her daughter, Jewel, it appeared as if lightning were *finally* going to strike. Both of her best friends had miraculously managed to find men for their independent, career-minded daughters among the clientele their businesses serviced.

It was Maizie's plan initially, and Maizie's future son-in-law came to her looking for a house and a pediatrician for his daughter. She sold him the first and introduced him to the second—who just happened to be her daughter, Nikki. Theresa found Jackson when she catered a dinner for him. Theresa's daughter, Kate, and Jackson were going to be married soon, as well.

As for her, she'd given up all hope of finding someone for Jewel. But now she had her chance. Christopher Culhane not only needed his house cleaned, he needed help finding someone—which was Jewel's forte.

Incredibly excited, Cecilia smiled. Karma had finally found her.

"I know a very good private investigator if you're interested." She did her best to sound nonchalant, even though her heart had just gone into overdrive, taking her pulse with it.

The relieved expression on her client's face had her almost giddy. Cecilia had a *very* good feeling about this.

Jewel smelled a rat.

Much as she would have liked to say, "Thanks but no thanks," when the offer had been presented to her, she wasn't exactly in a position to turn down business when it came her way. Even if the referral *had* come from her mother.

She sighed as she drove to the address she'd hastily written down after her conversation with her mother. There was no denying that times were tough for PIs these days. Suspicious wives were deciding that, for the time being, it was better to live with unfounded fears than to pay to find out that those qualms were right on the money because that would only lead to a divorce. And divorce, for now, was just too expensive.

Since most of Jewel's money came from shadowing cheating spouses, that didn't leave very much for her to do. Before her mother had called her with this case, she had actually been debating asking her if the cleaning service her mom ran needed any parttime help. She hated being idle, not to mention running the risk of falling behind in her monthly bills.

This job was like a stay of execution—with a bonus. For once she didn't have to trail anyone to a sleazy motel and wind up feeling as if she needed to take a shower because of what she'd had to witness and record.

Still, the referral *had* come from her mother and she knew all about the pact that her mother had made with her lifelong best friends. All three of them—Maizie, Theresa and her mother—were determined to get their daughters married. Her mother, and consequently, *she*, was the last woman standing.

That did *not* bode well for someone who valued her privacy and her life as much as Jewel did.

"This is legitimate?" she'd asked her mother not only over the phone, but in person, as well. Having swung by her mother's office to see her face-to-face, she'd scrutinized the older woman for any telltale signs of this being a setup.

Cecilia Parnell had sworn to the name and address' authenticity, ending with the ever popular, "If you can't believe your mother, who can you believe?"

What made this so-called case somewhat suspect was that her mother had given her an address, rather than a phone number.

What was *that* about?

Jewel would have preferred calling first, but her mother had said that the man was in dire need of a private investigator, so calling him, rather than coming directly over, was just an extra, unnecessary step.

What made it more suspect was that her mother had taken it upon herself to arrange the initial meeting, saying, "It's not as if you've got all that much taking up your time these days, right? There's no schedule for you to reshuffle."

Sad, but true, Jewel thought.

She would have loved to demur and contradict her mother's assumption, except that she really did hate lying unless it was in the line of duty to secure information for a client.

Besides, her mother had an uncanny ability to know when she was lying. There was no point in even trying.

So here she was, pulling into the client's driveway on a fall morning, about to take a case partly against her better judgment. But what choice did she have? None, that's what, she thought darkly.

Getting out of her well-maintained vehicle, she walked up to the front door and rang the bell.

Maybe it wouldn't be so bad, she reasoned, mentally crossing her fingers.

When the door opened, Jewel found herself meeting the gaze of the most solemn-looking child she'd ever seen.

The boy appeared to be waiting for her to speak first.

"Hi," she said brightly.

There wasn't even a hint of a smile on the small, sad-looking face. But, apparently a well-mannered child, the boy did echo her greeting back at her, albeit devoid of any cheer.

"Hi."

Obviously, the bulk of the conversation, at least for now, was going to rest with her, Jewel thought. She smiled at him and resisted the urge to stroke his silky-looking hair. Instead, she squatted down to his level so that they could be eye-to-eye.

"I'm Jewel. What's your name?"

The little boy shook his head, his dark hair swinging almost independently. "I can't tell you."

That took her aback for a second. And then she understood. "Because you can't talk to strangers," she realized. "Good for you," she praised. The boy continued looking at her with the oldest eyes she'd seen in quite a while. "I'm here to see, um—" Jewel looked down at the paper she was holding. She'd made her mother spell the last name so she'd get it right. "A Christopher Culhane." She folded the paper into a small ball with her thumb as she looked back at the boy. "That's your dad I'm guessing."

The boy shook his head from side to side.

"I'm his uncle," a man supplied for him, coming to the door. He appeared a little breathless, as if he'd been moving furniture—or exercising.

Crying "uncle" was exactly what crossed her mind, except not in the sense of the word that referred to family. She thought of it more in terms of surrender.

Her mother's taste had definitely improved, Jewel thought, covertly taking in Christopher Culhane's features. The man was tall and dark and he made the word *handsome* suddenly turn into a dreadfully inadequate description.

"Can I help you?" Culhane asked patiently, resting his hands on the boy's whisper-thin shoulders as if to anchor him in place.

Don't get me started, Jewel thought. The next moment, she was tamping down her runaway thoughts. She'd learned a long time ago that all that glittered was definitely not gold.

"Actually, I'm here to help you," she told him. When his expression only became more quizzical, she said, "I'm Jewel Parnell." She held out a business card as if to dispel any doubt as to her identity. "You were expecting me."

What he was expecting, Chris thought, was a man. The woman who'd miraculously made his sister's house habitable again had told him about a Jay

Parnell. He realized now that she hadn't been using a name, she'd used an initial.

Still, he heard himself asking, "You're the private investigator?"

"I'm the private investigator," Jewel assured him, then added cheerfully, "Would you like references?" This wasn't the first time she'd been on the receiving end of a disbelieving stare.

"Well, actually…"

"Say no more," Jewel assured him. Opening her oversize purse, she took out a bound folder and handed it to him. "These comments are from all my satisfied customers."

Maybe it was the odd frame of mind he found himself in, but her words presented too much of a straight line for him to pass up. "Where are ones from your dissatisfied customers?"

"There aren't any," she informed him with a touch of pride. Her mouth curved ever so slightly as she lifted her chin.

He looked at the folder and then the woman. What did he have to lose, he decided, except for some time? Besides, he welcomed having someone else in the house to talk to besides the boy.

Stepping back, Chris gestured for her to enter. "C'mon in."

Chapter 2

Jewel looked around as she made her way inside. The house appeared neat and clean, but aside from the vase filled with wildflowers in the center of the coffee table—her mother's touch, she'd know it anywhere—the room was devoid of any real personal touches. It struck her as rather sad.

Her own apartment all but shouted: Jewel Parnell lives here! It wouldn't have been home otherwise. There were knickknacks picked up from years of vacations, photographs documenting both her own life and her mother's, beginning from the time she was a little girl. These were the kinds of things that generated warmth and ultimately gave a place personality.

This house looked clean, but there was no detectable warmth. It didn't give off the aura of a house where a child was being raised.

Her mother had deliberately refrained from giving her any details about the case—utterly out of character for the woman—when she'd given her the name and address of her client. The only thing her mother had told her was that the man was trying to locate someone. Her mother had also said that she'd mentioned that she knew someone who specialized in finding people. Mercifully, her mother hadn't added "usually in sleazy hotels." It might be true, but it wasn't anything Jewel really wanted advertised.

The one thing Cecilia Parnell definitely hadn't mentioned was the little boy who was now watching her intently, as if at any given moment, someone were going to ask him to re-create her likeness from memory.

There was a lot going on behind those dark brown eyes, she decided. She'd never given much credence to the phrase "old soul" until just now.

"This is a nice place," Jewel finally commented in order to break the ice.

It was the boy rather than the man who answered her. "Now." When she looked at him, raising one quizzical eyebrow in a silent query, the boy lifted and lowered his shoulders. "Mom didn't like to clean much," he told her protectively. "But I tried to do it for her when I could."

Her heart going out to the boy, she couldn't hold back her questions any longer. "What's your name?"

"Joel," he told her solemnly.

"My name's Jewel. Jewel Parnell," she said, shaking his hand as if he were an adult. "Now that we're not strangers anymore can you tell me how old you are?"

"Five," he told her.

He sounded more like he was twenty-five, she thought.

Jewel turned toward Culhane and asked, "So what can I do for you?"

But again it was the boy who answered. "Uncle Chris wants you to find my dad."

If ever she'd heard a more mournful-sounding voice, Jewel couldn't remember when.

Because the little boy seemed to be a great deal more forthcoming than the man he'd identified as his uncle, she addressed her next question to the boy. "Did your dad suddenly disappear?"

"Only if you think of three years as being 'sudden.'" This time, it was the man who answered.

Jewel took a step back so she could focus on both of them at the same time and let either one field the questions. It would also help her avoid getting a crick in her neck.

"Any particular reason you want to find him now, as opposed to three years ago?"

"My mom said that we were better off that he was gone."

This was like a tennis match, except that the other team was playing doubles to her singles. Moreover, the boy's reply didn't really answer her question. Why now after all this time?

"I see. His mother is your sister-in-law?" she asked, looking at Chris.

"Sister," he corrected.

Okay, he was doing this for his sister. She could understand that. Family members often took over when the affected member was too upset to function. Something had happened recently to change the dynamics and she'd get to that by and by, she promised herself.

"Could I talk to your sister?" she requested, glancing around as if she expected the woman to be standing back in the shadows.

"Not unless you conduct séances as a sideline."

Chris couldn't help the bitter edge that entered his voice. Maybe he couldn't blame Rita for having an aneurysm, but he could blame her for everything that had come before, for not listening when he'd begged and pleaded with her to go into rehab and make an attempt at reclaiming her life. If not for herself, then for her son. At the time, he'd offered to pay not just for the stint in rehab, but for someone to stay with Joel, as well.

All she had to do was get better. But for that to happen, he thought, she would have to have *wanted* to get better. And she didn't. He was certain that, at bottom, Rita didn't think she deserved to be happy.

Damn it, Rita, why did you throw it all away? Why would you do *something like that? You had a son, for God's sake.*

Jewel could all but feel the tension radiating from the man who would be her client if she decided to take the case.

If, she mocked herself. She knew damn well that unless the man turned out to be a direct descendent of Satan or was numbered among the undead, she was going to take his case. She needed the money.

She also needed to get as much information out of

him as possible. She didn't believe in privacy when it came to solving a case or in leaving stones unturned. She always made it a point of knowing what she was getting into and how she was going to maneuver through it. Her first case, which involved tailing a cheating spouse, had taught her that. The wife had failed to mention that her husband was a decorated Marine sniper who felt incomplete without his sidearm somewhere within reach. She'd almost gotten her head blown off when he'd seen the flash from her camera and, enraged, had come charging at her.

Given what Culhane had just said about séances, she could only arrive at one conclusion.

"She's—" Jewel was about to say "dead," but because the boy was standing there, she inserted a euphemism. "Passed away?"

Jewel needn't have tiptoed around the issue. The boy confirmed her suspicion. "My mother's dead."

"I see." *Tough little guy,* Jewel thought. "When did this happen?" She looked from Mr. Tall, Dark and Handsome to the sad little human being standing beside him. The question was up for grabs.

"Two days ago," Chris told her. And he was still trying to catch his breath, he added silently.

"And the funeral?" Jewel wanted to know. "When is that?"

Chris suppressed a sigh. He felt as if everything were crashing in on him. Right now, ordinarily, he'd be at his office at the university, which seemed to be under siege half the time he was there. He was always grading papers or working on his latest textbook collaboration, that is, when he wasn't taking appointments with students. He didn't mind helping them, but the ones who sought him out were generally of the female persuasion, all interested in signing up for private tutoring sessions. Some weren't even taking any of his classes.

Still, fending them off was preferable to this situation. Dealing with death and the consequences that arose because of it was something he'd discovered that he was not any good at.

He reminded himself that he had to call back the funeral director. And find someone to conduct the ceremony, he realized. He didn't like feeling overwhelmed like this.

"Day after tomorrow," he told her, although he saw no reason for her question. He was asking her to find his brother-in-law, not his sister.

Pleased, Jewel nodded. "Good, then it's not too late."

He had no idea what she was talking about. Not too late for what? "Excuse me?"

Rather than repeat herself, she pushed forward. "How many obituaries did you run?"

What did that matter? "Again, excuse me?"

"Obituaries," she repeated, enunciating the word more slowly. "Those are stories in the newspaper that are usually put out by the family to notify the general public that—"

He cut her short. "I know what obituaries are," he retorted, then stopped. "Sorry, didn't mean to snap at you," he apologized. "I'm a little out of my element here."

This had to be hard for him. She remembered

what it had felt like when she'd lost her father. She and her mother had gotten through it by leaning on each other, as well as their friends. "Isn't there anyone to help you?"

"I'm helping him," Joel piped up solemnly.

She looked down at the boy. "I'm sure you are." She said it without sounding patronizing. From the little she'd picked up, Joel seemed to be a lot more capable than some adults she'd dealt with. "But this is probably all new to you, too," she suggested delicately with a kind smile. "I guess you'll just help each other along." She shifted her eyes back to Culhane. "About the obituaries…?"

Chris shrugged. "There's no point in putting them out." He glanced at Joel and decided to omit the fact that, for the past four years, Rita had predominantly been involved with drug pushers and users, none of whom would come to a funeral, thank God. "From what I gathered, Rita kept to herself a lot the past few years. She didn't have any friends."

Jewel glanced to see how the boy was dealing with that. There was no change in his demeanor, but she thought she noticed an even more stricken look in his eyes.

"This runaway ex-brother-in-law you're looking for, if he lives or works anywhere in the county, he might read the obituary and come to the funeral."

Chris thought about Ray. He'd never met anyone more self-serving and self-involved. "What makes you think he'd come?"

"Any number of reasons," she assured him. "Disbelief. Curiosity. Remorse. You'd be surprised how many different reasons there are for people to come to a funeral. It's not all about paying last respects."

Culhane's expression bordered on dark, she thought.

"You're assuming that he can read," was his bitter comment.

"Or has someone to read to him," she supplied without skipping a beat.

The answer brought the first semblance of what would have passed for a semi-smile to his lips. It seemed, she noted, to soften his entire countenance. It also made him look younger, more approachable.

Why hadn't any of her professors ever looked like that, she wondered.

Her comment made him come around a little, which, in turn, had him realizing that he hadn't even offered her anything. "Hey, I'm sorry, this whole thing has thrown me for a loop. Would you like something to drink?"

"No." A smile played on her lips as she looked toward the living room and the sofa there. "But sitting down might be nice."

Chris felt like an idiot. Despite occasional lapses when he was preoccupied with his work, he wasn't normally this socially awkward.

"The sofa's comfortable," the boy told her with the solemnity of someone delivering a sermon at High Mass on Sunday.

He threaded his small fingers through hers. Here was a boy who'd already learned how to take charge, not because he was pushy, but because he'd had to.

"It's right here," Joel told her, leading her to the sofa.

"Thank you," she said with sincerity, smiling at

him as she sat down. To her surprise, Joel remained standing, as if he wasn't sure he wanted to join her.

Culhane sat down in the love seat that was adjacent to the sofa. "Joel is holding it together better than I am," he confided.

Jewel gave herself a moment to study him more closely. "Were you and your sister close?" she asked sympathetically.

"Once," he recalled. And it felt as if that had been a million years ago, Chris thought. He could hardly remember Rita the way she'd once been. "Before things went spiraling out of control," he said tactfully, glancing at his nephew.

"And when did that start happening?" Jewel wanted to know.

Chris hesitated for a moment, then looked again at Joel. He couldn't speak freely with him around. He had a feeling that the boy was absorbing every word and he didn't want to be responsible for making him feel any worse than he already did.

He pointed toward the family room. "Joel, why don't you go and play a video game?"

The boy remained standing where he was. "I don't have any."

Chris stared at him. That was impossible, he thought. He had specifically sent Rita extra money for the boy's birthday and earmarked part of it for a game console and several of the more popular games. He'd said so in the note he'd included. He would have called if Rita would have taken his call, but after hearing the receiver on the other end being banged down a couple of dozen times, he'd learned his lesson.

"You don't?" he asked incredulously.

Joel shook his head. "No."

"Well, I just happen to have a portable game console in my purse," Jewel announced. Out of the corner of her eye, she saw Culhane looking at her quizzically as she took it out. "It's something I use while I'm doing surveillance." Which happened a lot more frequently than she was happy about. She never liked being inert for long. "That can be deadly dull and playing with this keeps my mind sharp."

She could see that Culhane looked skeptical, but she didn't bother explaining that the console also supported brain teasers and ways to test IQ skills. She wasn't trying to justify having one to him, she just wanted to explain why she had one in her possession.

Joel was looking at her uncertainly. She surrendered the video game player to him. "Okay, now why don't you take that into the family room?" Jewel suggested. "That way, you can play without having us disturb your concentration."

Joel gave her a look that told her he saw through the ruse, but played along anyway.

"I take it that you sent Joel a game console," she asked Chris the moment his nephew was out of earshot.

"I sent my sister money to buy him one," he corrected, then looked at her, slightly mystified. "How did you know?"

She laughed softly. "It wasn't hard to put the pieces together." When he still looked at her doubtfully, she added, "Mostly that surprised look on your face gave it away."

"You looked surprised, too," he pointed out.

She didn't argue. "Moderately so because all the kids I know or have dealt with eat, sleep and breathe video games. You, on the other hand, looked as if something that you took to be a given had just turned out to be wrong. There's a difference."

"Obviously," he commented, then shifted so that he could scrutinize her a little more closely. She was sharp, he'd give her that. Or maybe she was just good at coming off that way. "That's a pretty good card trick."

He was testing her, Jewel thought, maybe trying to see if she were quick to take offense. He was going to be disappointed.

"I don't do card tricks," she countered with an easy smile. "I'm a student of human nature. And I get straight A's most of the time."

She paused for a moment, trying to read him. There were a lot of signals coming off the man. Anger, grief, confusion. All of which were completely understandable, she thought.

Jewel wondered which would win out in the end. Or was this all going on as he tried to come to grips with what had just happened? It had to have changed the dynamics of his world.

"So, do I have the job?" she asked. "Or do you want to reserve judgment on that until you check out my references?" She nodded toward the folder she'd handed him earlier.

He waved away the second part of her words. He

was going on his instincts. Besides, he was in no mood to have to conduct interviews. "You've got the job."

"All right, about the terms—"

Again he waved his hand. "Mrs. Parnell already told me your rates."

"Oh, she did?" She tried very hard not to sound annoyed. Her mother had no business quoting her going rates. Since when did her mother even *know* what her rates were?

He nodded. "She said they were reasonable—and if I didn't think so, to call her and she'd handle it. She said the two of you have a close working relationship. I take it you've done a lot of work for her?"

"In a manner of speaking," Jewel allowed. "She's my mother." He looked somewhat surprised. "Does that make a difference?" she asked.

He thought a moment, then shook his head. "No."

"All right, since that's out of the way, I'm going to need as much information as you can give me."

"About Ray?" he asked.

"About everything," she specified. She thought she saw him clam up. Privacy issues? "Your sister, your missing ex-brother-in-law, your nephew. The first thing I'm going to do is contact the local papers to run that obituary tomorrow. For that, I'm going to need her full name, her date of birth, if there are any other surviving siblings—"

"No."

"Or children—"

"No."

The piece was going to be short and sweet, she

thought. Didn't matter, she'd find a way to dress it up a little.

Jewel took out a digital recorder from her purse. Placing it on the coffee table, she switched it on. "Okay, I don't want you to hold anything back. Tell me everything that comes to your mind when you think of your sister."

The device began recording. It had nothing to work with but silence.

Chapter 3

Jewel raised her eyes. He didn't look like a man who was trying to sort out his thoughts. He looked more like a man who was resigned to remaining silent.

"The recorder works better if it has something to record," she told him gently. "Though it might happen someday in the future, right now, technology hasn't advanced enough so that machines can record a person's thoughts."

This was hard on him. Anger had merged with a porcupine-edged sense of guilt. Would she be alive today if he'd insisted on continuing to come around? If he'd made Rita see a doctor...

Chris blew out a breath. "I don't know what to say," he admitted.

What was it about the sight of a digital recorder

that made so many people, even talkative ones, freeze? Jewel wondered.

"This isn't going to make it into any archives or be preserved for posterity," she promised him. "It's just to help me remember what you said. Again," she prompted gently, "the key word here is *said*." She gave him a starting-off point. "Did you ever actually meet Joel's father?"

Did she think he could amass this kind of animosity through hearsay alone? "Oh, yeah. I met him."

The way he said it told her that he'd disapproved of his sister's husband right from the very beginning. But she still asked her question anyway. "What was your first impression?"

He shrugged, struggling to keep the emotion out of his voice. "For Rita's sake, I wanted to like him. But I saw that he was loser, as well as a user. I knew that somewhere down the line, Rita was going to regret getting involved with him and—"

"Hold that thought," Jewel requested. Much as she really hated doing it—she had a feeling that it was going to be hard to get Culhane started again—she held her hand up to temporarily stop him from continuing.

Jewel felt rather than saw that the boy had drifted back into the room. Turning, she saw him standing in the doorway, holding the portable video game player in his hands. His attention wasn't riveted on the screen, it was on them.

This wasn't anything a boy should hear about his father, Jewel thought. At least, not at this age. Five was very young to have your illusions crushed, no matter how mature you seemed.

Beckoning the boy closer, she smiled at him and asked, "Is there something wrong, Joel?"

The boy crossed to her, holding out the unit she'd given him. He looked chagrinned as he admitted, "I don't know how."

Was it the game that was stumping him? Or was there something else? Was he just casting about for an excuse to come back in? "Don't know how to what?" she asked him kindly.

Joel sighed, thrusting the unit into her hands. It obviously embarrassed him to admit this. "To play with this."

"Don't any of your friends have one of these?" He shook his head. Though she'd asked the question, Jewel found that a little difficult to believe. Did he hang out with Amish kids? "They don't have one of these?" she repeated to make sure she understood what he was telling her.

"No," Joel said in a small voice. "I don't have any friends."

That hadn't occurred to her. He was too young to be a loner. "What about at school? Nobody there that you talk to or like to hang out with?"

There was a blank expression on his face. "I don't go to school."

This time, it was Chris who was caught off guard by what Joel said. He looked at his nephew, stunned. If anyone belonged in a school, to have his potential maximized, it was Joel. "You're kidding."

"Mama said I needed to stay home with her," Joel

told him matter-of-factly. "She said she needed me to help her with things."

"What kind of things?" Chris wanted to know. Just how badly had their lives disintegrated? Again he upbraided himself for letting things go the way they had. Why hadn't he made it a point to force Rita to mend fences so that he see for himself what was going on in her life?

The small shoulders moved up and down beneath the washed-out T-shirt. "Breakfast. Lunch. She said she liked the way I washed the clothes," he volunteered, obviously clinging to the offhanded praise.

Jewel could see that the revelation affected Culhane. He was probably struggling with the guilt that all this dredged up. Momentarily putting her interview with him on hold, Jewel shut off the recorder, made eye contact with the boy and patted the place next to her.

"Come sit by me, Joel," she coaxed. Dutifully, he did as he was told, looking somehow even smaller as he sat beside her. "I'm sure your mother really liked having you around and that you were a great help to her, but you do need to go to school. It's important that you learn things, like how to read and—"

"I know how to read," Joel interrupted.

"You do?" She doubted if the boy was capable of lying. "Did your mama teach you?"

Again, Joel shook his head, looking very solemn. "Alakazam taught me," he told her.

The name sounded like something a child would make up, Chris thought. Was he talking about some imaginary friend? "Who?"

Still maintaining eye contact with Joel, Jewel responded to Culhane's question. "That's the name of a character on a public broadcasting station program. It's one of those shows that's geared to help kids learn basic things, like reading, and adding and subtracting simple numbers. I have a feeling that your sister might have relied on the TV to act as a baby-sitter for Joel. Thank God for programs like that," she added, smiling at the boy.

Jewel glanced in Chris's direction. "You're going to need to enroll him in school," she told him. The unexpected news brought a frown to his lips. He probably hadn't a clue about things like registration, she thought. Handsome as hell, the man made her think of the absentminded academic. "Your wife handles these kinds of things?" she guessed.

The question seemed to come out of the blue and threw him for a moment. "What? No. I don't have a wife," he added.

"I see." Of course he wasn't married. For a second, she'd forgotten that her mother was the one who had brought them together. It would have been the first thing Cecilia Parnell would have ascertained before she started the wheels turning. "Would you like me to help you get him registered?" she asked. The moment the offer was on the table, Culhane looked incredibly relieved. It was all she could do not to laugh at his expression. "I'll take that as a yes."

Joel fidgeted beside her. When she looked at him, he appeared far from happy. "What's wrong, honey?" she asked the boy.

"Do I have to go?" he asked sorrowfully.

Rather than impress upon him that it was the law, Jewel tried to make it sound like something that he could look forward to.

"You'll like going to school," she promised. "You get to play games and meet other kids your own age. You'll make friends," she promised.

But he didn't look so sure. Joel's apprehensive expression remained. "What if they don't like me?"

She looked at him as if that were just not possible. "What's not to like?" she asked incredulously. Jewel grinned broadly at him, refraining from tousling his very silky dark hair. "You're a cool guy," she declared. Then, inclining her head as if she was about to share something exclusive, she said, "Let me let you in on a secret. You just talk to them about things they're interested in and they'll like you."

His eyes widened just a little. "Really?"

In an exaggerated motion, she crossed her heart. "Really. I have it on the best authority." And then Jewel nodded at the portable video game player he was still holding in his hands. "Would you like me to show you how to play that?"

The shy expression was back, as was the small, uncertain voice. "Yes, please."

"Love those manners," she commented, then raised her eyes to Chris. "You don't mind, do you? This'll only take a minute." And then she added with another grin, "No extra charge."

It hadn't occurred to Chris to even worry about the cost. He felt far too out of his element with everything else that was going on to worry about being charged for the extra time it might take to show his nephew how to use a video game player.

He urged her on with an absolving wave of his hand. "Go ahead."

She turned her attention back to the boy. "You heard the man. Let's get to it. Now, you have to hold it like this." Jewel demonstrated what she meant, then took Joel's small fingers and arranged them on either side of the game player.

Getting the dexterity part under control took longer than she'd expected, but once that was mastered, Joel caught on very quickly. She had a feeling he would. She had him playing the game in no time, conquering aliens with subdued relish.

Once he was entrenched in the game, rather than send the boy back to the family room to play, Jewel decided that it might be a better idea not to distract him. She motioned for Chris to adjourn to the kitchen with her. That way, they could keep an eye on Joel and she could still conduct the rest of the interview. If she were going to find Ray Johnson, she needed as much information as Culhane could possibly give her.

Sitting down at the table for two, the recorder once again in position, Jewel turned it on for the second time and said, "Now, where were we?"

Instead of trying to recall what he'd said to her, Chris commented, "You're pretty good at this, aren't you?"

"Tracking people down? Actually, I am," she told him. Not that she'd had all that many missing persons cases, but the few that she'd had, she'd successfully located.

To her surprise, Chris shook his head. "No, I mean talking to kids."

"Oh."

She looked over toward the living room. His nephew was sitting on the sofa, his small face screwed up with concentration as he worked his way from one level to the next with, whether he realized it or not, amazing speed.

Jewel shrugged off his observation carelessly. "They're just short people," she told him. "And I still remember being a kid," she confessed. She had an all-encompassing empathy that served her well in her line of work. "Besides, your nephew seems extremely bright. I think if you have him tested, you'll probably find that he's very gifted. Possibly even a genius."

Chris glanced over toward the boy. "I really hope not," he said with feeling.

She didn't quite follow. She would have thought that someone like him, a college professor, would have been thrilled.

"Why not?" she asked, curious. "Taking tests is a lot easier when you're gifted. Cuts down on hours and hours of cramming," she added, remembering all-night study sessions that still didn't yield the results she'd hoped for. While she had a mind like a sponge when it came to certain things, studying dry subject matter had never come easily to her.

He was still looking at the boy. "If you happen to

be different in any way, people tend to think of you as being strange."

Jewel studied Culhane for a long moment. "Speaking from experience?" she finally guessed.

This wasn't why he was hiring her. He didn't want her delving into his life, he just wanted her to find the boy's father. "What kind of information did you say you needed?"

She saw the "No Trespassing" sign being posted as clearly as if he had pounded it into the ground right in front of her. But if that was the way he wanted it, that was fine with her. She was curious, but it wasn't terminal and besides, everyone deserved to keep his privacy intact.

She checked the recorder to make sure it was on. "Tell me anything you can remember about your sister's husband. Let's start with where he worked. Do you remember the address?"

"He didn't work," Chris corrected her. "At least, not during the years he was with Rita."

She was familiar with the type. "Did he *ever* hold down a job?"

Chris nodded. That was how the whole thing began. "He used to work in a garage. Rita crashed her car and her insurance company sent her to this repair shop they had a contract with for an estimate. That's how she met Ray. He was the one who worked on her car. He got fired a couple of weeks after that." He frowned, remembering. "She thought it was romantic."

"Romantic?" Jewel echoed. She didn't see the

connection. Getting fired seemed like it was anything but romantic.

Chris nodded. "He was fired for blowing off his job to hang out with her. She was nineteen and very young for her age."

Unlike her son, Jewel thought. "And that's the extent of Ray's work history?"

Chris shrugged. He knew it wasn't much to go on and it frustrated him. But then, if there'd been a wealth of information, he would have been able to locate Ray himself. "As far as I know."

"Would you happen to remember the name of the garage?" she asked, mentally crossing her fingers.

"No, but I do remember that it was on Fairview and Carson. I dropped her off to pick up her car." He should have done it for her, he thought. If he had gone in her place, then all of this might have never happened and Rita would still be around.

Even if the boy wouldn't have been.

Jotting down the information, Jewel nodded. "That's a start. Do you have a photograph of Ray?" she asked hopefully. "I noticed that there weren't any photographs around."

"When they divorced, Rita burned all his pictures. Said it was part of the healing process." She'd always been a great one for burning pictures once someone was out of her life. Chris imagined that she'd burned the few she had of him when she'd banished him from her life, too.

Jewel surprised him by nodding. "I've heard of that," she said.

Chris laughed shortly, recalling the incident. Rita

had already been heavily into drugs and alcohol. And their relationship was on a downward spiral because he tried to get her to stop.

"Rita almost burned the house down," he told her. "Fire department had to come to put out the fire." He knew that for a fact because her homeowner's insurance wouldn't pay to repair the damages, so he covered the expenses out of his own pocket. "Luckily, they caught it in time so it wasn't a complete disaster."

Right now, there was only one thing that Jewel was interested in. "So then there are no photographs left at all?"

"Yeah, actually there is," he said wearily. She looked at him, waiting. "I have one."

"You?" She wouldn't have thought, given how he felt about the man, that he would have a photograph of him.

Chris nodded. "It's a wedding picture," he explained. "She gave it to me and I never got around to tossing it. Rita was in it," he added unnecessarily.

She knew that was the reason he'd kept it. Not because he was sentimental but, quite possibly, it might have been the only photograph of his sister he had in his possession.

"Good thing," Jewel said. "I'll need it as soon as possible."

"No problem," he told her. "I don't live that far from here."

She glanced over to where Joel was sitting. Now that he'd gotten the hang of it, the boy seemed to be completely engrossed in the video game he was playing. She didn't want him to be disturbed so soon.

"Why don't we get a few more of the questions out of the way before you go retrieve that photograph?" she suggested. Not waiting for Chris to answer, she went on to the next question. "Do you know if Ray ever served in the army or if he was employed anywhere that might have kept his prints on file before he married your sister?"

"He was never in the army," Chris told her, "but he was arrested, so his prints have to be on file with the police department."

This man was sounding more and more like a winner. No wonder Culhane's sister had divorced him. She wasn't feeling all that good about looking for Ray, but she supposed, as the boy's father, he had a right to know that Joel's mother had died. And there was always the infinitesimal chance that the man had changed.

"What was the charge?"

"Drunk and disorderly," Chris recited. That had been the beginning of the end of his sister's marriage, he recalled. "Rita called me in the middle of the night and begged me to bail him out."

She could tell that wasn't his automatic reaction to the situation. "And did you?"

He snorted. In his opinion, jail was too good for Ray. "If it was up to me, I would have had them throw away the key."

"You didn't answer my question," she pointed out. Jewel studied him for a moment and had her answer.

He had a soft spot in his heart for his sister. This had to be killing him. "You bailed him out, didn't you?"

Chris shrugged, frustrated. "She was crying. I was afraid she was going to start drinking again. She was pregnant," he explained.

Pausing, Jewel jotted down a few more notes for herself, then looked up at him. "You sure you want me to find this guy?"

He nodded. "I'm sure. If you don't find him, social services is going to take Joel."

Had she missed something? "Maybe I'm being dense here," she said slowly, "but aren't you Joel's uncle?"

Chris knew where she was going with this and it made him uncomfortable to discuss it. "Yes, but I can't raise him."

It was making less sense, not more. "Again, maybe I'm being dense here, but—"

He cut her off. "I don't know the first thing about raising a kid."

"Most first-time parents don't," she countered. "Kids don't come with instruction manuals. I'm told that you're supposed to learn as you go along."

Maybe, but there were more problems than just that. The idea of being responsible for the care and feeding of another human being, for his very welfare, made him uncomfortable. He wasn't prepared for something like that, didn't feel up to it. Look how he'd dropped the ball with Rita.

For the first time since his parents had died, he was glad that they weren't around so they wouldn't have to see this.

"I'm never home," he told the woman with the luminous eyes who was apparently waiting for more. "With all my work at the university, home is just some place I sleep. Occasionally."

She took all this in quietly, trying not to be judgmental. "If you don't mind my asking, exactly what is it that you do for a living?"

"I teach physics at the University of Bedford."

"A noble profession," she commented with a nod. "And that's it?"

"I'm also collaborating with some other professors on a revised physics textbook, and I just had a paper published in a professional journal."

She waited and when he said nothing more, she pointed out, "Physics professors have children."

His eyes went flat. He wasn't hiring her because he wanted to be challenged. "Physics professors usually have wives first."

He sounded irritated, she thought. She'd overstepped. Again.

Jewel held up her hands as if she were pushing back a blanket because the room had suddenly become too warm. "I'm sorry, I didn't mean to sound as if I were trying to talk you into something. It's just that, from the sound of it, Joel's father isn't exactly going to be up for father of the year, especially if he hasn't come around to see his son since he walked out—"

"He hasn't," Chris assured her.

"And you know this for a fact how?"

He glanced toward the living room. He genuinely felt sorry for the boy, but his situation was what it was. He couldn't take Joel in for more than a few days. Maybe a week. It wouldn't be fair to either of them, especially not to his nephew.

"Joel told me."

She looked over toward the boy and caught herself wondering what Joel thought about all this and how he'd react to being reunited with the father who had apparently wanted no part of him.

For the time being, she kept the rest of her thoughts to herself.

But her heart went out to the boy.

Chapter 4

Ray Johnson's features were etched into Jewel's mind as she quietly surveyed the surrounding area in the cemetery, searching for Rita Johnson's errant ex-husband.

It was a sunny Southern California day, but it was atypically muggy. Humidity was rarely a factor in the weather, but every once in a while, it made an appearance just to remind the transplants why they had all migrated here.

There were several other services going on at the same time at the cemetery. Jewel covertly scanned the mourners at each gravesite to see if Ray was there, hanging back so as not to be noticed, watching the woman he had supposedly once loved being buried.

She bit back a frustrated sigh. As far as she could

determine, Ray Johnson wasn't anywhere within the vicinity. That wasn't to say that he still might not come.

If he'd read the obituary.

Some people devoured the obituary page, happy to have cheated the Grim Reaper for another day. Others felt it was bad luck to even glance through the obits. Still others were oblivious to its existence.

She supposed it had been a long shot.

Because Chris had been convinced—and rightly so—that Rita's death wouldn't suddenly bring out friends from years gone by who had lost touch with her, and because his sister and the religion she'd been brought up in had had a falling out a long time ago, he saw no reason to go through the charade of a church service. Instead, he asked one of the priests at St. John the Baptist Church to say a few words over Rita's casket before it was lowered into its final resting place. He did it more for Joel than for Rita.

And maybe, Chris allowed, he'd done it a little for himself, as well.

So now, two days after he'd initially hired her, Jewel, Culhane and his nephew were standing at Rita Johnson's gravesite, listening to Father William Gannon offering up prayers and speaking with professional compassion about someone he had never met.

At least, Jewel thought, it had begun with the three of them and the priest. She'd stopped at the deceased woman's house and offered to take both Culhane and his nephew to the cemetery. Culhane had started to demur, saying he was going to drive, but Joel seemed to brighten up a little when he saw her. After a moment of silence, Culhane had thanked her and accepted her offer for a ride to the cemetery.

The priest was just beginning when Jewel saw a woman in black coming up the slight incline, moving quickly despite the fact that her heels were sinking into the grass with each step she took. Leading the way, the woman was followed by two other women, also dressed in black.

The very picture of compassion, Cecilia Parnell came straight to their tight little threesome, her gaze unwaveringly focused on the little boy who stood between his uncle and Jewel.

For one moment, Jewel was almost speechless. She'd thought after all this time that her mother had run out of ways to surprise her.

Obviously, she'd been wrong. "Mother, what are you doing here?" Jewel finally asked.

There was no hesitation on Cecilia's part as she smiled warmly, first at her former client and then at his nephew.

"I'm being supportive of Chris and Joel," Cecilia answered simply. "Worst thing I can possibly imagine is having a loved one die and then adding to that hurt by having no one attend her funeral service," her mother explained.

Jewel supposed she bought that. Sort of. "And Maizie and Theresa?" she asked, nodding at the two women who were just joining them. Theresa looked a little winded.

"They think the same way I do," Cecilia assured her daughter. Turning toward Chris, Cecilia made the introductions before Jewel could. "Chris, Joel," she smiled again at the boy, "these are my very dear best friends, Maizie Sommers and Theresa Manetti."

"Otherwise known as the Greek Chorus," Jewel murmured under her breath. The affectionately voiced remark still earned her a sharp look from her mother.

Each woman shook hands with Chris and expressed her sorrow at his loss. They both included the boy as well, treating him with the same sort of compassion they would have shown to another grieving adult.

Father Gannon cleared his throat. When they looked in his direction, he said, "If I may continue."

"Of course, Father. Forgive the interruption," Theresa apologized for all of them, stepping back beside Maizie.

Rather than stand by her daughter, Cecilia chose to stand on the other side of Chris, the latter and Jewel flanking Joel.

"Anyone else coming?" Father Gannon asked.

Chris raised a quizzical eyebrow in her direction. When she shook her head, he said, "No, no one else."

"All right then," Father Gannon said, and resumed the service.

It was over almost immediately, even though Father Gannon added several more prayers for Rita's soul.

Scanning the outlying area one last time, Jewel glanced down at the boy at her side. It seemed to her that Joel remained amazingly dry-eyed. He hadn't brushed away or shed a single tear from the moment the service began. By contrast, she noticed that her mother sniffled a couple of times into her handkerchief and Theresa was struggling to keep from sobbing. As was Maizie.

All of them, Jewel felt certain, were remembering other, far more personal funerals. Each woman had buried a husband years before she thought she would ever have to. Funerals brought that kind of haunting emptiness back. It was to each woman's credit that she had come out to give a small boy comfort.

Even Culhane, who appeared to have steeled himself against what was going on, had eyes that shone with tears he just barely managed to keep from falling.

Only the boy remained stoic throughout the entire brief ceremony. It was almost eerie, Jewel thought. She was tempted to ask Joel why he wasn't crying, but she refrained.

The service completed, Father Gannon, a large hulk of a man, shyly made his apologies. "I would stay longer, but there is a baptism I must get to."

Chris nodded his head. "A far happier occasion," he agreed as he slipped the priest an envelope with a check for his trouble.

Pocketing the envelope, Father Gannon hesitated a moment longer. He looked from the man to the boy. "If either of you find that you need to talk…" Handing Chris a small card with both his cell number and the church's phone number on it, Father Gannon allowed his voice to trail off.

Chris dutifully pocketed the card without looking at it. It could have been the business card for a local arcade for all he knew.

"Thank you, but that won't be necessary," Chris assured him.

Cecilia backed up his statement by saying, "He and Joel won't be alone, Father."

Jewel gave her a dark look, praying that Culhane took that as an offer on her mother's part to serve as a compassionate ear. She, on the other hand, knew exactly what her mother meant. She was offering *Jewel's* services. The matchmaker in her mother never died, never rested. Instead, it had gone into overdrive now that Nikki and Kate had "found their soul mates."

As if such a thing really existed.

She'd tailed enough cheating spouses to know that the opposite was far more likely to be true. More than 50 percent of all marriages were doomed from the start. She sincerely prayed that Nikki and Kate would be luckier than most people in their choices.

Father Gannon took his leave and Jewel made a final sweep of the immediate area. The man she was looking for was still nowhere in sight. Either from lack of knowledge, or for some other, more complex reason, Ray Johnson hadn't shown up to pay his last respects to the mother of his son.

Placing his hand on Joel's shoulder to guide the boy out of the cemetery, Chris turned to the trio of older women. "Ladies, I'd like to thank you for coming here today—" He got no further.

"Oh, but we're not leaving you and Joel just yet," Cecilia informed him. There was just the appropriate touch of cheerfulness in her voice. Not so much that it detracted from the solemn occasion, but just enough to indicate that things *did* have a way of getting better.

"I brought food," Theresa volunteered. "We can set it up once we get to your house."

Chris had no idea what to make of these women, two of whom had been complete strangers before today. There was no reason for them, or for the woman whose cleaning company had worked a miracle on Rita's house, to put themselves out like this. He was nothing to them and neither were Joel or Rita. He liked things that made sense and this didn't.

But there was no denying that, along with the confusion, their actions did generate a measure of warmth within him.

Still, he felt he had to protest, even though he sensed that it was futile. "You really didn't have to go out of your way like this."

Jewel felt obligated to intercede. She'd grown up regarding her mother's two best friends as her aunts and, in a great many ways, they were closer than real family. She also knew the way their minds worked—all of their minds. It was only after she, Nikki and Kate had graduated from high school that she came to realize that these kindly faces hid three very devious minds. Each woman was bound and determined to see her daughter and her friends' daughters blissfully wedded with 2.5 children and a white picket fence—and the sooner the better.

Since Nikki and Kate were now, according to the old-fashioned phrase, "spoken for," Jewel was the only holdout, if she didn't count Theresa's son, Kate's brother. She had secretly hoped that they would focus on Kullen because he was older than she was, but apparently age in male years was not the same as age in female years. Consequently, she had become the target of choice.

Well, not today, Jewel thought stubbornly. *And not here.*

"It's what she does," she told Chris. "Theresa runs a catering service. And Maizie," she added, nodding toward the most animated of the threesome, "is a Realtor. If you decide, down the line," she added expressly for Joel's sake, "to sell either your house or your sister's, she'd be the one to see. She's very good at what she does." Her eyes swept over the three women. "They all are."

"We didn't come to talk business," Cecilia quickly interjected, as if to blot out the effect of her daughter's words. She looked pointedly at Chris. "We came to help any way we can."

Jewel knew that she meant it. "No use fighting it," she advised her client. "Just let them feed you and fuss over you and Joel a little. Otherwise, they'll stay here until you do. They're very stubborn that way. Trust me, I know."

"Sounds like good advice to me." The edges of his mouth curved ever so slightly.

He did appreciate what Cecilia and the other women were trying to do. And if they came over to the house, that meant that he wouldn't have to be alone with the boy. It had been four days since he'd been summoned to the hospital by the police, four days in which he'd been with the boy and he still had no idea what to say, what to do with Joel or how to behave around him. Women were better at this sort of thing, he thought. Even the private investigator he'd hired was better at forming a connection with his nephew than he was.

Added to that, he had to admit that the lack of any sort of display of grief on the boy's part did disturb him.

"Why don't you ride in my car with me and the other ladies?" Cecilia suggested, looking down at Joel. "I'm not sure I remember exactly where your house is. I need someone to give me directions. Can you do that for me, Joel?"

Joel took his cue like a pro and nodded his head. "Okay."

It was a ruse, Jewel thought, suppressing her annoyance. Her mother was deliberately arranging it so that she and Culhane wound up alone in her car. Her mother didn't need directions, she had a natural, uncanny sense of direction. In addition to which, she also had a GPS mounted on her dashboard that provided alternate routes in case of any traffic snarls or whimsical acts of God and/or nature.

But Jewel knew that she couldn't very well come out and say that. Especially after her mother had successfully convinced Joel to switch vehicles.

It's a car, Mom, not a deserted island. Being alone with the man for ten minutes isn't going to make him want to live happily ever after with me. Or me with him. Especially since there is no such thing.

But she wouldn't mind sleeping with the man, she realized as she stole a glance at the broad shoulders and chiseled, square chin. *After* she located his brother-in-law and closed the case, she silently emphasized.

Squaring her own shoulders, Jewel led the way to her car.

She marched like a soldier, Chris noted, aware of the cadence of her footsteps. He caught himself wondering about her, some of his curiosity, he silently admitted, raised because of the appearance of the other women.

His had been a family in turmoil, more dedicated to shouting at one another and slamming doors to show their displeasure. His parents, he knew, were good people. They just weren't good parents. He supposed he should count himself lucky that he'd turned out the way he had. But why him and not Rita?

Why couldn't he have helped Rita?

At the very least, he should have stopped her from marrying Ray, a move that was, in his eyes, the beginning of the end for her.

Buckling up, Chris glanced at the private investigator he was counting on to help him reclaim his orderly life. He waited until she'd pulled out of the parking space and was weaving her way onto the main road before he said anything. "He wasn't there."

Jewel didn't have to ask. She knew Culhane was referring to his ex-brother-in-law. "Not that I could see, no."

Impatience foiled his ability to stifle a sigh. "Now what?"

Jewel was watching her mother, who was up ahead. After all these years, the woman still drove with a lead foot. You'd think that she would have learned to slow down a bit, be more careful. People complained about older drivers behaving as if they had molasses in their veins. Her mother drove as if she were in training for the Indy 500.

"Now I'll see if I can find out anything from his former employer at that garage you mentioned, the one where your sister first met her ex. Who knows? Maybe the guy stayed in touch with Ray, or gave him a referral when he went looking for another job."

"Another job?" His tone told her he thought that was reaching.

"Man's gotta eat and pay his bills."

Ray had probably found another woman to take advantage of. That was what he was good at. Survival—and falling through the cracks. "And if that doesn't pan out?"

"There are other ways to go," she assured him, deliberately keeping her words vague.

She half expected him to ask her to elaborate. When he didn't, she took a split second to glance in his direction. He was clearly preoccupied. It didn't take much to guess at what was on his mind. She'd seen him watching Joel at the service and the cemetery. The boy's behavior mystified him.

She could see it in their brief interaction at the cemetery. "Don't worry about it."

It took a second for her words to penetrate. When they did, he had no idea what she was referring to. "What?"

"I said don't worry about it," Jewel repeated. "Everyone deals with grief in his own way." She took a guess. "Maybe it's still not real to Joel. Maybe he still believes his mother will walk through the door." She shrugged. "Or maybe he thinks that it's not manly to cry." She glanced at him again just before she made a right turn. "You didn't cry," she reminded him quietly.

She noticed that Culhane squared his shoulders. Was he being defensive, or had she struck a raw nerve? "I don't believe in displaying emotions in public."

Although part of her wanted to explore that a bit further, Jewel let it drop. "Maybe Joel feels the same way."

"He's five," Chris pointed out, emphasizing his age.

That had nothing to do with it. "And he's looking to the only male role model he has."

"Me?" Chris asked incredulously. They'd only been together for four days. People didn't form attachments in four days.

But, obviously, his private investigator saw it differently. "You," Jewel confirmed.

Chris snorted. "You're wrong. The last time I saw Joel, he was two years old. How can I be his role model? He has no memory of me."

"Maybe, maybe not. I can remember something that my mother tells me happened when I was only eighteen months old."

Now she was just making things up. If this was the way her mind worked, maybe he'd been a little too hasty in hiring her. "That's not possible."

"The brain is a very strange organ," Jewel informed him. She pressed down on the accelerator.

Her mother was pulling farther and farther away. "Everything that's ever happened to us, every song we've heard, everything we've ever seen, is imprinted there somewhere." She shouldn't have to be telling him this. "You're a scientist, you should know that."

"Not exactly my field of expertise," he countered. Chris took a breath, reconsidering her argument. It seemed almost impossible. "So you think he's trying to imitate me?"

"He's trying to be a man, and you're the closest role model he has. You heard him—he has no friends. Consequently, there are no fathers in his life, no one to take cues from." She smiled, turning down another block. "Until you came along."

"Four days ago," he emphasized again.

"The length of time doesn't matter," she insisted. "You saw him. You're here now and he absorbs things like a sponge."

"So you're telling me that if I cry, then Joel will cry?"

His was the voice of disbelief, she thought. You could lead a horse to water, but getting him to drink was a completely different matter. "Maybe."

"Well, I'm not crying," he told her firmly. He couldn't. If he let his guard down for one second, if he started to remember...

There was nothing to be gained from that, he silently insisted.

"No one's telling you to."

The hell she wasn't, he thought. "Rita knew what she was doing. Knew that she was throwing her life away. Turning her back on her education, on every-thing our parents wanted for her—" That was prob-ably part of the reason she'd turned her back on it, he thought.

The mention of the senior pair brought up more questions in Jewel's mind. "Where are your parents?"

"They're dead," he said matter-of-factly. "My fa-ther was literally hit by a Mack truck and I think my mother just died of a broken heart six months later. She felt as if she had nothing to live for. They argued a lot, but they loved each other."

That didn't make any sense to her. Her mother had been distressed when her father had died, but she never lost her focus as a mother.

"But Rita was still alive," Jewel argued.

He lifted a shoulder in a vague half shrug. "In a manner of speaking. I wasn't the only one Rita cut ties with. She didn't like to have to sit through lec-tures."

Who did? Jewel thought. "I'm sorry."

The last thing he wanted was pity. "There's no reason for you to be sorry," he told her.

She looked at him for a long moment. They'd ar-rived at his late sister's house and she still had to park, but this took precedence over that. "If you think that," she told him, "then I'm even sorrier."

Chapter 5

The moment Maizie, Theresa and Cecilia walked into the house that had known very little laughter and joy in the past several years, the three women did what had come naturally to them all their lives: they took control.

As Jewel stood back and watched, these power-houses in three-inch heels took charge not just of the space, but of the boy and his uncle, as well.

Resistance is futile, she thought with barely hidden amusement. She wondered if either, especially Culhane, knew that they never stood a ghost of a chance. Deceptively petite and innocent looks to the contrary, the ladies were formidable forces to be reckoned with. She knew that firsthand.

While Theresa served the food she'd prepared

for the occasion, Jewel saw her mother moving about, straightening whatever had somehow gotten out of place since the last time she had been here. That left Maizie to entertain Joel, something she did with aplomb. The fact that Nikki's mother had been a grandmother-in-training from the moment her daughter had graduated from medical school certainly didn't hurt.

That left Jewel with Culhane.

Just the way she knew her mother and the two women her mother had shared her innermost secrets with since the third grade wanted it.

Too bad this isn't going to go anywhere, ladies, she thought. The man was charmingly unaware of his seductive sensuality, which was an excellent—not to mention rare—quality, but she got the impression that he wasn't in the market for a relationship, and God knew that she wasn't. A memorable night of torrid sex, sure, but a lasting relationship? That was like pursuing a unicorn. It was a mythical thing that didn't exist except in fairy tales and dreams.

"This really isn't necessary," Chris was protesting again as Theresa handed him a plate of food she'd just put together.

Behind the women were an array of casserole dishes and warming trays filled to capacity, which might easily have fed a small village if the occasion arose. Theresa had never believed that the words *food* and *moderation* belonged in the same sentence. Or the same room.

"Don't protest," Jewel advised, accepting her own

plate from Kate's mother. "It won't do you any good and besides, it keeps them busy and off the streets."

She glanced about the room, now so neat it almost hurt. Maizie was cheering Joel on as he played his video game—Jewel had insisted that he keep hers so that he could practice. And because she had run out of things to tidy, her mother was now rinsing off the serving spoons despite the fact that they all knew they were going to be used again almost immediately.

"Somewhere," Jewel commented with a shake of her head, "Donna Reed is looking down and smiling."

Her mother's eyes narrowed as Cecilia focused in on her. "There's nothing wrong with dusting off old-fashioned skills, Jewel. Sometimes a person just needs a break from the fast-paced modern world." Cecilia turned toward Chris for backup. The narrowed eyes were gone, replaced with a wide, warm smile. "Don't you agree, Chris?"

Engrossed in the process of having a piece of prime rib melt away on his tongue, Chris was momentarily distracted. When he saw Cecilia looking at him, he realized that she'd asked him a question and he had missed it completely. "Excuse me?"

Jewel came to his rescue. He might be a learned college professor, but he wasn't a match for a card-carrying member of the triumvirate.

"Mom, he's just taken a bite of Theresa's prime rib. The man'll agree to anything," Jewel pointed out. She grinned at Chris, waving him on. "Never mind, just eat. My mother was just advancing one of her favorite theories."

Over in the corner, their eyes on the small screen in the boy's hands, both Maizie and Joel suddenly cheered. Joel had defeated the alien force and made the world safe for humanity once again.

Maizie was the louder of the two.

"This is a very sharp young man," Maizie announced, congratulating Chris. She looked at her companion. "What grade did you say you were in? Because I think you'll be ready for high school the day after tomorrow."

"I'm not in a grade," Joel told her simply.

"You're not?" Maizie asked incredulously. She looked at him, confused. "How's that possible?"

"Because I'm not in school," Joel answered. There was a touch of self-consciousness to his reply, as if he now realized that this wasn't right.

There was a skeptical expression on Maizie's face when she looked over toward Jewel and the boy's uncle. "He's not in school?"

"No," Jewel answered before Chris could. She didn't want the man being badgered, and whether they knew it or not, the triumvirate had a tendency to badger. "But that's being handled."

Maizie looked relieved. "You've enrolled him?" she asked Chris.

"Not yet," he admitted.

"Has he had his—inoculations?" Maizie changed terms at the last moment. Because her daughter was a pediatrician, Maizie was more up than most on certain requirements that school-aged children had to meet before they were even allowed to register.

But Joel was not content to let the world roll

right over him. He had questions. Especially when things pertained to him. "What's in-noc-ulations?" he wanted to know.

Jewel sensed that sugarcoating it would only earn his distrust once he found out what the word meant. So she gave him the truth.

"Shots," she told him despite her mother waving her hand behind the boy's back to make her stop. "You go to the doctor and he or she gives them to you to keep you healthy."

Instead of displaying fear, the way Maizie and the other women clearly anticipated, the boy merely shook his head. "Not me."

She made a guess as to his meaning. "You've never had a shot?"

Joel shook his head again, his bangs sweeping back and forth across his forehead from the force of his denial. "I never went to the doctor."

"You must have been one very healthy boy," Cecilia commented in surprise.

Joel shrugged, as if he really didn't know if that was the case, one way or another. "Mama said I could get well by myself."

The three older women exchanged looks tinged with sadness that there were mothers out there who were only focused on themselves and consequently hardly paid the least attention when it came to their children's welfare.

However, it was Chris who voiced their collective concern out loud. He couldn't believe what he was hearing. "Your mom *never* took you to a doctor?"

Joel looked as if he didn't understand what all the

fuss was about. He'd never known any other life but
the one he'd led, causing him to believe that this was
how things were done.

"No."

Chris could feel his temper rising. Apparently,
the loving, caring sister he'd known had died not the
other day but a very long time ago.

"Ever?" he pressed.

"No." Joel fidgeted, sensing his uncle's barely
contained displeasure. "Don't get mad at her, Uncle
Chris. I was okay," he insisted.

"He's not mad, honey." Standing up, Jewel crossed
to the boy and put her arm around his shoulders.
"He's just concerned about you, that's all."

"I can call Nikki," Maizie volunteered. "I think
she can find out if Joel's ever received any of his
required immunizations. There's some database or
something they can access for that," she explained
with a careless wave of her hand. "I'm sure she can
see him tomorrow," the woman added brightly.

"Who's Nikki?" Chris wanted to know.

"Maizie's daughter," Theresa volunteered.

"And an excellent pediatrician," Maizie interjected with pride.

"Tomorrow's Saturday," Jewel pointed out. They
probably wouldn't be able to get things moving until Monday.

But Maizie was undaunted. "Doesn't matter.
Nikki'll see him," she promised with confidence.
"She owes me. I gave her life. I'll call her and let her
know what's up so she can get started," Maizie said,
taking out her cell phone.

Because she sensed his bewilderment, Jewel looked over toward Chris. She was right. He was wearing a mystified expression. The threesome took a lot of getting used to once they got going. They certainly could be overwhelming at times.

Her eyes met his. "They all think like this," she explained. "It comes naturally to them. They're über-mothers to the nth degree."

He glanced in Joel's direction. Now it was the woman who had brought all the food—Theresa he thought her name was—who was fussing over the boy. And the poor kid was lapping it up like some flower someone forgot to water for a very long time.

Chris's heart went out to the boy. "Über-mother," he repeated almost to himself. "That's not such a bad thing."

She could only laugh and shake her head. The man was a newbie. "You say that now. Try living with it for a while, *then* come back to me."

Belatedly, Jewel realized how the last part of her sentence sounded—as if it were an open invitation to Culhane, or at least an assumption that they were going to have an ongoing relationship rather than just a one-time client-investigator interaction. That was *not* what she was trying to convey.

Because she didn't know how to backtrack gracefully without being obvious or sticking her other foot in her mouth, Jewel took the only option that was left to her—she changed the subject.

"Maizie's daughter is a great pediatrician. If anyone can get Joel's chart up-to-date, she can," she promised Chris enthusiastically. "That way, there'll be no problem getting him registered for school. You can have him in a kindergarten class in a week, if not less," she concluded.

Chris looked from Jewel to the triumvirate and then back again. "Which one?" he wanted to know. His world revolved around the university. He hadn't a clue when it came to elementary schools in the area. "Which school do I take him to?"

The question sounded deceptively simple. At first. "The one closest to the house," Jewel told him. "Maizie is very good at knowing which neighborhood is in what school district." The information she was giving him didn't seem to enlighten Chris. The thoughtful frown remained and deepened just a little. "What's wrong?"

The woman was missing a very basic point, he thought. "If you don't find Ray in the next few days, which address do we use for Joel?"

To her, that was a minor point. There weren't *that* many elementary schools in Bedford. It was a very desirable place to live, but in comparison to many of the surrounding cities, it was still in its infancy. "Didn't you say you lived nearby?"

"Not all that nearby," Chris confessed.

And he had no idea if his house and his late sister's were even in the same school district. He had a feeling that they probably weren't. Nothing was ever simple when it came to Rita, he thought.

He lowered his voice, as if to spare Joel from hearing this. But the boy had stopped what he was doing and placed the handheld console on the coffee table. He was very aware that he had become the topic of conversation and was intently listening to his fate being bandied about.

"Staying here for a few days to help Joel deal with this situation is one thing," Chris was saying, "but all my reference books, my notes for my research, all that's over at my house."

Jewel didn't see any of this as a problem. The situation was fluid. The main thing was to get the boy into a school where he could take his first steps toward a formal education.

"All right, why don't you use that as Joel's address for the time being?" she suggested, then flashed the boy an encouraging smile. "When I locate his father, things can be adjusted."

She'd counted on support from her mother and the other two women. She'd forgotten how unpredictable they could be.

"Uprooting the boy so much won't be good for him," Theresa said quietly.

Jewel was about to protest that it wouldn't be for that long, but Chris had already turned toward the woman and asked, "What do you suggest?"

"Since your intent is to find the boy's father, and he'll likely move back in, why don't you use this house as an address?" Cecilia suggested.

Drawn into the discussion, Maizie temporarily shut her cell phone as she raised another point. "What if Jewel can't find his father?"

Cecilia frowned at the mere suggestion that could happen. "Jewel could find an angel's shadow if she had to."

"Luckily, I don't have to," Jewel murmured under

her breath, then turned toward Chris, covering her embarrassment with a quip. "My mother's just the tiniest bit prejudiced."

Rather than agree, or laugh, Chris surprised her by saying, "Hey, enjoy it while you have it." It earned him the approval not only of Theresa, but of all three of the women. Despite their thriving careers, all three were first and foremost mothers.

Cecilia beamed and patted Chris on the shoulder. "I knew I liked this young man the minute I saw him."

But Maizie had another wrench to throw into the plans. "What if Jewel finds him and he doesn't want to move back into this house? What if the man wants to take Joel to live with him instead of the other way around? He's got to be living somewhere," she pointed out.

This was getting out of control, Jewel thought. She held up her hands as if to physically stem the flow of words.

"Stop, stop," she pleaded. When the growing noise level died down, she addressed her suggestion not to any of the three women, but to Chris. After all, the decision, no matter how long they debated it, was ultimately his. "For now, why don't we just register Joel in this school district? That way, he can meet some of the kids in the neighborhood. If things change, we'll deal with them then."

She realized her mistake the minute the words were out. She'd said *we*.

She'd just injected herself into the mix. While she did work closely with any clients she took on and checked in with them regularly, once a case was over, so, for the most part, was the contact. In this particular case, she didn't want to inadvertently make her mother think that there was any sort of a match being struck here in the long run—or even the short run.

"I mean, *they'll* deal with them then," she deliberately corrected herself. She avoided looking at Culhane, afraid of what she might see in his eyes. Amusement, surprise or apprehension—none of it was something she would have moved into the "win" column.

It was Maizie who finally broke the silence and gave Jewel's idea the seal of approval.

"Sounds like a plan to me," she agreed. Holding up her still-dormant cell phone, she said, "I'll make that phone call now." There was a sliver of a question in her voice as she once again opened up the phone. She glanced at Chris to see if he concurred.

Feeling somewhat at loose ends, he nodded.

Maizie moved toward the kitchen, punching in the numbers that would connect her directly to her daughter no matter where she was.

Looking bewildered, Joel tugged on the hem of Jewel's blouse. "What's happening?"

He'd gotten overwhelmed, she thought. *Welcome to the club, kid.* It took effort not to get lost in the verbal back-and-forth pitches.

"Well, it looks like the short of it is we'll be getting you some friends," she told him.

Because that would be where, hopefully, this project would end: with his enrolling in kindergarten and making friends with at least a few children in the class. To her, that was more important than what address he used.

Her words did not get the reaction she'd hoped for. Joel looked upset. "I don't need any friends," he told her.

"Everyone needs friends," she told him kindly.

Jewel knew that the boy was probably afraid, and she could understand that. Being the "new kid" anywhere was an uncomfortable feeling. It was worse when you were a kid—even a brilliant kid.

As she made her pronouncement, she couldn't help glancing in Chris's direction. She had a feeling that, despite his kneecap-melting good looks, Christopher Culhane was a bit of a loner himself.

"Hey, wait, I *do* have friends," Joel told her suddenly.

This was a complete 180-degree change from a couple of minutes ago. She didn't picture the boy as someone who would deliberately tell a lie—especially one that was so blatant and easily disproved.

"You do? Who?" she wanted to know.

Joel never hesitated. Instead, he looked very solemn as he made the revelation. "You. And the nice ladies here."

Damn, but he was good, she thought. This time, she gave in and affectionately ran her fingers through his hair. She was pleased that he didn't flinch or pull back. "That's very sweet, Joel, but we're all adults, honey."

That response only confused him. "I can only be friends with kids?"

She knew that sounded way too confining to him.

Plus she had a feeling that, given his maturity level, Joel was probably currently stuck somewhere between the world of adults and the world of children. An unfortunate outsider to both. He was most likely safer among adults. They might ignore him or dismiss him, the way his mother probably had, but at least adults wouldn't ridicule him the way kids did with someone who was different.

Still, the longer that was put off, the harder it would be for Joel to blend in, even a little.

"Of course not," Chris told him firmly. "You can be friends with adults."

The way the man said it reaffirmed her suspicions that he had experienced the same sort of situation when he was Joel's age.

"Your uncle's right. You can be friends with anyone you want," she assured the boy.

Joel's eyes met hers. "So you're my friend?"

She saw that Chris was about to say something that would relieve her of this responsibility, but she answered faster.

"You betcha." She flashed him a grin and put her arm around the slight shoulders. "I'd be honored to be your friend, Joel."

She was rewarded with a bright, sunny smile.

"It's all set," Maizie announced as she shut her cell phone and crossed back to the others. Her eyes swept over both Chris and Jewel. "Nikki can see Joel in her office tomorrow morning at ten. She'll give him a physical and any immunizations that he hasn't had yet."

The boy's bright, sunny smile faded.

Chapter 6

Jewel had no intentions of accompanying Chris and his nephew to Nikki's office. She didn't want either of them, especially Chris, to feel as if she were pushing her way into their inner space. But just as she was about to leave her apartment that morning to attempt to track down Ray Johnson's former employer, her cell phone rang.

Putting down her keys, she fished her phone out of her pocket and glanced at the caller ID. It said "Private," which meant that it could have been anyone. The wide field ran from her mother's landline all the way to various political volunteers begging for contributions in order to keep their party strong.

Though the temptation to ignore the call was great, given her line of work, Jewel really didn't have that luxury. You never knew when another client might be calling—or an anonymous tip might be coming in. She already had several feelers out regarding her present case.

The first thing that had come to her attention was that there were over 653 Ray Johnsons in the country, with more than 220 of them in California. And those were only the ones who were listed. She was sure the number was at least double that amount.

But only one of them was Joel's father.

She had her work cut out for her.

Suppressing a sigh, Jewel flipped her phone open. "Hello?"

"Jewel?" A deep male voice rumbled against her ear. She realized that her hold on the phone had tightened in response. "This is Christopher Culhane. I hate bothering you…"

Ah, if you only knew… The man bothered her in ways he undoubtedly didn't suspect, but she wasn't about to let him know that.

Instead, she cheerfully reminded him, "You're the client, which means that you're paying for the privilege of bothering me anytime you need to." Maybe he'd remembered something that would help her locate his ex-brother-in-law. "So, what can I do for you?"

His answer had nothing to do with finding Ray. "Joel says he doesn't want to go to the doctor."

He'd struck her as a man who was in control of the situation—as long as the situation involved adults. This was something else again. He hadn't a clue when it came to dealing with someone under five feet tall.

Okay, she could be sympathetic, Jewel thought.

"Kids usually don't," she told him. There was a pause on the other end of the line. A very pregnant pause. Like he was trying to find the right way to ask and not be blunt. Taking pity on him, she decided to bail him out. "Would you like me to go with you? I could meet you at Nikki's office."

The relief she heard in the man's voice told her she'd guessed right. But apparently he still had a problem.

"I'm not sure he'll believe me if I tell him you'll be there." He lowered his voice, leading her to assume that Joel was within earshot. "I get the feeling that my sister broke most of her promises to him. He's not overly trusting."

Once shattered, trust was a hard thing to rebuild. If the most important person in his life didn't keep her word, how could he think that anyone else would? She could see where the boy was coming from, even as she sympathized with Chris's problem.

"Put Joel on the phone, Chris," she requested. "I'll talk to him." The next moment, she heard the sounds of the phone being shifted and handed over.

"Hello?" a small voice said hesitantly.

She kept her own voice cheery. "Hi, Joel. It's Jewel. What's this I hear about you not wanting to go to the doctor this morning?"

"I'm okay, Jewel," the boy insisted. "I don't need a doctor."

Poor kid. He probably thinks he's going to be tortured. "We talked about this, remember? You need to get certain shots before you can go to school. It's to keep you from catching some pretty nasty stuff."

Joel had a counterargument. "I won't catch anything if I don't go to school."

That was fast. "And waste that brilliant lawyerlike mind of yours? No way. C'mon, Joel," she coaxed. "Don't tell me a big, strong guy like you is afraid of an itty, bitty needle."

"I'm not afraid of a needle," he told her with feeling. "I'm afraid of having it stuck into me."

Wow, she thought. *This kid could be president by the time he's twelve.* Jewel looked at her watch. It was getting late. According to Maizie, Nikki had said she'd meet the boy and his uncle at her office at ten. They needed to hit the road. Soon.

"Tell you what. I'll be by in a few minutes and take you and your uncle Chris to the doctor. Dr. Connors is coming in just for you, Joel," she reminded the boy, thinking of the manners he'd displayed. She played on that. "It wouldn't be nice if you didn't show up. You don't want her to come all that way on a Saturday for no reason, do you?"

She heard the boy's deep sigh. "No, ma'am."

"Atta boy," she declared, grinning. "I'll be right there."

Joel and Chris were waiting for her in the driveway when she pulled up. Chris definitely looked relieved and the moment he saw her, Joel's face lit up like a decked-out Christmas tree.

It didn't take much for her to realize that although he might have needed a male role model, the boy was simply starved for female attention. That was one of the reasons he'd responded so well to her mother and her mother's friends. With his own mother gone,

Joel had no one to fill that emptiness and he was at loose ends.

If she was given to thinking with her head instead of her heart in situations like this, she would have wondered if perhaps she was doing more harm than good, interfering with the potential bonding process between Joel and his uncle.

But all she knew was that when the little boy's face lit up like that just because he saw her, something reacted inside her in response, a warmth that spread all through her.

She knew her mother would have had some comment about that being her biological alarm clock going off, but she knew it couldn't be that. She liked kids but she'd never experienced that overwhelming desire to have any of her own. Or a husband for that matter.

It was only human to respond to someone who looked that happy to see you, she silently argued. There was no ticking clock involved.

"Hi!" Joel cried, running up to the car, his dark eyes dancing.

"Hi, yourself," she laughed as he opened the door and scrambled into the backseat.

A child his size was supposed to ride in the rear passenger seat, but she was surprised that Joel hadn't tried to sit up front with her. The little boy's capacity for self-discipline, not to mention the extent of the things he seemed to know, just kept on surprising her.

"Sorry to put you out like this," Chris apologized as he got in on the front passenger side.

"Just all part of the service," she assured him cheerfully.

"Really?" he asked. Since he'd never had the need to hire a private investigator before, he had no idea what the job description actually entailed.

Her grin told him that she was kidding. It also, he became aware, evoked an entirely different response from him than he was prepared for. He forced his mind to focus on the business at hand: getting his nephew to the pediatrician for his immunizations.

"I'm making this up as I go along," Jewel admitted. "But so far, it seems to be working out," she told him. Her foot still on the brake, she turned to look in the backseat. "All buckled up?" she asked Joel.

"Yes, ma'am."

She nodded her approval, then glanced to her right. "You, too, Uncle Chris. We're not moving until you have your seat belt on."

It had completely slipped his mind. As he reached for the seat belt, he realized that he was reaching in the wrong direction. Switching hands, he tugged on the seat belt until it was secured around him.

"Not used to riding shotgun?" she guessed, hiding her amusement.

"What?" The term caught him off guard for a moment. "Oh, no, no I'm not. I'm usually driving," Chris explained.

"Would it make you feel more comfortable if you drove to the doctor's office?" Foot still on the brake, she lifted her hands from the wheel to indicate that she didn't mind letting him take over.

It was on the tip of his tongue to say yes, but then, because she'd offered, Chris refrained. He didn't want her to think that he was one of those macho types who needed to pound his chest every fifteen minutes or so just to prove how virile he was. Why he should care what she thought of him was something that he didn't pause to explore. Things were complicated enough already.

"No, that's okay," he told her. "I'm fine with you driving. Besides, you're the one who knows the way."

They weren't exactly traveling to a secret lair, she thought, pressing her lips together to suppress an amused grin. "It's the medical building in Fashion Island."

To her surprise, Chris shook his head. "Afraid I'm not familiar with the area."

It hadn't occurred to Jewel that *anyone* who lived in Southern California was unfamiliar with Fashion Island in Newport Beach. It had been around for *years*. Each year at Christmastime, the merchants outdid themselves when it came to decorating, trying to top the year before. She could remember her parents bringing her there to see it all when she was a little girl. It had become a tradition that she and her mother continued even after her father had passed away. She was extremely sentimental about the area.

"Were you born here?" she asked, curious.

"Here?" Chris echoed.

"In Southern California," she elaborated.

He realized what she was getting at. He didn't get around much. His work ate up his time. "I'm a native," he told her. "But I'm afraid I never had much time for malls and those kinds of places."

She found that almost impossible to believe. "Even as a kid?"

"Especially as a kid," he countered with a dry

laugh. He tried to picture his parents chauffeuring him, as he heard that parents did these days with their kids. He drew a blank. "I had no way to get there."

She was about to say that his parents were supposed to be the ones who brought him to the mall as a kid, but the point he was making penetrated. She was beginning to understand why his late sister had such poor self-esteem. And why she hadn't been that much of a mother herself. Rita Johnson lacked role models. Chris and Rita's parents obviously never spent much time with them.

It made her wonder why some people ever became parents at all. It wasn't as if there were no birth control available, or, barring that, no adoption agencies eager to place healthy babies.

Not wanting to press the issue, or possibly open up old wounds, she deliberately changed the subject and looked fleetingly over her shoulder at Joel. Apparently lost in thought, his expression was pensive.

"You'll like Dr. Nikki," she assured him. "She's one of my two very best friends, and she just loves kids."

Joel pressed his lips together grimly and barely nodded. His eyes were wide as he looked around, taking in the scenery. They were traveling down MacArthur Boulevard. The road ahead dipped down, allowing drivers to see the Pacific Ocean in the distance. It was a cloudless, sparkling morning and Catalina, looking like a whale sunning itself, was clearly visible.

Jewel made a left into a parking lot. They had arrived.

Unlike weekdays at this time, there were an infinite number of parking spaces for her to choose from. Only a handful of cars were in the lot, belonging to either physicians or dentists who kept Saturday hours and their patients.

Getting out of the vehicle, Jewel opened the rear door on Joel's side. "Ready?"

Taking a deep breath, and then another when the first one didn't seem to help, Joel nodded. He looked like someone about to walk to his own execution.

"Ready," he said in a voice that squeaked.

Jewel pretended not to notice as she put her hand out to him. "Then let's go and get this over with," she said cheerfully.

"Over with," Joel echoed, nodding vigorously.

Instead of walking abreast of them, Chris fell back and brought up the rear.

She looked natural with his nephew, he thought. Maybe, if his ex-brother-in-law continued to be missing after, say, a month, some kind of an arrangement could be made with this woman to look after the boy. Given the way she got along with Joel, maybe she might even consider becoming his guardian. As he observed the two of them, it was obvious to him that Joel seemed to be a lot happier and more open around Jewel than around him.

Which was fine, Chris silently argued as they got on the elevator. He could see why Joel liked her. She was effervescent, bubbly, while he…well, he was more like orange juice. Healthy, stable, but definitely not bubbly.

Because there was no one else to get on or off,

the elevator came to its destination almost a second after they'd gotten on.

"Follow me," Jewel said, and she led the way to the doctor's office.

Not much of a hardship there, Chris thought.

Nikki opened the door herself when Jewel knocked. The honey-blonde looked from Jewel to the two people with her. She nodded a greeting at Chris, but her attention was focused on the small boy standing beside him.

Nikki's bright, electric smile materialized the moment she made eye contact with Joel. "This must be my new patient," she said warmly. Placing one hand on his shoulder, she ushered him in. "I've heard good things about you, Joel."

"You have?" he asked incredulously, his eyes wide.

"I have," she confirmed. "Why don't you and I and your uncle step into Exam Room 1 and we can get all this technical stuff out of the way. After that, if you'd like to ask me some questions, or just talk, I'm all yours."

"Can Jewel come, too?" Joel wanted to know. It was then that Nikki noticed the boy was still clutching on to Jewel's hand tightly.

"I think we might have enough room for her," Nikki answered with a smile. "Let's go in and find out." Turning, she led the way through the empty waiting room to the door that admitted them into the exam area.

"Your friend's just like you," Chris commented, lowering his head to Jewel's ear as he walked behind all of them.

Jewel was fairly certain that he didn't realize it, but when he spoke just now, his breath feathered along the side of her neck. It instantly created a warm shiver up and down her spine, which took considerable effort to stifle. At least from being outwardly visible.

Inwardly was a different matter. It spread its tentacles all through her, leaving no part of her unaffected.

It had been a long while in between men, she thought. Though she told herself that all she was after was earthshaking, mind-blowing sex, down deep she knew she still had to feel something—respect, admiration, a more than passing attraction, *something*—for the men she went to bed with.

For one reason or another, it had been a long time since she'd "felt" anything at all.

That certainly wasn't the case now.

Jewel cleared her throat before responding. "I take that as a compliment," she told Chris. The man would never know how much effort it took to sound so nonchalant and unaffected, she thought, quietly congratulating herself.

"Well, you passed with flying colors," Jewel told the boy some forty-five minutes later when the three of them were walking out of the eight-story building. "See, I told you that you would."

Glancing down at Joel, she saw the way the boy was looking at his left arm, the site of his inoculations. His expression seemed to indicate that he was deciding whether or not it hurt. He needed to be distracted. "I've got an idea," she said suddenly. "Why don't the three of us hit the ice cream parlor?" There were several outdoor places and shops geared toward confection and all the things that went with that. "My treat," she added, slanting a glance toward Chris and hoping to disarm any protests before they formed.

But Chris wasn't ready to take her up on her offer so quickly, even though he realized he'd been battling a rather intense attraction to her for the past forty-five minutes.

Or maybe because of it.

"We've inconvenienced you enough," he pointed out.

"Inconvenienced?" she echoed incredulously. "Seeing Joel is never an inconvenience," she told him, her eyes on the boy. "And when you add ice cream to that, well, there's just nothing better."

"You like ice cream?" Joel asked, surprised. Pleased.

"Like it?" she echoed. "Ice cream's my biggest weakness." Jewel grinned. "Never met a flavor I didn't like."

For his part, Joel looked as if he'd just fallen in love. "Really?"

Jewel traced an X over her breast and then held up her hand as if she were taking a solemn oath. "Absolutely."

It was only after the fact that she noticed that Chris was looking at the area where she'd traced the X. She felt herself growing warm despite the chill in the October air. Because of the medical complex's close proximity to the ocean, there was always a breeze.

"And after we get our cones, we can take a walk on the beach," she said. She was fairly certain that

Joel hadn't done any of these aimless things, things that should have been part of a Southern California boy's life at this stage.

"Beach?" Chris questioned as if she had just said they were going somewhere halfway around the world.

Possibly there were two people who'd had deprived childhoods, she amended. "Yes, beach. You know, water, sand, the occasional seagull flying by making screeching noises."

He had things to do and research to catch up on. This would just be idling time away. Yet something kept him from saying that. Instead, he asked, "Aren't we keeping you from something?"

She took his tone to mean he was afraid she was on the clock. "I'm not charging you for this," she told him.

"That's not what I meant," he replied. Things were beginning to feel even more jumbled than they already were. Edges that had been so sharp before he'd found himself rushing to Blair Memorial were now dull and blurred. "It's just that we've taken up too much of your time."

Jewel looked at him for a long moment, wondering what kind of things were going on in his head. She hadn't said anything to indicate that she felt put out or taxed by any of this. She could only assume that he was using it as a cover.

"I'll let you know when it's too much," she promised as they all climbed into the car. Jewel twisted around in her seat, looking at the boy sitting behind her. "Right now, I have this huge craving for an ice cream cone. How about you, Joel?" she wanted to know.

Joel pushed the metal tongue of his seat belt into the slot. "Yes, please," he replied.

That was all she wanted to hear. Jewel started up her vehicle. "Never could pass up sweet talk like that," she told her passengers with a grin.

To her surprise, Chris put his hand on the steering wheel, preventing her from pulling out of the parking space. She looked at the man quizzically, waiting.

"Only on one condition," he told her. His expression looked pretty somber.

"And that is?"

"I get to pay."

Her mouth curved then. She'd been prepared for something far more serious than a tug-of-war over the check.

"You're on," she answered.

"On what?" Joel wanted to know, confused.

On very shaky ground, apparently, Chris silently answered as the woman in the driver's seat said, "It's just an expression, honey. It means I'm taking him up on his suggestion."

"Oh."

Joel's curiosity might have been sated, but his was just taking hold, Chris thought as he stole another glance at the woman on his left. He had a feeling this was just the beginning.

The question remained—of what?

Chapter 7

"None for me," Chris demurred when they walked into the small, old-fashioned ice cream parlor that backed up onto the beach.

Possibly because it was still early, the shop was only filled with sunshine. The six tables were all empty.

Taking out his wallet, Chris pulled out a twenty and, reaching around Jewel, he placed it on the stainless-steel counter just in front of her. "But you go ahead and order anything you want."

Jewel turned around to look at him. The whole point of coming here was to get ice cream cones. For *all* of them. "When was the last time you had an ice cream cone?"

He didn't see what that had to do with anything. "I can't remember."

Jewel frowned. "Now that's just plain wrong," she told him. "I know you're not lactose intolerant because I saw you eat two slices of Theresa's cheesecake after the service." Theresa's cheesecakes were twice as rich as anything available on the open market. "If you can eat that, you can eat any dairy product." She turned back to the teenager behind the counter. "He'll have two scoops of rocky road, please."

In compliance, the teenager pushed two teeming scoops of rocky road onto a sugar cone. He carefully handed the creation to Jewel who in turn passed the cone on to Chris.

"Enjoy."

It wasn't a suggestion, it was a direct order.

Looking down at Joel, Jewel smiled encouragingly. "Okay, your turn. What'll you have?"

He thought for a moment. "Can I have two different kinds of scoops?"

"Absolutely," she guaranteed enthusiastically. "Even three different kinds of scoops if you want," she told him with a wink. "But you have to promise to eat *really* fast so the ice cream doesn't melt all over you."

"Two's enough," he answered her with the solemnity of a seasoned diplomat. "What's your favorite?"

She didn't hesitate. "Mint chocolate chip."

Joel said nothing, he just nodded. Standing up on his toes, he looked down into the various vats of ice cream. Confronted with over twenty flavors, Jewel assumed it was going to take the little boy some time to make up his mind. Instead, he made his choice quickly—one scoop each of mint chocolate chip and rocky road, a mixture of her choice and what she'd picked for Chris.

Jewel couldn't help wondering how much of that was because Joel liked the flavors and how much represented his desire to bond with both of them.

No doubt about it, he was a very complicated little boy.

"Okay, now what?" Chris asked once they each had their cones and he had collected his change.

Jewel thought she saw a hint of amusement in his eyes. Good, the man wasn't as wooden as he would have liked her to believe. "Now we eat our ice cream cones as we walk."

"At the same time?" Chris deadpanned, holding the door open for her and Joel.

Definitely amusement, she decided, walking out. "That's the general idea, but the ultimate choice is yours," she quipped. "Oh, and you might try enjoying yourself," she added.

"I don't need an ice cream cone to enjoy myself," he told her.

"No, but it doesn't hurt," she said, taking an appreciative lick of the top scoop on her own cone. Ordinarily, she didn't lick her ice cream, she took bites of it until it was gone. It disappeared faster that way, but she also got to enjoy it more quickly.

Jewel slanted a look at him as they proceeded down a short, sloped alleyway between two weathered bungalows, making their way to the beach just beyond. The sky, so bright and blue just a short while ago, was now overcast, hovering like a gauzy shroud over the horizon.

"I'll bite," she finally said. "What *do* you need to enjoy yourself?"

There was no hesitation. The world of science had been his haven for as long as he could remember. "Understanding a new concept that I never understood before."

It took her a second to make sense of what Chris was telling her. "You're talking about physics, aren't you?"

He nodded. "Science is very pure and its frontier is really endless. There's always something new to learn, to understand."

She could appreciate getting wrapped up in the pursuit of knowledge—but not to the exclusion of everything else.

"But while it might keep you up at night," she pointed out cheerfully, "it won't keep you warm."

He didn't see where she was going with this. "That was never a requirement."

She moved her shoulders in a vague shrug. "Maybe it should be," she countered. Before he could say anything in response, she turned her attention to Joel. They'd ignored the boy long enough, and while he didn't seem to mind, she minded *for* him. "Well, we're one step closer to getting you registered for school, Joel. Are you excited?"

He didn't answer. Instead, he emulated her earlier movement and made his thin shoulders rise and fall in a careless shrug.

"Maybe a little afraid?" she guessed. The look

on his face as he raised his eyes to hers told Jewel she was closer to the truth than the little boy really wanted to admit.

He was deeper than children his age, she thought, but then, most children his age hadn't had to be a parent to one of their parents.

"It's okay to be afraid," she told him.

He stopped walking and looked up at her in surprise. "It is?"

"Uh-huh." She kept walking and Joel fell into step beside her on her right while Chris continued walking on her left. "As long as you don't let that fear make you hide from things," she qualified. "You've got to stand up to your fears and show them who's boss."

"What fears have you stood up to?" Chris asked, curious.

She hadn't expected him to interject a question. "Fear of failure."

She aroused his curiosity. People usually didn't. He found that interesting. "And have you? Failed?" he added.

"Nope, not yet," she answered brightly. Her shoe came in contact with something in the sand and she glanced down to see what it was. "Oh, look, Joel. A seashell." Jewel stooped to pick it up. It was small and, unlike so many other shells, it was in one piece, although heavily encrusted with sand. She blew on the shell to loosen some of the sand and then held it out to the boy. "If you hold it up to your ear, you can hear the ocean."

Instead of placing the shell to his ear to see if

he could indeed hear the ocean, Joel turned and pointed toward the waves that were ebbing and flowing against the shore. "But the ocean is right there."

She pressed her lips together in order not to laugh. "When you take the seashell home," she told him, "you can still hear the ocean." There was a skeptical expression on the boy's face when he looked down at the shell. "I think," she said to Chris, lowering her voice as they resumed walking, "I have more to find than just Joel's father."

He wasn't following her. "Oh?"

"There's a missing childhood that needs to be restored," she told him, watching Joel as the boy walked a few steps ahead of them, at the moment engrossed in the way the waves were hugging the shore.

Chris didn't understand her concern. "There's nothing wrong with being serious."

"Once in a while, no," she agreed. "But all the time? He's five years old, Chris. At five, he shouldn't be analyzing statements for accuracy. He should be running around, playing games he made up and laughing."

Chris looked over toward his nephew. There were pictures of him in an old family album stored on his bookcase at home that could easily have been photographs of Joel. Moreover, he could relate to the way the boy behaved.

"My guess," he speculated, "is that he hasn't had a whole lot to laugh about."

Chris was probably right, she thought. "Well, then, he needs to be given something to laugh about." Jewel looked at him pointedly.

Oh, no. He was too busy to take on another responsibility. This was only temporary. "Talking to the wrong person," Chris replied. He finished the last of his cone. "He's just staying with me until you locate his father."

She suppressed the urge to tell him that Joel was his blood and that he should help him, not regard him as a hot potato to be passed to whomever was there to take him. Instead, she told him, "Time is relative. A lot can be accomplished in a short amount if you do it right." She wasn't making an impression, she thought. "Ever see *The Lost Weekend?* Ray Milland plays an alcoholic who got stone cold sober in a forty-eight-hour period."

Chris snorted. The actor's name was vaguely familiar only because his mother liked to watch old movies when he was a kid. "That's Hollywood back when things were oversimplified."

"True," she freely admitted, "but it's harder to kick a drinking habit than it is to laugh."

He supposed, in some twisted, convoluted way, that made sense. But he had a more basic question. "Do you get this involved in all your clients' lives?"

The answer to that was no. "Most of my clients are suspicious, sometimes vengeful people I wouldn't want to get involved with on a personal level," she told him. And then she smiled. "This is really a nice change from that." She'd felt herself becoming involved the moment she looked into Joel's sad brown eyes.

"So the answer's no?" he asked. He preferred things to be black and white.

"No, I don't usually get this involved," she confirmed, then added, "I try very hard to keep my distance from people like that. Their lives are usually toxic."

"Then why do you do it?" he wanted to know. "You seem like a bright, intelligent person. There's got to be something else you could do for a living."

Probably, she acknowledged. But nothing that she would have wanted to do. She felt that investigation was her calling. Briefly, after graduating with a degree in criminology, she considered joining the police force. But she never liked taking orders.

"I'm good at this," she told him. "Good at getting to the bottom of things, at seeing what other people miss. At tracking down cheating spouses," she added with a sigh. Gathering evidence for divorces was, at the moment, her bread and butter. She could only hope that things would change soon. "It pays the bills, and every once in a while, I find a case that gets to me," she admitted. Jewel paused, looking at the boy. And then she turned her gaze pointedly to the man walking beside her. "If you ask me, I think you both need each other."

"What I need," he corrected, "is to get back to my work at the university. You can help me do that by finding his father."

It was what he had hired her to do. Who knew things would evolve to include another layer? Either way, it wasn't her place to force her sense of values on him.

"Right." Her cone finished, Jewel wadded up the

napkin in her hand. "Speaking of which, I guess I'd better get back to that."

She was about to call out to Joel to tell him that they were getting ready to leave, but Chris stopped her. "Wait."

Had she missed something? Jewel glanced around, but saw nothing that would make Chris want to pause. "For what?"

Instead of answering her, Chris took the napkin she'd just balled up from her hand. Opening it, he raised a section to her lips and gently wiped away the trace of green ice cream from the corner of her mouth.

As he eliminated the telltale drop, Jewel found herself holding her breath. Her eyes were on his. A warmth had slipped over her.

For a split second she'd thought...

But there was no reason to believe that anything out of the ordinary would happen. That was just her imagination running away with her.

She blamed it on the romantic comedy she'd watched on cable the night before.

"You had some ice cream there." Chris felt he needed to explain. He gave the napkin back to her.

She wasn't aware of taking it. "Thank you," she murmured.

The words, the moment, seemed to hang between them. It almost felt as if time had stood still for just a heartbeat.

Which was silly, because why should it? The man hadn't kissed her. He hadn't even touched her except through a napkin, for God's sake. Why did she suddenly feel like some virginal adolescent at the end of her very first date, waiting with baited breath for her first kiss?

She was light-years past that innocent, inexperienced girl. So why were her palms damp and her fingertips tingling?

Chris was still looking at her curiously, so she fumbled for words to explain. And because she was who she was, she told him the truth. And tried to make light of it.

"Funny, I thought you were going to kiss me."

She came so close to the truth, it caught him completely off guard. He had no idea that mind reading was part of her services.

"Why would I do that?"

She dismissed the idea with a shrug. "I don't know. Because you wanted to?" she guessed, still trying to keep the exchange light.

She didn't know the half of it, Chris thought. He wasn't sure why that was, either, but there was no denying—at least not to himself—that he had wanted very much to kiss her.

The feeling was as much a shock to him as it would have been to her had he said anything out loud. It had come over him out of the blue without any warning, like some rolling earthquake that left people shaken long after it was over. Shaken and doubting their own reactions.

"And if I had kissed you?" he pressed, wanting to hear her response.

What was he asking? Did he want to know if she would have protested? Not hardly. She was a flesh-

and-blood woman, not some heroine in an eigh-
teenth-century melodrama.

"That's easy," she told him. "I would have kissed
you back."

He nodded, unaware that he was smiling. Broadly.
"Good to know."

It left her wondering if he had just given her a
glimpse of things to come.

"Joel," she called out to the boy. "We're going
home."

"Whose?" he asked as he joined her.

Good question. "Yours." *At least it's yours for the
time being.*

"Thanks for coming on such short notice," Chris
repeated when she dropped them off at the house
some twenty minutes later.

Being ready at a moment's notice was no big deal
for her. Jewel considered it one of her assets. She
laughed. "I'm a private investigator. The only kind
of notice I get is short."

The sound of her laughter threaded through his
system, putting him at ease. He realized that, without rhyme or reason, the sound created a feeling of
well-being within him.

He forced himself to focus on her reply, not the
effect she had on him. He still thought that hers was
a strange choice of vocation for a woman. For so
many reasons. "I never knew a woman who could
get ready fast," he told her.

"How many women *have* you known?" She caught

her lower lip between her teeth. *That was a really dumb thing to ask, Jewel,* she upbraided herself.

Rather than get annoyed—or give her an inflated number—Chris resorted to an answer he thought she'd find acceptable, given her line of work.

"You're the private investigator," he told her. "You figure it out."

She paused, debating whether or not to give voice to her thoughts, or just to take the easy way out and say she'd get back to him on that. But it had been a rather strange morning. She decided she had nothing to lose by being honest with him.

"Your looks tell me that there should have been a lot of women in your life." She let him mull over the compliment for a moment before concluding, "But your dedication to your profession would seem to make that unlikely."

The latter was far closer to the truth than the former. "So which is it? A lot? Or none?" he asked.

"I'd split the difference." She glanced at her watch. How had it gotten to be so late? She'd only planned to give up an hour, not half the day. "I'm sorry, I've got to get going," she told him. Joel had stepped out of the vehicle and was now quietly standing beside his uncle, his beautiful brown eyes fixed on her. "I'll see you Monday, Joel," she promised. "You and I and your uncle have a date with Venado's school principal." She saw the concerned look create a small furrow between his eyes. The same one, it occurred to her, that Chris displayed when he was thinking. "Don't worry. That'll hurt even less than the shots."

Joel looked as if he doubted that, but he didn't

contradict her out loud. "Can we go for another walk on the beach when we're finished?"

She knew that there were things she needed to do and that she could have easily turned the boy down. But she didn't want to. Just because she didn't want kids of her own didn't mean that she didn't like the species, she thought with a grin.

"Don't see why not." She looked over to her client. "Is that okay with you, Uncle Chris?"

He'd almost kissed her on the beach. Only enormous self-control and the need for self-preservation had saved him from that huge mistake.

But what about next time?

Next time was going to have to take care of itself. Chris nodded. "I suppose it can't do any harm."

Jewel flashed a grin. "It can only do some good. See you Monday, men," she said as she threw the car into Reverse and pulled out of the driveway.

She smiled.

It was going to happen. She was certain of it. One way or another, it was going to happen. Either while the case was still in progress, or afterward—she wasn't certain about the timing—but she knew it was going to be soon.

And hot. Very, very hot. He might be a man of few words but she had a feeling that he was a man of many moves.

She and Chris were going to make love. She could feel it in her bones and had never been so sure of anything in her life. Sure of that, and the fact that the person who had invented ice cream should be nominated for sainthood.

Chapter 8

Always an early riser, Chris had already been up for almost three hours, and working for more than two of them, when he thought he heard the doorbell ring. Sitting on the sofa, deep in concentration, he looked up at the front door and frowned.

It was Sunday. It wasn't usual for people to just drop by unannounced during the week, much less on the weekend.

And then he remembered.

He *wasn't* home. He was in Rita's house. Maybe whoever was at the door had just come across one of the obituary notices that Jewel had sent out to the local newspapers and they were dropping by to see if it was true.

Well, he wasn't going to find out just sitting here, frowning, he told himself.

With a sigh, Chris put aside the scrap of paper he was currently making notes on.

First there was chaos, then there was order, he thought, looking around at the snowstorm of papers, envelopes and napkins he'd pressed into service, now scattered all over the coffee table. There were equations and/or notations on all of them. In their present state, he was the only one who could make any sense of what was there.

As he began to rise, Joel ran by him, heading toward the door. The boy looked almost eager.

"I'll get it," Chris called out to his nephew. He didn't want him getting into the habit of throwing open the door whenever someone knocked or rang the doorbell.

To his surprise, the boy didn't attempt to open the door. Instead, Joel scrambled up on the love seat that had its back against the window and peered out to see who was on their doorstep.

"It's Jewel!" Joel announced with the first bit of excitement he'd heard in the boy's voice.

"Jewel?" Chris echoed as he approached the front door.

What was she doing here? He didn't recall the private investigator saying anything about meeting with him today. Last he'd heard, she said she was coming along with them on Monday to get Joel registered for school.

Coming along.

The words mocked him. The woman wasn't "coming along," she was leading the way and he knew it. And he was damn grateful that she was. He hadn't a clue who to turn to for help when it came to doing all the ordinary things that having a five-year-old in your life entailed. He freely admitted that he would have been completely lost without her.

Opening the front door, Chris greeted her with "Were we supposed to get together today?"

"Hi, to you, too," she replied, amused.

Joel was right beside his uncle, shifting his weight from foot to foot, making no secret of the fact that he was happy to see her.

"Hi, Jewel!" he exclaimed even before she walked into the house.

Jewel grinned at the boy. "Now, that's a welcome," she pronounced. "Hi, yourself." She glanced up at Chris. "And to answer your question, no, we didn't make plans to get together today. But I like delivering my updates in person instead of over the phone." That wasn't entirely true, but he didn't have to know that. Let him think that she believed in the personal touch at all times. "Besides," she held up the two bags she'd brought with her, a warm, delicious aroma emanating from them, "I thought you might be running low on food, so I brought over breakfast. French toast, waffles, sausages *and* coffee," she recited.

She was about to place both bags on the coffee table, but she stopped before they made contact. The disarray registered. Her mother would have turned the mess into neat piles of paper in about five seconds. Ten tops.

"Making yourself at home I see," she commented. The next moment she was heading for the kitchen, which was still clutter-free, she noted.

"I was just working on something," Chris told her, following her into the next room.

"So I see," Jewel answered. She placed the bags on the kitchen table and turned toward him. "You want the food or the news first?"

Joel answered for both of them. "The food," he piped up.

"Food it is." That would have been her choice, too. Jewel's mouth curved as she raised her eyes to Chris's for a moment. He looked a little surprised. Obviously, the man wasn't accustomed to anyone making choices for him. "You've gotta be fast around a five-year-old—even a superintelligent one." Affection was spreading out long, slender fingers through her as she looked at Joel. The little boy in him was beginning to surface. There was hope.

"I'll keep that in mind," Chris murmured.

He opened first one cabinet, then another as he searched for plates. Rita's so-called system still hadn't quite sunk in yet, despite the number of days he'd already spent here. Cutlery took him a couple more moments to pinpoint as he opened several drawers before locating it. He finally placed plates and utensils on the counter in front of Jewel.

Though he'd made no comment on the choice she'd offered, Chris realized that he was in no hurry to hear the news Jewel was referring to. It wasn't that he'd settled in or gotten attached to the boy; it was just that if Jewel had managed to locate his ex-brother-in-law, it occurred to him that there would be no excuse to see her any longer. The thought of not seeing her anymore, he was surprised to realize, disturbed him.

Which disturbed him even further. Ordinarily, he didn't form attachments quickly.

So Chris did what he'd always accused the rest of the world of doing—he procrastinated. Until yesterday, he'd been eager to receive any news that would lead him to Ray. Now, he wasn't all that sure. There were mixed feelings swirling around in him.

The woman was fast, he noted. Just like that, the food Jewel had brought over was out of the bags and on the plates, waiting to be consumed.

With only minimal encouragement, Joel picked the French toast.

"These are good," Joel told her with wide-eyed wonder that she found both amusing and endearing.

"Glad you like them," she said. "French toast is my favorite breakfast, although I do like trying to fill up all the tiny spaces on a waffle. That way, when I eat the waffles, they're always extra sweet. How do you like yours? With syrup? Fruit?" she prompted when Joel didn't say anything.

Finally, he shrugged as he speared another piece of the French toast. "I don't know. I never had them before."

That was almost un-American, she thought, keeping the comment to herself. But if he'd never had waffles… "And the French toast?"

Joel shook his head, but he kept on eating. "No, never had that before, either."

She frowned. Some of her best childhood memories had taken place around the breakfast table. "What did you have for breakfast?"

He shrugged again, quickly making short work of the pieces on his plate. "Anything I could find. Cereal sometimes," he added with an uncertain smile.

Something else they had in common, Chris thought. "I was a freshman in college before I realized that people ate anything besides cereal for breakfast," he told Joel.

The boy smiled and, just for a second, Chris felt as if he and Joel were sharing a moment. Something inside him stirred.

Meanwhile, Jewel was trying to relate and having a difficult time. Breakfast had always been there for her, as was love. She looked from the boy to his uncle. "You're kidding."

"Hardly ever" was Chris's deadpan response.

It took her a moment to realize that he was making a joke. Jewel laughed. "Sorry, forgot who I was talking to." Joel, she noticed, was already polishing off his portion. There wasn't even any syrup or powdered sugar left on the plate. "Can I interest someone in seconds?" she asked, looking pointedly at Joel.

The moment she asked, the little boy pushed forward his plate, a hopeful look in his eyes. He wasn't nearly as shy as he'd been when she first met him and that was a very good sign. She *knew* that there was a real boy under all that solemnity and knowledge. He just needed to be brought out.

"You got it," she told him. This time, she gave him a waffle instead of French toast.

Joel eyed the waffle for a moment, then hesitantly asked, "Can I have it your way?"

"Coming right up."

Very carefully, Jewel filled each and every square hole on the waffle's surface with maple syrup. There was just the right amount to accommodate one waffle. But that was enough.

Joel happily started to chew his way to satisfaction, beginning on one end and working his way to the other side.

"How about you?" Jewel turned toward Chris. "Can I interest you in seconds?"

What she could interest him in, Chris realized, his eyes covertly sweeping over the curves of her form, had nothing to do with food for the body. Sustenance for the soul was more like it.

Startled, his thoughts came to a skidding halt. Since when did he think like that? Was losing his sister and realizing that his only earthly ties now resided in a five-year-old boy—a five-year-old boy he was trying to hand over to someone else—responsible for throwing him off this way?

Or was it something else?

At thirty-two, most people didn't think about mortality, but he did.

Now.

Was it just the need to leave behind a footprint, however faint, to prove that he had passed through this life? He didn't think that way normally, but there was nothing really normal about the past week he'd been through.

She was waiting for him to answer. Chris could see it by the way she was looking at him. "No, thanks."

Jewel wasn't ready to give up just yet. "More coffee then?" she offered.

He could always drink more coffee. There were days when he started working at seven in the morning and didn't come home until after ten at night. Those were the days that he literally ran on coffee. It kept him going.

"Sounds good," he agreed.

She paused for a moment, studying him before going for the aforementioned coffee.

Something was quite obviously on her mind. It stirred his curiosity. "What?"

"Do you pay some kind of tariff if you use more than a few words in any given sentence?" she asked.

He'd never employed a plethora of words—unless it was on a paper he was writing. But then physics begged for the usage of more words to make concepts clear.

"Why use twelve words when you can get your meaning across with two?" he countered.

"Oh, I don't know." She sat down opposite him again, nursing her own cup of coffee. "Some people call it having a conversation. Adding a little bit of light and shading makes it more interesting for most people." *But, obviously, not for you.*

He looked at her over the rim of his cup. "You take care of that for both of us," he pointed out.

She didn't dispute that she'd never felt the need to be brief. "Granted, but it's nice to have someone else in the conversation."

There was amusement in his eyes as he promised, "I'll work on it."

She grinned at him. *Baby steps were still steps.* "That's all I ask."

Chris took in a deep breath. He supposed that there was no point in putting off the inevitable. He was going to find out sooner or later and he'd always believed in sooner rather than later. This had been a departure for him.

But now it was over. So, as he sipped his coffee, Chris braced himself for what she'd initially come to tell him. "You said that aside from wanting to bring over breakfast, you had some news."

She'd almost forgotten. There was something about being around this strong, silent man that turned her into someone with the mental acuity of a dandelion in the wind. "In a manner of speaking."

Out of the corner of her eye, she noticed that Joel had once again cleaned his plate and was now listening to her intently.

"In a manner of speaking," Chris repeated. "I don't follow."

"Well, I don't really know if you can call it news," she explained, "if you have nothing new to add."

Two and two came together very quickly. "Ray's old boss hasn't heard from him," he guessed.

It had taken her two hours of talking and following the man around his shop as he worked to get that noninformation out of Bud Redkin. She nodded. "That about covers it."

"You think he's telling the truth?"

The question surprised her. Most people would have assumed that they were being told the truth. In her case, after the interview with Redkin, she'd checked the man out to see if he had any priors or if there had been any complaints lodged against him or his place of business. In both cases, the answer was no.

Which led her to her conclusion. "Yes, I think he was telling the truth. Redkin has nothing to gain by lying."

She was the expert, Chris thought. Part of him was disappointed with the outcome. The thing that gave him pause was that part of him *wasn't* disappointed. What was that about?

"So that's it?" he asked.

She couldn't gauge by his expression or tone if Chris was upset that she was unable to find Ray. But since Joel was within earshot, she refrained from asking. She didn't want the five-year-old coming away with the wrong impression. Genius or not, he still had feelings.

So she focused on business and reminded Chris what she'd said yesterday. "No, I still have other options to pursue."

She hadn't elaborated on that, he recalled. "Like what?"

She didn't like to talk about things until they were done, but she supposed that he did have the right to ask—and know. After all, he was paying for her services. "Like if Ray Johnson collected a paycheck any time since he left your sister, he might have filed a tax return." But she was taking nothing for granted. Even so-called law-abiding citizens sometimes "neglected" to file if they were getting paid off the books. And from what she'd gleaned from both Chris and Ray's old boss, Ray Johnson was not exactly a model citizen.

"What if he did?" Chris asked, for once taking a positive view. "The IRS isn't exactly known for their great penchant for sharing information."

Jewel took another sip of coffee and smiled over the rim. "There are ways" was all she said.

He found the mysterious smile on her face completely beguiling and stirring. He could feel its effects all the way down in his gut.

Maybe he was going off the deep end.

"What kind of ways?" he wanted to know, doing what he could to refocus his attention on why he'd hired her in the first place.

Jewel was shaking her head, her hair brushing along her shoulders. "Trust me," she counseled. "You're better off not knowing."

He interpreted her words the only way he could. "I don't want you getting caught doing something illegal on my account, Jewel."

"Don't worry." Instead of reassuring him that what she had in mind wasn't illegal, she just made him a promise. "I won't get caught."

She'd misunderstood, he thought. "No, I didn't mean—"

But Jewel started to laugh. "You have *got* to lighten up, Chris," she insisted, then smiled at him as she touched his shoulder. "Don't worry, this isn't anything that has a prison sentence attached to it." She still didn't want to get too specific. The less he knew, the less of a liability he was. "I'm just bending a few rules, not breaking any."

He didn't know if she was being honest with him, but he did know when to leave well enough alone. Not because he didn't want to be a co-conspirator or because he was such a straight arrow—there'd been a time when he wasn't. But if he knew what she was up to, he might feel obligated to stop her, and he had a feeling that Jewel Parnell was not a woman who was easily stopped. He'd rather not have that confrontation if he could possibly avoid it.

Jewel supposed he deserved a crumb more than he was getting. So she offered it to him. "I know a guy who owes me a favor and he knows a guy... Let's just leave it at that."

But she had raised another question in his mind, a question he wouldn't have normally wondered about. But for some reason he did when it came to Jewel.

"What kind of a favor?" he asked her.

She gave him just the bare bones. She had never been one to brag. "His sister was kidnapped in lieu of payment for some drugs. I made things happen to get her back."

Chris looked at her for a long, pregnant moment. Maybe he didn't socialize all that much, but he knew that most people would have turned that into a half an hour story, emphasizing their part in it and magnifying all their deeds. But Jewel just seemed to shrug it off.

Was that modesty?

Or was it something else?

"Now who's economizing on words?" Chris asked her.

Jewel responded with a grin. "Maybe your influence is rubbing off on me," she told him.

When she turned to say something to Joel since she'd left the boy out of the conversation, she suddenly realized that he was no longer in the room. That was really odd, she thought. She hadn't heard him leave.

And why *would* he leave? Every other time she'd interacted with Chris, Joel had stayed close by.

"Where's Joel?" she asked Chris. Maybe he had noticed the boy wandering off.

Anything Chris might have said in response to the question was drowned out by the sudden, heart-wrenching wail they heard coming from the rear of the house.

Jewel was on her feet instantly.

The cry had come from Joel.

Chapter 9

With Joel's distraught cry ringing in his ears, Chris rushed to his nephew's room, getting there just ahead of Jewel.

At the very least, he expected to find Joel lying on the floor, hurt and bleeding, a victim of some kind of bizarre accident. But, at first glance, there didn't seem to be anything out of order in the room. No books on the ground, covering him, no chair that had toppled backward with Joel as its occupant.

Instead, his nephew was standing in front of his small, secondhand bookcase, sobbing as if he were never going to be able to stop.

Though Chris was the first one to run into the room, it was Jewel who was the first to get to the boy. Dropping to her knees, she quickly looked him over to find the cause for this heartbreaking display of grief. Not finding any obvious injuries, she put her hands on Joel's heaving shoulders and asked, "Honey, what's wrong? What is it? Please tell me."

Joel couldn't answer her at first. The sobs were all but choking him. He was crying as if his heart had been shattered into a million tiny pieces.

Her hands still on his shoulders, Jewel quickly scanned the room, looking for clues. It crossed her mind that Joel might be having a delayed reaction to his mother's death. But what had triggered it?

"Is it about your mother, Joel?" Her voice was kind, coaxing.

Still trying to catch his breath, the boy could only point to the bookcase.

Jewel felt helpless and frustrated. Had Joel seen a photograph or something else that he associated exclusively with his mother? Was that what had brought on this uncontrollable flood of tears?

"What is it, honey? I don't see—"

And then, the second she said it, she did. She saw what had reduced the little boy to tears. Saw what had served as a catalyst.

In the middle of the books, knickknacks and things that only a little boy's imagination could turn into treasures, she saw a dingy-looking fishbowl. There was a crack on the side of the glass, near the top. But that had no bearing on its function as a home for the bowl's occupant. Or, more accurately, former occupant. For the turtle who had obviously been living there appeared to be dead.

There was no movement, no struggling on the

turtle's part. He was on his back, and his tiny feet were still.

Very gingerly, aware that Chris was watching her every move, Jewel reached into the bowl and extracted the turtle. She brushed a fingertip across his head, but there was no reaction. No attempt to bite her or to even pull his head into his shell. She had no idea what a turtle was supposed to feel like, but the one in her hand was room temperature. And very, very dead.

She laid him back down and turned to Joel. "I'm sorry, Joel. He's gone."

"He was my friend," the boy said in between hiccupping sobs.

Watching this, Chris was utterly stunned. "You're crying over a *turtle?*" he asked incredulously. "Seriously?"

Jewel could see what was coming. Making a quick decision, she said, "Excuse us for a second, Joel. I have to talk to your uncle."

With that, she took hold of Chris's arm and firmly pulled him into the hall. She could feel him staring at her in surprise, but she didn't want to take a chance on further hurting Joel's feelings. She understood what was going on, even if Joel didn't, and she needed to explain it to Chris. Things were *not* what they seemed.

"He didn't blink during the funeral," Chris said. "His *mother's* funeral. There wasn't a single tear before, during or after. Not one tear," he emphasized, holding up his finger. "And now, just because that stupid reptile croaks, Joel's crying as if his whole world is caving in on him."

He couldn't understand. Maybe Rita hadn't been the world's greatest mother. Maybe her name wasn't even in the top-qualifying one million. But how could Joel be crying for a turtle when he hadn't cried for his own mother?

"It *is* caving in on him," she assured Chris. "Now, be quiet and stop talking."

His eyes widened in disbelief. She was telling *him* to be quiet? Had the whole world just gone crazy?

"It's displacement," she informed him, her voice steely even though she was whispering. "Joel didn't cry after his mother died because being in restrained control of his emotions was the way he'd been taught to behave all his life. He has been the man of the house for as long as he could remember. He didn't have time for tears, for feeling sorry for himself. He had to take care of his mother.

"And when his mother died, he behaved as stoically as he always had, internalizing his grief. But the turtle was his pet. When he was playing with the turtle, he was just a normal little boy. A normal little boy with vulnerable feelings. When he walked into the room and found the turtle dead, that brave little soldier he was projecting just crumbled. Don't let this scene fool you. Joel's not just crying over losing his turtle, he's crying over everything. But predominantly, he's crying over losing his mother."

Chris considered what Jewel had just said. He supposed it was plausible. It wasn't as if he'd never heard of displacement. He just didn't associate that kind of multilayered response with a five-year-old.

"This PI license you have," he asked, a touch of

sarcasm hiding his concern, "does it come with a degree in psychology?"

Jewel smiled at him. He understood. "I minored in it," she told him. She didn't know if he realized that she was serious. "But it doesn't take a degree to connect the dots." Belatedly, she realized that she was still holding on to Chris's arm. With a twinge of self-consciousness, she released it, then turned around and walked back into Joel's room.

"Joel, would you like to have a funeral service for—" It suddenly occurred to Jewel that she didn't know what to call the expired turtle. "I'm sorry, what was your turtle's name?"

Joel wiped the dampness from his cheeks with the back of his wrist. "Mr. Turtle."

"Very neat and succinct," she said with an approving nod. "Would you like to have a funeral service for Mr. Turtle?"

His eyes darted toward the fishbowl, then back up at her. "Can I do that?"

She draped her arm around Joel's shoulders. "Of course you can. We can put Mr. Turtle in a shoe box— or wrap him up in a handkerchief the way they used to do in biblical times," she amended when she saw the disheartened look in the boy's eyes at the mention of a shoe box. Apparently, there weren't any to be had. One glance at the worn sneakers he was wearing told her that shoes hadn't been a priority for his late mother.

"They wrapped up people in handkerchiefs?" Joel asked, confused.

"They called them shrouds. They were big, white cloths, but for the sake of argument, you could say that they were made out of the same kind of material that handkerchiefs are these days." She looked over his head toward Chris. "I'm sure your uncle can donate a handkerchief to the cause so that we can bury Mr. Turtle in the backyard."

The idea of a funeral for a turtle had sounded rather absurd to him, but Chris told himself he wasn't going to say anything. Until she mentioned the word *bury.* Leaning into her, Chris whispered, "Do you have any idea how hard the soil is around here? It's like trying to dig into clay. Not exactly easy."

She wasn't about to be put off. Joel needed this kind of closure. Needed to feel as if he were in control of something.

"But you have muscles," she told Chris with a smile. She patted one of his biceps to reinforce her statement. "You'll manage."

Joel dried off the last of his tears, wiping away a trail that had made it all the way down to his chin, and ventured an almost hopeful smile in Jewel's direction. "Can we do it now?"

"Absolutely. All we need is a handkerchief and a shovel." She turned toward Chris, intending to collect the former. "Can you help us out here, Uncle Chris?"

Chris suppressed a sigh. He still thought that this was going a bit far, but if it helped the boy deal with his grief, displaced or not, he supposed he could go along with it.

Handing over his handkerchief, he said, "I'll go see if there's a shovel in the garage," and walked out of his nephew's bedroom.

* * *

In the end, Jewel prevailed upon Chris to go to the hardware store to buy a shovel. There wasn't one in the garage, and digging in the claylike soil with a spoon—the only thing in the house that came close to any kind of digging implement—would take much too long.

An hour later, armed with a shovel and a handkerchief, preparations for the funeral service got underway. Chris dug a small hole, swallowing a few choice words as he went about the chore.

For Joel's sake, Jewel saw to it that the ensuing service was conducted with all the solemnity of a real funeral. That included having a few well-chosen words said over the tiny, handkerchief-wrapped form that was now lying in repose in the shallow hole in the backyard.

She had Joel go first, and then she followed, giving the deceased pet his proper due as best she could. "We won't think of this as an end, Mr. Turtle, because it isn't. It's just the beginning. The beginning of a brand-new adventure. You've gone on to a place where there's always enough to eat and everyone gets along with everyone else. Rest well, Mr. Turtle. You've earned it."

She saw Joel gratefully smiling at her and she knew she'd struck the right notes.

Concluding her eulogy, she turned to Chris. When he made no move to say anything, she coaxed, "Your turn."

Chris scowled, confused. He was sure he'd heard wrong. "My what?"

"Your turn," she repeated. When there still was no response, she fed him the rest of the line. "To say a few words over Mr. Turtle," she prodded.

The look in Chris's eyes said she had to be kidding. That hope died the next moment as she continued to look straight at him, waiting.

The woman had a stubborn streak a mile wide, he thought. Stepping forward the way she and Joel had done, Chris kept his head bent, not out of any need to show respect for the dead turtle, but because if he looked up, he was certain his impatience at having to go through with this charade, for a *turtle* for God's sake, would be evident.

"I never got to know you, Mr. Turtle, but I'm sure you were a very good pet for Joel. Now you're in heaven. I guess you don't have to worry about anyone beating you in any races anymore. Enjoy yourself."

Jewel pressed her lips together to keep from laughing. Chris looked like the epitome of discomfort. He needed to be let off the hook. "That was very nice, Chris," she said softly. Turning to the boy, she asked, "Joel, would you like to throw some dirt on the shroud?"

"Like we did with Mama?" he asked.

She nodded. "Just like that," she assured him. She was rewarded with a look of pure contentment on Joel's face.

Bending down, he took a handful of dirt and threw it into the small grave. Jewel followed suit, making certain that she distributed the dirt evenly. Then she looked at Chris.

To her relief, he didn't roll his eyes the way she

had expected him to. Instead, he just bent down, took a handful of dirt and threw it on top of the handkerchief-wrapped turtle.

"I'll finish up," he volunteered.

She had been prepared to do it herself and smiled with no small relief when he made the offer. "That would be very nice of you, Chris."

Another voice joined hers. "Thank you, Uncle Chris," Joel said.

Chris caught himself thinking that the look on the boy's face made the whole charade more than worth it. Maybe Jewel did know what she was doing, he thought, as he slowly drizzled a shovel full of dirt over the tiny grave he'd just dug.

The satisfied feeling and warmth that ensued was a very nice dividend. Without realizing it, he slanted a glance at Jewel, because she was the heart of it all. Shining a light so that he could follow.

Jewel stayed with them another hour or so, but then she said that she had somewhere to be. Joel took the information in stride because he was five, but Chris had no such luxury to fall back on. He wondered what it was that she had to do and where she was going.

He came close to asking, but he didn't. Instead, he walked her to her car in the driveway.

"Thanks for being my interpreter," he said to her once they were outside. When she raised a quizzical eyebrow, he explained, "I don't speak 'kid' very well."

The admission made her grin. "You were one, once," she reminded him.

"I'll take your word for it," he answered. "My memory doesn't go back that far."

She wouldn't accept the excuse. "Sure it does. Just open yourself up and you'll remember," she promised. He obviously needed a little more convincing and prodding, she thought. "You were his age once, and I think the two of you have more in common than you realize."

He supposed that she might have a point. There were things that Joel said or did that stirred vague memories for him, memories that insisted on remaining teasingly just out of reach.

And then Jewel smiled at him. Really smiled. It was that smile that seemed to have generous helpings of sunshine in it. Just seeing it made him want to bask within its rays.

"You know, all disclaimers aside, for a novice, you did pretty well today," she told him.

He shrugged. The credit didn't belong to him. The sun was out now, having burned away the last layers of overhanging fog. A few stray rays were weaving themselves into her hair, giving it golden highlights. He caught himself wanting to thread his fingers through it to see if those strands felt any different from the rest.

"Only because I was following your lead," he finally managed to say, forcing himself to focus on the conversation. He didn't want her to go just yet. "You sure you don't have any kids?"

"Absolutely positive," she assured him. "It would be something I'd know. As for relating to kids, it comes easy to me. Maybe it's because I never grew up myself," she added tongue in cheek.

His eyes traveled the length of her form, a form that by any definition was nothing short of mouth-wateringly gorgeous. "Oh, you grew up, all right," he told her. "Trust me."

Chris's tone, unintentionally warm and sexy, sent another wave of heat zigzagging its way up and down her spine, rendering her momentarily speechless. It took her a minute to regain the use of her tongue.

"Was that a compliment?"

A compliment, not about the quality of her work, but about her body, sounded much too personal. The situation called for maintaining a professional distance between them, at least until he was no longer retaining her services.

"An observation," he countered.

"I see." He might be fooling himself, she thought, but he wasn't fooling her. She smiled indulgently. "Thank you for your 'observation.'"

He stared off over her head, his face expressionless. "You're welcome."

"What time do you want me over here tomorrow to help get Joel registered for school?" she asked.

The whole time, he thought.

That was when he realized that he really didn't want her to leave. She made dealing with Joel easier. With her here, he felt less out of his element, less like a fish out of water. It was better for the boy, too. And if he found her presence more than just passably pleasant, well, that was an added bonus.

The fact that this wasn't "business as usual" for

him was something he wasn't entirely willing to explore right now. But perhaps his sister's untimely
death had made him acutely aware that there wasn't
an infinite allotment of time available. Perhaps there
was more to life than just solving the perfect qua-
dratic equation.

But he knew that saying any of this would give
Jewel the wrong impression—or maybe the right
one; he didn't know. In any case, he couldn't afford
to have her know how attracted he was to her. Since
he was paying her for her services some sort of con-
flict of interest would definitely arise if he wound
up sleeping with her, as well.

Right now, he needed to keep things simple. And,
most importantly, he needed to have her find Ray. He
was fairly certain that she was good at her job. Once
his life was his own again, maybe then he would be
free to follow up on these feelings he was having.

So he pretended to think about her question, then
asked, "How does ten o'clock sound?"

She had always been, almost against her will, an
early riser, a habit she'd picked up from her mother.
"I can come over earlier," she volunteered. "That way,
you can get this registration over with and maybe get
a chance to put in some time at the university the rest
of the day." She knew he hadn't been there in a week,
ever since he'd found out about his sister's death.

The thought of touching base with the university,
of perhaps going in and teaching one of his classes,
was exceedingly tempting to him. Being a professor
had always been his goal. It was what he did, what
he was. But everything was up in the air right now.

Besides, what would he do with his nephew? He couldn't just conveniently stick him out of the way in a filing cabinet.

He was surprised that Jewel hadn't thought of that. "As much as I'd like to, I can't bring Joel with me to sit in on my classes, and I can't just leave him at home."

"I know. Monday my mother goes over her books, and then she and her friends have this poker game they play once a week. I think I can persuade her to alter her plans a bit to include Joel. He'll have three grandmothers-in-training fussing over him. How great is that?"

He should have known she would have thought this through. "Sounds good," he agreed. "You have an answer for everything, don't you?"

She looked at him. There was an ache inside her, an ache that felt as if it were growing larger every time she was alone with him. Logic dictated that she not act on impulse, but emotions told her the exact opposite, leaving her stuck in the middle, undecided and torn.

She knew there was no such thing as "happily ever after"; she'd had proof of that over and over again. But she also knew that there was the "enjoyable now." And now was all there was.

What would you do if I kissed you, Chris? Would you back away, saying there were lines not to be crossed, or would you kiss me back?

"No, not everything," she answered quietly, addressing his comment.

There was something about the expression on her face and the tone of her voice that spoke to him. Or, more accurately, that got to him.

And maybe that was why it happened, although he really wasn't sure. His reasoning process became a blur.

All Chris knew was that one moment, he was talking to her, the next, Jewel was in his arms and he was kissing her.

The way he really wanted to.

Chapter 10

Jewel was aware of everything. Of the look in his eyes, of her heart as it pounded. Of his mouth as it came closer to hers.

It was as if it were all happening in slow motion.

She was afraid that if she moved, if she so much as breathed, the spell would be broken and she'd be snapped out of this temporary, delicious fantasy that had somehow overtaken her.

But the moment his lips touched hers, she knew that this wasn't a fantasy.

It was real.

Very, very real.

Real enough to up her body temperature by at least several degrees. The last time she felt this hot, she'd had a raging fever.

Savoring the moment, the intoxicating excitement, she wrapped her arms around Chris's neck, gave herself up to the feeling and kissed him back.

He should be apologizing for taking liberties. And he would. In a minute. But Chris wanted to enjoy the moment, the overpowering sensation just a little longer. He was aware of his arms tightening around her, aware of the delicious taste of her lips permeating his consciousness. Jewel tasted of all things sweet and tempting.

A fire surged through his veins.

God, was he losing his mind?

Or finding it?

With effort, Chris made himself pull back—before he made another move forward that he was going to regret. Because he wanted to make love with her. And that was completely crazy, not to mention out of the question.

Avoiding her eyes for a moment, Chris coughed, clearing his throat. Buying some time.

"I'm sorry," he finally said, raising his eyes to hers. "I don't know what came over me. I don't have anything to say in my defense except that I haven't been myself lately."

It took her a moment to pull herself together and another to catch her breath. She could still feel her pulse racing. She was far from a novice at this, but no one had ever made her lose her train of thought before just by kissing her. It usually took a lot more "undercover" activity than what had just transpired to make her forget her name, rank and serial number.

There was no denying that Chris was sexy. He

had already gotten her blood going with just a look or a word, but she definitely hadn't been prepared for this. Talk about still waters running deep. This was like falling through a crack in the earth and encountering a subterranean wild river.

"Well, tell whoever was just substituting for you that's it's okay." *And make him come by again.* "I'm not about to go all 'indignant feminist' on you." She took a breath as subtly as possible. Her pulse was still sending out scrambled Morse code. "We're both consenting adults here." Searching for words in the jumble that now comprised her brain, she ran her tongue along her lips and tasted him again. Her stomach tightened in futile anticipation. "Very adult," she added under her breath.

He scrutinized her, as if uncertain whether or not to take her at her word. "So then you're not offended or angry?"

She grinned. Hadn't he gleaned that from the way she'd kissed back? "So far from angry that we're not even on the same continent."

"And you'll still come tomorrow?" he wanted to know, then quickly added, "For Joel?"

Even if I had to walk barefoot in the snow. "Count on it." She couldn't have pulled off a deadpan expression right now if her very life depended on it. The grin on her lips came from deep within her and it was far too difficult to suppress. The best she could do was repeat the words he'd just said. "For Joel."

He held the door open for her as she slid behind the wheel. "Thank you," he said.

No, thank you, she thought. Not trusting her voice,

she merely nodded as she started up the car and put it into Reverse.

Jewel had barely gotten back onto the road before her cell phone began to ring. Was it Chris? Had he decided to ask her to come back, using some flimsy excuse to make her return? She would have accepted anything, it didn't matter. But because of their situation, the ball was in his court and the play was his to make.

One eye out on the road, she fumbled in her glove compartment for her Bluetooth headset, something she hated dealing with but it was either that or pull off the road in order to answer her phone. There was a third alternative, but even if she wasn't hoping that the call was coming from Chris, she wasn't the type to let her calls go to voice mail unless she just couldn't get to her phone in time.

The cell was about to ring for the fourth time— at which point it *would* go to voice mail—when she finally pushed the silver button on her headset that allowed her to answer the phone.

She realized that she was nervous as she said, "Parnell Investigations."

"About time you answered. So, do you have anything 'new' to tell me?"

Daydreams unceremoniously bit the dust. It wasn't Chris on the other end of the call; it was her mother. Acting as if she knew what had just happened between her and Chris.

How in God's name had her mother known that Chris had just kissed her?

Calm down, Jewel. She's not a seer, she doesn't

know. She's just being Mom and checking up on you, the way she always does.

"Nothing new," Jewel said innocently. The light turned yellow and for once, she slowed down instead of flying through it. Talking to her mother always took the edge off her reflexes. It would be just her luck to have a car run a red light and come plowing into her. Better slow than sorry. "I'm still looking for Joel's father."

"And you're hoping to find him in Joel's house?" There was a touch of mocking in her mother's voice. "Do you think he might be hiding in the closet? Or possibly inside Chris's mouth? I assume that was why you'd locked lips with him, hoping to suck out Joel's father."

"How did you—? Okay, this is getting positively creepy now, Mom. How the hell did you know that he kissed me?"

"Don't swear, Jewel," Cecilia admonished. "I taught you better than that. As for how, you're not the only Parnell who's capable of finding things out, dear."

"You're not a Parnell, Mom," Jewel pointed out, a fact that her mother had repeated to her more than once. "At bottom, you're an O'Hara."

Cecilia snorted. "I put up with your father's mother for ten years before the old crone died. I earned that name."

Jewel remembered how trying and demanding her father's mother had been. There were several times when she'd been surprised that her mother hadn't just lost it and strangled the woman. Anyone familiar with Fiona Parnell wouldn't have ever blamed her.

"No argument here."

She heard her mother chuckle. "Well, now, that's a novelty."

Oh, no, she wasn't going to get sucked down this path again. "Are you going to tell me how you knew that Chris kissed me or are you going to continue to regale me with your snappy patter?" And then, before her mother could say anything to enlighten her, the explanation suddenly came to Jewel. She'd heard a car go by when Chris was kissing her. "You drove by, didn't you?"

Now that she thought about it, the vehicle had sounded like it was slowing down, but she'd just thought that it was a nosy person wanting to watch them kiss.

She'd been right. It *was* a nosy person. It was her mother. She should have known.

"That was you in the car, wasn't it, Mother?"

"I don't know what you're talking about."

She could almost see her mother tossing her head, her still beautiful hair flying over her shoulder. The woman could have been an actress.

"I'm talking about hearing a car slow down, then pick up speed and drive away. That was you. Don't bother to deny it." She shook her head. "Mother, what possible reason could you have had to drive by his house like some deranged stalker? They have laws against stalking in this state," she warned. "You could be arrested."

"Don't get so dramatic, Jewel. I wasn't stalking,"

Cecilia protested with a touch of indignation. "I was just going to stop by to see how they were doing. I had a batch of Theresa's chocolate chip cookies with me—she's experimenting again," she said by way of an aside. "But I got my answer at least as to how Chris was doing without having to stop the car."

Jewel braced herself. She could hear her mother's grin over the phone and she knew what was coming.

"So, I did good, didn't I, Jewel?"

She'd guessed right, Jewel thought. "Mom, if by that you mean that you were right to refer his case to me because you thought that I could find his missing ex-brother-in-law, then yes, you 'did good.'"

"You know perfectly well that's not what I mean, Jewel." There was more than a trace of impatience in her mother's voice.

"Maybe," she allowed. "But I'm not going to dignify what you're alluding to with an answer. Look, Mom, I'm on the road—"

"You have that thing, that greentooth—"

"Bluetooth, Mother," she corrected not for the first time. "It's called a Bluetooth."

"Whatever," Cecilia dismissed. "You've got that thing to talk into so the police can't give you a ticket." She got back to what she'd wanted to say. "Why do you have to be so stubborn about everything?"

"It's in my genes," Jewel answered matter-of-factly. "I get it from my mother."

"You like him, Jewel," Cecilia insisted. "I've watched you. At the cemetery, at the house. I can see that you like him."

Her mother was adopting far too simplistic a view

of things. It didn't matter if she liked him or not. She wasn't about to get involved in the manner her mother was hoping that she would. "That has nothing to do with anything."

"Yes, it does." Her mother's tone said she knew better. "If I wasn't the one who'd sent him your way, you'd probably be wondering if he was 'the one' by now. But because I arranged this, because *I* like him, you're digging in your heels and resisting getting involved with him."

Jewel didn't have time to argue. Besides, there was no winning when it came to her mother. "I *am* involved with him, Mom. I'm handling his case."

Her mother laughed shortly. "You should be handling something else."

"Mom!" Jewel almost swerved into the next lane. Fortunately, there was no car in that space. Recovering, she blew out a breath. She and her mother had an open relationship, but her mother had never been this bluntly direct before.

"You're not fourteen anymore—and even at fourteen, you were more knowledgeable than I was comfortable about. My point is that life is pretty short and if a decent, intelligent man crosses your path, you shouldn't immediately run the other way just because he has your mother's blessings. And if that man happens to be a hottie, well that's all the better."

Her mother was obviously going through her second childhood, Jewel decided. "I'm not comfortable with your calling a guy a hottie, Mom. What's come over you, anyway?"

"I'm worried about you," Cecilia said.

"Then stop worrying," Jewel told her. "There's nothing to worry about, anyway."

"If you were a mother, you'd understand. Mothers worry. It's what we do. And we don't stop until we're dead because there's always something to worry about. The fact remains that Christopher Culhane is very much a 'hottie' and if you pretend that you're not interested, some other woman's going to come by and snatch him up," Cecilia predicted.

"And then she can go through the divorce instead of me," Jewel concluded. This time, she pressed down on the accelerator, flying through the yellow light before it turned red.

"You're not even married yet, Jewel. Why would you even be *thinking* about getting a divorce?"

Her mother lived in a very sheltered world, despite everything she'd been through. She'd married her very first boyfriend. She and her two best friends remained married to the same men until the disclaimer, "til death do us part," became a reality. All three women had had good marriages. The world that existed these days was completely foreign to her mother and her friends.

"Because, sadly, it happens, Mom. It happens a lot." She thought of all the cases she'd handled since she began her career five years ago. Every one of the cheating spouse cases had ended in divorce. Those were devastating odds. "Do you think that most of my clients got married thinking they were going to be divorced within five, ten, fifteen years?"

She heard her mother sigh. "I can't speak for anyone else, Jewel."

"Sure you can, Mom." She almost missed her turn and made a sharp right at the last minute. The driver behind her blasted his horn. "You're trying to speak for me."

"That's different. I'm your mother. Everything you do is my business, whether you know it or not. Whether you like it or not," Cecilia added with emphasis. "Because if you're not happy, I'm not happy."

"I'm happy, Mom, I'm happy," Jewel said through clenched teeth.

"No one's happy alone, Jewel," her mother stubbornly insisted.

She had her there, Jewel thought. "I'm not alone, Mom. I have you. And my friends."

"That is not the same thing, Jewel, and you know it. I'm talking about someone to share your life with—and that doesn't mean a dog, either," Cecilia interjected quickly, anticipating her daughter's next words.

This was going to go on indefinitely unless Jewel took some drastic measures.

"What, Mom? What did you say? Sorry, Mom, I seem to be losing you. I'm going through an underpass." To underscore that, Jewel cupped her hand around the headset and made some garbled, swishing noises, doing her best to imitate static.

"I'll talk to you later," Cecilia said, raising her voice to be heard above the so-called static. With a sigh, she hung up the phone.

Jewel followed suit, shaking her head. Only her mother could make a promise sound like a threat, she thought. And this was only the beginning. She knew her mother wasn't about to back off. Not now that both her friends had finally been successful in their matchmaking efforts. They'd brought their daughters together with men they'd met through their chosen careers—even Jewel had to admit they were practically perfect for her friends in every way. So her mother was not about to just give up because she'd asked her to.

If anything, that was like waving a red flag in front of a bull. Her resistance just gave her mother more of an incentive to keep pushing. And no one under the sun could push like her mother could. Not even Maizie. Her mother could keep this up indefinitely.

She didn't have to ask to know that this—not running a house-cleaning service—was what her mother felt was her calling, her destiny. Her mother was going to get her married or die trying.

"I appreciate the effort, Mom," Jewel said out loud to her absent mother as she made her way up a freeway ramp, "but there are no guys out there who won't break your heart without a backward glance. All the good ones are spoken for or dead."

While she fervently prayed that Nikki and Kate had lucked out and gotten two very rare men who meant what they said about loving them until the day they died, she truly doubted that lightning would strike a third time in a given space.

These days, if you knew three couples, chances were better than even that two of those couples were on their way to getting a divorce for one reason or another. And if they weren't now, they would be soon. She should know. She'd handled the back end of too many cases, gathering proof for a spouse who was either vengeful, grieving or, on rare occasions, in denial, and she'd hoped that she could somehow prove that they had a right to be optimistic.

Those were always the toughest cases for her because, once she'd collected evidence to the contrary, she knew her news would not be well received. Once or twice she'd actually thought of lying, of burying the information and telling the client that her husband really was working late rather than seeing a younger woman.

But she had an obligation to her clients to do the best job she could, even if it ultimately meant that her report would be greeted with tears or rants.

What all these broken marriages and broken promises had taught her was that it was better just to enjoy the moment, to enjoy the temporary thrill. *Forever* was a word for storybooks. Realistically, it had nothing to do with the vows exchanged in a marriage. She had made her peace with that, which was why she wasn't even looking for the "perfect mate."

However, if she were looking for the perfect specimen of the male gender, she doubted that she could come up with anything better than Professor Christopher Culhane. On that score, her mother was right. She certainly wouldn't kick the man out of bed if the occasion arose.

She smiled to herself, thinking of her mother's response to that. More than likely, her mother would see it as the beginning of something lasting.

"Sorry, Mom," she said as she wove her way around a slow-moving SUV. "That's the best I can do."

The "best" seemed pretty good to her from where she sat, Jewel mused. The more she thought about it, the better it sounded to her. The very thought of winding up in bed with Chris, of making love with him, got her blood moving *very quickly* through her veins.

If the man made love the way he kissed, she might just have to invest in fireproof sheets if they wound up coming together at her place.

Her mouth curved as she thought about that. It was definitely something to consider.

Jewel shook herself free of the fantasy that was taking hold. Right now, she had to follow up a hunch she'd had earlier. She didn't want Chris to think that he was wasting his money by hiring her.

With effort, Jewel focused her mind on the case and not on the man who was asking her to find Ray Johnson. It wasn't easy, but after a while, she managed.

Chapter 11

Like an evening shadow slipping across a room, it slowly dawned on Chris that he was looking forward to seeing Jewel.

He told himself that it was only because she was so good with his nephew, understanding the boy in ways he couldn't even begin to fathom. And it was because of that, not any deeper, more personal reason, that he kept glancing at his watch every few minutes. When he wasn't looking at his watch, he was looking out the window, anticipating the moment that she'd pull into his driveway and stride up the front walk.

Somehow, he couldn't quite snow himself.

For the most part, Chris felt he was keeping his thoughts pretty much under wraps—until Joel's voice penetrated his thoughts. "Do you think that she won't come?"

"What?" Preoccupied, Chris only heard the question after several seconds had gone by. It was as if there were a five-second time delay going on in his brain.

Patiently—with far more patience than he felt—Joel explained, "Jewel said she'd be here."

Chris didn't know if Joel was distressed, or if he was trying to reassure himself—or Chris. In any case, Chris felt compelled to take on the role of the calm adult, even though he was hardly feeling calm.

"If Jewel said she'll be here, she'll be here." He glanced again toward the window, from this angle seeing only the withering olive tree directly in the front yard. "She's probably just stuck in traffic."

Joel took this as a plausible excuse, nodding his head. "It'd be easier if she stayed here."

"This isn't her home," he explained to the boy.

Joel looked at him as if the answer he'd just tendered didn't really make sense. "It's not yours, either, but you're here 'cause it's easier."

Chris laughed, shaking his head. He'd love to see this kid in high school on the debating team. "How old are you really?"

Joel's small eyebrows narrowed, scrunching together over the bridge of his nose. "Five."

Chris wasn't given to touching, to drawing in close, but something kept cutting through his reserve. He ruffled Joel's hair. "You're very bright, you know that, right?"

Joel nodded. When he responded, he sounded like a learned old soul. "Yeah, I know that."

It was at that moment that it occurred to Chris that

perhaps placing Joel in kindergarten in the public school system could be a disservice to the boy. He was far too bright to waste his time playing dodge-ball and making paper-clip holders.

Maybe he'd look into finding a private school that could develop the potential that was obviously there.

The next moment, he forced himself to pull back. One step at a time, Chris silently warned himself. First they needed to get Joel into a school, *then* he could look into someplace better.

Not your problem, he reminded himself. If Jewel was successful, Joel would be turned over to his father and Ray could handle the boy's education. He had a life waiting for him, Chris reminded himself.

The thought left him feeling oddly hollow.

"She's here!" Joel suddenly declared with no small measure of enthusiasm.

Chris hadn't seen or heard anything to indicate that Jewel had arrived. "So now you have x-ray vision?" he teased the boy.

"No, I heard her car," Joel tossed over his shoulder as he rushed to the front door.

"Okay, no x-ray vision, superhearing," Chris amended under his breath. Because, heaven knew, he hadn't heard the car—or any car—approaching. But Joel obviously had. Since he had told Joel not to open the door to strangers, the boy went through the motions of looking out the window beside the door to make sure that it was Jewel coming up the walk. It was.

Jewel's index finger had barely made contact with the doorbell before the front door was swinging open. The next moment, she found herself looking down at Joel's beaming face.

"Boy, you certainly are excited about registering for school." She laughed as the small arms went around her hips in a greeting hug. Her hand tightened around the cell phone she was holding to keep from dropping it. The call to her mother had almost made her late.

"No, about seeing you," Joel corrected, pulling her into the house.

At that moment, she thought, Joel was every bit the five-year-old. She put away her phone and paused to smooth down his ruffled hair. Out of the corner of her eye, she saw Chris approaching them and nodded a greeting. "Hi."

"Hi." The turquoise jacket and skirt made her look like a businesswoman. *A sexy businesswoman,* he thought, then pushed the idea away before it could run off with him. "Any luck locating Ray?" he asked, needing something to fill the quiet.

She shook her head as she slipped her arm around Joel's shoulders. "Sorry, not yet."

It made no sense to Chris why her words prompted a feeling of relief within him, but now wasn't the time to explore that. He merely nodded at the information and said, "We'd better get going. The appointment's for eight-thirty."

Joel looked up at Jewel rather than him. "I'm ready."

She smiled at the boy. "Yes, you certainly are." She struggled to resist the urge to ruffle the hair she'd just smoothed down. "Let's go," she coaxed.

Glancing over her shoulder at Chris as they walked out, she asked, "I'll drive. Okay?"

It made no difference to him. He wasn't one of those men who felt his car was an extension of his persona. It was just a means of getting from one place to another.

"Fine with me." As he approached her vehicle, he noted the new addition in the backseat. "You've got a child seat." Pausing, he looked from the seat to her. "You bought that?"

She opened the rear passenger door behind the driver's seat. "Had to if I'm going to be taking Joel anywhere. It's the law." Something that she had become aware of only yesterday. Before then, there had been no reason for her to pay attention to rules pertaining to children in cars. "Kids five and under have to sit in the back in a child seat—no matter how bright they are," she added with a wink at the boy. She nodded toward the seat. "Why don't you get in, Joel?"

He looked a little uncertain as he climbed in and shifted around until he was comfortable. "Where does this go?" he wanted to know, holding up the end of his seat belt.

"First we buckle you into the seat, then we put this around the seat," she explained, securing first the belt that came with the car seat, then the one that came with the car. "It's to keep you safe," she added as Joel looked down at the belts. She couldn't quite read his expression, but she could guess. Most kids didn't like restraints.

"How much do I owe you?" Chris asked as soon as he got in next to her.

Buckling up herself, she started up the car. "You mean the bill up until now?"

She'd quoted him a per diem rate, saying that it remained constant unless there were added expenses. She hadn't mentioned any of the latter so he was fairly confident he knew what that tally was.

"No, I mean, for the child seat," he clarified.

The seat was something she'd taken it upon herself to get. She wasn't about to charge him for it, not unless he wanted her to buy one for his car, too.

"It's okay. I've been meaning to get one." It was a lie, but it was a small one and in the larger scheme of things, Jewel felt she could be forgiven.

The thoughtful look on Chris's face bordered on a frown. "You have?"

"I'm thinking of expanding my clientele to include kids." The deadpan tone was so convincing that he almost believed her before he realized that she was pulling his leg. After a moment, the grin gave her away. "You never know when one of those things can come in handy. I plan on keeping it so, no," she told him, driving down the through street and out of the development, "you don't owe me anything."

He wasn't all that sure about that. She was helping him with Joel, putting herself out and doing things that he was fairly certain weren't part of her job description. Contrary to what she said, he owed her. A lot.

But, for now, he made no comment, merely nodding his head in response. Some things you couldn't settle up by writing a check.

* * *

"You just blew him away," Jewel declared a little less than two hours later as they were returning to her car. It was obvious when they arrived at Los Naranjos Elementary School that the principal, Dr. Randall Taylor, had very low expectations of the little boy who hardly spoke above a whisper when he was introduced. That soon changed as Joel read clearly and confidently from a third-grade reader.

Opening the rear door, she waited for Joel to climb onto his seat. "I don't think he's ever met anyone as bright as you before, Joel."

Looking down at the boy's face, she had a feeling that flattery was something new to him. He was absorbing her words like the drought-parched earth taking in the first rain in a very long time.

"You think I made a mistake, turning down his offer to have Joel skip a grade." It wasn't really a question Chris posed as he got into the car again. He had a feeling that he knew the answer.

He was wrong.

"I did for about five minutes," Jewel admitted. "But initially I didn't think it through. Now that I have, I realize that you're right." Starting the car, she paused to look at him before she released the brake. "You're probably speaking from experience, aren't you?" The fact that he didn't deny it spoke volumes. "How many grades did you skip?"

Chris shrugged. "Doesn't matter." Then, as she pulled out of the parking spot, he decided that there was no reason to keep the matter to himself. He wanted her to understand. "Two."

She thought as much. There'd been a look on his face when he politely thanked the principal for the suggestion, opting instead for a normal scholastic route for Joel for the time being, that told her there was a reason behind Chris's position. "Two different times, or all at once?"

"All at once." The laugh was self-depreciating, devoid of any humor. "Bad enough being the smartest kid in the class. When you're also the youngest by a couple of years…"

Chris didn't finish. He didn't have to. She had a vivid imagination and could certainly fill in the blanks.

She didn't attempt to hide her sympathy. "Must have been pretty rough for you."

There were times when pity and sympathy were difficult to separate. He wanted neither. He shrugged indifferently. "Could have been easier."

And he was trying to protect Joel from having to go through that, she thought. Rather than getting caught up with the academics of it all, trying to push his nephew to the outer limits of his abilities, Chris had wound up being more concerned with the boy's adjustment to the situation.

Well, well, well, Jewel thought, you learned something every day. Christopher Culhane was a good man. Better than she'd first guessed.

Joel spoke up suddenly. "This isn't the way home," he observed, watching the streets that whizzed by his window. "Are we going to the beach like you said?" he asked hopefully.

"Even better," Jewel responded, sparing just a second to look over her shoulder at the boy. "I have a surprise for you."

"What is it?" Joel wanted to know, eagerness and excitement pulsing in his voice.

"Well, if I told you, then it wouldn't be a surprise, now, would it?" Jewel asked, struggling to keep a straight face.

"No, ma'am. I guess not," Joel responded solemnly. Despite his resignation, his excitement was evident just below the surface.

Seeing life through the eyes of a child brought an optimistic sheen to everything, she thought. She'd almost forgotten what that had felt like. She had Joel to thank for reminding her.

Joel didn't have long to wait.

Jewel pulled up in her mother's driveway, and even before she turned off the ignition, her mother was coming out of the house, her arms opened wide in greeting.

She had to have been watching at the window, Jewel guessed. Some things never changed. She remembered her mother keeping vigil like that when she'd first started dating.

If the smile on Cecilia Parnell's subtly made-up face had been any wider, she would have had to rent a body double to accommodate the rest of it, Jewel thought, turning off the engine. She got out of the car and opened the rear passenger door.

"Remember the ladies who came to your mom's funeral?" Jewel asked him as she helped Joel out of the restraining belts. "Well, they thought you were so much fun to play with, they asked me if you could come by so they could have a rematch."

Although the thought obviously appealed to Joel, the shift in his expression told her that he saw a small problem with that.

"But I didn't bring the video game," he told Jewel in a whisper.

Jewel struggled to suppress her grin as she pulled the handheld player out of her purse. "But I did."

Joel eagerly took possession of the game, his eyes dancing. "You think of everything!" he declared happily.

The boy filled her with joy, Jewel thought, absorbing his happiness as it radiated out. She couldn't help glancing back at Chris. "This is one great kid."

She'd get no argument from him. Chris was becoming convinced of the same thing himself. He watched as Joel ran up to the trio of women and each took her turn hugging him. Chris noted that his nephew no longer just stoically took the displays of affection as if he were afraid they would vanish at any moment, but returned them, as well.

It looked as if Joel was set for the next few hours. Chris slanted a look toward the woman responsible for it all. "Does this mean I have time to go over to the university?"

"That's what it means. C'mon," she beckoned, already reopening the driver's-side door. "I'll drive you back to Rita's so you can pick up your car."

"Take your time, you two," Cecilia called after them. She already had Joel under her wing, literally and otherwise. "We want to enjoy Joel's company. You do the same with each other."

Jewel shut her eyes for a second, gathering strength. Wondering if anyone had ever died from humiliation. "See you later, Mother," she called out tersely.

As Chris buckled up and she started the car, she debated about whether to let the matter go or to say something to apologize.

Ultimately, she decided that the "hint" her mother had sent their way was much too blatant to ignore. "Sorry about that," she murmured, starting down the road.

He looked at her quizzically, apparently not following her line of thought. "About what?"

He was just being polite. It was like saying that he wasn't aware of the elephant in the room. "My mother and her parting comment."

It took him a second to make the connection. "Oh. That." The smile on his lips was a tolerant one. To him the apology was entirely unnecessary. "From what I gather—and I have no firsthand experience with this—Cecilia was just being a mother. She wants you to be happy."

She wanted to ask him what he meant by saying that he had no firsthand experience. Was *this* referring to a meddling mother, or something else? But she decided that perhaps he wasn't up to probing right now. She let it ride.

"What she wants is for me to be married," Jewel corrected.

His broad shoulders rose and fell beneath his jacket. "Maybe to her that's one and the same thing."

"Very astute of you," she acknowledged, a smile playing on her lips. "My mother, bless her, grew up in a completely different generation when the words, *'til death do us part* actually meant something. Now, if they mean anything, it's only because one spouse has killed the other." She bit back a sigh as she decided not to race through a swiftly changing yellow light.

Chris studied her profile as they waited for the light to change again. "And I thought I had dark thoughts."

"They're not dark thoughts," she protested, shifting her foot onto the gas pedal. "That's reality. I admit that, because of my line of work, I get to see a bigger share of disgruntled married couples who want nothing more than to be rid of one another than most people. But even if I didn't see them, they'd still be there," she pointed out. "If a tree falls in the forest, it still makes a noise even if there's no one to hear it." She used the familiar saying to make her point for her.

"Marriage doesn't mean what it used to. People don't stick together through thick and thin anymore. At the first sign of unrest or trouble, they're out of there, shedding mates like snakes shed skin." She hated this particular fact of life, but that didn't make it any less true. "My mother and her friends were a lot luckier. They didn't just marry good men, they married 'forever.'" Jewel blew out a breath. She was letting the subject get to her, and Chris was a captive audience. She shouldn't be subjecting him to this. "I'm sorry, I didn't mean to preach—or vent."

"I think venting probably fits the situation better.

But you know," he hypothesized, "statistically speaking, if fifty percent of marriages fail, that means that fifty percent of them succeed. You strike me as someone who's pretty determined. If you were to marry someone, it would be forever. You'd make damn sure of it."

Whether he realized it or not, he'd just succeeded in raising her spirits. "That's a very nice sentiment, Chris."

He didn't like being thanked and that was where this was headed. He offered a disclaimer. "Just an observation," he replied.

She caught another red light. At this rate, it was going to take forever to get him to his car, she thought. "You have trouble accepting gratitude, don't you?"

He pretended not to know what she was talking about. "Was that what that was?"

"That's what that was," she confirmed. The next moment, she turned a corner then pointed toward the house on the right. "We're here."

He looked out. "So we are. By the way, what time am I supposed to pick up Joel?"

"That's entirely up to you. I'm sure the later you come by, the happier my mother and her friends will be." Parking in the driveway, Jewel pulled up the hand brake. The engine was still running as she paused to let Chris out. With her free hand, she dug through her purse, searching for her cell phone in order to check something on her schedule.

Except that she couldn't. No matter where she felt around, she couldn't seem to locate the phone. "Damn, I know it's in here somewhere."

Chris paused by the car door. "What is?"

"My cell phone." She shook her purse a little, thinking it might surface.

"You had it out in the house," he recalled.

Right. Now she remembered. Jewel sighed. "And left it there."

"C'mon, I'll let you in," he offered.

Maybe it was her, she thought as she turned off the engine and got out, but for one moment, the words seemed to have the ring of a prophecy about them.

Chapter 12

The moment Chris unlocked the door for her, Jewel hurried inside the house.

Her cell phone was exactly where she thought it would be. Right on top of the coffee table where she'd put it when Joel ran up to hug her.

"Got it," she announced, putting it into the zippered compartment of her purse.

Slipping the purse's strap onto her shoulder, she glanced in Chris's direction, trying to gauge his thoughts. She didn't want him to think that she was scatterbrained. If he thought she had trouble locating her cell phone, he might have doubts about her ability to track down Joel's father.

"In case you're wondering," she told him, "I don't usually misplace my phone."

He shook his head. "Didn't think you did," he answered matter-of-factly. His eyes slid over her curves slowly. Right now, his thoughts were miles away from mundane things like misplaced cell phones. Or even getting back to work.

Right now, all his thoughts were centered on her.

On what it felt like to have her against him. That kiss the other day had set a great many questions in motion for him. Questions that would never have any answers, unless…

Jewel shifted slightly, a restless feeling suffusing her mind, body and soul. It was time for her to leave, she told herself. There were a couple of resources she needed to tap before she could put out more feelers.

Yet she wasn't moving, wasn't going out the door or even turning in that direction. Her eyes had met his and the moment they did, a nervous anticipation skittered around inside of her.

Because silence was stretching out between them, swallowing seconds, Jewel searched for something to say. Anything, no matter how inane. "Bet you can't wait to get back inside a college classroom."

He'd almost said "yes," but that would have just been an automatic answer, not a truthful one. A week ago, it would have been, but not anymore. A week ago, the University of Bedford constituted his whole life and he'd been content with that. At least, he'd *thought* he was content with that.

But now, completely against his will, his horizon had been expanded.

If he said "yes," then that would have been the end of it. She'd walk away to do whatever it was she was going to do and he'd drive over to the university, hours ahead of schedule.

He didn't want an end to it. Didn't want her to walk away. Not even for a moment.

"That's not a hundred percent true," Chris heard himself saying.

She wasn't quite sure she understood what he was saying. There were a number of conflicting signals going out, confusing the hell out of her. "I thought you lived and breathed teaching—when you weren't writing," Jewel tacked on.

"So did I," he freely admitted. He found himself taking another step toward her. And then another. It was almost as if he had no choice in the matter. "Looks like we both might be wrong."

"Oh?" She could feel her very breath backing up in her lungs. Or was she just holding it, waiting? "I don't think I quite understand."

Chris laughed softly, as if the sound was only intended for him. "That makes two of us." With effort, he tried to wall off his emotions, tried to back away. But he remained where he was, far too aware of her proximity, far too aware of *her* for his own good.

Or hers.

"I'm keeping you." He was doing his best not to let this happen. "You have an appointment."

The words left her lips in slow motion. "Actually, I don't." She hadn't been definite in her plans, telling her contact only that she would be dropping by some time on Monday. That left it wide-open, which was just the way she liked it. Free to come and go as she pleased. So why wasn't she going? "But you have a class," she reminded him.

"Not until three o'clock." He glanced at his watch, although he was already well aware of the time. "It's only ten forty-five."

The corners of her mouth curved slightly. "With that much time, you could walk to the campus."

"Or do something else entirely," he countered quietly.

Her mouth went utterly dry. So dry she was surprised that she managed to push the single word out. "What?" Her heart was hammering so hard, it was about to break the sound barrier. Cries of "Mayday" echoed in her brain.

Chris gently cupped her cheek with his hand. Time froze and completely stood still. Nothing moved but her pounding heart, which was threatening to vibrate right out of her chest.

As he began to lower his mouth to hers, she had the answer to her question. "Oh, that," she murmured breathlessly.

His lips were a fraction of an inch from hers when her response stopped him. *Was* he assuming too much? "I can back away if you—"

Chris never got a chance to finish.

He thought he heard Jewel warn, "Don't you dare," but he wasn't sure because the next moment, her hands were framing the sides of his face and *she* was pulling *him* into a kiss.

Pulling him into her space. Into her world.

Her lips locked on his as she rose up on her toes

so that they could both feel the full impact of the heated contact.

When she finally drew back to allow them both to catch their breath, he did his best to try to keep the moment light, even while his head was spinning and his blood surged madly through his veins.

"Is that because you found your phone?" Though he did his best not to show it, he ran out of breath by the next to the last word.

"As good an excuse as any," she told him, fighting back a grin. "I was always taught to celebrate the little things."

Damn but he wanted her.

None of this was making any sense to him. He wasn't acting like himself. But there was no going back, no pulling away.

He took her into his arms, drawing her closer. "By all means, let's celebrate."

And that was how it began.

How her entrance into a brand-new, shining world she had never quite experienced before started. There'd been other men, although not nearly as many as she had pretended, but never once did the ground disappear beneath her feet, never once could she recall being filled with an anticipation she couldn't really control.

And never once, at the very end, when the magic and the starlight had passed and it was all over, had disappointment *not* been hovering somewhere in the wings, waiting to pounce and overtake her.

Disappointment didn't even put a toe into the water this time, didn't cast a *hint* of a shadow.

What was there was fire, heat, a dizzying sense of satisfaction even as the next bombshell had already begun to form.

Again.

She'd never lost her sense of orientation before, never felt so excited, so overwhelmed that she completely lost track of the sequence of events.

Oh, she knew they'd started out fully dressed in the living room and wound up stripped, panting and sealed together, sweaty and passionate, in the master bedroom. But how was unclear.

What she *did* remember were sounds and sensations and the feel of his hands, surprisingly strong, yet incredibly gentle, running along the length of her body. But if she were asked to verbally re-create what had happened, moment by moment, there was no way she could.

Urgency had been her companion, cheering her on as she reached one plateau after another, always believing that this was the end of it, only to discover that there was more. More sensations to absorb, more crescendos to savor, each of them echoing hard throughout her entire body.

With his hand on the Bible, vowing to speak the truth and nothing but, Chris couldn't have said what had come over him. Why, when he should have been reaching for his worn briefcase, he found himself reaching for her instead. But suddenly, the need to be alone with her, the desire to make love with this woman who was so completely different from anyone he'd ever known, had been so overpowering that he knew that this was something he couldn't even *begin* to ignore.

Chris had never been one to seize hold of life before. Instead, he had gone along his quiet path, giving himself up to science. He liked things that made sense, no matter how long it took for him to arrive at the conclusion.

This, this made no sense at all.

But it felt wonderful.

He couldn't remember ever feeling this alive before. Or, he realized as he gave in to another surge of impulse and brushed his lips along the tantalizing length of her body, feeling this happy.

Unable to hold himself in check any longer, Chris drew his body up along Jewel's until his eyes were looking down into hers.

And then he took her.

Or she him.

He wasn't certain of the order, all he knew was that he couldn't ignore the demands of the rhythm that had taken him prisoner, holding on to him tightly. The rhythm echoed faster and faster until, suddenly, he was propelled into another world where two people became one and nothing else made sense but that.

He was vaguely aware of her crying out, and the sound vibrated in his head even as the heated embrace of euphoria receded inch by cooling inch from around his body.

Chris became aware that his arms were wrapped around her, as if that sole act could stave off the onslaught of reality. He wanted the feeling of euphoria to remain forever.

But even as he thought it, the feeling was breaking up, expiring like the bubbles in a bubble bath after their time was past.

"I didn't hurt you, did I?" she heard him ask, his warm breath brushing up against her skin. Heating it all over again.

"I don't know," she admitted. "This is the first out-of-body experience I've ever had." And she fervently hoped it wasn't going to be the last. She wasn't naive enough to believe that this was the beginning of the rest of her life, but she was hopeful enough to pray that there were a few more moments like this left for her before she and Chris went their separate ways.

Raising her head, she leaned her arm across his chest and then rested her chin against it.

Her eyes danced as she deadpanned, "Was it something I said?"

He'd been afraid that he'd gone too far, presumed too much. Hearing the teasing question brought a sense of relief to him.

"No," he answered honestly. "It was something you did."

If she'd somehow triggered this wondrous experience, she needed to know. That way she could do it again. "What?" she pressed.

"You were," he replied. When she looked at him, puzzled, he repeated, "You just were."

Jewel needed more of a hint than that. She ran

her fingertip along his lips. She was arousing him. She could see it.

"Were what?" she pressed.

"You. You were you. And magnificent," he whispered just before he drew her head down to his. Her mouth down to his.

The lovemaking began all over again, with even more pulsating excitement this time because each knew what was waiting for them just around the corner. And because time, ever an enemy, was growing short. Life was waiting for them just outside the door.

They made the most of the moment.

Late that afternoon, when Chris arrived to pick Joel up from Cecilia's house, he saw that Jewel's car was parked at the curb.

She was here.

A dozen or more feelings instantly sprang up, assaulting him from every angle. It had been difficult enough to keep his mind on his lesson plan as he stood at the front of his classroom. If he forgot a word or two, or missed a beat, he knew it would be attributed to his having lost his sister. All his classes had been informed by the substituting professor why he hadn't been there for the past few sessions.

But how was he going to pretend that nothing monumental had happened between the two of them when he walked into Cecilia's house and caught his first glimpse of Jewel?

And his second glimpse and his third?

How was he going to pretend that he wanted to do

something other than sweep her into his arms and start the lovemaking process all over again?

He felt as if someone had slipped into his body and transformed him.

Jewel could feel the pulse in her throat going haywire—or at least it seemed that way—the moment she saw him take command of the room.

She did her best to appear nonchalant when Chris walked into the living room after her mother had opened the front door to admit him.

Her best was not good enough.

Maybe this was a bad idea. Maybe she should have gone straight to his sister's house to give him a progress report. Encountering him here, under the watchful eyes of her mother and her mother's fellow yentas, the same day that Chris had made the earth move for her might not have been the smartest thing she had ever done.

Even if she could exercise steely control over herself, her mother, bless her, had a sixth sense when it came to the vibes given off by a man and a woman.

And Maizie was even worse. The only one who wasn't as tuned in to those things—and was more thoughtful about making her suspicions public— was Theresa. Although, Jewel reconsidered, not to hear Kate tell it.

She forced a smile to her lips and tried to sound as distant as possible as she told Chris, "I just wanted to let you know that I think I might be on to something."

The look on Chris's face told her that he wholeheartedly agreed. That, as far as his opinion went, she most definitely *was* on to something.

She was quick to set him straight. "About the location of Joel's father," Jewel stressed, lowering her voice.

"Oh. Good." The first word reflected that he was still somewhat stunned to see her. The second word so lacked feeling and enthusiasm that she thought he hadn't really heard her. That *was* why he'd hired her, wasn't it? To find the boy's real father.

"I have to follow it up," she continued, "but it seems to be the first solid lead I have."

He remembered her saying something about tracing the man through his IRS filings. Was that what she'd done? And why didn't he feel a sense of relief or happiness at the thought of locating Joel's father? This was what he'd wanted. To pass the obligation of taking care of another human being onto someone else.

Had his wiring gone so far off-kilter today that nothing made sense to him?

"Well, that's good news, isn't it?" Theresa asked slowly, looking from Jewel to Chris and then back again. It was obvious by their expressions that neither of them saw this as particularly good news. Theresa smiled as she exchanged glances with Cecilia.

"Yes. Of course. Good news." Chris was parroting the words. Who would have ever thought that such a small woman could upend his world? And at his age. It just didn't seem possible.

And yet, it was true.

He looked strange, Jewel thought. As if all four cylinders of his engine weren't firing correctly. "Is something wrong?" she asked him, concerned.

"No, nothing," he assured her a little too quickly. "I'd better get Joel home," Chris said suddenly. "He's got a big day tomorrow."

Apparently oblivious to the conversation going on around him up until this moment, Joel's head snapped up. His small eyes darted from his uncle to his new—and only—best friend.

"Jewel?"

There were so many things she heard in Joel's small, reedy voice. It didn't take much for her to know that what he needed most was reassurance. "Sure, I can come with you tomorrow to drop you off."

He didn't look the least bit surprised that she had read his mind. "And pick me up?"

Chris looked on, somewhat surprised by the exchange.

"And pick you up," Jewel confirmed with a wide smile. "And in between, you're going to have a great time," she promised the boy, putting her arm around the small shoulders. She slanted a look toward his temporary guardian. "Isn't he, Uncle Chris?"

Chris's eyes met hers over the boy's head. "Absolutely."

One glance at the boy's face told them that Joel was far from convinced.

She had her work cut out for her, Jewel thought. But she worked best under pressure. "Want me to come over tonight?" she asked the boy.

Both Joel and his uncle said, "Yes," their voices overlapping.

Jewel grinned. Her eyes went from the grown

man who'd lit up her world to the little boy who lit up whenever he saw her. She deliberately avoided looking in her mother's direction—or the direction of either of the other two women. She wasn't up to dealing with their knowing expressions.

"You got it," she told the two males in the room.

Unable to avoid it, out of the corner of her eye she glanced toward her mother and saw the smug, satisfied look. It was enough to make her want to shout, "It's not what you're thinking!"

But, unfortunately, it was.

It was *exactly* what her mother was thinking. And that, truthfully, was the only fly in the ointment for her because, although she dearly loved the woman who had given her life, Jewel knew what Cecilia Parnell was capable of. If she grazed the ball just once, it encouraged her to take a thousand swings at bat. And even though they might all turn out to be misses, her mother would keep on swinging until she had another hit, however minor, to her credit.

Her only salvation, Jewel thought, was that once Chris was history, as he surely would be, she would tell her mother that there was nothing between them except for Joel.

But even as she thought it, she had a feeling her mother wouldn't believe her.

Chapter 13

Before the week was out, Chris felt that he had, in essence, reclaimed his life. He was back teaching at the university and he was once again working on the college textbook. But life was not without its surprises.

He discovered, much to his amazement, that what had once sustained him and given him purpose now just wasn't enough. He looked back over his years in the academic world and was mystified that he had ever thought that his life was full. It wasn't. There was an emptiness at the core, an emptiness that he now realized he had unconsciously tried to ignore by filling his time with work. Perpetual work.

He published papers, did research and occasionally volunteered to take over classes for vacationing fellow science professors. All, he now knew, in order to avoid coming face-to-face with the truth: Man could not live by job devotion alone.

There was a need for balance that could only be arrived at by filling that all-consuming hole with family. With the fulfillment that being needed on a personal basis brought. Providing a home and emotional support for his nephew had made all that clear to him.

But even being both mother and father—temporarily, he reminded himself—for the boy did not sufficiently fill up the hole. For that to happen, there had to be something more.

There had to be Jewel.

She completed the unit.

Completed him.

Even as he thought that, Chris turned to face Jewel, silently warning himself not to get too attached to any of it. That at any moment, everything could change in a heartbeat. The way it had with Rita's death. Except that this time, it would be Joel's departure that would bring about the change. The boy would be leaving if his father were found. As would Jewel, because finding Ray was what she'd signed on for. There would be no reason for her to keep meeting with him once that was accomplished.

Unless she wanted to.

Chris sighed, staring up at the darkened ceiling. He was a novice at this, at keeping the fragile pseudo—family unit together, alive and well. One misstep and it would all be over, shattered beyond repair.

He now knew what a tightrope walker had to feel like, trying to inch his way from one end of the rope to the other without falling. Without losing everything. The very thought made his gut tighten. Almost to the point where he couldn't breathe.

Chris shifted in the bed he'd commandeered— Rita's bed—and slowly turned back to the woman beside him. The woman, partly to present her reports verbally, partly in response to Joel's perpetual requests to see her, had taken to coming over every evening after five o'clock. They would all have dinner together and then they would take turns, when he didn't have papers to grade, helping Joel with his homework.

Chris smiled to himself. The first time that happened, he'd expressed surprise that there actually *was* homework in kindergarten, but obviously the school believed in working with young minds right from the start. And that was a good thing.

So one of them would help the boy with his homework and thus a pattern was created. First they'd all spend time together, then after Joel was tucked into bed and read to until he fell asleep, Jewel and he would carve out their own private heaven, making love with a passion that said things that neither of them had yet ventured to voice aloud: that they knew this was just temporary. That they were making the most of the time they had together. Storing memories for the time when they would no longer *be* together.

She could feel Chris looking at her. Studying her. Jewel turned into him, her naked body brushing up against his.

Odd how quickly she'd grown so comfortable around him, she thought. There was no awkwardness in the silences that occasionally occurred between them, no sense of urgency to fill the air with conversation.

But even though there was no awkwardness, she sensed that there was something bothering him. Something he was having difficulty putting into words.

"Something on your mind you want to talk about?" Jewel coaxed softly.

He was beginning to think she was a mind reader. She always seemed to know when he was holding things back. "What makes you say that?"

Jewel raised herself up on her elbow and ran her fingertips lightly along the furrow that had formed between his eyebrows. The same kind of furrow that Joel had when he was thinking.

"You're pensive," she told him. "As if you don't know how to phrase whatever it is that you're wrestling with."

That was as good a summation as any. Chris sighed. "Maybe I don't."

"Just spit it out," she encouraged, then teased, "There won't be any points off for bad grammar, I promise."

He wasn't getting anywhere silently chewing on this. Making up his mind, he plunged in. "You haven't found Ray yet."

Was that what this was about? That so far, despite her best efforts, she hadn't been able to produce Joel's father? She hadn't given up by a long shot.

"We're not out of options yet," she told Chris. "One of the people I know is putting me in touch with—"

"Maybe we should stop looking." Now, that surprised her.

She didn't understand. Chris had been so adamant about locating Joel's father when he'd first hired her. Not that much time had gone by. What was going on? Why had he changed his mind?

"Why would we do that?"

He gave her reasons, going about it as if he were proving a theorem. "Look at it logically. If Ray had wanted to be part of Joel's life, he would have found a way to stay in contact with him. Phone calls, birthday cards, postcards if he's traveling. Something," he emphasized. "After all, Joel's his son. That's supposed to mean something. Instead, there hasn't been anything in three years. Three *years*. For all intents and purposes, it's like Ray just dropped off the face of the earth. Maybe he doesn't *want* to be found."

It made sense. But all this was true when he hired her. She had a feeling that there was more.

"What else?" she prodded.

Chris slowly blew out a breath before answering. One hand under his head, he tucked the other around her and brought Jewel closer to him.

"Bringing Ray back after all this time will just toss Joel's life into chaos again. Ray may be his father, but he's a complete stranger to Joel. It would be like putting him into a foster home. I can help supplement his education and, in case you haven't noticed, the kid lights up like a Christmas tree every time he sees you. Joel's happy now, possibly for the first time in his life, and I don't think I have the right to spoil that for him. To shake things up for him by bringing his father into it."

He paused. Was he being selfish or altruistic? He wasn't really sure. All he knew was that he didn't think that changing things again so soon after Rita's death was a good idea.

"Maybe we should just let sleeping dogs lie," Chris said.

"Maybe," Jewel acknowledged. She knew he didn't want to hear this, but it had to be put out on the table. "But what happens if that sleeping dog wakes up and wanders into your lives?"

Puzzled, he turned into her. "What?"

She spelled it out for him. "What if Ray comes back on his own for whatever reason and finds out that Rita's dead and his son's being raised by the brother-in-law he's always felt inferior to?"

Her assumption caught him off guard. He looked at her, confused. "What makes you think he felt inferior to me?"

"Things I picked up on while trying to locate Ray." Jewel sat up to look at him, ignoring the fact that she was nude from the waist up. "We might never be able to find Ray, but we have to continue trying as long as there are still avenues to pursue." She didn't go into details, but she was fairly sure that she was on the right track. "Because if we just call it all off, I guarantee you're going to spend the rest of your parental life looking over your shoulder, expecting Ray to just show up one day and take Joel from you, maybe just out of spite. Trust me. You don't want to have to live like that."

Chris slowly shook his head. "No. You're right. I don't."

And because it was the middle of the night and nothing could be done about it one way or another right now, he set the matter aside and focused on her. On the lightly bronzed beauty sitting up next to him and looking like a goddess.

He felt his gut tightening all over again. Tightening out of need and radiating far-reaching fingers of desire all through him.

"How did you get to be so wise?" he wanted to know, slipping his hands on either side of her waist.

She grinned. "Dumb luck most of the time. Instincts make up the rest of it," she added.

Chris was now lightly skimming his palms and fingers along her waist and inching his way up to the sides of her breasts. Desires and needs flooded through her, making her ache for him all over again, even though they had already made love, not once but twice. And only a few minutes ago she'd thought she was too exhausted to breathe.

But from out of nowhere a fresh, new burst of energy emerged, drenching her and energizing her all at the same time.

Leaning over, she brushed her lips lightly against his. Once, twice and then again, each pass lingering just a second longer than the last.

He cupped the back of her head, bringing her closer to keep her from ending the kiss too soon.

The kiss deepened.

As he savaged and savored her mouth, Chris could feel his self-control ebbing away. She could reduce him to a mass of passions so quickly he hardly knew how it happened.

Only that it did.

He'd never known anyone like Jewel before and, most likely, never would again. She was an anomaly he couldn't begin to understand. Being who he was, he promised himself that someday he would unravel this enigma that was Jewel Parnell.

But not tonight.

Tonight there would only be a third round of lovemaking. There was no room for anything else. Tomorrow with its cold reality was still light-years away from here, he promised himself.

With a swift movement, Chris shifted their positions and suddenly, she was the one on the bottom and he on top. Moving his body in a gentle, familiar rhythm, he paid homage to every soft, pliable, damp inch of her, grazing her body with his fingers and his mouth.

Starting a fire that mere water couldn't begin to put out.

She shouldn't be doing this. Sleeping with Chris had long ceased being about just enjoying herself and scratching an "itch" that was distracting her. She was sinking into that place where she *needed* this to keep on functioning. Needed to have this man make love with her. Needed to feel his lips on hers, needed the wondrous high that only he seemed capable of creating for her each and every time a climax shuddered through her.

It was that old catch-22. The more she made love with him, the more she wanted to make love with him. She knew she needed to stop, to walk away while she still could…

Who was she kidding? That window had long since shut. She *couldn't* walk away.

And yet, she knew she couldn't stay, either. To stay would be to invite the tarnish to come, as it did with each relationship that was out there.

Better to have all this live on in her memory, perfect and wonderful, than to have it disintegrate right in front of her, turning sour the way she had seen so many relationships do, time after time.

If she continued like this, all she was doing was setting herself up for a fall. For an all-consuming, crashing disappointment.

Nothing lasted forever. Or even came close.

But, oh, it was so hard to be strong when the fire inside her belly threatened to eat her alive.

Later. She'd think about it later.

When she could think.

Because right now, Chris's very presence was blotting out her ability to form coherent thoughts. Even short ones.

There was only one cure for that. And it was temporary at best.

Threading her arms around his neck, Jewel arched her hips to admit him and gave herself up to the revelry that hovered such a short distance away, waiting to swallow her up.

"So how's it going?" Kate asked breathlessly. Two steps ahead of Jewel, she had just taken a seat at the small table she'd commandeered for their semiregular get-together at the coffee shop that was located across the street from Nikki's hospital.

Every week or two, she, Jewel and Nikki tried to meet at least for coffee to touch base with one another. But a last-minute patient emergency had Nikki calling to beg off today, so it was just Jewel and Kate this time around. Until recently, they'd used these meetings to commiserate about their marriage-minded, interfering, matchmaking mothers. But of late, the lament had proven to be no longer necessary, since two of them were now, much to their mothers' unending joy, engaged to be married.

Kate set down the two coffees she was carrying and slid one across the short length of the table to Jewel.

Her eyes were dancing as she said, "I hear Aunt Cecilia sent you a man you couldn't refuse."

"Who told you that?" Jewel asked sharply. Hands wrapped tightly around the container, she was about to take a sip but stopped dead at Kate's question.

"I don't have a 'single' informant," Kate told her. "Like everything else, it came in threes. Aunt Cecilia, Aunt Maizie and my mother, all of whom have declared, separately and together, that this guy—Christopher Culhane is it?—is the 'perfect catch.'" She took a healthy swallow before leaning in to Jewel. "Your mother even showed me a picture of him." Kate smiled, pleased for Jewel. "He's very good-looking." She winked at her friend. "If I wasn't so crazy in love with Jackson, I might have even Indian-wrestled you for this guy."

Jewel was still digesting the previous part of

Kate's statement. "A picture? Where did my mother get a picture of him?"

A horrifying scenario presented itself to Jewel. Her mother posing Chris like some artist's model in a nude sculpting class. She could feel her cheeks heating and picked up the cup again. She could blame the shift in her skin tone on the hot coffee if Kate noticed.

"Actually," Kate amended, "she showed me a page out of the University of Bedford's last yearbook. They had the professors listed separately. A physics professor." She gave a low, appreciative whistle. "I must say I'm impressed."

She had to nip this in the bud now. The last thing she wanted was for either one of her almost-married best friends to come up and lavish pity on her once she and Chris went their separate ways—as they inevitably would sooner or later.

"There's no point in being impressed," Jewel told her dismissively. "There's nothing going on."

Jewel had a tell, an unconscious giveaway when she was lying to someone she cared about. A tic in her right cheek would start up. She knew it was all but dancing now.

Kate kept a straight face. "Oh?"

Jewel shrugged. She and Kate, as well as Nikki, had been friends since birth. Maybe even since conception. Keeping things from either of them had never been easy for her. She could hide the truth from her mother far more easily than she could from her friends.

So with a sigh she said, "Well, there's 'something'

going on," she was referring to their nightly love-making sessions, "but there's nothing going on if you get my meaning."

"Possibly, in some alternate universe," Kate allowed, "but here, in this one... Huh?"

She spelled it out to Kate. "Okay, Chris's a hell of a lover, but you and I know that being a fantastic lover doesn't add up to 'forever.'"

Kate clearly wasn't about to dismiss the man that quickly. "It could, given other attributes."

But Jewel remained firm in her convictions. "I'm not going to set myself up for a fall, Kate. You and Nikki might have lucked out, but there's only so much luck out there to be had."

"It's not luck and you know it," Kate insisted. "A relationship—any relationship—takes hard work and determination and a real willingness to compromise. A lot," she underscored.

"All true," Jewel allowed, but she had a different perspective on the matter, one she'd learned from her long, tedious hours of surveillance. "However, all those heart-broken, cheated-on spouses who hire me, they thought they all had that extra-special relationship, too—until they suddenly had the rug pulled out from under them and landed hard on their bruised hearts."

"Then tack the rug down," Kate advised matter-of-factly. She reached across the table, putting her hand on top of Jewel's. "At the very least, Jewel, don't declare whatever it is that the two of you have going on dead while it's still got a breath of life left within it. I'd hate to see you miss out on something wonderful because you're afraid."

"I'm not afraid," Jewel protested with feeling.

Kate's pager went off. She glanced down at the number on the tiny LCD screen. The moment she did, she rose to her feet. "Looks like I'm out of time, Jewel. They want me in court. Think about what I said," she requested with feeling. "Oh, by the way, the coffees are paid for," she tossed over her shoulder a second before she hurried out the door.

"I am *not* afraid," Jewel repeated with more feeling, saying the words to her friend's retreating back.

But she knew she was.

Chapter 14

This definitely was *not* the reaction she'd expected.

Having moved heaven and three-quarters of the earth, reaching out to people she hadn't been in contact with for some time now—in some cases several years—Jewel had finally managed to pinpoint the location of Joel's father. Ray Johnson was currently living in Las Vegas under an assumed name and doubling as a dealer/bouncer at one of the lesser-known casinos.

She was fairly proud of herself for being able to track the man down by using the thumbprint on his California driver's license. He'd allowed that license to expire, but on a hunch she'd put the thumbprint into the system and run it through a number of different databases. While nothing came up in either the military service database or the one that listed felons across the country, a match kicked out in the database that kept prints on hand for everyone employed by the gaming industry in Nevada.

She'd remembered thinking that it was lucky for them that working at a casino required having your fingerprints taken.

Now it didn't seem to matter.

"What do you mean, forget it?" she asked Chris incredulously.

"Just that, forget it," he repeated. Thinking she might be afraid that he was going to renege on their initial arrangement, he added, "I'll pay you for your time and any extra expenses you might have incurred trying to locate Ray."

This really didn't make any sense to her. She remembered how eager he had been to get out from under the responsibility of caring for his nephew. "So you don't want me going to Las Vegas to bring this guy back?"

"No."

Even if he'd changed his mind about the responsibility portion, he knew that it was only right to let the man know what had happened. "I thought we already had this conversation," she said, addressing his back as he paced about the room.

It was late. Verifying her information had taken a while and she'd arrived here only in time to say goodnight to Joel. Consequently, bedtime had been stretched to the limit, but eventually, Joel fell asleep. And then she had dropped her bombshell.

"We did," he agreed.

She caught his hand to keep him from continuing to pace. It was like talking to a moving target at a shooting gallery. "And the outcome," she reminded Chris, "was that you agreed that I should keep on looking for Ray."

"That was when I didn't think you would find him," he confessed. He shouldn't have underestimated her. "Now that you have…" His voice trailed off for a moment, then he continued with conviction. "I don't think it's in Joel's best interest to have his father back in his life. Ray was short-tempered, argumentative and I'd call him dumb as a post, except I'd be insulting posts everywhere. If Joel goes to live with him, I guarantee that the boy will be put down every day of his life. He's already smarter than his father ever was and Ray doesn't like to feel inferior."

She stared at him, confused. "If you felt that way, why did you start this? Why did you have me even looking for the man?"

"Because I didn't think it through," he answered honestly, then owned up to something even more unflattering. "Because I was just thinking of myself. I wanted to get back to my life, to the way things were. Except that's not enough for me anymore," he admitted. "I like coming home and hearing Joel tell me about his day. It gives a whole new meaning to everything. I can nurture him," he said with feeling. "Ray, or whatever he's calling himself these days, can't. *Won't*," he underscored.

She held her hands up to stop him from saying any more. "Hey, you're preaching to the choir here."

He was relieved to hear that. "Then we can just forget about this?"

Surprise shot through him when he saw her solemnly shake her head. "No."

He didn't understand why she was refusing his request. "But I thought you said you agreed with me."

"I do, but that doesn't mean that you can just forget about Ray—who, by the way, now goes by Dennis Carter," she interjected. "Because if we don't get a signed document from the man, saying he relinquishes all parental rights to Joel, the lovely world you're projecting in your head runs the very real risk of blowing up at any given moment—without warning."

She'd grabbed his attention right at the beginning. "A signed document?"

Jewel nodded. Tired from her long day, she sank down on the sofa. "That's what I said."

He was silent for a long moment, turning the matter over in his head. "Do you think Ray'll agree?" he finally asked.

She thought they had a very good shot at it. "From everything you've told me about the man, I think it's a safe bet. He sounds like a selfish jerk and it really bothered me that you were willing to just hand Joel over."

"Well, I'm not anymore," he emphasized. Rather than sit down next to her, he perched on the sofa's arm, restless. "But what if he doesn't sign away his rights? What if he decides, for whatever strange reason, to give fatherhood another shot? By going to him, we'll be letting him know where to find Joel."

She tried to assuage Chris's fears by using his own arguments on him. "As you said the other night, if he had been interested in getting back in touch with Joel, he would have tried to reach out to him at some point. An official document filed with the court will buy you peace of mind. I can have one of my friends—she's a family lawyer and, coincidentally, Theresa's daughter," Jewel interjected, "draw up the proper legal papers for you. We can be on the road tomorrow if you like."

He laughed shortly. "What I'd like," he told her, "would be to never have started this in the first place." He played the words back in his head and realized what was wrong with that path. "But, then, I wouldn't have met you, would I?"

Her smile was soft.

Jewel hadn't changed her mind about the situation. She knew what they had was only temporary, but she could certainly cherish it for all she was worth while it lasted.

"No," she agreed, "you wouldn't have."

Never one to count chickens before they had not only hatched but had also shed their downy fuzz and grown feathers, he still allowed himself a moment.

"I guess having to see Ray again is worth it." His eyes drifted over her, taking possession. "Especially considering what I got in the bargain." He laced his fingers through hers. "You said you think we can be on our way tomorrow?"

She nodded. "Just as soon as I have Kate draw up those papers for Ray to sign."

Chris had to admit, if only silently to himself, that he felt a little uneasy about getting in contact with Ray. The man might just decide to retain custody out of spite. But he knew that Jewel was right. This had to be done.

"Do it," he told her. "Get the necessary papers drawn up."

He sounded as if he were steeling himself off, she thought. "You know, if you'd rather not have to deal with this character, I can go to Vegas as your representative. There's no need to put yourself through this if you don't want to."

But Chris was already shaking his head, turning down her offer before she finished.

"No. I need to see him, to make sure he understands that if he does take Joel, I'll be all over his Neanderthal hide if he so much as causes that boy a single moment of unhappiness."

She wondered if he knew how heroic he sounded, making himself Joel's champion.

"Road trip it is," she agreed. "I'll be back here with the papers tomorrow morning," she promised.

He missed her already and she hadn't even walked down his driveway yet. It amazed him how much his life had changed in such a very short span of time. How much it had changed and how much that didn't seem to bother him.

He supposed that you never stopped learning.

"Jewel," he called after her. When she turned

around in response, he'd already caught up to her. "One for the road," he said in answer to her quizzical look. And then he kissed her.

Jewel was not alone the next morning when she came to pick Chris up. Her mother was sitting in the passenger seat beside her, opting to go in Jewel's car rather than taking the sky-blue-and-white MINI Cooper she loved so dearly.

There could only be one reason for that, Jewel thought. More talk time this way.

She'd called her mother early this morning, asking if she was up to babysitting Joel for the day. Her mother was giving her an enthusiastic "yes" before she even finished the question.

Jewel had hardly backtracked out of her mother's driveway before she started having second thoughts about her impulsive decision. Maybe she should have asked Theresa or Maizie to babysit instead. Cut from the very same fabric as her mother, the two other women at least held themselves in check around her. Not because they weren't each hopelessly enamored with the happily-ever-after scenario they'd all bought into, but because they tried not to come on too strong with someone who wasn't their actual daughter. She knew that neither Theresa or Maizie would be sitting beside her, wearing a smile so smug that it was off the charts.

"Isn't Chris *everything* I said he was?" Cecilia asked, like someone who already had the answer.

"You didn't say anything, Mom," Jewel reminded her tersely. "I should have known better."

"But he's everything I ever wanted for you," Cecilia said with a heartfelt sigh. "Tall, dark and handsome with an intellect that's every bit as impressive as his biceps."

Jewel eased her foot onto the brake at a light that was still yellow in order to look at her mother. "Just when did you see his biceps?" she wanted to know.

In response, Cecilia merely gave her a mysterious smile that would have been the envy of the *Mona Lisa*. "You don't expect me to give away all my secrets, do you, darling?"

Her mother was making it up as she went along, Jewel concluded, and the more she reacted to what was being said, the more liberties with the truth her mother was going to take.

"No, I certainly don't," she answered with a serious expression. "Just make sure that Joel gets to class and then remember to pick him up. I'm not sure how long we'll be—and *don't*," she emphasized pointedly, "tell me to stay the night."

Cecilia allowed a touch of despair to enter her voice. "If I have to tell you that, then somewhere along the line I must have gone horribly wrong with your education."

"Your heart's in the right place, Mom," Jewel acknowledged, changing lanes to avoid a slow-moving vehicle, "but your methodology could use a lot of work. Every time you push, I get the overwhelming desire to dig in my heels."

Cecilia frowned. "Even if you miss out on the perfect relationship?"

"Even then." And then she relented slightly. "I

didn't say my reaction was a good one, just that I had it." Her mother sighed and Jewel could almost hear the older woman shaking her head. But they'd arrived at Joel's house. Despite the dauntingly long drive that loomed ahead of her, most of it probably in soul-depressing traffic, Jewel cheered herself up with the fact that she wasn't going to have to deal with her mother's penchant for matchmaking for the rest of the day.

Stopping the car, she got out and crossed to the front door. Her mother was right behind her.

Having heard them drive up, Chris opened the door less than half a minute later. "Thanks for doing this, Cecilia."

"My pleasure entirely, Chris," she responded with feeling. "And don't feel you have to come rushing back right away," the woman added. "Joel and I will be just fine holding down the fort until you're here again."

"Where are you going?" Joel wanted to know, drawn to the doorway by the sound of their voices. It was still early and he'd just finished eating breakfast. He didn't need to get ready for school for another twenty minutes.

"Just a little road trip, Joel," Jewel told the boy, opting for the simplest explanation. She'd forgotten how curious he'd become, asking questions until he was satisfied.

"A little road trip to where?"

"Las Vegas," Chris told him.

"Did you know that they have over a thousand chapels in Las Vegas?" Cecilia asked innocently.

Jewel had never bothered doing a head count of the number of chapels in the gambling capital of the country. "I'm sure it's not that many, Mother," Jewel replied tersely, giving her a warning look.

Her mother smiled in response, completely ignoring the "back off" look in her daughter's eyes. "All it takes is one."

Fighting back a wave of embarrassment as she debated whether or not to commit justifiable homicide, Jewel looked at the man she'd come to pick up.

"Let's go before the traffic gets really bad," she said, although she knew it was already too late for that. It was Friday and there were always people trying to get a jump on a long weekend. The traffic would most likely be bumper to bumper.

Unaware of traffic patterns when it came to Vegas, Chris nodded, pausing only to say a few parting words to Joel. "You be good, Joel, and do whatever Mrs. Parnell tells you to do."

"She lets me call her Cecilia," Joel told him happily.

"I'm letting you call her Mrs. Parnell," Chris pointed out, his meaning clear.

"Yes, sir. Mrs. Parnell," Joel repeated.

"Grandma might be a compromise," Cecilia suggested, not quite managing to carry off an innocent expression.

"In what universe?" Jewel challenged, then held up her hand before her mother could utter a comeback. "Never mind. I'm not getting sucked into a debate. We have to go."

Cecilia placed a delicate hand to her chest. "Why Jewel, whatever do you mean?"

Jewel gave her a dark look, but made no reply other than a generic, "See you later," which she actually directed toward Joel before turning on her heel and hurrying out to her vehicle in the driveway.

Chris had just barely made it into the car before she was pulling out of the driveway. She wanted to get away before her mother could say something else to embarrass her beyond all measure.

"You'll have to forgive my mother," she told him, straightening the steering wheel and throwing the car into Drive. "I think she overdosed on her 'Pushy Mom' pills today."

"I hadn't noticed." Chris meant to keep the grin to himself, but he failed, undermining his words to the contrary.

She didn't have to look; she could hear the grin in his voice. "And if I believe that, you have a bridge you'd like to sell me."

He laughed. "No, no bridge. Actually, I'm rather grateful to your mother."

This was going to be good, she thought. "Go ahead, I'm listening."

"Other than the fact that she recommended you as a private investigator, her 'innocent' remarks did manage to get my mind off the reason for this little road trip in the first place." He didn't want to contemplate the fact that, despite Jewel's assurances to the contrary, there was a very real possibility that things could go horribly wrong.

Jewel stole a quick glance in his direction. "Worried?"

"Yes." There was no point in denying it. "Very," he added.

"Don't be." Taking her right hand off the wheel, she patted his knee reassuringly. "Everything's going to turn out just fine."

If only he could believe that. "I forgot, you're an optimist."

"Only way to face life," Jewel answered him with feeling.

"And if Ray decides that he wants to have Joel come live with him?" Despite all his efforts, he couldn't shake himself free of that scenario.

"If it comes to that, optimist or not, I'm also very good at pointing out the downside of things," she assured him. "By the time I get finished with the man, he'll be making an appointment to get a vasectomy within the hour. And you can be sure that he'll be *more* than willing to sign the legal document I have in my purse."

He remembered what she'd said last night. "Then you did get it?"

"We wouldn't be going if I hadn't." Kate hadn't exactly been overjoyed to have Jewel pop up on her doorstep at almost midnight last night, but once she'd been filled in, Kate had understood and forgiven her for her inopportune timing. As had Jackson. "It's all nice and legal and signs over all parental rights to you."

"You do think of everything." There was admiration in his voice.

The corners of her mouth curved. "God knows I try," she told him.

Chris laughed softly and she caught herself reveling in the sound before she silently told herself she had to stop doing that, stop absorbing little bits and pieces of things he did, things he said. Women in love did things like that and that wasn't her. She had her feet firmly planted on the ground, Jewel insisted, and knew what she was doing.

Having fun until the fun ran out.

"I'm going to hold you to that," Chris was saying.

"Fine." *As long as you hold me, I don't care what the reason is.*

The thought galloped through Jewel's mind before she could stop it. It made her nervous.

Because it made her vulnerable.

Chapter 15

Lucky Lady sounded more like a name for an up-and-coming racehorse than a casino, but that was the name the refurbished establishment's new owner had affixed to it. His hope, no doubt, was that luck would indeed materialize, luring a healthy crowd of second-tier gamblers away from the bigger casinos that tended to lavish attention only on very high rollers.

Business, Jewel had learned in her quick investigation, was only fair to moderate. It was the kind of place that someone like Ray Johnson, a.k.a. Dennis Carter, could safely get lost in.

They reached Vegas at a little after one in the afternoon. The high density of traffic migrating from Southern California to the city known for sin and glitter had made the journey particularly draining, especially when it came to a complete standstill.

Entering the city, Jewel turned on her GPS unit. The pathfinding machine glibly told them where to turn and when, allowing Jewel to take in some of the scenery, instead of exclusively searching for street names. What she viewed made her decide that the city's mesmerizing magic only came out after sundown. Vegas in the daytime looked like an aging showgirl. What the night successfully hid, the daylight brought out, accentuating the telltale flaws that time had etched.

"Are you sure you got the right name?" Chris asked, looking at the front of one lesser-known casino after another as they drove past them. "I've never heard of the Lucky Lady."

Neither had she until she'd done a little more research. The high-end casinos were the ones that garnered publicity, but gambling was an across-the-board, equal opportunity addiction and opportunists made the most of it, providing avenues for the rich and the definitely-not-rich alike.

"When was the last time you were in Vegas?" Jewel asked.

Chris paused, trying to remember. "Six, seven years ago," he finally admitted. "Maybe a little longer." He'd gone to attend a convention for university physics professors. He'd come away thinking too much energy was being wasted in one place, but he kept that to himself.

"Things change here daily," she told him. "A year ago, the Lucky Lady was called the Royal Flush or something equally inane. Ray—or Dennis, take your pick—hasn't exactly come up in the world, but at least he's working now." Coming to a red light, she turned to look at him. "Want to stop for lunch first?" she offered.

He shook his head. He doubted if he could have kept it down. But then it occurred to him that he wasn't the only one to consider here. "Unless you do," he amended.

She was hungry, but she could wait. "Business before pleasure," she replied. The light turned green. "According to the map I looked at earlier—"

"Turn right, here," a disembodied voice instructed. "Final destination on right."

"This must be the place," she murmured.

There was one lone valet in a somewhat rumpled uniform sitting on a stool against the wall. When he saw them pull up, he came alive and hurried over to the sedan.

Ordinarily, it was against her basic principles to have someone else do for her what she was perfectly capable of doing for herself. But parking here, even in the daytime, would be tough for a seasoned magician to pull off. Jewel surrendered her vehicle and her keys to the gawky valet who looked as if he'd only begun to shave that morning, accepting a receipt in return.

"Park it near the front," she told the valet. "We won't be long."

The look on the tall, thin young man's face told her that he might be unseasoned, but he'd heard that before. With effort, he slid his long frame into the vehicle and murmured, "Yes, ma'am."

She and Chris walked up to the front doors of the

casino in strained silence. She stopped just before entering and looked at him. "Ready?"

No, he wasn't. He would rather have skipped this entirely and just continued with this new life that had been thrust upon him, but he knew that Jewel was right. Not notifying Ray or securing legal custody of his nephew would leave him open to a life fraught with unease. He'd be forever waiting for the other shoe to drop without having so much as a clue when that might be.

"Let's get this over with," he answered.

She nodded, noting that he'd deliberately avoided repeating the word that she had used. Jewel went in first.

They worked their way past the squadron of machines affectionately—and not so affectionately—referred to as one-armed bandits. The minute she spotted the bar, Jewel picked up her pace and crossed to it. Any bartender worth his paycheck knew everyone.

The stocky bartender stopped massaging the slick countertop as she approached and gave her his best smile. "What's your pleasure, little lady?"

"Information," Jewel replied with a smile that matched his. She took out a photograph of Ray she'd printed up from the DMV archives. "Does this man work here?"

The bartender shook his head, clearly about to plead ignorance, when his eyes caught the twenty peeking out from behind the photograph she'd laid down on the bar. Picking up the photograph, he took a closer look.

"Yeah, that's Dennis." Setting the photograph back down, he closed his hand around the twenty.

"Is he here today?" Chris asked.

"Saw him earlier," the other man confirmed, then pointed off to the right. "He's over there, at the black-jack table. Dealing," he added.

Jewel slipped the photograph back into her pocket. "Thanks."

"Come by anytime," the bartender told her as she walked away. "I'll give you a drink on the house."

"That's probably not all he'll give you," she heard Chris mutter under his breath.

It took an effort for her to suppress the grin that rose to her lips. It almost sounded as if Chris were jealous. But she knew better. Jealousy was for people in a relationship. They were just two ships docked at the same port for a limited time, and she was going to have to keep reminding herself of that until it sank in. Especially since everything appeared to be com-ing to an end.

As they approached the blackjack table, she noted that Joel's father seemed to be struggling not to ap-pear as bored as he obviously was. Currently, there were two men at his table. One looked as if he'd spent his life perched on a stool at one casino or another, and the other was a couple of decades younger, wet behind the ears and searching for his fifteen min-utes with Lady Luck. Both men were watching Ray deal as if their very lives depended on the next turn of the card.

Six-four and stocky—he'd obviously gained weight since he and Rita were an item—with dark hair and small, narrow eyes, Ray looked up as Jewel came to the table. Interest instantly flared in his gaze.

"Take a seat," he told her, his tone low and velvety.

"We came to talk," Chris said, taking his place beside her.

Ray's seductive smile instantly faded. His eyes darted around the two people, as if he expected to see someone else with them. It didn't take much to figure out who it was he was expecting.

Looking around, he called out to someone just to his left. "Kelly, can you take over for me for a few minutes?"

The woman looked annoyed and on the verge of saying no when her eyes came to rest on Chris. An appreciative smile slowly worked its way through the frown.

"Sure, why not?" The smile faded when the man who had caught her attention moved away from the table at the same time that the dealer did.

"How did you find me?" Ray hissed at Chris the moment he'd placed enough space between himself and the other casino employees.

"The credit goes to Jewel," Chris told him, nodding at the woman beside him.

Anger rumbled in Ray's voice and colored his features. "I haven't got any money for Rita or the kid, if that's what you're here about. I'm barely getting by—and I've got a wife to support. I've got a decent enough life now. I ain't going back."

"I'm very happy for you," Chris said flatly, his expression conveying the exact opposite.

"I ain't going back," Ray repeated with more feeling. "You can't make me."

"No one wants you to go back," Jewel assured him, wondering what it was that Chris's sister ever saw in this Neanderthal.

"Then what are you doing here? And where's Rita?" he asked suspiciously, obviously still thinking she might pop up at any moment.

"Rita died." She could hear the pain in Chris's voice, even though his expression never changed. Rita's ex seemed to be oblivious to it, apparently unaffected by the news.

"Died? Of what?" he asked suspiciously.

"A brain aneurysm," Jewel answered.

"Yeah, well, that's too bad." Ray shrugged carelessly as he glanced back toward his table and the disgruntled woman who was covering for him. "We've all got to go sometime. Look, I've got to get back to the table. I've already taken my break. They don't like you to abuse the rules here."

But Chris wasn't about to let him go just yet. They had unfinished business. "Aren't you even going to ask about Joel?" he demanded.

Ray shrugged again. "What about him?" he asked indifferently. And then his eyes narrowed as a realization occurred to him. "Is that why you're here? To pawn the little wimp off on me?" His mouth twisted as if the very thought of dealing with his son repelled him. "Well, you can just forget about it. My wife's pregnant. She's expecting twins." It was obvious that the news was not a source for celebration for him. "I've got more than I can handle."

"We'll make this quick and painless," Jewel said, getting in his way as he tried to leave again. Fishing around in her purse, she grabbed and held up the papers that Kate had drawn up for her. "Just sign this and you can go on with your life."

Ray frowned as he regarded the document suspiciously. "What's that?"

"Legal papers pertaining to your parental rights to Joel." For the sake of brevity, she summarized the contents. "It says that you're giving them up freely."

Ray's dark eyes darted back and forth from his former brother-in-law to Jewel. "And then I'm not responsible for him anymore?"

"And then you're not responsible for him anymore," Jewel guaranteed, nodding her head.

"Hell, yes, I'll sign it. Give me something to write with," he declared eagerly, feeling his pockets as he searched for a pen.

Taking one out of his breast pocket, Chris thrust it into Ray's hand. "Here."

Ray looked around for a surface to write on, and Jewel turned around, offering up her back for him to use. He lost no time in signing the papers.

"Done," Ray declared, giving her the document and Chris the pen. "Now get the hell away from me before I get in trouble," he snapped.

The look Chris gave him could have shot daggers. "Gladly," he bit off.

Ray turned on his heel, about to walk away. But then he paused and turned around again. "Hey, he's not worth anything is he? The kid?"

"Not in the way you mean," Chris answered

coldly. He could envision himself wrapping his hands around the man's thick neck and choking the life out of him. Chris took hold of Jewel's arm, hurrying her away. "C'mon, I need to get out of here before I do something really stupid."

Jewel found that she had to rush in order to keep up with him. "Like what?" she prodded as they made their way out of the casino.

"Like strangle that piece of dirt with my bare hands."

She'd seen better-matched battles. "He's got about thirty pounds and four inches on you," Jewel pointed out tactfully.

"Rage has got to count for something," Chris retorted.

The last thing she wanted was to have him go ballistic. "Put it behind you, Chris," she urged him. "You've got custody of Joel. That's all that matters."

He took a deep breath and then let it out. The anger he felt on Rita's behalf, as well as Joel's, began to subside a little.

Collecting himself, he corrected her last statement. "Not all."

"A big part of it, then," she amended. This wasn't the time or place to split hairs over semantics. "Why don't we go somewhere, grab a late lunch and celebrate?" she suggested, then added a word that put everything into perspective. "'Dad'?"

For a moment he appeared to be rolling her words over in his head. And then he nodded. "Sounds good to me."

"Great, because I am really starving," she told

him, doing her best to sound cheerful and upbeat despite realizing that she'd lost sight of the fact that their association was about to come to an end. If not now, then very, very soon. The goal had been achieved. That meant that she was no longer of any service to him. They could each go their separate ways and move on with their lives, emphasis on *separate*.

"You're awfully quiet," Chris commented. Immediately after having lunch they'd hit the road and, unlike the trip out, were making great time. He'd noticed that as she'd turned on the engine, she'd also turned on the radio. Music, not conversation, had filled the air for the past few hours. "I'm not used to that with you."

She was surprised that it had taken him this long to notice. With a half shrug, she gave him a vague excuse. "Just thinking."

She did her thinking out loud. At least, that was what he'd come to expect. This was something different. "About?"

"My next case."

Next case, as opposed to this one. Was that all this had been to her, he caught himself wondering. Just a case? Now that it was solved, her attention had shifted to another puzzle, another challenge. An uneasy feeling wafted through him.

"You have something lined up?" he asked, trying to discern if he was being paranoid or if he had a good reason to feel this way.

She avoided his eyes and stared at the road

straight ahead as she nodded. "Came in a couple of days ago," she added.

"Does that mean you'll be busy?" *And that I won't be able to see you?* he added silently.

"Very." The single word came out in a rush and emphatically.

He felt a chill running down his spine. She was telling him that it was over. Just like that.

"Okay," he said slowly, as if he was tasting the word and found it bitter.

Okay. Chris had accepted the lame excuse she'd given him. Maybe he even welcomed it, she thought. Just like that, without a challenge, without a protest. He was okay with it, okay with not seeing her because she was "busy."

Dammit, what did she expect? She *knew* that their association, that what had happened between them, those few, precious weeks, had all just been temporary. She'd told herself as much over and over again. Hell, she'd walked into this knowing it was finite.

Why couldn't she have gotten the message through to her damn heart?

Jewel let out a long breath slowly, struggling to focus on the road. They'd made excellent time and were almost home. All the traffic had been headed toward Vegas. Hardly anyone was coming back this soon.

And then, before she knew it, the trip was over. Just as their time together was over. She was pulling up in his driveway.

And her mouth felt like cotton.

Chris got out on his side. It took a second before

he realized that she wasn't moving. She was still sitting behind the steering wheel. Moreover, the engine was still running.

Rounding the hood, he came over to her side. "Aren't you coming in?"

She wanted to, but it was only putting off the inevitable. Trying to revive something that had already been declared dead. And besides, her mother was inside. One look at her face and her mother would know what was going on. And knowing her, her mother would make some sort of comment. Or worse, try to keep them together.

She wasn't up to that.

"No, I'll pass, thanks." Her voice was flat, devoid of emotion. "I'm kind of tired. Besides, this is your moment," she told him, trying to smile. "Yours and Joel's. I don't want to get in the way."

She was brushing him off, Chris thought. Her mind was obviously made up. He wasn't about to beg and embarrass both of them.

Stepping away from the vehicle, he said, "Don't forget to send me the bill."

Like she cared about the damn money. "Right. When I get around to it," she answered vaguely. "I'm going to be very busy."

"So you said," he acknowledged woodenly.

Jewel pressed her lips together, forbidding herself to cry. "Tell Joel goodbye for me." She threw the car into Reverse. If she stayed a moment longer, threats or no threats, she was going to cry.

Chris turned away, not wanting to watch her

leave. His heart felt like lead in his chest as he unlocked the front door.

There was music playing in the background. Cecilia had the radio on as she was finishing up the dishes. The moment she heard the front door, she hurried toward it and was there as Chris walked in.

"Hi. You're back sooner than I thought," Cecilia said, greeting him with a warm smile. She glanced behind him, but he was already closing the door. "Is Jewel parking the car?"

"No," he answered stoically. "Jewel's on her way home."

"Home?" Cecilia echoed as if the word made no sense to her.

He didn't want to talk. Everything inside him felt shell-shocked. He'd thought…

He'd thought like an idiot, Chris upbraided himself. Jewel was a bright, vibrant woman who thrived on excitement. Who generated it wherever she went. He had to have been crazy to think she would have been satisfied with a college professor for more than a few weeks.

"Yes, she left."

There was a finality to the word, to his tone. Cecilia stared at the young man she had handpicked for her daughter. She knew Jewel inside and out. The parts that weren't like her were like her late husband. If Jewel had left, it was because she was afraid. Afraid of getting hurt. Damn that job of hers.

"And you let her?" Cecilia demanded incredulously. Incensed, she shot straight from the hip. "Have you lost your mind or am I completely wrong about you and you don't care about her? Because, like it or not, my daughter loves you, Chris Culhane. All you have to do is look at her face to know that."

Chris opened his mouth to defend himself and then stopped. Suddenly, all the pieces just came flying together. How could he have been so stupid? So caught up in his own imagined hurt that he hadn't read between the lines? Hadn't seen what was right there in front of him? Cecilia was right. He *had* lost his mind. Temporarily. But it was back now. And he was ready to reclaim what was his.

"Stay with Joel," he tossed over his shoulder, heading for the door.

"No problem." Cecilia hurried after him to lock the door. "Just get it right this time," she called after Chris.

"I fully intend to." It was a pledge to himself. And to Jewel.

Chapter 16

Tears were streaming down her face as she drove. Jewel cursed herself.

She thought she was tougher than this. She would have sworn to it if anyone had asked. But tough people didn't cry when the inevitable happened. Not when they knew it was going to happen all along.

Jewel couldn't stop crying even as she struggled to get herself under control.

She'd been right all along. She *knew* it was going to be like this.

So why did being right hurt so damn much?

It wasn't as if this were a surprise. Sitting on the sidelines, gathering proof, she'd seen it happen time and time again. Two halves of a whole coming apart. Sometimes six months after the marriage, sometimes twenty years. But it happened. Over and over again it happened.

Hadn't she said right from the start that all relationships were doomed?

Okay, not all, she reminded herself, but most. The word *most* had been the culprit, the reason she'd let her guard down. *Most* whispered that there was a chance, however small, that she and Chris could somehow beat the odds.

Who was she kidding?

She wasn't a gambler, not when it came to something like this, to matters of the heart. To forever.

She stifled a sob that tried to break free.

Dammit, she had to stop this, had to stop tearing up and falling apart or else she was going to run into something or cause a collision.

Blowing out a shaky breath, she wiped her eyes with the back of her hand.

Maybe she needed to take a break, a vacation. There *was* no other case; she'd lied to Chris. She only wished there were so that she could get her mind off this soul-wrenching ache she felt in the pit of her belly. She desperately needed something to keep her occupied. But since there was no case, maybe she'd just take off for a few days…

And do what? a small voice in her head demanded. *Think?*

That was all she needed, endless days stretching in front of her with nothing to do but think about how empty she felt inside. How hollow.

Ordinarily, if things were getting her down, or she needed to get away, she would get in touch with

Nikki or Kate and go with one of them, or both, for a weekend mini-vacation.

But there was no doing that now. Both of her friends were deeply involved with the men in their lives. Any "getting away" would be done with their fiancés, not her. She was the odd girl out.

How had she become the fifth wheel without even knowing it?

Jewel blinked and looked around. She was on the freeway, heading for home. She didn't even remember getting on the on ramp. Apparently, the car was on automatic pilot, she thought.

As was she.

Maybe it was better that way. She needed to stay numb, removed, until she was finally up to dealing with this.

Until the pain was no longer unbearable.

Chris couldn't quite figure it out. How had Jewel managed to get so far ahead of him in such a short time? Only a couple of minutes had gone by, but by the time he'd come rushing out, she was nowhere in sight.

Jumping into his car, he had to all but floor it to even get a glimpse of her. It took another eight minutes of one eye on the road, the other on the lookout for any police cars, to catch up to her.

When he finally did, pulling abreast of her car, Jewel seemed to be oblivious that he was even there. Whether she really didn't see him or was just pretending, he had no idea. What he *did* know was that he was determined to get her to pull over.

Still driving parallel to her vehicle, Chris rolled down the passenger window, leaned on his horn and shouted, "Pull over!"

Stunned, confused and startled to see him suddenly all but at her side, a whole host of emotions raced through Jewel as she maneuvered her car onto the right shoulder of the freeway. The moment she did, he pulled over, as well, parking behind her.

Getting out of the car, she wondered if there was something wrong with either Joel or her mother, both of whom were still at the house.

"What's wrong?" she asked him the second he got out of his car and headed for her. "Did you forget something?"

The sound of cars whizzing by made it hard to talk above a shout. "Yeah, you."

She raised her voice, certain she'd heard wrong. "What?"

"You," he repeated, reaching her. "I got so caught up in everything that I thought it would just continue going right and then I thought—" This was all getting too complicated. "Never mind what I thought. Your mother set me straight."

She had no idea what he was talking about. "My mother?" This had all started with her mother. When would that woman learn to stop meddling?

"Yes." Even standing next to her, he had to shout to be heard. The noise from the cars all around them swelled. "She asked me if I was crazy."

He was still not making any sense, she thought. "And this set you straight?"

"Yes."

She shook her head, but that didn't clear it. Or change things. She just wanted to get away. "What are you talking about?"

Traffic was slowing down now, as motorists began to watch the minidrama playing out on the shoulder of the road.

"Your mother made me realize that I was crazy to let you go without a fight."

"'Let me go'?" she echoed in disbelief. "I thought it was pretty clear that you were trying to tell me it was over."

"Where did you get that idea?" he demanded incredulously. "You were the one who called this just another case."

She *was* guilty of that, she thought. "This *wasn't* just another case, but I didn't want you to think that I expected something."

"What if I expected something?"

She shook her head, unable to make the words out. "What?"

"What if *I* expected something?" he repeated, raising his voice even more.

Her heart refused to settle down and beat normally. "Like what?" she heard herself asking.

"Like spending the rest of my life with you." He took her hands into his. "I'm old-fashioned, Jewel. I don't want to just sleep with you. I want to wake up with you, have breakfast with you, make plans with you—I love you and I want to marry you. You've filled my life the way I never knew was possible. Don't make me feel empty again."

Anything too good to be true wasn't—hadn't that

been the first thing she'd ever learned? So why was she rooting for Chris's side, praying he'd say something to convince her?

"Now," she told him. "You want to marry me now, but once whatever you're feeling right at this moment vanishes, once you think things over—"

"I'll still want to marry you," he insisted. "And I'll still want to *be* married to you."

And then, amid the snaking evening traffic, on the shoulder of the road, Chris took one of her hands in his and got down on one knee. "Jewel Parnell, will you marry me?"

Self-conscious, aware that traffic was at a virtual standstill and every set of eyes were now on both of them, she tugged on his hand. "Chris, please, get up," she pleaded.

But he shook his head, remaining where he was. "Not until you tell me you love me and say yes."

She looked up, as if searching the sky for strength. "Of course I love you. I wouldn't be this miserable if I didn't love you."

"*Love* and *miserable*—not exactly the two words I wanted to hear in the same sentence," he told her. "Again, will you marry me?"

She pressed her lips together. Could he actually be serious? About wanting her for all time? "I don't have a choice in the matter?" she asked.

His answer was short and firm. "Nope."

She was losing the battle, but she gave it one more try. "You don't know what you're saying."

"That's where you're wrong. I'm a physicist. I *always* know what I'm saying."

He had no idea how much she wanted to believe him. How much she wanted to be convinced. But she didn't want to wake up some morning only to find him gone. "You haven't thought this through."

"Oh, yes, I have," he contradicted. "Would you like to see the flowchart?"

He got her then. "You made a flowchart?"

He grinned. "With colors and everything."

A motorist leaned out of his car and shouted, "Hey, lady, say yes already!" To underscore his point, he hit his horn, hard. The sound was echoed over and over again as other drivers joined in.

Within moments, there was a cacophony of car horns beeping.

Dammit, she was melting. *Please don't let me regret this.* "You really want to marry me?"

He nodded, his eyes solemn. "I really want to marry you."

"And *stay* married to me?" she emphasized.

"And stay married to you," he echoed.

She let out a long breath slowly. She was going to follow her heart. He was right, she had no choice. "Then I guess I'd better say yes."

He rose to his feet, still holding her hand. "Sounds good to me," he told her before kissing her.

The sound of blaring horns grew louder, but this time, it was the drivers' way of cheering.

At least, that was the way the evening news reported the story later that night when Cecilia taped it. She fully intended to share the tape with her future grandchildren someday.

Epilogue

Joel's eyes moved from his uncle to the woman he'd come to adore. The woman he'd secretly been afraid was going to leave. Except now they were saying something different to him. Something that made him feel very excited.

"You're going to marry my uncle?" he finally asked Jewel in a small voice. That was what they'd been saying to him. That and all this stuff about permission. That's why he was confused. Grown-ups never asked a kid for permission to do anything.

Jewel wanted to marry Chris with all her heart, but there was more than herself to consider here. She knew that. Knew, too, how important it was to feel as if you mattered. Even if you were only five. Feelings had no age limits.

She wanted Joel to know that he mattered. To both of them. And he always would.

"Only if you say yes," she told him.

Joel looked at her, still a tiny bit confused. "You want me to marry you, too?"

Exchanging glances with Chris, Jewel stifled a laugh as she looked back to the boy. "In a way, yes. If I marry your uncle, we're going to be a family, Joel. You, your uncle and me."

"Is that okay with you, Joel?" Chris asked. He looked as serious as Joel ever remembered him look-ing—except that there was a smile in his eyes. A smile that made Joel feel warm all over.

A family. He, his uncle and Jewel. A real family. He liked the way that sounded. Liked the way that felt in his stomach.

"Okay," he told Jewel. "I'll marry you, too." And then he put one stipulation on his consent. "But Uncle Chris does all the kissing."

Chris laughed as he pulled them both into his arms. "You got it, Joel."

And then, to show his nephew he meant it, he kissed his bride-to-be.

* * * * *

We hope you enjoyed reading

READY FOR MARRIAGE

by #1 *New York Times* bestselling author

DEBBIE MACOMBER and

FINDING HAPPILY-EVER-AFTER

by *USA TODAY* bestselling author

MARIE FERRARELLA

Both were originally **Harlequin®** series stories!

Discover more heartfelt tales of family, friendship and love from the **Harlequin Special Edition** series. Romance is for life, and these stories show that every chapter in a relationship has its challenges and delights and that love can be renewed with each turn of the page!

HARLEQUIN®

SPECIAL EDITION

Life, Love and Family

When you're with family, you're home!

Look for six *new* romances every month from **Harlequin Special Edition!**

Available wherever books are sold.

When Harper had gone back to work a few days after
the funeral, Ryan had offered to be the one to get up in
the night with Oliver so that she could sleep through. It
wasn't his fault that she heard every sound that emanated
from Oliver's room, across the hall from her own.

Thankfully, she worked behind the scenes at *Coffee
Time with Caroline*, Charisma's most popular morning
news show, so the dark circles under her eyes weren't as
much a problem as the fog that seemed to have enveloped
her brain. And that fog was definitely a problem.

"Do you want me to get him a drink?" she asked as
Ryan zipped up Oliver's sleeper.

"I can manage," he assured her. "Go get some sleep."

Just as she decided that she would, Oliver—now clean
and dry—stretched his arms out toward her. "Up."

Ryan deftly scooped him up in one arm. "I've got you,
buddy."

The little boy shook his head, reaching for Harper.

"Up."

"Harper has to go night-night, just like you," Ryan said.

"*Up,*" Oliver insisted.

Ryan looked at her questioningly.

She shrugged. "I've got breasts."

She'd spoken automatically, her brain apparently stuck somewhere between asleep and awake, without regard to whom she was addressing or how he might respond.

Of course, his response was predictably male—his gaze dropped to her chest and his lips curved in a slow and sexy smile. "Yeah—I'm aware of that."

Her cheeks burned as her traitorous nipples tightened beneath the thin cotton of her ribbed tank top in response to his perusal, practically begging for his attention. She lifted her arms to reach for the baby, and to cover up her breasts. "I only meant that he prefers a softer chest to snuggle against."

"Can't blame him for that," Ryan agreed, transferring the little boy to her.

Oliver immediately dropped his head onto her shoulder and dipped a hand down the front of her top to rest on the slope of her breast.

"The kid's got some slick moves," Ryan noted.

Harper felt her cheeks burning again as she moved over to the chair and settled in to rock the baby.

Fall in love with A FOREVER KIND OF FAMILY by Brenda Harlen, available May 2015 wherever Harlequin® Special Edition books and ebooks are sold.

www.Harlequin.com

H HARLEQUIN®

SPECIAL EDITION

Life, Love and Family

Save $1.00

on the purchase of
A FOREVER KIND OF FAMILY
by Brenda Harlen, available
April 21, 2015, or on any other
Harlequin® Special Edition book.

Available wherever books are sold, including most
bookstores, supermarkets, drugstores and discount stores.

Save $1.00

on the purchase of any Harlequin® Special Edition book.

Coupon valid until June 30, 2015. Redeemable at participating outlets in the
U.S. and Canada only. Not redeemable at Barnes and Nobles stores.
Limit one coupon per customer.

52612363

Canadian Retailers: Harlequin Enterprises Limited will pay the face value of
this coupon plus 10.25¢ if submitted by customer for this product only. Any
other use constitutes fraud. Coupon is nonassignable. Void if taxed, prohibited
or restricted by law. Consumer must pay any government taxes. Void if copied.
Millennium1 Promotional Services ("M1P") customers submit coupons and
proof of sales to Harlequin Enterprises Limited, P.O. Box 3000, Saint John,
NB E2L 4L3, Canada. Non-M1P retailer—for reimbursement submit coupons
and proof of sales directly to Harlequin Enterprises Limited, Retail Marketing
Department, 225 Duncan Mill Rd., Don Mills, Ontario M3B 3K9, Canada.

U.S. Retailers: Harlequin Enterprises
Limited will pay the face value of
this coupon plus 8¢ if submitted by
customer for this product only. Any
other use constitutes fraud. Coupon is
nonassignable. Void if taxed, prohibited
or restricted by law. Consumer must pay
any government taxes. Void if copied.
For reimbursement submit coupons
and proof of sales directly to Harlequin
Enterprises Limited, P.O. Box 880478,
El Paso, TX 88588-0478, U.S.A. Cash
value 1/100 cents.

5 65373 00076 2   (8100)0 12022

® and TM are trademarks owned and used by the trademark owner and/or its licensee.
© 2015 Harlequin Enterprises Limited

NYTCOUP0415

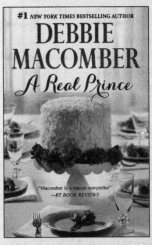

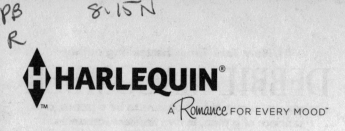